Historical fiction

CW01025039

DECEPTION

JAN STIRLING LOCKE

CRANTHORPE
MILLNER
PUBLISHERS

First published by Cranthorpe Millner Publishers (2024)

ISBN 978-1-80378-217-1 (Paperback)

www.cranthorpemillner.com

Cranthorpe Millner Publishers

Printed and bound by CPI Group (UK) Ltd
Croydon, CR0 4YY

I dedicate this book to Fenham Library, Newcastle upon Tyne, for permitting a precocious reader to join the "grown-ups" section of the library long before I was of an age to do so. I found part of Helen's story on the shelves there and kept it close to me.

"The wrongs which we seek to condemn and punish have been so calculated, so malignant, and so devastating, that civilization cannot tolerate their being ignored, because it cannot survive their being repeated."

Justice Robert H. Jackson (1892 – 1954)
Chief United States Prosecutor at the Nuremberg trials of Nazi war criminals following World War II.

"I cannot tell how the truth may be;
I say the tale as 'twas told to me."

Walter Scott (1771 – 1832)
Scottish historian, novelist, poet and playwright

INTRODUCTION

When we think of the Resistance in France between the years 1940 to 1944, our perception is fashioned by its representation in the many films we watch depicting the exploits of brave men and women in their resistance to enemy occupation, by the stories we read in books and by the true life accounts of the survivors, now so few in number, of those times. There was, of course, the popular comedy series *'Allo 'Allo!* which I thoroughly enjoyed, albeit in the knowledge that it was in no way representative of the realities of life in France under the Occupation.

The common perception of the Resistance as a single cohesive entity is a false one. For most, if not all, of those years of occupation by the brutal Nazi regime there was no uniform "Resistance", but instead resistance comprised disparate groups with a range of political affiliations and objectives, united in the common goal of if not driving the occupying army from France, at the very least making their stay as difficult and unpleasant as possible. Only a minority of the population felt they had to oppose the occupation. Most decided just to watch and wait and somehow "get by" in the hope that the Allies would come to their rescue. Also, the deprivations of the Occupation inculcated apathy and passivity in the people of France – when their children were malnourished and there was a shortage of even the most basic necessities, survival took precedence over resistance. And for those who did resist, in the form of direct action against the Nazis and their Vichy collaborators, by sabotaging rail networks and infrastructure and assassinating military personnel, the penalties were severe and the perpetrators faced death, deportation or imprisonment. Reprisals and hostage-taking inevitably followed such acts and for many French people, the price of violent resistance was just too high and seen as futile in the face of the overwhelming strength and resolve of the occupying German command.

The Resistance became more effective when links were formed with the Free French army in exile in Britain and with the SOE, or Special Operations Executive known as Churchill's Secret Army. Highly secret RAF flights transported trained saboteurs and intelligence specialists into German-occupied countries, as well as dropping military supplies and money to resistance groups.

But resistance took many other forms: depriving the Germans of the food they demanded by selling it on the black market was one way and misdirecting Germans when asked for directions was another. Far less recognised were the efforts of the brave people who risked their lives to hide in their homes and outbuildings those evading captivity and death, in particular the Jews of France who soon after the Occupation became subject to the same persecution meted out to Jews throughout the German-occupied counties of Europe.

I cannot talk about resistance without also mentioning its antithesis, its evil twin if you like: collaboration. As with resistance, this did not exist as a single definable entity, subject to limits or boundaries. In many cases, the boundaries, the lines in the sand, were blurred, as I hope this book will affirm. Collaboration at its worst was the supine acceptance by Pétain and the Vichy government to the partition of France, which led to the subjugation of its population and the persecution and murder of its citizens, in particular its Jewish citizens. Equal to this were those ordinary citizens who denounced their neighbours, resulting in arrests, imprisonment, deportation and murder of Jews, resistance groups and critics of the occupiers.

Also, in this top tier of collaborators were the *gendarmes* who, in full knowledge of their ultimate fate, enthusiastically arrested their fellow citizens, Jews and resistants, and delivered them up to deportation and death. The infamous internment and transit camps of Drancy, Pithiviers, Gurs and others were operated by *gendarmes*. When in 1943 the Germans took over the Drancy internment camp, inmates reported a great improvement in conditions, albeit that they were nevertheless deported to Auschwitz from there. The *gendarmes* arrested and oversaw the detention of over 13,000 Jewish men, women and children, including new born babies, in the Vel' d'Hiv in the week following the roundup of the 16th and 17th of July 1942. Throughout that time, in the oppressive heat of summer, those imprisoned were denied water, food and sanitation, and from there they were deported to Auschwitz.

Collaboration through their close relationships with German Nazis included prominent literary figures as well as those in the arts, entertainment and fashion industries, including Coco Chanel and Louis Vuitton.

Collaboration Horizontale, or having sexual relations with the occupying enemy, was considered a shameful crime and a betrayal of the values and standards of morality that French women were supposed to uphold. In the eyes of those French men who had been forced into slave labour in Germany or who were prisoners of war during the Occupation, it represented a challenge to their virility and potency. Jealousy and outrage on the part of French men and women at the sight of women consorting with German soldiers led to the disgraceful scenes following the liberation of France by the Allies, in which women accused of *Collaboration Horizontale* were stripped, beaten and had their heads shaved by angry mobs.

Many of these women had enjoyed truly loving relationships with the German occupiers. This was inevitable as women were forced to billet soldiers in their homes, they worked in shops, hotels and bars serving the soldiers and officers and they worked as housekeepers and hotel maids for the troops. They would not have considered that there could be any conflict of ideology in the love affairs that developed; indeed it was entirely natural for relationships to develop in the circumstances. Many of the women involved in affairs with the occupiers were simultaneously resisting the occupation by helping

Jews evade arrest and helping the resistance. Furthermore, no one could foresee how the war would end, particularly during the early years of the Occupation when an Allied victory was far from assured.

Paradoxically, prostitution was openly tolerated by the Vichy regime and brothels throughout France were well-regulated and flourished during the Occupation. The Vichy regime did not consider sex workers as real women, but idealised the homemaker and mother, and fidelity to French men was integral to this ideal. Another example of this double standard of morality is the fact that French men returning from imprisonment and forced labour in Germany were not victimised for having had sexual relationships with German women while there. It was only women who suffered the wrath of the *tondeurs* and their enablers.

I hope this book will provide some insight into the risks ordinary people took in their determination not to be collaborators, not to be bystanders, as their fellow citizens were dragged from their homes by their own police officers and sent in cattle trucks to the killing camps in Eastern Europe. The tragic irony is that the trains taking Jews to these camps were SNCF trains, the company initially financed by the Jewish Rothschild family who themselves were targets of the Nazi regime.

Although this book is a work of fiction and any resemblance to actual people is entirely coincidental, it is based on an account I heard as a child.

PROLOGUE

19th July 1944
Normandy

She knew it would not be long before they came for her, to punish her for *collaboration horizontale*.

The years of occupation by the Germans were almost at an end. Bombs had been falling upon the city and its surroundings since the beginning of July. She knew there was little left of Caen now – the city had been the object of Allied attention from the moment the first soldier landed on D-Day and the Germans had committed most of their panzer divisions in determined defence of it. The combination of allied bombing raids and ground combat had reduced the city to ruins and caused civilian casualties in the thousands.

She rarely ventured into the streets. It was too dangerous. There were rumours of sniper attacks by young French women, the lovers of German soldiers, who were fighting resistance groups and allied troops. In the hasty evacuation by the remaining panzer and artillery units, horses and carts had been requisitioned to replace the trucks that were needed at the encroaching front line. As Calais and the northern beaches had been the anticipated landing of an allied invasion, and Hitler convinced by his clairvoyants that this would be so, the Germans had been ill-prepared for a landing this far south. That it should have come to this allowed her a wry smile.

However, a disagreement between General von Rundstedt, Commander-in-Chief in the West, and General Field Marshal Rommel regarding a strategy of defence of the coasts had added to the catastrophe. The former, as she had overheard, saw that the imperative should be to engage in a land battle with any allied invasion, far from the coast and where the Tiger tanks would be most effective. The enemy should be drawn into German defensive positions. Rommel, on the other hand, favoured placing armoured divisions close to the coast, immediately behind the beaches, the Atlantic Wall as it was known, to prevent the Allies from getting a foothold on occupied territory.

As it came to pass, Rommel had not been in Normandy on the 6th of June but in Germany to celebrate the birthday of his wife and to get an interview with Hitler to promote his plan, in the knowledge that Hitler's inclination was to follow the advice of the most recent general to get his ear. But he was too late. The Allies had landed in Normandy at dawn and Von Rundstedt could not get Hitler's approval to move the panzer reserves as the latter was asleep, no doubt under the influence of his usual cocktail of drugs, in Berchtesgaden, at his "Eagle's Nest" retreat. Rommel did not get his interview and Hitler's clairvoyants were wrong.

Even when the Allied forces had taken the beaches, Hitler continued to assert that this was a mere diversionary tactic and that the main invasion force would land at Pas-de-Calais and refused to permit Rommel to move reserve units south. He had misjudged and been misled.

The *Kommandant* had emptied the house of all documents and radio equipment – the Guadagnini cello now stood with its companions along the wall of the library, ignored and unloved.

His leave-taking was hurried – the approach of the allies to the outskirts of the city necessitated a rapid retreat to defensive positions. As she watched him drive off to command his panzer division, she felt the child make its first fluttering movements deep within her.

The *Kommandant* had not looked back.

*

The shaving of a woman's head as a punishment for adultery had its origins in biblical times and was customary in Europe from the medieval period. By removing the woman's most conspicuous seductive feature, her hair, the woman was then publicly shamed and her wrongdoing was revealed to all. Its reintroduction in the 20th century became a commonplace retribution and humiliation meted out to women who had relations with a member of an enemy occupying power. Following the Allied liberation of Europe, women who were accused of consorting with German soldiers were routinely stripped, shaved, and often tarred and feathered, before being paraded through the town by jeering crowds.

They dragged her out of the château and drove her to the main square in Caen. Her tormentors, the *tondeurs,* included many women whom she knew to be petty collaborators, and worse. She recognised *Madame* Aubert, a seamstress who had long coveted the Singer sewing machine belonging to her rival in the town, *Madame* Judit Kaczwynski. The latter, along with her three daughters, made wedding gowns for the affluent families of Caen. Aubert felt her business had suffered since the family had settled in Caen and had informed the local *Gendarmerie* that although *Madame* Kaczwynski's husband, Jacques, was a practising Catholic, his wife was Jewish. The code of Jewish Law states that the child of a Jewish mother is Jewish, regardless of the father's religion. *Madame* Aubert used this knowledge to denounce the family. As a result, all four women, the youngest of whom was only seventeen years old, were arrested by the *gendarmes* and taken to the infamous transit camp at Drancy.

As soon as the *gendarmes* had dragged the women from their apartment, *Madame* Aubert entered and removed the object of her envy.

She reflected on the cost of that machine, certainly that of four innocent lives. It had been well known by that time that Drancy was a transit camp and from there the inmates were taken by train to be murdered in Auschwitz. The communist underground newspaper *J'accuse* – copies of which would mysteriously appear in sacks of potatoes, bags of flour and various other concealments – had a cover story in the summer of 1942 stating that 11,000 French Jews had been exterminated at Auschwitz since March of that year. Deportations of Jews from France began on the 27th of March 1942 – they had been promised resettlement in a homeland for Jews in Eastern Europe. The editor of *J'accuse*, Adam Rayski, learned of the true fate of those deported following contact with an escaped slave labourer from Poland.

Jacques hanged himself from the balcony above the courtyard where the family lived. The attempt by a local priest to plead for their release had not deterred the *gendarmes* in the execution of their duty; their allegiance was to the edicts of the occupying German authorities.

1

The rain is unrelenting. It started long before the crowds had begun to gather in the square to commemorate the 60th anniversary of the D-day landings. The remains of the Mulberry Harbour are barely visible through the dense cloud cover. The sombre mood of the occasion is reflected in the dismal weather. This is how Helen remembered the 6th of June 1944.

She has arrived early and with the help of her granddaughter has secured a seat on the raised benches behind the barriers and above the space which will shortly be filled with families and friends of the veterans who survived the D-day landings and the battles that followed.

This is the first time she has come to an anniversary, although enough invitations have been offered over the years.

Sixty years ago. So much of that time is too painful to contemplate and the years have not erased the memories. Many here today would have been part of that. Do they ever speak of it? Amongst themselves? To their children and grandchildren?

And what of the decades of silencing those who returned from the camps? And the narrative of President De Gaulle, that the entire French nation had been united in resisting the occupation by Germany?

It was 1995 before the President of France, Jacques Chirac, acknowledged the role the French state had played in the persecution of Jews and other victims during the German occupation. There were so many levels of the state that had been complicit: from the bureaucrats who drew up the lists of Jews to be arrested, to the *gendarmes* who dragged them from their homes, to the prison guards at the internment camps at Drancy, Pithviers, Gurs and others, to the bus companies that transported them to the train stations and to the train company, SNCF, that transported them to "Night and Fog", to their deaths.

The country that had fervently embraced the Rights of Man had been willing to witness those rights removed. One decree followed another, debarring them from professions, forbidding them entry to places of entertainment, relegating them to the last carriages on the metro and eventually herding them into cattle trucks. The Germans had not requested cattle trucks – this initiative came from SNCF. French trains driven by French drivers conveyed the deportees to their deaths.

But of the recorded 75,000 Jews deported, 3,000 had returned. She remembers one *retournee* who staggered off the train at Caen, emaciated and partially sighted after two years of imprisonment and broke down in tears, questioning why she had returned when her children and husband, who had also been arrested, were dead. But someone was able to tell her that her two daughters were alive – they had been cared for by an elderly couple in Lisieux and she herself had organised this. The family were united when the husband returned in 1945.

Such stories were rare. Those returning from the camps more often than not discovered that they were the sole survivor of a once large and happy family. And for those who had escaped arrest and deportation, waiting for days at the station in the hope of the return of a loved one, that hope more often than not was extinguished on the Red Cross list of those confirmed as dead. Many of the returned could testify as witnesses to the deaths. The testimony of one survivor heaped more horror onto the grief of the bereaved family. He related the gruesome details of how the man, a medical doctor with a practice in Caen and father of two children, had met his death in an act of savage brutality. The details of this would haunt the family forever. Perhaps it would have been kinder to have spared them the details of their father's death. But the sadism of the German Nazis needed to be revealed to the world and the perpetrators held to account.

For those who survived in hiding, it had been a time of terror. The fear of betrayal, the torment of knowing that others, family and friends, had been killed. The knowledge that they had died because they had followed the rules and registered with the authorities, or been betrayed by a neighbour with a grudge, or a jealous colleague. Breaking the curfew to eat *crêpes* with a neighbour led to a family's arrest and deportation. A neighbour noticing the mother of the family leaving her house after 9 p.m., informed the local *gendarmes* who arrested her. As soon as it was discovered she was Jewish, the entire family was arrested and sent to Drancy, from where they were taken to Auschwitz and murdered.

The square is decked with the flags of all the victorious allied countries and before long, the mood will be lifted by the military bands and the march past of those veterans still able to do so.

The parade begins with veterans accompanied by current members of their regiments proudly holding the flags and saluting the representatives of the governments and royal families on the dais.

The veterans of an RAF squadron march close to where she is sitting. She sees him. A sharp intake of breath and she shakes her head in disbelief. He is unmistakable. He carries his 84 years well. They are of an age, as they were at that time. The brief contact they'd had when it was all over described battles and flights beyond Normandy. And then silence. She thought him to be dead, although silence was part of the operation. The war had been over for thirty years before the flights, which Air Vice-Marshal Harris had disparaged as "transporting ragamuffins to distant spots" were admitted to and given the recognition they deserved. De Gaulle had branded the agents as mercenaries and expelled them from the country while celebrating the achievements of the Resistance.

And what of the collaborators and her own place in the narrative?

Her granddaughter picks up her sudden agitation.

'What's the matter, Granny?'

'Nothing, nothing at all.'

She smiles at her granddaughter, who mirrors herself at that age.

'It is so amazing, isn't it? Do you think anybody from those days will be here?'

She squeezes the girl's hand. A brief shiver, which her granddaughter will attribute to the cold, and her mind drifts back to those far-off days. Sixty years; a lifetime for some, and a foreign country to those who survive.

PART ONE

Helen

2

I grew up surrounded by love. As the only child of a country doctor and his French wife, I enjoyed their undivided love and attention. With my mother, I was "*La Petite Poire Belle Helene*". I spoke French with Maman and English with a distinct Scots "burr" with my father. My parents met in Cambrai in 1916 during the Great War. Dr James "Jamie" Douglas, a newly qualified doctor, was working as an army medical officer close to the front line. Soon after his arrival at the hospital in Rue Léon Gambetta, a group of volunteer French nurses arrived to work there. My mother, Marie-Claude Dubois, was one of them.

There had been little opportunity for socialising or any kind of formal courtship but they were attracted to each other from the beginning. Neither spoke the other's language with proficiency. But Marie-Claude's tireless commitment to the care of the wounded and dying, despite the gore and the screams of pain from the appalling wounds they had sustained, and her gentle way with the traumatised victims of that senseless and brutal war moved him first to admiration and then to love. In turn, Marie-Claude felt an immediate fondness for the gauche red-headed Scotsman. She knew that he had been called up as a commissioned officer upon graduation from Edinburgh University Medical School. She guessed that nothing in his medical training could have prepared him for the bloodiness of the battlefield and the mangled bodies he had to attempt to restore to some kind of life. There was the tacit acceptance amongst nurses and doctors alike as to when a man screaming to be allowed to die, with injuries beyond hope of repair, should be allowed to do so, and with as much dignity and relief from pain as possible. These times were not spoken about. There was no time for anguished soul-searching as more mutilated casualties were stretchered in.

They married in 1919, at the little church in the village of Sainte-Honorine-de-Ducy, in the Calvados region of Normandy, where Marie-Claude's family had farmed for generations. Jamie's family's Scottish Presbyterian denomination was not an obstacle to the marriage. His family were not regular worshipers at Foulden Parish Church in the Scottish Borders, and the fact that their only son had not only survived the war but had also found a decent and beautiful girl to marry overcame any reservations they might have had. The Catholic Church's stipulation that any children born of the marriage would have to be bought up as Catholics caused some disquiet. There was no Catholic school in the village where my father would join his own father in his medical practice. But this was something my parents knew they would manage when the time came. For the moment there was much to celebrate. The whole village came to toast the young couple with a *vin d'honneur* and Scots and French guests ate and drank to the health of the young couple well into the warm August night.

I attended the village school in Foulden until the age of eleven. On Sundays, *Maman* and I were driven by Papa in his Model T Ford to the Catholic Church of Our Lady and St Cuthbert in Berwick-upon-Tweed for Sunday mass. Papa would pass the time walking along the nearby beach at Cocklawburn where the castles of Bamburgh and Lindisfarne could be seen on a clear day.

My childhood was rich with music. I learned French and English nursery rhymes and folk stories in both languages as well as popular folk songs. I could sing traditional melodies and play them on the piano. *Maman* had studied piano at the Conservatoire in Paris. This was unusual for a farmer's daughter, as girls were expected to help around the farm and to marry into a farming family, but my grandparents, Catherine and Michel, had encouraged her musical talent, and from the age of ten had been happy to wave her off at Bayeux Station every Saturday, where she would take the train to Paris to stay with *Tante* Mathilde and have lessons with a professor of piano at the Conservatoire for three days of the week. I had inherited my mother's musical talents and this gave my parents much pleasure.

Papa enjoyed reading to me and from a young age, I knew of the works of Sir Walter Scott but also the many heroic stories of my Scottish heritage.

My favourite story was the one told to me by Papa, that of my ancestor and namesake Helen Gloag, who in 1769 left her village in Perthshire to cross the Atlantic to start a new life in America. He told me that I resembled my ancestor who had the same red hair, pale skin and green eyes. The earlier Helen had been captured by pirates, the fearsome *Salé* pirates of Morocco, and sold into slavery. But her beauty caught the attention of the master of the household and she was sent as a gift for the Sultan of Morocco, Sidi Mohamed, whose fourth and favourite wife she became. Papa had a letter that Helen had sent to her family in Perthshire, telling of her life, first in the harem and then as the wife of the Sultan. There had been many such letters and people had marvelled at the fortunes of the local girl who some hailed as the Empress of Morocco. Helen's eventual fate was unclear. It was possible she had been killed along with her two sons following the death of Sidi Mohamed. His successor was a violent and cruel man, and it was often the fate of wives and concubines to be killed by the new sultan. I hoped that my ancestor found a way to escape; surely providence would have ensured her survival.

I also enjoyed knowing how close Scotland and France were historically; the "*auld alliance*" between the two nations was reflected in the happy marriage of my parents. Many of the words used by the local people had their roots in the French language, such as "dinna fash yersel" meaning do not get angry or upset by something which had its roots in the French *se facher*, to get angry. There were others too. To "blether" *Maman* explained came from the French *bavarder*, to chatter or gossip. And I loved the story *Maman* told about the origin of the word marmalade. Mary, the daughter of King James the 5th of Scotland and his French wife, Mary of Guise, went to France to marry the young King Francois the 2nd. While there, she would ask for a special dish of oranges and sugar to be served to her whenever she was unwell. So it became commonplace, according to *Maman*, that whenever she asked for this dish, her servants would say "*Marie est malade*" (Mary is ill) which in time became marmalade.

At the age of eleven I was sent to board at a convent school in Newcastle-upon-Tyne. These were not happy times; I missed my parents and my home overlooking the fields and pasture lands of the Tweed Valley with the Cheviot Hills in the distance.

The nuns were strict and uncompromising. I was forbidden to speak or sing in the language of my mother and my Scots *burr* aggravated the nuns who called me a barbarian. The fact that I was left-handed seemed to be anathema to them. The pen would be wrenched from my left hand and forced into my right hand. Any attempt to use the hand that was natural to me to write with was met with a slap of the ruler.

I found the hours spent praying in the chapel, kneeling on the hard benches while reciting prayers by rote, tedious and stultifying. So much of the education centred on deportment, elocution, reading the classics, some basic mathematics and religious instruction. Aspects of the latter I found perturbing, particularly the use of the words "Deicide People" to describe Jews. I had never encountered such a terminology. My parents observed their respective religious faiths, and my father minimally so, but there had never been any mention of ill feelings towards those of other religions. I put up my hand during the "Doctrine" class to ask the meaning of the words and to opine that they seemed to be very unfair. Wasn't Jesus himself a Jew?

The nun taking the lesson called me to the front of the class and slapped me on both hands with the ruler. I was then tasked with writing "The Jews Killed Christ" 100 times as a punishment for being a "heretic", as the nun labelled me. I was instructed to report to Reverend Mother the following day to explain my insolence, and to confess my heresy to the priest at Friday's Confessional.

This incident made me conscious of the casual use amongst my school friends and teachers of words and phrases that denoted varying degrees of antipathy towards people of the Jewish faith. Acts of meanness when sharing the weekly "tuck boxes" sent by parents to supplement the meagre fare provided by the school elicited the epithet "Jew" towards the offending girl. I began to challenge this but was met with incredulity. They simply had no idea why I should find such banter inappropriate or offensive.

I discussed this with *Maman* and Papa during the school holidays and they told me that they were proud to have a daughter with such a strong sense of justice and respect for the dignity of others – and brave enough to defend my principles. This early sense of justice would in the course of my life prove prescient.

Maman explained that her best friend at the Conservatoire had been a Jewish girl called Odette whose family lived close to Caen in Normandy. She had stayed with Odette's family many times. Her father had fought in the Great War and been awarded *Le Croix De Guerre*, The War Cross, for his brave actions at Verdun. They had kept in contact by letter over the years. Odette's parents were now dead. They had been killed by a car outside their apartment in Paris. Odette had recently married. Her career as a pianist had taken precedence over marriage at a younger age but she had met and married a cellist in the Paris Opera orchestra and was expecting their first child.

3

July 1938

My parents were waiting for me on the northbound platform of
Berwick-upon-Tweed Station. My school days were finally over, to my
great joy and relief. I had excelled academically, gaining distinctions
in all my School Certificate subjects as well as distinctions in my
Higher School Certificate. I was looking forward to spending the
long summer days relaxing in the garden, watching the apples ripen
and riding the ponies we kept in the field adjacent to the orchard.
I had been offered a place to study medicine at Edinburgh University,
Papa's Alma Mater. This was a great achievement as there was a strict
quota system for female medical students and I was one of only three
accepted that year.

It was late in September, two weeks before I was due to commence
my studies at the university. *Maman* and I were in the garden having
tea while watching the sunset over the orchard. The trees were still
heavy with ripe apples. Our neighbour, Scott, had been around to
fill up a basket of especially sweet ones for the horses; *Maman* and
I had been carefully storing the cooking apples and pippins in boxes
in the cellar.

Maman made a suggestion that took me completely by surprise.

'Papa and I are wondering if you would consider waiting a year
before taking up your place at the university. He has discussed this
with the provost and they both agree that it would be wise for you to
be another year older before you begin your studies. We know how
important it is for you and we are so very proud of you, but to go
from the convent to a big university seems such an enormous step for

a young girl, especially since you will be surrounded by young men and this could be...'

Here, *Maman* faltered. There was an awkward pause, and she took a sip of her tea. I was sure that what *Maman* really meant was that I would be overwhelmed in a male, well, mostly male, environment and of course, in the way of all mothers, was worried about what the nuns would have coyly described as temptations of the flesh.

As was common in those far-off days, I had been taught very little in matters of sexuality. At the age of eleven, I received a small blue book which was distributed by the nuns to each girl in my class. Within the book were admonitions to keep as pure as The Virgin Mary, how to wash the "private" parts of the body and the changes our bodies would soon undergo as we became women. The admonition of purity warned against sitting on a boy's knee and other "acts" which could be provocative. This had been a great source of amusement to the girls and provoked much speculation as to what these acts could involve.

At the age of fifteen, we were presented with a green book of otherwise identical size and format. This gave more detail regarding purity but also explained in a simple sketch the differences between the male and female "private parts" and a brief explanation of how they are used in the procreation of children. The Virgin Mary and purity was mentioned frequently in the text and this caused some confusion as to how Mary managed to have a baby and remain "pure" and a virgin. The nun tasked with answering any questions raised by the contents of the green book averred that this was an Act of Faith, a basic tenet of the Holy Catholic Church (her words) and the lesson was brought to an end.

There were occasional "hops" at the convent with boys from the nearby St Cuthbert's Catholic School for Boys invited as suitable partners for the girls. These were strictly chaperoned and the door to the sports hall where they were held was closely guarded by the nuns to ensure that all contact between the sexes was irreproachable.

But this did not stop various crushes from developing between the participants, and notes found their way over the school wall suggesting clandestine meetings and promises of undying love. These were much treasured by the recipients and the source of great envy by those who were not the objects of such passion.

Maman put her cup down and looked lovingly at me. She told me that she never ceased to marvel at how the setting sun reflected my red-gold hair. She had heard Papa telling the story of the earlier Helen, to whose same red-gold hair had attributed her Arabic name in the harem as *Schem-she-dah,* meaning break of dawn. In this light, it was also the colour of sunset.

She waited for my response.

'But, *Maman*, I have worked so hard for this. You and Papa were so proud when I was accepted. What has changed? And what will I do for a year? I can't stay at home doing nothing. I could help father with his practice, I suppose, but it is not what I thought you wanted. And I want to be a doctor. Perhaps I will return to Foulden and take over the practice eventually or perhaps I could do more. I am only eighteen and it seems that there is so much of the world that I know nothing about and that I could be part of; qualifying as a doctor would give me the chance to do these things.'

I struggled to find the words. I did not want to hurt my parents. Perhaps they had missed my company during the long terms at school in Newcastle. Not for the first time I felt the burden of being their only child. If I had siblings perhaps things would be different, their love more divided, less focused on me.

When I was two years old, *Maman* gave birth to a baby boy who lived for four days only. I had been too young at the time to appreciate the tragedy and sorrow of this. When I was much older, *Maman* took me to the tiny grave in the village churchyard and explained how my brother had seemed healthy at birth, a beautiful dark-haired baby boy, but who after three days started to struggle for breath. The diagnosis of heart failure had meant that he could not be saved and he had died in *Maman's* arms. My parents always celebrated Jamie Michel's birthday on the 12th of April, but the 16th of April was always a day of great sadness which did not diminish over the years. I learned to respect *Maman's* need for support in her grief which would often erupt in episodes of intense crying. Papa was more self-contained and would take me for a long walk in the hills at these times. As I got older, I often reflected on this this. Was it to protect me from *Maman's* anguish or his way of escaping from his own sorrow?

Maman took another sip of her tea.

'I have a proposal,' she said.

Maman explained that her friend, Odette, now had two daughters: Céleste aged six and Séraphine aged four. Odette was working as a pianist at the Paris Opera Ballet School. This, she explained, had been surprising, as her friend had graduated with the gold medal from the Conservatoire and had for many years been a concert pianist in much demand throughout the capital cities of Europe. This employment at the Paris Opera meant that she had to travel to Paris from Caen every day and was not at home until late in the evenings. She had chosen this work, apparently, as her husband, Stefan, was the principal cellist in the orchestra of the Paris Opera. This enabled them to travel together for work and have a family life in Caen. But now the two little girls were too old to be with their *nounou* and needed a *gouvernante* to care for them while their parents were working in Paris. Odette wished the children to learn English while being in the care of a responsible young woman. This arrangement would only be for a year, after which time both children would be attending *ecole maternelle*.

Odette had asked *Maman* if I would consider taking on the role of a governess to the children for that period of time.

Maman also explained that Odette's husband, Stefan Erhart, was from a German Jewish family who had moved to Paris to escape the hostility towards Jews since the rise to power of Adolf Hitler and the National Socialist Party.

'I have talked about this with your father and he was worried about the situation in Europe, but since our Mr Chamberlain came back from Munich with the promise of "Peace in our Time", he is confident that all will be well and that France will be a safe place for you to spend a year. We both agree that you will benefit from this year in France.

'Caen is a very beautiful city and Odette and Stefan have a lovely home close to it. I have stayed there many times. When her parents died, Odette inherited the house. She is *une fille unique*, as you are. It seems from her letters that she has lost contact with the rest of her family. The children by all accounts are charming.

'You will be able to visit your grandparents in Calvados. Their village is not far from Odette's home. They will be delighted to see you. It has not been possible for them to travel to Scotland to visit us. There is always so much to do on the farm. Since the Great War, there has been a shortage of young men to help your grandfather with the land and cattle. Of course, we have sent photographs and letters but they would be so happy to finally meet *La Petite Poire Belle Helene*.'

6

So it was decided. *Maman* accompanied me on the train from Berwick to London. At Victoria Station, I took my seat on the boat train that would cross the channel and take me to the Gare du Nord in Paris. There I would be met by Odette and travel with her by train to Caen.

By the time the train pulled into the Gare du Nord I was exhausted; the sea crossing had been rough and the couchette cabin full of noisy children returning to school in France. I longed for a hot bath and a comfortable bed.

The platform was crowded with excited families greeting each other. Mothers who had sent their children to relatives in Britain for fear of war in Europe were delighted to bring them home now that peace was assured. I struggled with my enormous suitcase along the platform towards the *sortie*. I had seen photographs of Odette and knew that Odette had a recent one of me, but in this immense sea of people how would we find each other?

Then I saw a tall slim lady running towards me, her blonde hair escaping from a barrette. She was carrying a bulging satchel from which music scores threatened to escape onto the platform.

'*'Élene*, I am so sorry. My rehearsal ran over time. I so wanted to be here when the train arrived.' She hugged me and took my suitcase from me.

'*Pauvre petite*. You must be so tired. How pale you are. Now, we must get a taxi to Gare Saint-Lazare and soon we will be in Caen. You will see some of Paris. I will ask the driver to make a special detour around the Arc de Triomphe and the Tour Eiffel.'

I fell asleep in the taxi so the Arc and Tour would have to be enjoyed at a later date. Odette secured a first-class compartment on the Cherbourg train which would stop at Caen two hours after leaving Gare Saint-Lazare.

My first impression was of the green undulating countryside which reminded me of my home in Berwickshire. This brought a prick of tears and a surge of nostalgia for my life there. The endless stretch of fields with recently harvested crops of wheat and barley interspersed with hedgerows and farmhouses were built, as Odette explained, with typical Caen stone, not so different from the houses of my village.

The train pulled into the Gare du Calvados, the main train station in Caen. A porter opened the door and took care of my suitcase. Once outside the station, Odette looked around for a taxi and soon we were driving at speed through the narrow streets of the city. The houses seemed to rise vertically from the *trottoir* – from the gaily painted shop fronts at street level to the higher levels of apartments above.

Odette pointed out the great castle, Le Château de Caen, which she explained had been built by *Guillaume le Conquerant*, William the Conqueror, in 1060, six years before his invasion force won the Battle of Hastings and the crown of England. We drove past the great churches of St Pierre and the Abbey Saint Étienne and a short way along a narrow road out of the city. We entered a village named Sainte-Genèvieve-sur-Orne and shortly after, turned into a wide *allée* lined with lime trees, their leaves now in the full golden radiance of autumn. The lawns on either side were beautifully manicured and interspersed with glorious shrubs. Narrow paths lined with flower beds led to a large tiered stone fountain which sprayed water into a wide pond. In the distance, I could see late roses climbing over an old brick wall. And then we were in front of the house, a magnificent three-storey building in cream-coloured stone with a high-pitched roof and round tower attached to one side. It was the most beautiful house I had ever seen.

'Welcome to Château des Tilleuls,' said Odette.

7

A young uniformed maid showed me to my room, insisting on carrying my suitcase. Odette had instructed me to wash and rest and that the family would be ready to greet me as soon as I had recovered from the journey. But not wishing to keep the family waiting too late into the evening, I had a quick wash, changed into clean clothes and made my way down the wide, ornate balustrade staircase to the room that Odette had shown me when we arrived. A fire burned in an enormous fireplace and seated around it were Odette, a handsome older man and two little girls. All stood up when I entered the room. Odette introduced me to her husband, Stefan, and the girls. She explained that for tonight we would speak in French but at meal times thereafter English would be spoken. When Céleste and Séraphine were in my charge, English would be their language of communication. She was very precise about this and I felt slightly intimidated. Life at home in Berwickshire was more relaxed; I did not have to consider language in this way. If Papa was around we spoke English, and if *Maman* and I were alone we spoke French. But for me, there was no difference, there was only one language.

Odette then rang a bell summoning a maid who was told that the family was now ready to eat.

The dining room was as magnificent as the salon. High gilded ceilings with paintings and portraits on the walls, another vast and ornate fireplace and large doors opening onto a terrace from which the fountain could be seen.

During the meal, Odette explained the history of the house. The original château had been built during the reign of the Valois kings of France. Ruins of the original château, the remains of the tower, could be found in a corner within the walls of the rose garden.

'*Interdit aux enfants,*' she said, wagging a finger at the two well-behaved little girls sitting on either side of me.

She told me how the original château had been a sanctuary in the days following the St Bartholomew's Day massacre on the 24th of August 1572. Huguenots escaping the massacre had been hidden there by the sympathetic Count, Le Comte d'Harcourt, who owned the château at that time. I had not studied French history in any depth, but I knew that the massacre had taken place in Paris during the celebrations of the marriage of Margot, the daughter of Catherine de' Medici, and Henri, King of Navarre. The latter was a Protestant, as was his entourage, but the French court was Catholic. Fighting had broken out between the two religious groups, leading to the massacre of over 10,000 Huguenots. Many managed to escape and return to Navarre.

Odette told of a family of ten who had been rescued by the Count. They had been hidden in the château until the fighting ceased and then given safe passage under the Compte's protection to their home in Navarre. But the Compte's action was denounced by a treacherous serving girl and the château was burned to the ground by a Catholic mob from the nearby village. Only the direct intervention of King Henri, who was made aware of the Compte's courage, saved his life. But he and his family were forced to live in reduced circumstances on the land.

The d'Harcourt family fortunes improved during the reign of the Bourbon Kings; greatly so, because during the reign of Louis the 14th, the Sun King, a d'Harcourt daughter became his favourite mistress for a time. The Château des Tilleuls was built during this period and the gardens were designed by André Le Nôtre, the principal gardener to King Louis.

The French Revolution in 1789 and the terror that followed led to the deaths of the entire family and the château and estates became derelict.

I was astounded by Odette's vivid description of the massacres and the explanation of the rise and fall of the fortunes of the d'Harcourt family. This would not have been a conversation in front of children in Berwickshire. But I was fascinated by it all, and in my youthful enthusiasm for adventure longed to explore the ruin in the rose garden.

'There is a book I believe in the library about the history of our château. Perhaps you can look for it. It is very old, as are many of the books. You must take great care not to damage it. It will be written in *Moyen Français*, the French of that time, and so not easy to read.'

Odette went on to explain that her grandfather, Lev Abramsky, had bought the derelict château in 1891 and that she had been born here. Her grandfather's family had been successful fur traders in Odesa, Ukraine, but had moved to France in 1881 to escape the pogroms against Jews that followed the assassination of Tsar Alexander the Second in March of that year. The Jews were officially blamed for his death by his successor, Tsar Alexander the Third, and the persecution and massacre of Jews, which lasted for three years, was actively encouraged by the Tsar.

Lev and his wife, Rivka, had originally settled in Rouen where there was a large Jewish community and a magnificent synagogue. His business prospered, he and Rivka became French citizens and he had been in a position to buy the derelict château and restore it to its former beauty.

Odette explained that her own mother had been her grandparents' only child and had inherited the château and estate around it. She had married a distant Abramsky cousin whose family had also moved from Odesa to Paris. Her father, Leon, a French citizen by birth, had fought in the Great War and been awarded *The Croix de Guerre* for outstanding courage in the Battle of Verdun. Her father was Leon Abramsky and thus she had been able to retain the Abramsky family name. She, Odette Abramsky, had married Stefan, who had been born in Berlin and whose family, the Erharts, were all professional musicians or distinguished professors at the university there.

Stefan's father had been awarded the Iron Cross First Class for rescuing his commanding officer under enemy fire while defending the Hindenburg Line at St-Quentin in 1918. The family were immensely proud of him and his father had enjoyed wearing the medal at regimental reunions and festivals such as Heroes Memorial Day. The restrictions placed on Jews in Germany under Adolf Hitler's Nazi regime had deprived him of these opportunities. Since 1937, Jews were forbidden to leave their homes on public holidays and festivals.

The family had counted themselves friends of the great Austrian conductor, Herbert von Karajan, who was now principal conductor of the Berlin Philharmonic Orchestra. But most of Stefan's family were now in Paris or London. Only his younger sister, Gisela, remained in Berlin with her children. She was married to a German Catholic, Joseph, whose father, Isaak, was Jewish but who had converted to Roman Catholicism in order to marry Joseph's mother, Elsa. The children had nevertheless been brought up in the Jewish faith despite the disapproval of Joseph's mother and her family.

I expected Odette to say more on this subject but perceived a tension between the couple and thought it tactful to indicate that I was tired and would like to be well slept before taking charge of the children the following morning.

Odette agreed immediately, but added, 'But you must remember, 'Élène, our religion is passed through the mother. Even if my *Maman* had married a Catholic French man or me, *et voila c'est une belle pensée, oui*? it would be so.' She winked mischievously at Stefan.

8

Despite bouts of homesickness I quickly settled into my new life. Odette and Stefan took the 8 a.m. train from Caen to Paris every day and returned every evening in time for *diner*, except on concert or recital nights when they either returned close to midnight or stayed in Paris with Stefan's family who had a large apartment in the 6th Arrondissement, Saint-Germain-des-Prés. Odette promised to take me to stay there at Christmas time to see the beautiful decorations on the Champs Élysées.

I set up a classroom area in the nursery where the little girls had slept as babies under the care of their *nounou*. It was now a playroom with an enormous dolls house in the style of the château with miniature furniture replicating the furniture in the Château des Tilleuls. A magnificent rocking horse the size of a Shetland pony stood in front of the high windows which overlooked the rose garden. There were boxes of toys of every description. There was a small bathroom attached to the nursery and a cupboard which was concealed in the panels of the walls. The children were proud to show me how to find it, by counting the panels along from the window to the door. I looked inside and saw that it was large enough for at least four adults but was shocked to see a key on the inside of the door; the girls could lock themselves in there. I took the key from the lock and put it away in a drawer.

I started by setting up a chalkboard and writing the alphabet in English, teaching the different vowel sounds. This did not work as the girls became restless and preferred to talk in French to each other.

I wrote to *Maman* to request that my English fairy tale, nursery rhymes and poetry books be posted to me, as well as the piano music for the Scottish and English folksongs I had learned as a child. There was an old upright Pleyel piano in the nursery. The library had a beautiful Bösendorfer grand piano which Odette used for practice and to accompany Stefan on his cello.

The books took a fortnight to arrive but were a great success. The girls loved the rhythm of the poems and rhymes and soon learned to memorise them. I found ways of making the phrases from the fairy tales and nursery rhymes, which were beautifully illustrated in the books, relevant to their play and activities. Most successful of all was teaching the girls traditional Scottish songs and ballades. They were soon singing *The Skye Boat Song* to my accompaniment on the piano.

All meals during the day were prepared by the family cook and served in the nursery by one of the maids. After *déjeuner,* the girls were to sleep for a couple of hours. Once I had settled them, I was free to do as I pleased around the château. I explored all the rooms, many of which were fully furnished – but the furniture was covered in dust sheets as though waiting to be brought to life. The tower rooms were very interesting; they afforded views across the city to the Canal de Caen à la Mer, the short canal which connected the city to the town of Ouistreham and the English Channel, La Manche.

The tower was, in fact, a turret as it did not start at ground level but was attached to the second floor of the house. It was clearly a decorative feature, although I imagined that it could be used as a lookout for approaching enemies and even as a defence in attack, or as a prison for a fairy-tale princess. I imagined Rapunzel letting her long golden hair down for the prince to climb up. This was not a story I had read to the children as I was worried about frightening them with stories of witches. Rumplestiltskin had also been put to the bottom of my pile of fairy tales. Goblins and witches could wait until the girls were older.

On the Saturday mornings that Odette and Stefan were at home, I would organise a little concert in the nursery for them. Both were thrilled at the progress the children were making in English and their singing.

Odette's reaction to a tune I played on one such Saturday surprised me. As a child, I enjoyed listening to music on Papa's phonograph. One song in particular attracted me with its plaintive melody and the myth associated with it. The *Lorelei* told the story of a beautiful maiden on a rock on the Rhine whose song and beauty enticed sailors to their deaths. I had an English translation of the words to the song but had not yet taught it to the girls. Nevertheless, they loved the melody and Céleste could already pick out the notes on the piano. Odette stormed up to the piano as I was playing and slammed it shut, nearly trapping my fingers.

Her face was contorted with anger as she shouted, 'I will not have that song in this house! Do not ask me why. It is enough that I have ordered this.'

With these words, she took the music from its stand on the piano and left the room.

I was bewildered and near to tears. Stefan appeared to be equally so.

He put his arm around me and tried to comfort me with the words, 'It is possible someone in her family died in a shipwreck, I have no idea, but this is a song my family also loved. It has been banned in Germany because the words were written by a famous Jewish poet over one hundred years ago. The music was once very popular in my country and played in cafés, restaurants and on pleasure boats on the Rhine.'

The rest of the day passed as normal. Odette invited me to join the family for the Saturday walk around the gardens and was as charming and amiable as ever.

9

I had been sensitive to the fact that the family were Jewish and that my Catholicism might cause some difficulties for them, but Odette had allayed my unspoken concerns regarding the issue of religion from my first day with the family, explaining that she and Stefan observed their religion only in as far as was compatible with their life as French citizens. They observed the Sabbath, she explained, only if it did not conflict with their musical commitments in Paris.

Odette had been instructed by *Maman* that I should attend Sunday mass every week and have my confession heard at least once a month. I had inherited Papa's relaxed approach to religion, which was in contrast to *Maman's* devout Catholicism. I did not wish to oppose her diktat, but I enjoyed cycling every Sunday morning to hear mass at the beautiful church, Église Saint-Pierre, in the centre of Caen. The church was close to the castle and its gothic architecture, ornate façade and huge spire made a striking contrast to the immense stolidity of the 11th century Norman castle, built for defence rather than worship. The interior of the church was no less magnificent, with massive gothic arches, elaborate side altars and carvings representing scenes from medieval folktales.

As in the little church in Berwick, the mass was said in Latin. My confession was often heard by *Père* François, an elderly priest who had trained for the priesthood at Ushaw College in Durham. His maternal grandmother had married an English man and settled in the university city of Durham. She had persuaded him to study there rather than in France. He was delighted to meet *"La Petite écossaise*" as he called me, and enjoyed the opportunity to speak English with me. He seemed equally pleased to learn that I was living with a Jewish family, particularly one so prominent in the city. He expressed concern for the events occurring in Germany, the *soi-disant* liberation of German-speaking territories in Czechoslovakia and the Anschluss of Austria.

'But we should not worry for France and Britain. Hitler has promised no further expansion. We have trust in the treaty he signed. It is for the Jews who have to live under his rule that I am concerned.'

His words prompted me to relate my memories of the words used to describe Jews at my school, and the casual use of the sobriquet "Jew" as an insult and explained how shocked I had been by this.

'It is good that you think like this, Helen,' he responded, 'and have the courage to defend your sentiments. There may come a time when this is tested.'

When I think back to that long ago day, of my innocence and naivety, I could never have imagined how *Père* François's words would prove to be prophetic.

10

On the Friday evenings that Odette and Stefan were at home, they celebrated the Jewish Sabbath. Odette's grandparents had spoken Yiddish and the family continued to call the day *Shabbos* rather than the Hebrew *Shabbat*. I was always invited to join the family and was more than happy to do so.

As soon as the sun had set, the household would gather in the dining room. The family was joined by the cook and the two maidservants, both of whom were granddaughters of the cook. Stefan would light candles and recite a blessing, Kiddush, over a cup of wine. Then there was a second blessing over two plaited loaves of bread, challah, followed by a ritual hand washing before eating the bread. A simple meal of either chicken soup, or gefilte fish and then several courses of meat, vegetables and desserts followed. The same meal and blessings were repeated the following day for lunch, but at dinner time, the third meal, there was no Kiddush.

For the family, such Saturdays were an opportunity to spend time together. They walked around the gardens with the children, enjoying the time they were able to have with them. Odette wrote letters and played music, as did Stefan. Shabbos finished on Saturday evening following the Havdalah blessing.

Shabbos weekends were also an opportunity for me to have some free time. One Saturday at the beginning of November, I went to visit my grandparents in their village, Sainte-Honorine-de-Ducy. They were delighted to finally meet their granddaughter and to introduce me to my many aunts, uncles and cousins who lived nearby. Michel and Catherine had now retired and my Uncle Damian and his wife, Amélie, now ran the farm with the help of their sons, my cousins Martin and Jacques. Both were married to farmers' daughters and had young children.

The farmhouse was enormous with many *dépendances*, which included cattle sheds, a stable block, a vast milking parlour and huge barns stacked with hay. *Grand-père* Michel still preferred to use the pony and *carriole* to travel to the nearby market town of Caumont-l'éventé, but Damian and Amélie met me at Bayeux Station in their 1934 Citroën 7A. They delighted in telling me that Grand-père Michel was certain that cars were a passing fancy and that in time his beloved horses would once again rule the roads.

I joined my cousins, Agathe and Guylaine, in feeding the chickens that fussed and pecked around the coops in the back garden of the farmhouse. My cousins were the same age as me but had not had the same educational aspirations. Both looked forward to marrying local boys. Agathe was already engaged to a boy in the neighbouring village of St-Paul-du-Vernay, whose family ran a small garage and car repair shop.

My visit coincided with the annual village *Méchoui* when despite the cold, the whole village gathered on the field next to the church and a lamb was spit-roasted and shared, along with other meats and salads. Games were organised for the children and a great deal of cider and Calvados, the local apple brandy, was drunk.

Amélie explained that *Méchoui* was, in fact, the name for a North African celebratory meal of roast or clay oven-baked lamb, but the word was used throughout France for an occasion such as the one that day.

Damian drove me back to Caen in the evening while Amélie stayed to milk the cows. Odette invited him in for coffee. I knew they had met many times during their youth when Odette and Marie-Claude gave recitals in Caen and Bayeux, but I was surprised that Damian seemed hesitant in giving Odette the formal kiss on both cheeks. He had shaken hands with Stefan but appeared slightly bewildered when he saw Odette. But I reasoned that many years had passed since they had last met and Damian was probably in awe of the grandeur of the surroundings. He politely refused the invitation to stay for coffee.

11

On another Shabbos Saturday, a couple of weeks after my visit to my grandparents, I offered to help the cook and her granddaughters in the kitchen. The family were reading in the library and I did not wish to intrude on their time together. After we had cleared and washed the lunch dishes, the younger girls, Ruth and Ellana, left to walk around the town and I stayed to talk to the cook. Leah was a lady in her sixties and over cups of tea she told me how she and her husband, and six children, the youngest only seven years old, had fled from their home in Odesa just before the pogrom of 1905. Many of her friends and relatives who had stayed behind died in the massacre of Jews. I was not familiar with the word *pogrom* and asked her what it meant.

'It is the word to describe an organised massacre of a group of people, usually because of their religion or ethnicity; in our situation, because we were Jews.'

She continued, 'There had been other pogroms before and we had learned how to recognise the mood of the city, the warnings that we were in danger. Some Jewish families had armed themselves with guns and knives and women prepared sulphuric acid solutions. We knew what had happened in Kishinev in 1903 and we were afraid. We were so poor that during Passover, many of us, including my family, had to beg other Jews for the money to buy Matzoh for the Passover meal. Yet the Russians accused Jews of taking all the wealth from the city and blamed us for all the problems in Russia, where there was a war at that time with Japan. Because of the war, Odesa suffered a loss of trade and there were strikes in the factories, workers and students were protesting in the streets, political groups were fighting each other and there was growing opposition to the Tsar.

The Battleship Potemkin arrived in June 1905 and this made the situation worse. Its crew mutinied because of the bad conditions on the ship. Thousands of citizens of Odesa went to the port area to view the battleship and workers rallied to the cause of the sailors. The Cossacks arrived and started shooting the workers. My own brother was shot dead on the 15th of June. Fire was started in the wooden buildings of the port and people, both Jews and non-Jews, were trapped in the fire. The Cossacks shot them as they tried to escape.

A few days after this, a newspaper article blamed the Jews for the massacre and demanded that Jews pay for the damage to property and personal loss. The article demanded that all Jewish apartments in the city be searched for weapons, otherwise, the city would be taken over by Jews. It was another attempt to blame Jews for trouble and to incite violence against us.'

Leah took a sip of her tea and asked me, 'Surely you know what has happened in Germany? You have heard of *Kristallnacht*? The Night of Broken Glass?'

Leah explained how between the nights of the 9th and 10th of November there had been a pogrom against Jews in Germany and Austria. About 30,000 Jews had been arrested and taken to camps and over 1,500 synagogues burned or pillaged. Many Jews had been murdered. The windows of Jewish shops and businesses had been broken and Jewish cemeteries in Germany and Austria destroyed. This had been in retaliation for the killing of a secretary at the German Embassy in Paris by a young Jewish man who was aggrieved that his family was being forced to return to Poland.

'The German government used this to whip up anti-Jewish sentiment and a full-scale pogrom followed, and now Jews are being actively persecuted, imprisoned and deported.'

Leah put her cup down and looked at me intently.

'So, you see, Helen, how easy it is for Jews to be the scapegoats when a government decides it wants to exclude a group of people from the lives they should be able to live. The Germans put police officers in civilian clothes into the crowds to stir up what they called the "Righteous anger of the German people against the Jews". We must pray that this does not come to pass here in France.'

I was shocked, realising that I had no idea of what was happening outside of my world in Château des Tilleuls.

'So what happened next in Odesa?' I asked.

'It became more violent throughout the summer and into the autumn. My husband could see what was coming. We packed our few belongings and enough food for three days and left the city under the cover of darkness on the night of the 18th of October. We had two hand carts between us: in one, my husband pushed the younger children, and in the other, I pushed the food and clothing and whatever we could manage to take with us; the older children helped. In one day, we crossed the border into Roumanie and changed all the roubles we had saved to buy train tickets, and after three days we arrived in Paris. My husband's cousin was a chef in a hotel in Paris and he arranged papers for us – without his help, we would have been sent back to Odesa. After a few years, we could become French citizens. My grandchildren were born in France and here we have been free to practise our faith and work.'

'And what happened after you left Odesa? Did your relatives and friends survive?'

'The day after we left, the full pogrom started. Shooting between the various groups broke out and the crowds became convinced that the Jews were responsible and the murders and mutilation of thousands of innocent Jews began. My friend, Elena, was hung from her window by her legs to watch her six children being murdered on the street below. Non-Jews who had been friends with their Jewish neighbours for generations turned on them, denouncing them to the pogromists, who raped and cut open the stomachs of pregnant women and slaughtered infants in front of their parents.

'Perhaps I should not tell you of these things, Helen, but this is what can happen when evil and hatred are allowed to have their way. Many policemen and soldiers wearing civilian clothes watched and participated in the massacre, as in Germany a week ago.'

However hard I tried, I could not conceal my revulsion at what I had learned from Leah. I thought of the woman, Elena, watching her children being murdered. These events were beyond my imagination. In some way, I could relate the horror of it to the stories I had learned of the Highland Clearances following the 1745 rebellion. The Duke of Cumberland's men had been brutal in their reprisals against those Scots who had supported the Stuart Pretender, Charles Edward Stuart. The events led to many Scots leaving their homeland to travel to America, as had my ancestor, Helen Gloag.

I thought back to my childhood. Apart from relating how they had met, my parents never talked about the Great War. As a child, while looking in an old trunk for dressing up clothes, I found Papa's regimental jacket with its medals. When I asked him about it, he gently requested that I not ask about those four years. I guessed from the look of anguish that briefly crossed his face that there were memories that he found too terrible to talk about.

'How did the pogrom end?'

'Following complaints by the British and French Consuls, the city governor ordered the commander of the garrison to get the pogromists off the streets and this ended the worst of the massacre. But, for many months, it was not safe for Jews to be out of their homes. Many of those who survived the pogrom left for other countries in Europe or to America soon after.

'You should understand, Helen, that there are always people who will find an excuse to persecute us. The Tsar at that time did not make a law against the Jews but he did not care enough to protect us. This gave the Jew-haters the chance to do as they pleased. It has always been so and I fear it will be so again.'

'But you are safe here in France, are you not? The French Government protects Jews by law and the *gendarmes* obey the law.'

Leah put her cup down and said, 'Our safety will always depend on who makes the law.'

12

It was a chilly afternoon late in November when I made my first visit to the ruined tower in the rose garden. The air was redolent of the smell of burning leaves from the bonfire the gardener had made on the other side of the walled garden. This evoked memories of the bonfires celebrating Guy Fawkes Night in my village in Berwickshire. *Maman* had not approved of the celebration due to its anti-Catholic sentiment but had nevertheless allowed me to join in the festivities, which I knew to be very small in scale compared to south of the border.

Odette and Stefan had not returned from Paris the previous evening due to a performance at the opera. Once the children were settled for the night, I went into the library to look for the book Odette had mentioned. The library was another magnificent room with bookshelves lining the walls and ladders placed by each shelf. Leather sofas and armchairs were disposed around the room and oriental rugs in rich reds and gold lay on the polished wood floor. A Bösendorfer grand piano stood in the bay of the high-arched windows. The fireplace, as in the salon and dining room, was massive, but whereas those in the other rooms were marble, this one was of ornately carved wood. Leah was occasionally tasked with lighting the fire in the evenings if Stefan wished to occupy the room. She offered to do so for me, but not wishing to put my friend to any trouble, I declined. It was Leah's time to relax as well.

It took me a long time to locate the book as there seemed to be no order or cataloguing system to the shelves, but eventually, reaching high up from the top of one ladder I saw it: a leather book with the name of the château engraved in faded gold lettering. I carefully moved it from its place on the shelf, shaking the thick layer of dust that shrouded it as I did so. The fleeting thought that no one had read this book for centuries crossed my mind as I curled up in one of the armchairs and began to read.

It was well past midnight before I replaced the book on the shelf. It had not been easy to read as the pages were stiff with age and penetrated with dampness in places. The Middle French had not been too difficult to decipher, but in any case, it was the illustrations that interested me far more than the text. The drawing of the original château revealed it as being smaller than the more recent one but fortified to withstand attack. It had a tower attached to the structure but this was clearly a watch tower and the lower walls were sunk into a ditch to protect them, as one illustration revealed, from cannon fire. Of more interest to me was a series of drawings showing the existence of underground tunnels which appeared to be deep in the earth, well below the lower walls. There were pages missing in this section, but a final drawing revealed a winding staircase that appeared to be below one of the tunnels. I was intrigued and impatient to discover more about the ruin and determined to explore it the following day.

The tower was in the far corner of the rose garden. It was evident from the tangle of ivy and brambles that the gardener felt that this part of the garden was not worthy of his attention. The area was in the shadow of an enormous Pendunculate Oak tree, which Odette had explained was at least 400 years old. I had noticed that the tower was not visible from any of the windows of the house – either the oak tree obscured it or the fact that the walls of the rose garden were so aligned to deflect the view from the house towards the corner opposite, where sunlight and roses were abundant.

The approach to the entrance was difficult due to fallen masonry, with much of it covered by patches of lichen, moss and piles of slimy rotting leaves. There was a partially paved pathway under the leaves, but this had deep fissures which were difficult to negotiate without stumbling, as I did many times.

Once inside I shivered in the dank air. Centuries of neglect had left wide cracks and holes in the clay walls and a foul mess of droppings evidence that birds were nesting and roosting there. A few rotted timbers were all that remained of the original gothic roof arches and piles of leaves had fallen through its gaping hole. The place smelled of decay and abandonment and the floor littered with the remains of dead birds and mice in varying stages of putrefaction.

Enormous cobwebs hung from corners and beams. A huge black spider scuttled under a pile of leaves. I loathed spiders and had always dreaded the spider season at home. This usually began towards the end of August in Berwickshire, particularly if the weather was wet. My family home was part of a former nunnery and the old walls seemed to harbour a multitude of spider colonies of various shapes and sizes. The huge black ones were my most feared as I knew they could bite if threatened. One of my childhood friends had picked one up to show me how harmless it was and had been bitten for her efforts. It was their suddenness, which was how I saw it anyway. I would go to the sink in the chilly bathroom and find one climbing out from the plughole. Most revolting of all was to wake up and find one scuttling across my eiderdown. *Maman* instructed me to leave a glass of water by my bed as it would attract the spiders away from me – "but do not, *ma petite*, drink from the glass or *voila*, you may drink the spider."

I shuddered despite the fond memory of *Maman's* wisdom. But I always placed a glass of water next to my bed, out of my reach, wherever I was.

Odette had given no indication as to where the Huguenots had been hidden in the old château, or how they had managed to live there for so long undetected and I had thought it wise not to ask her. Odette would fear for my safety or that I might be tempted to take the children there to explore.

I looked around; there were no obvious doors to any other part of the ruin. According to the illustrations in the book, the tower had been built into the side of the earlier château in much the same way as that on the present château. Presumably, it had been a much larger structure in its time and used as a look-out or for defence.

It was a mouse that caught my attention. It appeared from among a pile of leaves in the middle of the floor. I jumped, not that I was afraid of mice as they were common enough in the barns of my home. They were rarely seen in the house as our family cat was an adept predator. My movement caused the mouse to disappear back under the pile of leaves and debris on the floor. Almost simultaneously, a gust of wind exposed the part of the floor the mouse had emerged from: a trapdoor with a rusted metal ring on top. There was a small hole on one side; clearly the route the mice used for access below and above.

I cautiously pulled at the ring, half expecting the trapdoor to disintegrate as I did so, but I pulled harder and the door opened up, revealing a set of steps which descended into a narrow tunnel. The tunnel looked wide enough for me to crawl into. Curiosity overcame my revulsion as I brushed away cobwebs and mouse droppings and gently eased myself through the trapdoor and onto the steps below.

There was enough of the setting sun to light up part of the tunnel, and as my eyes adjusted to the darkness, I could see that it widened and descended a considerable way underground from another set of steps a few yards away from the entrance. Without a torch, I could not explore further as it would soon be pitch dark and the family might note my absence and worry about me.

I pulled myself back through the trapdoor, covered it with layers of leaves and resolved to return on another day.

13

December brought cold winds and frost to Normandy. The old oak tree, now bare of leaves, looked menacing; a nightmare behemoth despoiling the gardens that had been so carefully planted and nurtured. I had planned to revisit the tower as soon as possible, but the entrance to the tower was even more treacherous; the paving and rubble were covered with rank leaves which had blackened in the frost. I decided to delay my next visit until the weather was warmer and the days longer.

The close proximity that year of Christmas and the feast of Chanukah meant that I was very busy preparing the children for the festive season, and, of course, trying to temper their excitement on account of both events.

Odette had explained that *La Fête de Hanoucca* was a moveable feast in the Jewish calendar, in much the same way as Easter in the Catholic Church. It was a lunar-determined feast, in contrast to the Roman Catholic calendar which determined a fixed date for Christmas as the 25th of December. *Hanoucca* in 1938 began on Saturday the 17th of December and ended on Sunday the 25th of December.

Odette explained that *Hanoucca* means dedication but that it is also known as the Festival of Lights, celebrating the victory of the Maccabees over the much larger Syrian army two thousand years ago, and the miracle at that time when a day's supply of oil kept the nine candles of the Menorah in the newly dedicated temple in Jerusalem alight for eight days.

Leah and her granddaughters were kept busy preparing the special *Hanoucca* food which would be eaten by the household over the eight days of the celebration, and my offer of help was gratefully accepted. Stefan's parents would be joining the family for some of the time during *Hanoucca*, as well as friends from Paris.

I remembered *Maman's* hectic activity before Christmas at our home. *Maman* would stuff a large plucked goose with her own recipe of goose liver and *confit* de gizzard. A tree would be sent from Papa's family estate and placed in the hall at the front of the house, where the family would spend a happy time decorating it with ornaments and lights. *Maman* would make mysterious shopping trips to either Edinburgh or Newcastle and return with parcels, all beautifully wrapped by either Jenners of Edinburgh or Fenwick of Newcastle. Papa's parents and an assortment of his aunts and uncles and their children would arrive on Christmas Eve and gather around for a meal. My father was an only child but there were plenty of "cousins" to compensate for that. We children would hang up our largest socks on the fireplace and reluctantly go to bed hoping to hear the sleigh bells during the night and see snow in the morning.

Papa always drove me and *Maman* to mass in Berwick on Christmas morning, while the other adults helped to prepare the Christmas dinner.

I knew that this year would be very different. *Hanoucca* would end on the 25th of December and intense bouts of homesickness frequently overcame my efforts to share in the family's anticipation and joy.

On the Friday evening before the first day of *Hanoucca*, Stefan brought the nine-candled Menorah to the main window overlooking the *Allee* and lit the first two candles. Odette explained that it was placed there as a tradition, to spread light to others. The centre candle, the Shamash or helper candle, would be used to light a candle from right to left on each evening of *Hanoucca* until all nine were burning.

Throughout the eight days of *Hanoucca*, I felt as though every day was Christmas Day. Presents were distributed among the household at every meal, at which we enjoyed beef brisket, chicken, potato latkes and matzo soup, as well as sweet and savoury kugel and the sweet fried dough balls filled with jam which Céleste and Séraphine so adored.

The gelt, the chocolate coins which were used to play games as well as eaten, reminded me of those that appeared in my Christmas stocking every year. Stefan's parents joined the family for the last days of *Hanoucca*. They spoke German with Odette and Stefan but were utterly charming to me and told me how impressed they were by their granddaughters' proficiency in English.

Stefan took a photograph of Odette, me and the children with his new Leica camera. Odette wore the diamond necklace that Stefan had given to her as a *Hanoucca* present as well as a gold bracelet inset with diamonds on her right wrist. I admired both and Odette explained that the bracelet had been her grandmother's.

'My grandfather exchanged some of his furs for the bracelet during their escape from Odesa. He and my grandmother were on a train with the family of a diamond merchant. The wife of the diamond merchant had been forced to leave her fur coats with her maid in Odesa. My grandmother loved to tell this story to visitors, that she had to conceal the bracelet in her underwear to cross the frontier into France otherwise *les douaniers* would confiscate it.'

But for me, the best moment of all was when an enormous fir tree arrived on the 24th of December and the children and I were tasked with decorating it with special baubles ordered from Paris by Odette.

14

The dark cold days of January seemed endless. Odette and Stefan were very busy with rehearsals and performances during the winter ballet programmes and Odette often stayed in Paris overnight.

Once the girls had settled for their afternoon rest I had the time for other projects. I often helped Leah in the kitchen and had become very friendly with her granddaughters, Ruth and Ellana. I was therefore very anxious when one afternoon I found all three women sobbing in the kitchen. Leah wiped her eyes and proceeded to tell me of a letter she had just received from her sister in Milan. Sara had left Odesa with her family for Italy soon after the pogrom of October 1905 and had been very happy there. The Jewish population, though small, had been established in Italy for centuries and Jews were well integrated in society there. Sara's son worked in one of Milan's biggest banks and her grandsons were training to be doctors.

'Sara's son has been sacked from his job and my grandsons have been sent out of the university. His wife is distraught; they will have no money and now their boys cannot work.'

I put my arms around the distraught woman.

'It is the same as in Germany. Since Mussolini, the prime minister, made his pact with Hitler, things have got bad for Jews in Italy. In November, the Racial Laws were brought in and now Jews cannot work in banks or public offices and Jewish students are banned from university. My sister's family are not allowed on public transport and Sara says the house will be taken from them. They are desperate but it seems they cannot leave the country. Sara also has news from

Germany where Jews are being arrested and sent to camps. They are beating Jews in the streets, even women and children. It is not only Jews who are arrested but anyone who speaks against Hitler and his laws. Hitler will not keep his promise of no further aggression – he is waiting for the moment to strike. Helen, if he decides to go to war, no country in Europe will be safe for Jews.'

I could find no words of comfort. I had recently received a letter from Papa. He too was worried about the situation in Germany and feared that war would be inevitable. *Maman* had written to Odette urging her to leave France with the family for the safety of their home in Scotland. Odette had allayed her concerns by telling her that France was a safe country for Jews, that the Rothschild family lived just outside Paris and that she and Stefan had performed there recently. Odette told me of *Maman's* offer saying "The Rothschilds financed the construction of the railways. We would not have our beloved SNCF without their help. There are many Jews in prominent positions in the government. Nothing bad will happen to *La France*".'

Leah's fears were not without justification. In his speech to the Reichstag on the 30th of January 1939, Adolf Hitler told the world that the outbreak of war would mean the end of Jews in Europe.

I heard the BBC report of his speech on the small Ducretet Thomson wireless I kept in my bedroom, a Christmas present from Damian and Amélie with whom I had celebrated *Réveillon*. This had been a very thoughtful present as they realised how much I had enjoyed listening to the wireless at home in Scotland.

Leah explained that since 1938, radio stations were allowed only three brief daily news broadcasts which meant that most people were unaware of the critical events taking place in Europe at this time. Newspapers and wireless news bulletins were tightly controlled by the French government to promulgate propaganda supporting its policy of appeasement towards Germany and Italy.

Now aware of the advantages of the wireless, I determined to follow the BBC news closely from now on and to keep the wireless a secret from the family.

15

In February 1939, a precocious spring brought a spell of warm sunshine to Normandy and I took advantage of it to further explore the tunnel. On this occasion, I took a torch and a penknife as well as gloves for brushing away the dreaded cobwebs and mice droppings.

The trapdoor was more difficult to open as shards of winter ice still filled the crevices between it and the stone floor. I pulled hard, my fingers aching with the cold in spite of the gloves, but finally, the door yielded and I was able to see down the steps and into the tunnel below.

The steps were very steep and frozen solid. I gasped in panic when my legs slipped into a void where two of the rungs were missing. Once in the tunnel, I moved cautiously, holding the top of my head to judge its height, and to avoid the cobwebs brushing against my hair.

It was bitterly cold. After the second set of steps the tunnel descended deeper into the ground and bifurcated. I decided to take the right fork – I would explore the left another time.

Deeper still I went until eventually I found myself in a room with a low beamed ceiling. The beams were pitted with woodworm in places but seemed otherwise secure. There was a small door on the opposite side from where I had entered. Its base was splintered and an animal had chewed through it in places. Despite the low ceiling, the room was not at all stuffy and I shivered in a sudden draught of cold air. The room had the mustiness of age but was otherwise clear of debris. The ridiculous thought that the former guests had left it in good order crossed my mind and with that thought came the certainty that this was the room that had afforded sanctuary to the survivors of the St Bartholomew's Day massacre. It was a room that had been built not to be found. Excitement and elation caused me to shiver. I thought of the Huguenots who had hidden here. At least it had been in summer; now the cold and damp were extreme.

I decided to try the door in the wall. The ring pull was stiff with time– rust had eaten into its fixings – and as I pulled I worried that it might break off completely. Suddenly, it gave and I was looking at a winding stone staircase. The stone treads were cracked and broken in places but still accessible. I could not see how far it ascended and my first instinct was to climb up and discover where it went. But it was getting late and good sense told me to retrace my steps in order to cover up the access to the tunnel before I was missed by the household. I returned to the trapdoor and into the fading spring light.

16

At the end of February, Odette and Stefan took the children skiing. They invited me to join them but I declined. It was my Grandmother Catherine's 70th birthday during that week and Damian and Amélie had arranged a surprise birthday meal for her with all the family in Bayeux.

With the family away on holiday I had more time to look around the grounds of the château, which apart from the rose garden I had not yet had the time to explore. The weather had suddenly turned much colder and the grey sky and flurries of fine snow presaged heavy falls by nightfall. I put on my warmest coat and gloves and set out towards an area of woodland which stood a short distance behind the kitchen gardens of the château. The gardener's cottage stood close to the woodland and a thin plume of smoke rose from its chimney. The gardener was in his early sixties and I had occasionally been with Leah when he delivered vegetables to the kitchen. His demeanour when he spoke to Leah caused me to sense an antipathy on his part. On one occasion, he reacted angrily when Leah pointed out that some of the potatoes she was peeling were bruised. I distinctly heard him mutter:

'They are good enough for the likes of you.'

This shocked me and I said as much to Leah.

She merely replied, 'This is how it is with him and his kind,' and continued peeling the potatoes, indicating that she did not wish to discuss the episode.

After that time I did my best to avoid the gardener, as I did that day, furtively edging around the edge of the rabbit-proof fence and taking a rough pathway distant to the cottage. The woodland became quite dense in places and I was anxious not to go too far from the house in case I lost my way. I made a note of every fork in the pathway and of any unusual plants or memorable features. Papa had taught me this from a young age – we often walked in the forests of the Tweed Valley, where he impressed on me the need for observation and awareness of the danger of becoming disorientated.

The woodland was very quiet and still. The only sound was the crackling of twigs and frozen leaves as I made my way through the dense canopy of bare branches. Ash trees linked arms with sessile oak and the grey ghosts of birch trees stood sentinel along another pathway. Rooks circled low dipping their wings as they landed on the barren branches. The air was filled with the tang of damp moss and the fusty odour of decaying fallen branches. A small plantation of Fraser fir trees, their branches tipped with frost, stood close to a mound of stones covered in lichen, which seemed to be the foundations of a long abandoned dwelling. The trees opened up to a small glade where a few early snowdrops were struggling to emerge.

The hoot of an owl alerted me to the time; it would be dark soon and I should turn back. And then I stumbled and fell into a tangle of brambles and frozen leaves. The toe of my boot had caught on something beneath the undergrowth. As I knelt down to release my foot I saw a rusty metal grill, the slats of which were warped in places and my boot had caught in one of them. I moved the brambles to one side and peered through the grate. It was too dark to see further than a few inches but I could discern a set of steps descending into the darkness. I pulled at the grate and it gave slightly but appeared to be attached to something beneath it. Intriguing though this was, I knew there was no time to investigate further, so I replaced the brambles and leaves, promising myself to return as soon as I could.

The following day, I set out early towards the woodland but saw the gardener cutting wood outside the cottage. I could see no way of getting into the woodland without him noticing me, so I changed my plans, deciding to make another attempt to explore the underground room. I returned to the house to collect the torch and a penknife and set off to the rose garden. On my way there I noticed for the first time another ruined building. This was on the north side of the great oak tree and would not have been visible when the tree was in full leaf. Also, it was some distance behind the tree and partially hidden by the wall of the rose garden. The ruins of a domed roof and part of the arched doorway could be seen through the gnarled branches of the oak. Odette had not mentioned this ruin. Perhaps it was connected in some way to the tower. Generations of her family had lived here so surely they would be aware of its existence. Perhaps Odette had been forbidden to explore ruins, as she had her own children. I would ask Odette more about the history of her home on the family's return from holiday.

17

There had been a fall of snow during the night which made the entrance to the ruined tower even more dangerous; the rocks and broken paving were now hidden and the piles of slimy leaves more perilous.

The trapdoor opened more easily this time and I made my way down the steps and along the tunnels to the room I had found on my previous visit. I took more time to look around it. It was cold and although the air felt damp, the walls were dry, which was surprising as the room was so far underground. There were draughts of air which, though musty, would have enabled the Huguenot fugitives to live comfortably while hidden here. The tunnels could have been used to bring food to them and also provide a means of escape.

As with the trapdoor, the door gave more easily this time. Another piece of wood splintered off as I heaved it open and I was looking at a spiral staircase carved into stone which wound clockwise around the walls of a narrow vaulted chamber. I noted that the steps were of differing treads and remembered a school excursion to The Castle Keep at Newcastle. The history teacher had explained that the castles of that era had steps which wound clockwise to enable the defenders' swords to reach the most vulnerable part of the attacker's body, and the uneven tread made it more likely for the enemy to stumble.

The staircase ended in an open space carved into the stone and above this was a rusty metal grate attached to an equally rusty hook on the wall. This grate enabled thin shafts of daylight and fresh air to filter through. I prised the grate free of the hook and using my penknife, cut back the brambles which clung tenaciously to it. I pushed hard; a pile of dead leaves and lichen fell through and I was looking at the glade of the previous day, this time covered in a layer of snow. I climbed through and after carefully replacing the grate and covering it with leaves and broken branches, I ventured further into the woods, all the time noting clumps of ferns, the rotting bark of fallen trees, anything that would enable me to navigate my return to the château.

The woods gradually gave way to open fields reaching far into the distance. A herd of cows shared a mound of hay in one field while other fields were ploughed, the brown earth of the furrows barely visible through their covering of snow. A cold silence hung over the landscape.

The snow began to fall more heavily as I made my way back through the woods towards the château, again avoiding the gardener's cottage. Smoke still rose from the chimney but the cottage was in darkness.

Then I remembered the trapdoor in the ruined tower. It would still be visible to anyone who ventured into the tower, as would my footprints in the snow. I knew that Leah kept a large broom in the cupboard next to the rear door to the kitchen; I could use that to sweep over my tracks once I had covered up the trapdoor. I ran into the kitchen to find Leah removing her snow boots, the broom lay against the wall, the snow on its brushes melting fast onto the tiled floor.

Leah smiled at me and said, 'It is done.'

She then turned to the pile of vegetables on the kitchen table, giving me to understand by her demeanour that she did not wish further discussion.

18

The family returned from their holiday and I resumed my life in the nursery with the children. Odette announced that she no longer wished them to have a rest period in the afternoon, explaining that she would prefer them to have more time to speak English with me and that *"en vu les circonstances"*, she would prefer them to have an earlier bedtime. She did not explain what these circumstances were and her manner precluded any temptation I may have had to enquire. I was concerned that Odette knew of my exploration of the ruins and wished to punish or deter me from returning there. Perhaps Leah had informed Odette on her return. But nothing in Leah's attitude that afternoon indicated that she disapproved of my activities. When I went down to the kitchen the following afternoon to collect *goûter* for the children, I asked Leah directly if this was the case. Leah reassured me that this was not so and calmly passed me the tray. As usual, it was covered with a white linen cloth and laid with napkins, a plate with thick slices of chocolate-covered bread and cups of milk.

Once the children had settled for the night, I had an hour before the return of Odette and Stefan to tune in to the BBC news. The German army had marched unopposed into Czechoslovakia the previous day and Hitler and other Nazi leaders were now in Prague. Hitler had made the chilling announcement that "Czechoslovakia has ceased to exist".

Neville Chamberlain had made a speech in Birmingham condemning Hitler for breaking the word he gave at the Munich

Conference and warned that Britain would strongly resist any further territorial expansion by Germany.

That evening, I did not hear Odette and Stefan arrive home and was startled by the bell for dinner. Now that the children did not stay up to eat *dîner* with their parents, it had become customary for Odette and Stefan to visit the night nursery to kiss the children and wish them *"dormez bien, mes petites"*. They would then invite me to join them at the table. It was now after ten o'clock, well past the usual time to eat. I went down to the dining room but hesitated at the door as I could hear a heated discussion underway inside. Odette seemed particularly agitated. But I knocked tentatively and opened the door. The conversation stopped abruptly as they greeted me, and soon Leah appeared with the serving dishes and the usual mealtime pleasantries were resumed. It was during the after-dinner coffee that Odette surprised me with an explanation for the unusual circumstances of the evening.

'Stefan is concerned for his sister, Gisela. She is now alone in Berlin. Her children have been in England since December and her husband has left her. Stefan wanted all the family to come here after the trouble in November but I refused. I told him that these things are not normal in a country such as Germany, the land of Nietzsche, Kant and Beethoven. But now Gisela's husband is divorcing her for a young Catholic woman and she has sent the children by train and ship to England. Stefan wants to travel to Berlin to bring Gisela here. I am against this. It will be too disruptive for our children. She needs to stay in her home and wait for the situation to improve. But he is determined to go.'

I felt very uncomfortable. Following my conversations with Leah, I did not feel I could concur with this manifestly optimistic assessment of the situation. Furthermore, Stefan looked extremely upset.

His voice was shaking when he explained, 'Gisela put the children on a *kindertransport*. On the 15th of November last year, after the terror of *Kristallnacht* in Germany and Austria, a group of British

Jewish and Quaker leaders appealed to Mr Chamberlain, your Prime Minister, to allow Jewish children to come to Britain without their parents, to escape from the terror and restrictions. It was agreed by your government that families in your country offered homes, and organisations in Germany helped families to get their children onto the trains. Gisela's children arrived on a ship called SS Prague at Harwich on the 2nd of December. They are now with my family in London. They are safe but my sister is not. She says they are taking Jews away in trucks; no one knows where they are going but there are terrible stories. I want to bring her here. Last night the phone rang here and it was Gisela. She was crying and begging for help.'

To my astonishment, Odette flung her napkin onto the table, stood up and abruptly left the room with the words, 'Do as you wish, it is nothing to me.'

I was shocked and could find no words of comfort for Stefan who looked upset and embarrassed by Odette's terse exit. I touched Stefan's arm lightly and silently left the room. I was bewildered by Odette's curt behaviour and lack of concern for a close family member. Since the death of her parents in 1930, Odette had apparently distanced herself from her Abramsky relatives. *Maman* had found this decision hard to reconcile with the memory she had of Odette's welcoming family home and the cousins she had met in the château. Only Stefan's family in Paris had been invited to the château at *Hanoucca* and no reference was ever made to the Abramsky relatives.

The following morning, Stefan was not at breakfast; he had gone to Germany to find his sister.

19

The days following Stefan's departure brought a great change in the family. The children missed their father and I was grateful for Odette's suggestion that I tell them their father was playing in an orchestra in London and would soon be home.

But Odette was spending far more time in Paris than previously and on the rare evenings she was at the family home, she preferred to lock herself away in her rooms, the red light on the hall telephone indicating that she was engaged in long conversations with someone. She did not mention Stefan at any time nor indeed express any concerns for his safety.

Meanwhile, I continued to follow the news on my wireless. As well as the BBC, I also tuned into Radio Normandie – but my greatest triumph was to find the wavelength for CBS and listen to William Shirer's broadcasts from Berlin. The latter told me of the growing tensions between Germany and Poland. On the 21st of March, Hitler demanded the port of Danzig from Poland, which was formally rejected by the Polish government a few days later. On the 31st of March, Britain and France agreed to support Poland in the event of a German invasion.

I wrote to my parents in April. Conscious that the anniversary of the birth and death of my brother was always a sad time in the family, I wished to reassure them that life in France was continuing as normal and that people were confident that the political situation between Germany and Poland would be resolved. In many respects this was true as by the middle of April, France was on the cusp of the warmest summer in memory. There was an air of optimism, with people determined to enjoy life to the full. In Caen, couples walked together along broad avenues which were fragrant with the blossoming chestnut trees.

Odette was rarely at home in the evenings now and I had sole charge of the two children. I increasingly sought out the company of Leah in the evenings, and she was as puzzled as I regarding Odette's absence. The telephone rang one night but as soon as I picked up the receiver, the line went dead. I waited and the phone rang a second time and I heard a man's voice. He sounded distressed but spoke in German and I could not understand what he said. I was certain that the voice was that of Stefan but again the line went dead. Since then, the telephone appeared to be disconnected; when I picked up the receiver there was only silence.

April was followed by an even more glorious May and I took the girls for picnics on the beach at Ouistreham. The miles of flat golden sand at low tide reminded me of the beaches in Northumberland, but the warm sea air was a welcome contrast to the chilly North Sea coast, where trips to the beaches, even in high summer, often required layers of woollen clothing, windbreaks and flasks of hot drinks.

Leah continued to receive letters from her sister in Milan, which described the increasing difficulties for Jews living there as well as more troubling political news. A treaty named the Pact of Steel signed by Hitler and Mussolini on the 7th of May provided for military cooperation between Germany and Italy.

'This is Hitler ensuring he has support for his ambitions,' opined Leah while she and I sat together in the kitchen late one evening. We no longer expected Odette to return for an evening meal and I was content to eat in the kitchen with Leah and her granddaughters. Leah proceeded to tell me that her younger sister and family were planning to emigrate to America. Sponsors among the Ukrainian Jewish diaspora in America were obtaining visas for those who wished to leave Europe. Her sister was trying to persuade Leah and her family to do the same.

'But my family have a good business in Caen; they are *Bouchers* and they are French citizens, as are my granddaughters, Ruth and Ellana. My other children are also here in France with their families. We had a Jew for Prime Minister – *Monsieur* Léon Blum was elected twice. This gave us hope, despite the actions of the *Camelots du Roi* and the *Action Française*.'

Leah explained that these groups were violent anti-Semites and had been responsible for attacking Blum and nearly beating him to death. I felt I could confide my possession of a wireless for which I did not have a licence. Leah did not indicate surprise at this disclosure but warned me to remove it from my room as soon as possible to a place of safety.

'You will find such a place,' she said, her face as inscrutable as the time when I went in search of the broom.

20

The 14th of July Bastille Day holiday brought crowds to the beaches, and bonfires and firework displays across the city. BBC reports described bombers of the Royal Air Force flying over Paris, as the French army, including several colonial armies, the Foreign Legion, Navy and Cavalry marched through the Arc de Triomphe and along the Champs-Élysées. They were accompanied by British Marines and Royal Guards. This display of unity in the face of German aggression instilled confidence in the nation. Surely Hitler would not dare challenge such an army.

Odette returned to the château at the beginning of August. She gave no explanation for her absence and did not make any reference to her husband's disappearance. She was as charming as ever towards me, thanking me profusely for my care of her daughters. She also ensured that Leah and her granddaughters were paid their wages, which were by now very much in arrears. I was allowed to spend a week with my grandparents and family in Sainte-Honorine-de-Ducy. It was the *moisson* – the exceptionally warm summer had produced an early and abundant harvest. With my cousins, I followed the reapers and raked the crop onto the carts and enjoyed the juicy apples that were ripe enough to be plucked easily from the trees in the orchards.

During this time I received a letter from Papa. This was unusual as letters were normally sent to the château. The contents of the letter also surprised me as I had given my father no cause for disquiet in my letters which I posted every Saturday from the post office in Caen. I had, however, been concerned that it was many weeks since

I had received letters at the château. It was the gardener who was responsible for collecting the mail and delivering it to the front door of the château. Odette and Stefan would then distribute the letters among the household. But these were not normal times at the château and I vaguely assumed that letters awaited me at the post office and intended to go there and enquire.

Papa's letter was full of foreboding.

My darling Helen,

I am writing to you with the full support of your dear mother who sends all her love to her only child.

We have written many letters to you over recent weeks but in none of your letters to us do you acknowledge their contents. Maman has written to Odette expressing the same concerns but has not received any response.

Furthermore, we have received a letter from a German family in London. They are caring for two children, a boy and a girl, who are the niece and nephew of Odette and her husband. The children arrived from Berlin on what has been named Kindertransport. Their mother, Gisela, is the sister of Stefan. As Jewish children, their lives were at risk, as are the lives of all Jews in Germany and in those countries that Hitler's Germany has invaded and occupied. We can only imagine the terrible decision that must have been Gisela's, to put her children into the arms of strangers in the desperate hope that they would reach a place of safety in a faraway country. They are safe with Stefan's cousins in London, but of Gisela, there is no news except that her husband, who is not of the Jewish faith, abandoned her for another woman.

And there is worse news to come. The Central Council for Jewish Refugees in London received news from a contact in Berlin that Stefan Erhart was arrested when he went to the former home of his sister. He has been imprisoned in a concentration camp at a place called Sachsenhausen. There has been no news of him since then. We do not know whether Odette is aware of her husband's situation. She has not responded to letters from Maman and the telephone at the château is not answered.

My darling daughter, we both urge you to leave France as soon as possible. Encourage, if you can, Odette and her daughters to do the same. As Jews, they will also be at risk. We have every reason to believe that Hitler's ambitions will be extended westwards. Hitler set out on his road to war years ago with violations of the Treaty of Versailles as well as other international agreements. While our government and other European governments were well aware of these violations of treaties, all preferred to make concessions to Hitler to avoid another devastating war, the consequences of which Maman and I are all too aware. We did not wish to lose another generation of young men. But with hindsight, this appeasement of Hitler has been a grave error of judgement. It has encouraged him to further his ambitions, to menace and to conquer. So, my darling child, we beg you to come home to us as soon as you are able.

I am sending this letter to the safe hands of your grandparents, Michel and Catherine. They will help you make all the necessary arrangements for travel.

With all the love a parent can send,
Papa and Maman

I read the letter again and then discussed its contents with Michel and Damian. With their support, I decided that I would return to Château des Tilleuls and persuade Odette to accompany me to Scotland together with the two girls. As there was a guarantee of accommodation and support for the family in Britain, there would be no problem with the government offices regarding their immigration. Having made this decision, I returned to the château the following day.

To my disappointment, I found that Odette had again left the château having given no reason for her departure and again leaving her two daughters. According to Leah, a car had arrived early the previous morning and Odette had been driven away by two men. There had been no evidence of coercion. Odette had been carrying a large travel bag and appeared to have been expecting the car. She had left an envelope on the table containing a month's wages for Leah and her daughters and a brief note for me instructing me to continue to care for her daughters at the château. She gave no details of her destination or any means of contacting her.

I had no alternative but to write to my parents explaining that I now must stay in France to care for the children who had been entrusted to me. But I remained optimistic that Odette would return and could then be persuaded to travel to Scotland and safety.

I decided to move my wireless to a small alcove in the tower of the main château where the rooms were unused and the furniture shrouded in dust sheets. Leah and her granddaughters rarely ventured up there. Ellana and her sister believed the tower to be haunted and while I had no such apprehensions, I decided I would encourage their fears, with a few embellishments of my own, to discourage others from venturing up here.

I carefully placed the wireless as Damian had instructed in order to receive the best possible reception. On the 23rd of August, I listened to William Shirer's regular broadcast on CBS radio. In the broadcast, Shirer reported a speech given by Hitler to Wehrmacht commanders, detailing an impending German invasion of Poland, and a planned extermination of the Polish people. The text of the speech had been divulged to a British diplomat by an informant in the German Intelligence agency, the *Abwehr*.

I shivered on hearing this. There could be no doubt as to Hitler's intentions. War was now inevitable. I wondered whether my parents had heard the same broadcast.

21

"A counter-attack" were the words used by Adolf Hitler and the German High Command to justify their attack on Poland at dawn on the 1st of September 1939.

I listened to the broadcast by William Shirer in the alcove in the tower. Hitler had given no specific information on the attacks by Polish forces and there was speculation that the "attacks" were incursions by SS troopers wearing Polish army uniforms. I shook with apprehension and disbelief. But I comforted myself with the hope that surely Britain and France would come to the aid of Poland and prevent Hitler and his armies from causing more suffering and emboldening them to further territorial claims.

I tried the telephone in the hall. Perhaps it was not too late to accept my parents' offer of refuge for Odette and the children. But the telephone line was dead again. I tried the one in Odette's room and found that it too was not working. Odette had been using the telephone up to the time of her latest departure from the château. I could do no more than await her return to report the problem with the telephone and hopefully persuade Odette to take up my parents' suggestion.

News of the attack on Poland had not reached Leah and her granddaughters. I found them working as normal in the kitchen when I went in to request breakfast for the children. I decided it would be wise to keep the news to myself for the moment and I would not divulge the location of the wireless either.

The children were upset by their mother's absence and I did my best to comfort them and keep to their usual routine. Once they were asleep, I went up to the tower and removed the wireless from its hiding place in the alcove. There was no broadcast from CBS, but I tuned to BBC London and learned that the German army had advanced further into Poland and that Hitler had not deigned to answer the ultimatums issued by the British and French governments to halt the invasion and withdraw his troops from the country.

Two days later, on Sunday the 3rd of September, I heard the solemn broadcast on the BBC by Neville Chamberlain.

This morning, the British ambassador in Berlin handed the German government a final note stating that unless we heard from them by 11 o'clock that they were prepared at once to withdraw their troops from Poland a state of war would exist between us. I have to tell you now that no such undertaking has been received, and that consequently, this country is at war with Germany.

Leah and her granddaughters were visiting family in Paris that day but returned late in the evening. They had heard the news and told me that a general mobilisation had been announced and men were reporting to army recruitment offices in Paris and Caen.

'You understand, don't you, Helen, that should the war go badly for France, we Jews will be scapegoats for what follows? Hitler has promised to exterminate our people.'

I tried to reassure her that the combined forces of Britain and France and their colonies would most certainly overwhelm the German armies.

'But, Helen, the people of France were not prepared for this. They had little understanding of the international crisis. It suited the government to distract them with music and comedy shows on the radio, and the same in the newspapers. Rather than provide information, they tranquilised public opinion and now people are mystified by what is happening. This will affect morale.'

But it seemed possible that it would be a swift victory for the Allies. The British Expeditionary Force and the French First Army were defending the Maginot line along the French border with Germany, and the French had made progress into the Saar region. The news of Poland's utter defeat without any active involvement by the Allies filled us with dread. A regime of terror had been imposed on the country with summary executions of civilians and internment of political leaders, university professors and priests. Jews were being forced from their homes and moved to designated areas in cities. Most of these reports came from CBS but it was becoming clear to me that foreign journalists in Germany were finding it difficult to report anything other than Nazi propaganda.

On the 7th of September, I heard William Shirer's broadcast from Berlin which he acknowledged would probably be his last from the capital. Using the words "in this one-sided war", he expressed his regret and frustration that Germany had been able to defeat the Polish army and subjugate the Polish people without any military opposition from Britain and France.

I felt saddened and disappointed. Shirer's broadcasts had been essential to my understanding of what was happening in Germany. Now I would only have BBC news and this was only available as the BBC Home Service and on a different wavelength from before now. And the now seemed so very different and frightening.

I spent time adjusting the tuning and also moving the location of the wireless within the alcove. The broadcast was now only available at night as a European programme, but it was reassuring to hear the clipped accents of the English newsreaders.

22

The autumn of 1939 reflected the sombre mood of a continent at war. Heavy rains followed the abundance of warm sunshine that had characterised the summer months of that year. I tried my best to distract Céleste and Séraphine from their sadness at the absence of both parents. I had no way of explaining their disappearance. Stefan was at best a prisoner in an internment camp or, at worst, tortured and dead in the hands of his German captors. Of their mother, there was only her inexplicable disappearances and distancing from her family. I could only hope that Odette was preparing the way for her children to escape the horrors of a probable German invasion of France.

As winter approached there was little news of the war. It seemed that the Allies were dug in along the borders, facing their opponents. But apart from minor clashes with reconnaissance patrols, no actual combat was reported. People I met in the streets of Caen described *la drôle de guerre* as a reassurance that both sides would retreat from conflict and peace and normal life would be restored. Although both neutral countries, Belgium and Holland fortified their defences and the BEF and French army received more equipment and training.

Early in December I left the two girls in the care of Leah in order to travel to Paris and visit Stefan's parents. The feast of *Hanoucca* was to start on Wednesday the 6th of December and I hoped to persuade the couple to celebrate the festival with their grandchildren. It was important, I reasoned, that festivals were celebrated despite the strangeness of the circumstances.

The apartment, in the 6th arrondissement, had been leased to them by Odette following the tragic death of her parents. I found the elderly couple in a state of extreme agitation having had no news of their son, Stefan, or of their daughter, Gisela. They were aware that Gisela's children were safe with family in London but were anxious about Céleste and Séraphine in the absence of their mother. They welcomed the opportunity to celebrate *Hanoucca* with their granddaughters and insisted that the festival should be held at their apartment.

Accordingly, I brought the two girls to Paris on the evening of Wednesday the 6th of December and Stefan's parents did their best to ensure that the festival was celebrated in all its traditions and spirit of joy. On the final evening, the 14th of December, we were joined by another family, which included a very lively boy of the same age as Céleste. A raucous game of hide-and-seek took place which came to an abrupt end when the boy fell from his perch on the cistern of the lavatory. It had seemed the perfect hiding place as it was located behind the door of the bathroom and thus far he had evaded Céleste's hunt for him. The scream and thud brought the family to his aid. He was unhurt but his fall had dislodged part of the water tank and some of the tiles above it. I used a small ladder beside the lavatory to climb up to inspect the damage and replace the tiles. To my amazement, I saw that behind the tiles was a cavity in which a gold bracelet bearing a rose gold Star of David was lying. I picked it up carefully. It appeared to be valuable but surely if this was the family's hiding place for treasures, there would be other items here too? I showed the bracelet to Stefan's mother who was completely mystified. It did not belong to her and must, therefore, be an heirloom of Odette's family. But why Odette had not removed it when she left the flat was inexplicable. She insisted that I take the bracelet with me on my return to the château and restore it to Odette.

Christmas passed with no news of Odette. I wrote to my parents with greetings for Christmas, the hope that the "phoney war" would be resolved and that Hitler, faced with the might of the Allied Forces, would retreat from Poland and peace would be restored. As I wrote this, I felt a sense of impending doom which was at odds with the hopes I expressed in my letter. It was only after posting the letter at the central post office in Caen, that I realised I had not mentioned the bracelet. *Maman* may have recognised it and been able to explain its concealment.

So, the bracelet remained unclaimed at the back of a drawer in Stefan's desk in the library where I had placed it on my return from Paris, and I forgot about it. I rarely ventured in there. It was too painful to see Stefan's cellos in their black cases, unopened and unplayed. They evoked images of coffins. I chided myself for such a superstitious fantasy but avoided the room nevertheless.

23

The marking of the New Year of 1940 was a subdued affair. I was again invited to join Damian, Amélie and my cousins for *Réveillon* and took Céleste and Séraphine with me. Once the children were settled for the evening, Damian and Amélie asked me about the situation at the château. They were as perplexed as I as to the whereabouts of Odette and assumed, as I did, that Odette must be making plans to evacuate her children in the event of a German invasion. Damian quietly advised me to keep my possession of the wireless a secret. He had learned that the private use of a wireless to listen to foreign news broadcasts was now banned in Germany and that punishment by beheading with an axe was the penalty for so doing. I shuddered with disbelief that such a cruel, barbaric practice could exist in modern times. I promised that the wireless could not be found and that I would take every care in the event of an invasion to ensure its concealment.

I was able to speak briefly on the telephone to *Maman* and Papa in Foulden. The telephone lines were very busy and it was in the early hours of New Year's Day that I finally managed to speak to them. They were reconciled to the fact that travel back to Britain was not possible at the present time, but hoped that peace would prevail and I would be able to return home and commence my studies at Edinburgh University. The optimistic tone of the conversation raised my spirits and we returned to the château with presents for Leah and her family and renewed hope for the future.

The BBC told of rationing in Britain and in March came the news that the German Air force had bombed the Royal Navy Home Fleet at Scapa Flow in the Orkney Islands.

Worse was to come. On the 9th of April 1940, Germany invaded Denmark and Norway. Denmark surrendered on the day it was invaded to avoid the bombing of the capital, Copenhagen. British and French troops fought briefly in Norway but engaged too late and by the 10th of April, the country had fallen fully under German control. Radio Normandie reported arrests of Jews and those who resisted.

This was followed by the German invasion of Belgium, Luxembourg and the Netherlands on the 10th of May. The German forces, supported by the Luftwaffe, surprised the Allies by pushing through the forested hills of the Ardennes, bypassing the defences of the Maginot Line on France's eastern border and reaching the English Channel.

On the 21st of May, the British Expeditionary Force became cut off from most of the French army. Dutch, French, Belgian and British forces became trapped between two German army groups and were squeezed into a pocket against the Channel coast. Unless an effective counterattack could be made, the only escape for Allied forces was by sea, through the ports of Boulogne, Calais, Dunkirk and Ostend. Millions of civilians were caught up in the fighting.

By the 26th of May, all the French and Belgian ports north of the River Somme, apart from Dunkirk, had been captured by the Germans and the evacuation of Allied troops from Dunkirk had begun. Belgium surrendered on the 28th of May and there was no doubt that Hitler would now turn his attention to conquering France.

I listened to this news with mounting horror and consternation. I felt an enormous weight of responsibility for the lives of the two children in my care and for those of Leah and her family. Winston Churchill was now the Prime Minister of Britain and his radio broadcast upon taking office warned of long months of struggle and suffering and the need for united strength. I felt unequal to the challenges that now faced me. In the absence of Odette, I had become the unofficial *châtelaine* of des Tilleuls.

My fears were realised on the 5th of June when the German army overcame the fortifications on the Maginot Line and then moved south with the obvious intention of taking Paris. Bombs fell on the city on the 10th of June and people began to flee the city in panic

I was desperately concerned for the safety of Stefan's parents. The following day, leaving Leah in charge of the children, I cycled to Sainte-Honorine-de-Ducy. I intended to telephone the couple using Damian's telephone, to persuade them to leave Paris for the relative safety of the château but I discovered that the lines to Paris were blocked. Damian repeated his warning about the wireless. He and Amélie were clearly very concerned for my safety and offered me accommodation at the farm. I refused, again citing my duty to the children. They wrapped up a couple of freshly killed and plucked chickens, some cheeses from the dairy and two bottles of Calvados and carefully loaded them into the pannier of my bicycle.

The sun was setting when I returned to the château. To my amazement, a large Mercedes sedan car was parked by the front entrance of the château. A man in a black leather coat sat smoking inside the car while another was helping Odette load suitcases onto the luggage rack at the back. The children stood by the car holding their favourite *doudous*.

A feeling of great relief swept over me. Odette had returned and was to take us all to a place of safety. I understood that many Jewish families were leaving for Portugal, which had remained neutral, or even driving to Switzerland, also a neutral country. I placed my bicycle against a wall and ran to embrace Odette. To my great dismay and embarrassment, Odette did not return my embrace but pushed me aside. The men could be seen smirking and whispering to each other as she did this.

I felt clumsy and foolish, and even more so when she said, 'I am taking the girls to where they will be among friends. You, my dear, will stay here and accept what will come. I have no further responsibility for you. Come, girls, it is time to leave. Kiss Helen farewell. We must be on our way.'

The girls clung briefly to me but clearly had been instructed to keep the parting as short as possible. I kissed their heads and tried to stop the tears that were welling up and threatening to course down my face. I resolved that I must be strong for them, wherever they were, and hope that the future would be kind to them.

Odette then spoke in German to the men. She placed the girls on either side of her in the rear seat of the car and the car started off down the driveway.

24

Leah gratefully accepted the gifts of food. There had been no meat available to buy in the market that morning. The people of Caen were panicking and buying up as much food as they could now that the war had reached France. She was as mystified as I by Odette's sudden reappearance and abrupt departure. Odette had not entered the kitchen or made any attempt to speak to either herself or her granddaughters. She had, however, visited the gardener and handed him a package.

'Money, I have no doubt. I do not trust that man and do not understand why *Madame* Odette permits him to stay here. He has no love for Jews and that is certain. Helen, you must help us. The Germans will be here soon. It is too late for us to leave and, in any case, there is nowhere that is safe for us in Europe.'

I held the woman in my arms but words of comfort were impossible. We both knew of Hitler's intention to exterminate all Jews and that it was only a question of time before the Jews of France would be subjected to the same horrors as those in Poland and every other country conquered so far.

I decided to go to confession that evening. My usual routine was to attend the church of Saint Pierre on a Saturday evening and have my confession heard by *Père* François, after which, we would stroll around the church gardens and speak English together. That evening, the church was full, with queues outside every confessional and the pews filled with people, no doubt praying for peace. But I waited my turn patiently in the pews next to *Père* François's confessional.

I began my confession in English, as a signal to *Père* François of my identity.

As soon as I had uttered the words, 'Bless me, Father, for I have sinned,' Père François interrupted me.

'Helen, you must return to the church at 10 p.m. this night. There are important matters to be arranged. Please do not ask any questions at this time. Leave the confessional, pray for a while in the church and leave. Go in peace, my child.'

I returned that night as I had been bidden. *Père* François admitted me by the door to a side altar. The church was now empty and the only light came from the chancel light on the main altar and the candlelight of the Lady Chapel. He beckoned to me to kneel with him at the Lady Chapel and spoke in whispers.

'Helen, you are in great danger. Your duty now is to Leah and her family. They must be protected from what will happen when the Germans conquer our country, as they most surely will. I know from Leah that you have discovered the secret room which gave refuge to the Huguenots centuries ago. You should prepare the room for her and her family and do your best to keep them safe there. You will be assisted in this by others and indeed others may also have need of sanctuary there. You are wondering how Leah and I know of this room, are you not?'

I nodded in assent.

'She told me of your explorations. There is another entry point which we will show you. You will need a new identity. As a British subject, you are an enemy of Germany and will be arrested and imprisoned, or worse. You will return here tomorrow at the same time when I will be joined by someone who can help you with this. Please do not ask any questions at this point. Now go, my child. We will meet tomorrow. Take care that the gardener does not see you leave tomorrow, nor indeed return this evening.'

I crept back to the château. The gardener's cottage was in darkness. I realised that I had not seen him since the departure of Odette. I went to the kitchen where Leah and her granddaughters had been joined by their mother, Raisa. Leah explained that her husband and son-in-law would stay above their *boucherie* to protect it from theft.

25

I returned to the church the following night. There was a news blackout on Radio Normandie but the BBC reported the rapid advance of the German army towards Paris. The door to the side altar was unlocked and except for the chancel light, the church was in darkness. The shaft of moonlight from the doorway lit up the Lady Altar as I nervously edged towards it. A figure emerged from the shadows of the altar and touched my shoulder, making me jump in alarm. I saw that the figure was not that of *Père* François but of a young woman of about my age. She gestured to me to sit on a pew and proceeded to inform me of the role I must now assume. She did not give her name and warned me that I would not be given the names of any I may encounter in the course of my activities. She had spoken in French but then surprised me by quoting from a poem by Rudyard Kipling.

"'Them that ask no questions, isn't told a lie...'"

To which I responded, "'So watch the wall my darling while the gentlemen go by.'"

The young woman smiled. 'That will be the code, this poem, in any communication with us.'

We continued in French. She handed me an identity card and using a small pocket-size torch, she showed me the name on the card as Gabrielle Doucet, born in Lisieux on the 2nd of May 1920. She explained that this young woman had died, together with her parents, in an automobile accident a year ago. Apart from an uncle, who the young woman explained was part of their group, she had no other relatives in France, certainly none in Normandy. The uncle had kept the identity cards of the family in the knowledge that they could be useful. The headstones of the family had been removed from the cemetery. I examined the identity card. The girl in the photograph had regular features and was wearing spectacles. Her identity card stated Gabrielle as *"Institutrice et femme de ménage"*.

'So, you are both intelligent and capable. That is perfect for your role,' said the young woman.

'But her hair was blonde and mine is red. There could be no mistaking that. And I do not wear spectacles,' I protested.

'The spectacles can be explained as only necessary for reading. But you will need to wear them occasionally, with ordinary glass, of course. As for your hair colour, I have what is necessary to change that.' She produced a bottle of peroxide. 'This you must use immediately on your head hair and, of course, in other areas if necessary.'

I blushed at this as I could not imagine myself in a situation where such drastic changes would be required.

The young woman smiled.

'Helen, or rather Gabrielle, you may be asked to do more than care for the family at the château. We do not know what war will bring and how we may have to adapt. *Père* François would find this conversation, shall we say, difficult, which is why I have been tasked with such details. Helen Douglas must disappear as soon as possible. It will be explained that she left with *Madame* Abramsky-Erhart and her daughters. You must speak French at all times and make no effort to contact your family in Scotland.'

'But what of my family in Normandy? Only recently I was with my uncle and aunt, and also my cousins?'

'Your cousins will be told the same story by your uncle and aunt. I spoke with Damian and Amélie today. They understand how anxious your parents will be but have promised utmost discretion. Gabrielle Doucet was appointed as housekeeper of Château des Tilleuls by *Madame* Abramsky-Erhart during her absence. We have every reason to believe that the lady will not be returning to the château in the near future. If she does, we can, shall we say, adapt to the situation at that time.'

The figure of *Père* François emerged from the shadow of the altar. He took my hand in his left hand and made the sign of the cross on my forehead with his right hand.

'Have courage, Helen. I know you to be brave and compassionate. Whatever you need to do to ensure the survival of those in your care, and for your own survival, will be righteous in the eyes of God. Know that you will be watched over by others who cannot be named and whom you can trust. I will leave you now with my young friend. She has further instructions for you.'

With those words, *Père* François left the chapel.

'So, Gabrielle, we must deal with the gardener. He is an enemy of the Jews in your care. He is in contact with groups in Paris who will be happy to welcome the German Nazis and do their bidding with regard to the Jews. Tonight, you will go to his cottage and kill him. You will set fire to the cottage with his body inside. Empty bottles of the delicious Calvados your Uncle Damian gave you will be found on the bench outside the cottage. It will be assumed by the *gendarmerie* and the *pompiers* that he drank too much and retired to bed with a lighted cigarette. Such things happen and it can be very sad, but this man will not be mourned.'

I was shocked beyond all reason by her words. I could not imagine myself as the perpetrator of such an act of violence.

'I cannot do this. Why me? If this is to be done, surely there are others who could do it?'

'This is your first test, Gabrielle. And it must be done. It may be asked of you again. It is better that you learn now. Take this and I will show you how to use it.'

The young woman took a small Beretta handgun from her bag and put it in my hands which were shaking so much that I nearly dropped it.

'There are eight cartridges in the cylinder, more than should be necessary. I bid you farewell and good luck.'

She kissed me on both cheeks and left the church.

26

Now alone in the church, I kneeled at the altar and prayed for the strength to do as I had been bidden and for forgiveness for what surely was a crime and a sin.

I then left the church and returned to the château. The lights were on in the gardener's cottage and I crept through the kitchen garden and hid in the shrubbery behind its rear door. To my horror, I realised that he was not alone; another man was sitting on the chair next to him by the fire. They were drinking and laughing together over a paper. I kept very still and was able to catch a few of the words in their conversation. They were talking about a list on the paper, a list apparently of all the Jews in the neighbourhood. The gardener snickered when his companion suggested that they find them before the Germans did and what fun they would have with the women. Their words appalled me; I had to act, to do as I had been instructed, but how? I could not shoot through the window and dared not risk making my presence known.

I returned to the château, collected a can of gasoline from the garage and a box of matches from the kitchen and then went back to my hiding place behind the cottage, where I made a small pile of brushwood next to the rear wall. I poured a small amount of the gasoline onto the pile and set it alight. It burned quickly and a cloud of smoke rose above the shrubbery. I heard the men inside exclaim and watched as they made for the rear door of the cottage. I waited until both men were through the door and in my eye line and fired the gun. The first shot hit the gardener in the chest and he stumbled to the ground. The second shot hit his companion between the eyes. He fell forward and did not move. The gardener struggled to his feet and looked at me in the eye. I felt his shock and hatred and knew that he could see into my soul. My instinct was to run from the scene, to hide, to do anything possible to wipe out my actions of that night. But I forced myself to return his gaze and fired the gun once more, this time hitting his left eye. He fell to the ground.

I waited until I was certain both men were dead and then started the difficult task of moving both bodies into the cottage. I worked quickly, as I knew that once rigor mortis had set in, my task would be more difficult. I managed to arrange their bodies convincingly by the chairs around the fireplace. I found bottles of wine in the cottage kitchen, poured the contents into the drain outside and placed the empty bottles on the floor beside the bodies. I then took the cigarettes from their pockets and placed them on the chairs. I poured the remaining contents of the gasoline can around the cottage and set it alight; it burned quickly and I made a hasty exit through the door. Once I was certain that the fire was going to destroy the cottage and its contents, I returned to the château, replaced the empty gasoline can in the garage and located the bottles of Calvados. These I decanted into one of Leah's massive preservative jars, took the empty bottles to the bench outside the cottage and left them there.

My first thought after I had accomplished this was that there had been no need to waste good Calvados. This surprised me. I started to laugh, hysterically, the enormity of my actions suddenly overwhelming me. Then I fell onto the grass and vomited, choking and sobbing, unable to believe what I had done, what I was capable of. Leah appeared beside me. She took me in her arms and held me close to her, stroking my hair. She told me that I must now hide for a while in the château. She would summon the *pompiers* and answer their questions. It was too soon for my new identity to be made known.

I watched from a window in the tower as the fire engine arrived to put out the blaze. I watched the following day when the *gendarmes* arrived to examine the ruins of the cottage and to identify the human remains there. I learned from Leah that no crime was suspected. The gardener was known to be a habitual drunkard and had several times been ejected from local bars for being inebriated and violent. They could not identify his companion of that night and it was assumed he was not a local man. The empty bottles and evidence of smoking were enough for them to conclude that the fire was accidental.

That night, I applied the peroxide to my hair. I asked Leah to cut it to just below shoulder length and to give me a fringe, or bangs as Leah called the style. I decided not to apply the peroxide to my pubic area; that could wait. I tried on the glasses and looked at myself in the mirror.

'Hello, Gabrielle,' I said.

PART TWO

Auriole

27

Auriole Ritter was born in the town of Beblenheim in Alsace in 1893. Her father, Otto, had a prosperous vineyard and her mother, Adelaine, gave piano lessons in the family home. Auriole spoke French with her mother and German with her father. Her father's family owned vineyards on the banks of the Rhine close to Koblenz, but in 1871 following the defeat of France in the Franco-Prussian war, Otto took advantage of the acquisition of Alsace by Germany to buy a strip of land in the Sonnenglaz, in the foothills of the Vosges Mountains. The Pinot Gris grapes he grew made a luscious wine close in type to the Sylvaner grape cultivated by his family for generations. Soon after purchasing the vineyard, he married Adelaine Meyer. The bride's family was opposed to the match as resentment towards the German victors was commonplace at the time. But the region had been under German rule in the past and intermarriage between the French and German-speaking communities was not infrequent.

The little town with its half-timbered houses and flower-decked balconies was enchanting and Otto's prosperity ensured that the Ritter house was the most imposing.

Auriole showed an early talent for the piano which delighted her mother and at the age of eighteen, she went to study at the Paris Conservatoire with Professor Louis Diemer. Here, she met Odette Abramsky and Marie-Claude Dubois.

Odette and Marie-Claude were close friends. Both had been private pupils of Professor Diemer in Paris before being of an age to be his students at the Conservatoire. Odette frequently stayed with

Marie-Claude's family in the village of Sainte-Honorine-de-Ducy in Normandy where the Dubois family had a large farm. In turn, Marie-Claude stayed at Odette's family home near Caen, a magnificent château with gardens, ruins and woodland to explore.

Odette, Marie-Claude and Auriole were the only girls studying with Professor Diemer. During the academic term, Odette lived with her grandparents in their apartment in the exclusive 6th Arrondissement, while Marie-Claude and Auriole were allocated a shared room at the convent Notre-Dames-des-Champs, close to the Conservatoire. At the weekend, Marie-Claude went home to her parents or stayed with Odette and her grandparents in Paris.

Neither Odette nor Marie-Claude felt eager to become close friends with Auriole, but as the only female pupils of the professor, it was inevitable that the three girls would spend time together.

It became apparent to Marie-Claude that Auriole was infatuated with Odette. She seemed to imitate her in every way possible, mimicking her performance technique and replicating recital programmes. On more than one occasion, an adjudicator criticised the professor for allowing two of his students to present identical programmes in a competition. Marie-Claude found this trait very disturbing. She tried to dismiss her concerns as a form of jealousy on her own part. Perhaps she resented Auriole's presence as fracturing the close friendship she had with Odette. Perhaps Auriole's behaviour was no more than an expression of admiration for Odette's greater talent. However hard she tried, Marie-Claude could not help but feel uncomfortable, but equally felt unable to express her concerns to Odette.

Auriole insinuated herself into invitations to the apartment of Odette's grandparents, where the couple were enchanted by her. Marie-Claude found this behaviour insincere, particularly as she had overheard Auriole speaking of Odette to another student as a "yid from the pale". Marie-Claude had never heard this expression before and sought advice from another Jewish student who explained it as derogatory. She found it difficult to reconcile this use of language with the charming guest who increasingly frequented the apartment.

The grandparents took great delight in remarking on Auriole's resemblance to Odette. Both were blonde and of the same height and build, with regular features and brown eyes. Odette always wore a gold bracelet inset with a rose gold Star of David on her left wrist. Auriole frequently admired the bracelet but observed that it was surely normal to wear such an ornament on the right wrist. Odette explained that it was traditional to wear it on her left wrist, but in any case, as she was left-handed, it was natural for her to place it on the left wrist and her gold bracelet watch on the right wrist. The Star of David bracelet was a family heirloom, given to the firstborn Abramsky daughter and to be worn at all times as an amulet to protect the wearer from ill fortune.

'My family suffered much ill fortune before they came to France and they still hold the superstitions from those days. I am not so much a believer in these fantasies, but I respect the family tradition.'

The grandparents also enjoyed speaking German with Auriole. Odette had never learned German, as her parents had insisted on French being spoken at home, but her grandparents explained that German had been the language of their education and favourite literature and they welcomed the opportunity to speak it with the charming *Alsacienne*.

Auriole appeared enthralled by the family history and even more so by the artefacts and treasures in the apartment. Many of these had been in the Abramsky family for generations. She was particularly attracted to a gold bracelet inset with diamonds worn by Odette's grandmother and even requested to try it on her own wrist. The grandmother hesitated before agreeing to permit this, explaining that it was a very valuable heirloom and part of the Abramsky family history. Odette's grandfather had exchanged some of his furs to obtain it in the flight from Odesa in 1881, and she, Rivka, had concealed it in her underwear to avoid its confiscation by customs officers at the border. While this was a source of merriment amongst the three girls, Marie-Claude was uncomfortable with the look of covetousness on Auriole's face as she placed the bracelet on her wrist and slowly removed it to hand back to the old lady.

But more troubling for Marie-Claude were the books and pamphlets that fell from under Auriole's mattress while the maid was turning it during the weekly cleaning service. Marie-Claude had left a music score in the room and had hurried back to retrieve it before her lesson. The maid was in the process of gathering the papers and books from the floor when Marie-Claude burst into the room and was embarrassed by the intrusion. To make amends, Marie-Claude helped her to replace the items but could not help but see the nature of the works. They included the anti-Jewish newspaper *La Libre Parole* and the book by Édouard Drumont *Jewish France*, as well as crude drawings depicting the supposed racial characteristics of Jews. She was shocked by what she saw and found it hard to understand the contradiction in the choice of reading material and the girl who appeared so enamoured of Odette and her family. She resolved never to mention her discovery to either girl but she was even more suspicious of Auriole's sincerity.

The years at the Conservatoire passed quickly. All three girls enjoyed the musical life of Paris and were regularly invited to musical soirees attended by the Boulanger sisters, Nadia and Lili. Odette became Nadia Boulanger's protégée and had master classes in musical analysis and sight singing with Nadia at her apartment in Rue Ballu. The girls mingled with professional musicians and other friends of Nadia from the musical community, including Gabriel Fauré and Igor Stravinsky. Both girls were invited to the premiere of Diaghilev's ballet *The Firebird*, with music by Stravinsky. Marie-Claude was delighted to have her programme signed by the two artists.

In June 1914, the girls were to perform their diploma recitals in front of an audience of professors, fellow students and invited friends and family. Marie-Claude had already decided that she suffered too badly from "stage fright" to consider a career as a soloist and was planning to train as a teacher in Caen. Nevertheless, her recital was well received and she was awarded a certificate of high merit. Odette's performance received a standing ovation. She was given the gold medal for that year and invited to be the soloist with the Paris Symphony Orchestra in a performance of Saint-Saëns' second piano concerto, her diploma recital choice.

When Auriole did not appear on stage for her recital, there was a great deal of consternation. Her name was on the programme and she had rehearsed her programme with the Conservatoire orchestra the previous day. Marie-Claude volunteered to return to their lodgings to discover the reason for her non-appearance. Auriole had shown no sign of illness that morning nor given any indication that she would not attend the recital. She asked one of the nuns to accompany her to their room, fearing that some accident may have befallen the girl and that she would need support in such a circumstance. But when they opened the door, they found that although her bed was neatly made and her possessions around the room, there was no sign whatsoever of Auriole.

Marie-Claude planned to begin her training as *Institutrice* at an *Ecole Normale* in Caen later in the summer. She returned to her parents' farm in Calvados, anticipating lazy summer days relaxing in the orchard and spending time with her cousins. This was not to be, as on the 28th of June 1914, in the Bosnian capital, Sarajevo, Archduke Franz Ferdinand, heir presumptive to the Emperor Franz Joseph of Austria-Hungary, was assassinated along with his wife, Sophie, by a Bosnian Serb.

A complex web of alliances and treaties between the major powers led to Germany declaring war on France on the 4th of August. Immediate mobilisation of men of fighting age meant that the young men who worked on the farm were conscripted into the army. Marie-Claude was needed to help with the *moisson*, the harvesting of the barley and wheat, as well as gathering the ripe apples from the orchard and storing them for eating through the winter. She helped her mother with the apple press, which would be put to use in the preparation of cider and the Calvados apple brandy. On the 5th of

September 1914, Russia, France and Great Britain concluded the Treaty of London as the Allied powers against Germany and Austria-Hungary. The war that was to become known as "The Great War" had begun.

Marie-Claude began her training to be *Institutrice* at a school in Caen a few days later. Her parents had insisted that they could now manage the farm without her help and that she should continue with her plans to train as a teacher. Her musical talents were much appreciated at the school, where she was called upon to play at assemblies and concerts as well as accompanying the school choir. Her list of private piano pupils grew steadily and she had a reputation for patience and gentleness with even the most recalcitrant pupils.

She received letters from Odette who was in Rome preparing for the piano Grand Prix de Rome. Italy had maintained a neutral stance in the war and Odette would not be returning to Caen until the December of that year, but was looking forward to being with her dear friend once more.

Following the first battle of the Marne in September 1914, wounded and dying soldiers arrived at Caen Station, where improvised hospitals were set up to receive them. Red Cross workers were there to help but were overwhelmed by the number of casualties and the severity of their wounds. Despite having no medical or nursing experience, Marie-Claude volunteered to assist them.

An encounter with an English lady called Grace Ellison changed the course of Marie-Claude's life. The lady was on her way to Bordeaux from Paris and had witnessed the tragedy of severely wounded men waiting at cold railway stations for whatever medical care they could get. She told Marie-Claude of her determination to bring trained and experienced British nurses to organise temporary hospitals on the battlefields of Northern France. These nurses would instruct volunteer French women in the treatment and care of the injured and dying and would most certainly be of lasting use to France.

In October 1914, Marie-Claude worked under the direction of Sister Emily Haswell in Rouen, where she learned how to dress battlefield wounds, the principles of antisepsis and the application of the Thomas splint in fractures. She was vaccinated against cholera and typhoid, and in 1915, as a fully trained member of the French Flag Nursing Corps, she was sent to The Order of St John Hospital in Étaples, close to the front line of the Battle of the Somme. Nothing in their training could have prepared Marie-Claude and her fellow nurses for the mangled bodies, the anguished cries of the wounded and the stench of gangrene and trench foot. In sub-zero temperatures, the medical and nursing teams strived to save men's lives while struggling against their own fatigue and illness.

On the 18th of November 1916, the Somme offensive drew to a close. Marie-Claude and her group were sent to Cambrai, to the hospital in Rue Léon-Gambetta, where she met the young Scots medical officer, Jamie Douglas.

28

Odette Abramsky and her family fascinated Auriole. They were well integrated into French society and had become wealthy, not only as a result of determination and hard work in their adopted country but also due to wealth accumulated over generations of success in trade. They also appeared to feel indebted for being welcomed into a country that valued such industry and thought nothing of displaying their wealth and sharing it with others. The magnificent apartment in the 6th Arrondissement with its works of art and treasures induced in her a grudging admiration but also an insidious feeling of resentment that a family of *émigrés* could have so much success and wealth. She suppressed these emotions in a simulated effusiveness towards Odette's grandparents at whose apartment she was made welcome along with Marie-Claude Dubois. She coveted the jewellery worn by Odette and her grandmother and could not resist requesting to try on the gold bracelet worn by the grandmother. The glint of the inset diamonds induced in her a feeling of euphoria – the possibility of owning such jewellery could be within her grasp.

Her own mother had very little jewellery. Although her father's vineyard was prosperous, her parents were cautious with money. The exterior of the Ritter house was imposing but the interior reflected their ascetic choice of living. This she understood was in no small way attributable to the vagaries of political fortune experienced by the inhabitants of a region which had so often changed nationality. Alsace was a combat zone, caught in the middle of two enemy nations, France and Germany. This doubtless inculcated certain vigilance, the need to protect their resources in an uncertain world. Her mother identified as Alsation, *Alsacienne*, and maintained as far as practicable her French identity, especially in practising her Roman Catholic faith. The majority of Alsatians were Catholics and perceived Germany as an anti-Catholic oppressor. Auriole was very close to her father; she shared his penchant for militaristic forms in society and his disdain for France and all things French. They both ridiculed *Madame* Ritter's attachment to her French heritage, but her mother maintained her *sang-froid* and was confident that, in time, Alsace would be returned to France. In the interim, it was important that Auriole spoke French and continued with her studies on the piano.

Her father stood for the office of mayor of Beblemheim in 1905 as a German nationalist. Auriole was too young at that time to understand it all, but his rhetoric drew much from the anti-Semitic sentiment that had followed the "Dreyfus Affair" in 1894, in which a Jewish army officer from Alsace, Alfred Dreyfus, was accused and subsequently court-martialled for passing French military secrets to the Germans. Dreyfus was sent as a traitor to Devil's Island off French Guiana and "The Affair" helped to create the kind of violent right-wing groups that presaged the rise of fascism in European politics. Anti-Semitic riots broke out in many cities, with hostile crowds incited by Jules Guérin and his newly formed *Ligue Anti-Sémitique*. Evidence that Dreyfus had been framed by his senior officers emerged, and in 1899, Dreyfus was pardoned and released, but the damage to public opinion regarding Jews had been done.

Otto projected himself as the deliverer of the people of Alsace from the threat of Jewish interference in government and the military. The influx of Jews to Germany to escape the pogroms in Odesa and Kyiv had caused a wave of anti-Semitism, as many ethnic Germans and French resented their success in business and their increasing presence in political life. Otto portrayed the Jewish population of Alsace as the enemy within to be blamed for all the injustices and ill fortune that befell the citizens of the country.

For the most part, Otto's rhetoric was disregarded and he was not elected. France and Germany were enjoying a period of peace and prosperity and fast becoming the industrial heartland of Europe. There was no appetite for any organised oppression of the Jewish population. But some did listen, including his young daughter, Auriole. She attended all her father's political meetings and distributed anti-Semitic magazines and pamphlets.

Much of Auriole's support for her father's campaign was on account of her resentment of a neighbouring Jewish family. The two daughters of the family were talented pianists and in a recent piano competition in Strasbourg, had been joint winners of the gold medal. Auriole had not reached the final round, despite her generally acknowledged greater talent. Furthermore, both girls were then offered scholarships at the newly established Juilliard School of Music in New York. There was great excitement among the citizens of the town, that such an honour and opportunity had been granted; none more so than that of their piano teacher, Auriole's own mother, which caused an even greater rift in their relationship. As a consequence, Auriole expressed a preference to spend more time with her father's family in Germany, and from 1909 until 1911 when she was admitted to the Paris Conservatoire, she studied as a private pupil with Hermann Zilcher at the Hoch Conservatory in Frankfurt. It was here that she met Heinrich Claß.

29

Carrying only a small valise and covering herself in a long hooded cape, she passed through the gates of the convent unnoticed by Sister Concierge. The letter had arrived in the morning post, which she had been able to intercept before the nun responsible for distributing the mail could see the postmark. She made her way to the Gare de l'Est on foot. Her absence from the recital would provoke a search, and cab drivers might be questioned during an investigation.

He would be waiting for her on the platform with the tickets. It would be good to be in Frankfurt again, among friends and those who espoused the same values and ambitions as herself.

The letter had been sufficiently abstruse to avoid suspicions on the part of Sister Cécile, who was known to open and censor letters arriving for "the young ladies". But she had understood her instructions completely. It was time for her to return to Germany, and her lover.

She had left Beblemheim in 1909 without regret. She had begun to despise her mother, for her triumphalism at the scholarships awarded to the Jewish pupils and her confidence that Alsace would one day be restored to France, a country that Auriole considered inferior to Germany.

Her father's tacit approval of her decision was evident by the letters of introduction he passed to her as she boarded the train at Strasbourg. Amongst these was the name Heinrich Claß.

Her father's family arranged for her to lodge in rooms close to the conservatory. Auriole soon realised how much spare time she would have to explore Frankfurt and to follow up on the introductions her father had given her. She met Heinrich Claß at a political rally held in the town hall of the Oberadd district of Frankfurt. There were very few women at the meeting and she was by far the youngest, and most beautiful. Claß was a passionate and eloquent orator, promoting the ideology of a pure Germany, free from the polluting influences of ethnic minorities, particularly Jews whom he described as an inferior race. He expanded this theme to include Slavs and called for the expulsion of Poles from Imperial Germany. But his central theme was the need for racial purity and the superiority of the German race, returning persistently to the theme that the Jews were subverting the integrity of Imperial Germany.

Enthusiastic applause followed his speech and afterwards, he mingled with the crowd of well-wishers. She took this opportunity to approach him with her father's letter. He took it from her hands and she felt his eyes regard her, the pretty blonde girl whose brown eyes reflected the intensity of his own gaze.

Heinrich was at that time 37 years old with a prosperous legal practice in Mainz. He was married to Helga, a pastor's daughter from Hamburg. She was five years older than him and since the birth of their only child, a daughter, she had become an obsessive *Hausfrau*, cooking, cleaning and preoccupied with the raising of their child. Helga had no interest in his political activities, and was of her father's opinion that Jews worshipped the same God as Christians and thus deserved tolerance as well as respect for their important role in German life. This infuriated Heinrich and the couple rarely shared a meal together and slept in separate rooms. The difficult birth of their daughter had precluded sexual relations for months and during that time, he had pursued his desires with other women. He now found his wife repugnant and Helga, for her part, was relieved to be free of his importunities, as she regarded them.

In front of him was a beautiful and appreciative young woman who embraced the same ideals as himself and who he suspected felt the same attraction to him as he felt for her. He was correct in this. They became lovers that night.

For the next two years they were rarely apart. Heinrich was careful to avoid a pregnancy and she was happy to play the part of mistress to the great man. She took on the role of secretary and was active in the production and distribution of anti-Semitic pamphlets at meetings.

In 1911, her piano teacher recommended that she apply to the Paris Conservatoire. Zilcher approached his former colleague and friend, Professor Louis Diemer, to recommend her as his pupil. She was reluctant to leave Frankfurt but her lover saw an opportunity in such a move: a loyal German nationalist associating with academics and potential friendships with influential families could have many advantages. He encouraged her to move to Paris and promised to visit her there whenever possible.

She found lodgings at the convent Notre-Dame-Des-Champs, where she shared a room with Marie-Claude Dubois, who had the same professor of piano as her friend, Odette Abramsky.

Heinrich returned to his wife in Mainz but maintained his position in the Pan-German League. Under his presidency, the direction of the league became more radical, promoting hostility to France and in 1911, advocating rearmament and a swift war, which would lead Germany to world power and territorial expansion. He described the Jews as the "enemy within" subverting the government and polluting the purity of the German Race.

Heinrich first saw Odette Abramsky at a recital given by Professor Diemer's pupils. He was introduced to the Professor and later to Odette as Auriole's uncle. He was struck by the uncanny resemblance of his lover to the young Jewish girl. Later that evening, he reflected on this and contemplated on its future potential. He made discreet enquiries regarding the Abramsky family and was impressed by the wealth and connections they had accrued during their relatively short time in France. He told Auriole of this when she joined him at his hotel the following morning. She had excused herself from classes on the pretext of illness. After their passionate reunion, he suggested that she cultivate her friendship with Odette and study her discreetly: her performance, style of clothing and mannerisms.

30

They arrived in Frankfurt in June 1914. Heinrich allowed himself a brief "honeymoon" with her and then set her to work translating into French his most recent book, a hypothetical treatise on how he, as Kaiser, would promote Pan-Germanism, imperialism and anti-Semitism.

During this time, Heinrich introduced Auriole to Walter Nicolai, a senior intelligence officer in the Imperial German Army who had recently been put in charge of the German military intelligence service, the *Abteilung*. Nicolai shared Heinrich's fervent nationalism and made no secret of the fact that he was impressed by Auriole: she was fluent in both French and German, loyal to Germany and demonstrated ability in observation and surveillance. The latter he had perceived during their walks together in the woods outside Frankfurt where he had also tried, albeit unsuccessfully, to seduce her.

Following the outbreak of the war between the Allies and the Central powers in August of that year, Heinrich felt vindicated; he was certain that Germany would be victorious and that this war would justify his theories of German supremacy as a world power.

Walter Nicolai visited the couple in Frankfurt. His proposal that Auriole should train as a spy was greeted with enthusiasm; she was keen to play her part in the war effort. Heinrich's presence was required in Berlin, where his zealous nationalism would be useful in influencing public opinion. Patriotic fervour reached a peak when

Germany successfully overran Belgium and took the port city of Antwerp in October 1914.

A few days later, Walter Nicolai accompanied Auriole to the train station in Berlin, where she joined a group of three other young women on a train to Antwerp. There they were enrolled at the spy school of the *Kriegnachrichtenstelle,* The War Intelligence School, headed by Elsbeth Schragmüller, alias *Fraülein Doktor.* Schragmüller had been tasked by the military authorities to recruit and train spies to be sent throughout France. Auriole was the perfect recruit: fluent in French, intelligent and, as Elsbeth soon discovered, possessing a photographic memory, she excelled at all the skills taught at the school. She learned how to develop secret codes and create invisible ink and miniature handwriting to enable messages to be hidden in accessories such as umbrellas and shoe heels. She also learned how to kill.

Under the code name "Elise", she was able to infiltrate the spy networks of Britain and France operating in the occupied territories of France and Belgium. Her fluency in French and seductive charms facilitated her assimilation into groups determined to disrupt the offensive of the hated German occupiers. One of her many achievements was to limit the impact of French saboteurs crossing from the neutral Netherlands, whose main purpose was the destruction of the railways bringing troops and supplies to the battlefront.

Her affairs with various high-ranking French military officers provided vital information for the *Abteilung.*

31

Following the defeat of Germany and the signing of the Armistice on the 11th of November 1918, Auriole returned to her lover in Berlin. Heinrich was bitter and disillusioned by what he considered capitulation in the face of victory and saw it as a betrayal of the German people, blaming those he described as subversive elements in the country, in particular, the Jews.

By 1922, Auriole was tiring of her lover. But life in Berlin was exciting: Heinrich set her up in an apartment in Admiralsplast, where she gave piano lessons but continued to support his writing, translating much of it into French for distribution among the rising numbers of anti-Semitic organisations in France.

While poverty shaped the lives of many of the city's inhabitants and political tensions often exploded in street violence, Auriole found herself caught up in the vibrant social life that epitomised the "Roaring Twenties" in Berlin. She frequented the nightclubs and bars, which had proliferated since the end of the war, and became part of a set of young people who felt liberated from the constraints of the pre-war years. It was at one such venue, the Moka Efti, where she met Erika Canaris and was invited to join in her birthday celebration.

The two young women were close in age and during the course of the evening, discovered each other's interest in music. Erika was an accomplished violinist and married to Wilhelm Canaris, a naval commander and decorated war hero. Canaris, as Auriole discovered, was also active in naval intelligence. She was invited to soirees at the Canaris villa to play piano and accompany cello and violin sonatas, which were attended by friends and colleagues of the Canaris family. A young naval cadet who was also a talented violinist was invited to join the musical soirees. His name was Reinhard Heydrich.

Born into a musical family, Heydrich was in his early teens during the Great War. When Germany lost the war, he followed his family's example in blaming the Jews for his country's defeat. Heydrich was influenced by the German *Völkisch* movement and its belief in the supremacy of the blond-haired, blue-eyed Germanic people, which he resembled. He took delight in associating with violent and anti-Semitic groups and joined the *Freikorp*. At the age of 18, he began work as an officer cadet in the Kiel naval dockyard and six years later, was promoted to first lieutenant. He served as a signals officer attached to naval intelligence under the command of Wilhelm Canaris.

Heydrich had a reputation as a womaniser but had been described as a man with "a cruel, brave and cold intelligence, for whom the truth and goodness had no intrinsic meaning". In other words, he was a man very much of the same character as that of Auriole. They became lovers.

Auriole had maintained her association with Walter Nicolai throughout her time in Berlin and she introduced him to Heydrich. Heydrich's experience in naval intelligence impressed Nicolai and in 1929, he and Auriole were recruited to the counter-espionage section of the *Abwehr*.

In the same year, Auriole and Heydrich joined Adolf Hitler's Nazi party. A year later, now aged 28, Heydrich became a member of the *Schutzstaffel* known as the SS, the elite organisation of black-coated young men chosen on the basis of their racial characteristics. An interview was arranged for him with the new SS Reichsführer, Heinrich Himmler, who was planning a rival intelligence service to the *Abwehr*. Himmler was impressed by Heydrich's self-confidence and determination and appointed him as head of the SS security service, named the *Sicherheitsdienst* or SD, and Auriole took on the role of his secretary.

Work began in a small office with a single typewriter, but due to Heydrich's fanatical zeal, it soon grew into a vast network of informers, creating dossiers on anyone who might oppose Hitler, as well as information gathering on Nazi party members and Storm Troopers or SA leaders. Both Heydrich and Auriole had a taste for gossip and they maintained folders of rumours and details of the private lives and sexual activities of top Nazis. Auriole was adept at planting hidden microphones and cameras.

But, by this time, Heydrich's interest in Auriole as a lover was fading as another much younger woman had caught his eye. Lina von Osten was 19 years old, blonde with blue eyes, and thus the epitome of Himmler's Rhine Maiden ideal. She was also an enthusiastic member of the Nazi party. Heydrich's marriage to her was encouraged by Himmler. Heydrich's reputation had been compromised by a scandal during his time as a naval intelligence officer. Older members of the Nazi party were uncomfortable with a man who had been dismissed from the Navy in disgrace due to "behaviour unbecoming in an officer and a gentleman". This had involved a young woman he had seduced and promised to marry, only to abandon her. Marriage to a young woman such as Lina would quell all possible reservations party members might hold against a young man who showed such ruthless diligence in the cause of National Socialism.

Auriole accepted the situation with equanimity, after all, she was still young and beautiful enough to attract other lovers and Heydrich had made it clear that he still needed her as his assistant.

But it was Himmler himself who in 1930 suggested an alternative role for Auriole. She was to return to France and be a "sleeper agent", a potential asset if required in future action. This would require a change of identity in order for her to access influential and wealthy people, and possibly play a covert role in subversion and agitation – in other words, to be an agent of influence. She expressed concerns that she risked exposure due to her activities as a double agent during the Great War, but Himmler mildly said, "I have the utmost confidence in you. Target your identity and eliminate all who could challenge it."

PART THREE

Helen

32

As soon as the *gendarmes* had finished their investigations of the ruins of the cottage, we set to work removing quilts, blankets, bed linen and towels from the closets of the château. Leah advised leaving a few items behind. It would look suspicious, she reasoned, if the closets were completely empty.

There would be no way of heating the underground room during the winter months, but with adequate blankets and warm clothing it should be possible to survive the cold. A supply of mattresses mysteriously appeared at the kitchen door the following morning. Under the cover of darkness and with the help of Raisa and her daughters, we carried these together with quilts and blankets to the underground room.

Leah showed me the other entrance to the room. It was located in the ruins of the former chapel beneath the stone altar. A trapdoor beneath the altar opened into a wooden stairwell and on into another tunnel. This descended to the junction with the tunnel I had found earlier. It took all night to move the beds and bedding into the room. Leah emptied the store cupboards of preserved fruit and vegetables and filled buckets of water from the well. We put buckets to use as lavatories in a corner of the room and placed dressing screens from the bedrooms of the château around it. I promised to empty the buckets regularly.

In my guise as Gabrielle, I attended confession the following evening and requested oil lamps from *Père* François. I hurried back to the château in time for the BBC broadcast; the news could not be worse. The Germans had broken through the French lines across the Somme and Aisne rivers and were approaching the outskirts of Paris. There was mass panic in the city and people were loading up cars, wagons, handcarts and perambulators in a desperate effort to escape the approaching German army and salvage what they could from their homes. The panic spread and towns and villages south of Paris became deserted. The BBC named this mass evacuation the "Exodus".

I learned of the evacuations from Dunkirk. British Expeditionary Force troops were still on the beaches awaiting rescue. Many had been killed in strafing by the Luftwaffe while they awaited evacuation, but bizarrely the German tank divisions were not involved in the attacks. The rumour was that Göring had persuaded Hitler that the Luftwaffe could annihilate the retreating troops without the help of the armoured divisions. Heavy cloud cover had made this impossible for over twenty-four hours and facilitated the rescue effort. Many thousands had been rescued by naval vessels and by civilian small boats. I felt a thrill of pride for my countrymen. It must have taken enormous courage to cross the channel in a fishing boat or leisure craft to rescue the stranded soldiers in the face of constant bombardment from the German planes once the cloud cover had lifted. I also learned that many British soldiers had escaped from the beaches and would doubtless be finding ways to return to Britain. I guessed that the Germans would be aware of this and be hunting for them. I vowed to do whatever I could to help my fellow countrymen if the opportunity arose, and prayed for their safety.

Leah decided that the night of the 13th of June should be the last the family would stay in the château. By the following day, the underground room would be fully equipped with bedding and food supplies, and it would be better that they were installed safely before the inevitable arrival of the German army to Caen. Leah fretted about her husband and son-in-law, but I promised to visit the shop regularly to check on them and pass on discreet messages. She hoped that the men would join them as soon as I considered it necessary.

We raised our glasses, which contained the delicious Calvados supplied by Damian, to the defeat of Germany and our own survival.

At dawn the following day, the 14th of June, German soldiers marched into Paris. Parisians watched in silence as the well-dressed and healthy young soldiers marched down the Champs-Élysée to the sound of a military band. They were followed by waves of tanks, motorised infantry and more troops. The German flag was hoisted over the Arc de Triomphe and swastikas adorned all government buildings. French time was advanced by one hour to bring it into line with Berlin and the German mark was fixed at more than twice its pre-war level.

News spread to Caen that the Germans were behaving with utmost propriety, in contrast to the savagery that had marked the invasion of Poland. It seemed that this was due to the passivity of the population. Once it became evident that there would be no revolt, the Germans assured the Parisians that property would be respected and the curfew, which had been set for forty-eight hours, was immediately lifted. But the telephone exchange was now in German hands and all weapons were ordered to be handed in.

Radio Normandie was back on air and there was no edict preventing the possession of a wireless. The news reported the *politesse* of the German soldiers. They were shopping in the Galeries Lafayette for stockings, shoes and perfume and being scrupulous in paying for everything. They were even handing out chocolates to children and setting up soup kitchens in various parts of the city. The 14th of June was unseasonably warm and people stopped to listen to military bands playing Beethoven under the chestnut trees of the Jardins des Tuileries.

I visited the *boucherie* owned by Leah's husband and son-in-law, where I found them to be in good spirits as trade had been brisk but without the panic buying of previous days. The local farms had supplied chickens and other meat in plentiful supply and there was an air of optimism in the city. After all, they told me, France had been occupied before, in 1814, 1870 and 1914. There had been looting and chaos at those times. Now they were amazed at how civilised the conquerors seemed to be.

33

As I was ostensibly alone in the château, I cancelled all deliveries of food and shopped discreetly in the town. I made sure that I did not frequent the same shops and businesses – it was too soon to become recognised by local people. "Trust no one," had been the advice of the young woman in the church.

"'Don't you tell where no one is, nor yet where no one's been,'" I responded, with a smile.

With no visitors expected at the château, Leah felt it safe for her family to venture out into the rose garden and enjoy the sunshine. I worried about Ruth and Ellana. It seemed unfair for them to be kept underground, particularly as Ruth was already thin and pale. I spoke to *Père* François about this during my now weekly confession.

I began my confession in the normal way, but added, 'People will think I have many sins to confess, that I am here so often.'

'Do not worry, my child. There are many in this town who feel the need to unburden their sins onto me with greater frequency.'

I was sure this had been said with a smile. The screen of the confessional did not permit me to confirm this. I confided my concerns regarding Ruth and Ellana. *Père* François promised to consider the possibility of finding an alternative refuge for them. He told me to return to the church the following night, as there would be further instructions for me.

I left the booth and knelt to do my apparent penance. As I got up to leave, I noticed an elderly woman looking closely at me. The woman slowly got to her feet and I realised she intended to speak to me. To hasten away would only serve to raise the woman's suspicions, so I waited outside the church for the woman to approach me.

'Surely you are the young woman who was *gouvernante* at the château. I saw you with the children many times. But I understood the family had all left. They were Jews; they knew what would happen when the Germans came. I was waiting for that time. I would be the first to show where the Jew house was. But you look different. It is the hair and the glasses, but you are still as then.'

'No, *Madame*, you are mistaken. I am employed as *femme de ménage* at the château. The family and the *gouvernante* have left, for Switzerland, I believe. I was appointed to keep the château in good order for when they return. Yes, *Madame* Erhart noted at my interview my likeness to Helen, the English girl. But I am Gabrielle Doucet and I have my identity card to show you if you like. But really you are mistaken *Madame*; I should not have to prove who I am and no young woman likes to be compared to another. Surely you remember that from your own youth?'

I tried to keep my voice steady and to put a glint of humour into my last sentence. But my heart was beating wildly and I felt faint in the heat of the church garden. My identity had been challenged already. I was not equal to this subterfuge. How soon would it be before others perceived the same?

I returned to the church the following night. This time a young man was waiting for me. He used the phrase from Kipling and I made my response.

I started by relating my encounter with the old lady at the church. He promised to make enquiries as to her identity and suggested that I should wear, as many women did, a large mantilla over my face and head. Up to then I had only worn a small silk kerchief when attending mass or confession. He advised that I would need to be careful and to avoid shopping for food close to the church; no doubt the woman lived in the vicinity of Saint Pierre and I would be likely to encounter her again. I agreed that this was a good plan. He thanked me for my care of Leah and her family but warned me that the situation could only get worse for Jews and those who tried to resist the German occupation.

'France is no longer a safe place for Jews or for any who are brave enough to oppose the Germans. For the moment, they are behaving as though they are the saviours of France rather than the aggressors. Believe me, Gabrielle, they have been preparing for the occupation of France for a long time. Hitler is determined to have his revenge for the Treaty of Versailles. His generals did not approve of the behaviour of the *Gestapo* in Poland, and Hitler has agreed that the SS and their security police, the *Gestapo*, do not accompany the troops into France. But this will not last; *Reichsführer* Heinrich Himmler will not wish to have his SS and SD excluded, and it will not be long before they will be here and the terror will begin.

34

On the 16th of June, the Prime Minister of France, Paul Reynaud, resigned. He and his government had fled when the German army entered Paris, first to Tours and then to Bordeaux. He handed power to Marshal Pétain who, as the hero of Verdun in the Great War, was much loved by the people of France. At 12:30 p.m. on the 17th of June 1940, Pétain announced on the wireless that he had agreed to be the new head of government and that he was asking Germany for an armistice. There was to be no more fighting and the French people were to fully cooperate with the German authorities.

'Now the Germans will be making the rules. As I said that day, our safety depends on who is making the rules.'

Leah was sitting under the wall of the rose garden where the others had joined her in enjoying the warm June sunshine.

'We Jews will be held responsible by the people of France for this catastrophe. And Pétain is no friend of Jewish people.'

I was equally pessimistic. I knew that posters were being put up on the walls of buildings in Paris and all major cities, including Caen, reading, "Have confidence in the German soldier". The poster depicted a handsome young German soldier holding a child in his arms, presumably a French child.

I had listened to the call to arms by General Charles de Gaulle, transmitted by the BBC on the 18th of June. The message was on behalf of the Free French Army, many of whom had escaped to Britain before the fall of France or from Dunkirk. His message was heard by few on that day but was repeated on the 19th and 22nd of

June. At that time, most of the millions of people who had left their homes as the German army approached were now making their way back to those homes in the north. De Gaulle pronounced sternly that it was a crime for French people to submit to their occupiers and an honour to defy them. "Whatever happens, the flame of the French Resistance must not and will not be extinguished."

I felt somewhat ambivalent when I heard this speech – from the safety of a BBC studio, these were easy words to say, but for those who would suffer the brutality that would surely follow any resistance, it was an entirely different matter. I noted that De Gaulle did not mention the reasons for France's defeat. His message was that France was not beaten and would live to fight another day.

I asked myself if I would be equal to the challenge of this call to resist – and then I remembered the gardener and his friend.

I was more discreet when shopping in Caen. I went to the markets late in the day, when there were fewer people on the streets, and avoided the area around the church of Saint Pierre. A beautiful black lace mantilla that covered my head to my shoulders was left in a package by the rear door to the château.

'I look as though I am in mourning in it,' I described to Leah.

On the 22nd of June at 18:36, in the Forest of Compiègne, the Armistice was signed by officials of the Nazi party and the government of the French Republic. There was no doubt in anyone's mind that the choice of venue for this humiliation of France was Hitler's moment of revenge. The choice of Compiègne and the use of the same railway carriage that had been used when Germany signed the 1918 Armistice was his moment of triumph and scorn.

I listened to William Shirer's broadcast from Compiègne in which he described Hitler's face as "afire with scorn, anger, hate, revenge and triumph".

Under the terms of the Armistice, France was now carved into two distinct areas: an Occupied Zone comprising three-fifths of France, which included the Channel and Atlantic ports, and a so-called Zone Libre. The Occupied Zone contained the whole of northern and western France, whereas the Zone Libre in the south was to be left relatively free of German troops. The French government would now be based in the spa town of Vichy. The Germans would have control of the channel ports, heavy industry and raw materials. Alsace and Lorraine were annexed once again to Germany, and the men were conscripted into the German army.

Marshal Pétain and his chief minister, Pierre Laval, a renowned anti-Semite, were set to put in place the French state in which a "New France was to arise from the ashes of defeat". This New France would be Catholic, conservative and authoritarian, with respect for discipline and obedience to the new order. Pétain's words following his meeting with Hitler left no doubt in anyone's mind as to how the Vichy regime would conduct its affairs: as a vassal state of Nazi Germany.

I am embarking today on a path of collaboration, with honour, to maintain French unity.

'And we will be the first to be blamed for this break up of our country,' said Leah. 'There are many who have been waiting for this opportunity and now their time has come.'

Leah was correct in her prediction. Within days of the Armistice being signed, posters bearing the words "Our enemy is the Jew" were put up on the walls of buildings in Paris and Caen. Young "guards" hung around Jewish shops to intimidate customers and by August, the ransacking of Jewish shops and businesses had begun. The *gendarmes* did nothing to prevent this. The Germans were short of their own police officers and had instructed the *gendarmes* to resume their duties. At the beginning of the occupation, the *gendarmes* had been told to hand in their weapons; now they could take them back. A few resigned on principle, some chose to "*se boucher le nez*" and just obey orders, but others saw active collaboration with the Germans as a path to promotion.

The atmosphere in the city of Caen was consistent with that in all the major cities of the Occupied Zone. Newspapers were strictly censored and most news arrived by word of mouth. It appeared that the initial relief at the politeness of the German occupiers was giving way to fear and uncertainty. More Germans arrived to govern and they commandeered houses, hotels, schools and entire streets. Sections of hospitals were closed to all but German patients and many restaurants and cinemas were closed to all except German personnel. They seized cars and furniture and requisitioned petrol. They plundered and pillaged at will and the French people had no way of redress.

The German military administration was also responsible for civil affairs in the Occupied Zone. This would be divided into *Oberfeldkommandanturen* with an *Oberfeldkommandur* and *Feldkommandur* in command of each. The holders of these positions could requisition a local château as the headquarters for the administration.

Feldcommandur General Karl von Werstein was appointed to the Calvados region of Normandy and on the 2nd of July, he and his guards, adjutant, orderlies and team of secretaries arrived at the Château des Tilleuls.

I heard the approach of the armoured vehicles and saw the flag-decked staff car as I was crossing the rose garden. The vehicles swung in an arc around the front entrance of the château and came to a halt. I watched as a tall grey-green uniformed officer stepped out from the passenger door of the vehicle, which was held open by a saluting soldier. I watched as he gazed at the château and then at the gardens. He and his entourage then mounted the steps to the front door of the château. I gasped in amazement when he rang the bell; I had heard that German officers usually took possession of properties by breaking down the door. I hurried unseen through the back door, smoothed my hair in front of the hall mirror, took a deep breath to calm my nerves and opened the front door.

'*Bonjour, Monsieur Le Kommandant, et bienvenue au Château des Tilleuls.*'

I bowed my head in an appropriately obsequious gesture as I said the words.

Von Werstein bowed in response and then gave the detestable Heil Hitler salute. I did not feel obliged to reciprocate but bowed my head again and repeated my words of welcome.

In accented French, Von Werstein explained that he was now in command of the château.

'I understand, *mademoiselle,* that the château belonged to a family of Jews. Can you explain, please, where they are and what is your role in this place?'

I watched his grey-blue eyes look me over from head to toe as he said those words. I felt naked beneath his gaze, and more vulnerable and afraid than I had ever felt in my life.

'I am Gabrielle Doucet. I was employed by *Madame* Abramsky-Erhart to take care of the château when she and her children departed. I do not know where they are and it is not my business. My only concern is that I have not been paid since they left.'

With these words, I managed a disdainful sneer which I hoped would persuade the *Kommandant* of my distaste for my former employers.

It seemed to work. He smiled and said, 'A good and faithful servant! I am sure you can help us here. You are familiar with the château and that is useful. Be assured that we will not neglect your payment. So, for now, *Fräulein* Gabrielle, if I may address you as such, you will show us where we should make our rooms and then be prepared to take charge of the domestic affairs of the château, as you have clearly done so well thus far.'

I tried my best to maintain my composure but nevertheless, my voice shook as I thanked Von Werstein for his offer. No doubt he would attribute this to the honour he was bestowing on me. For this I loathed him but at least it meant that I could stay at the château.

The remainder of the day was spent allocating rooms to the *Kommandant's* advisors and security detail. The latter were mostly young infantry soldiers. I locked the nursery and hid the key. This room had a partial view over the rose garden and I could not risk being observed going to and coming from there. I gave the *Kommandant* the bedroom that had been occupied by Odette and Stefan and suggested the library and salon for his offices. There were two female secretaries in his entourage, both dressed in military grey uniforms. They set about immediately and efficiently unpacking typewriters and papers. A communications officer set up phone lines. From what I could understand, one line was direct to Berlin, another was a line to Paris and other administrative centres throughout France, and one was for his personal use. The German flag and the swastika now flew above the château.

Later that day, the *Kommandant's* personal cook arrived. I showed him the kitchen where he was shocked by the empty shelves. I hastily excused this as a result of the looting that had taken place as the German army was approaching Paris. The valet was equally unimpressed by the lack of bed linen. The same excuse seemed to satisfy him.

To the secretaries, I allocated the bedroom that had been Céleste and Séraphine's room. The young women spoke French and asked me about the tower. One expressed the possibility that it would afford nice views over the city and countryside. I gave a shiver and told them that it was reputedly haunted, which proved an effective deterrent to the desire for a view.

I offered to help the cook with shopping for provisions and to be on hand to help around the house. Shopping for food would give me an opportunity to communicate with the group. Up to now, I had only met a young woman and a young man in the church, but I assumed there must be others.

I wondered if my friends in the underground room knew of the arrival of the *Kommandant* and his troop. Surely they would have heard the vehicles? I looked out of the window and down the driveway. Armed sentries stood at the entrance to the drive. I would have no way of covertly leaving the château, day or night. I decided that religion would provide an excuse to leave the château. I tentatively knocked on the door of what was now the *Kommandant's* office and was admitted by one of the secretaries. The *Kommandant* was in the process of placing photographs on his desk – *no doubt his wife and children*, I thought to myself. He smiled at me and indicated that I should take a seat on the chair opposite him. Again, I felt his gaze on me. I touched my hair instinctively – surely the red-gold was not visible. No, it could not be as I had recently peroxided my hair. I explained that today was the anniversary of the death of my grandmother and that on this day it was my normal practice to attend evening mass at the church where she had been buried. I held his gaze for a short time and then modestly lowered my eyes.

'Of course, you may, *Fräulein*. If you wish, I can send one of my soldiers with you for protection or if not now, at some other time perhaps.'

I was horrified by the suggestion but meekly responded, 'Thank you, *Herr Kommandant*. Today, it will not be necessary. The church is quite close to the château and I prefer to be alone on such days. But, yes, in the future, I may ask this of you.'

I bowed my head by way of valediction and turned to leave the room.

It was only later that I realised that the *Kommandant* had not done the detested Heil Hitler salute.

36

I took my mantilla from my room, set off for the church and arrived just as confession was finishing. I knew that *Père* François would leave his booth and then go to the sacristy to prepare to say the evening mass. I waited in a pew close to his confessional booth until he came out and then, crossing myself as I did so, left the pew to genuflect in the aisle, causing *Père* François to hesitate. He acknowledged me with a brief nod of his head and entered the sacristy door at the side of the altar.

I left the church and walked along the garden path that bordered the church wall – there was a door to the presbytery at the end of the wall. I looked around to make sure I was not being followed. The door was unlocked and I made my way in tentatively. Perhaps *Père* François would not receive me. There were only ten minutes before the start of mass. But I need not have worried, as *Père* François was waiting for me and he ushered me silently into the sacristy.

'Stay for mass and sit in the pew at the back of the church, on the left-hand side. You will be contacted by one of the group. My child, you are in great danger, as are all who you are caring for. But the situation is not hopeless. These are terrible times for France, and indeed for the world. We must do our best to counter this evil. Much will be asked of you and you must choose whether you wish to play your part or not. This is a matter of conscience. But if you choose to follow the instructions you are given, remember that yours is the righteous path and you will be forgiven. Now, return to the church, my child. I will offer this mass for you.'

I found his words puzzling but returned to the church as instructed. My mantilla completely covered my head and shoulders and as the church was full, I looked about to see if the old lady who had challenged me that day was in the congregation. If she was, no doubt she would be at the front of the church. The elderly usually arrived early and sat in the pews at the front to be first to receive communion and a shorter distance to return to their seats. There were three others in the pew I had been directed to and I had to make my way into the middle of the row. A young woman with a baby was sitting at the end of the row. The baby was fretting despite the mother's attempts to soothe it. Next to her sat another young woman who appeared to be annoyed by the disturbance caused by the baby. The latter gestured to me that she wished to move away from the baby. The other occupant of the pew was a middle-aged man who did not raise his head from his missal. I immediately acquiesced and sat beside the young mother. As the congregation stood up for the reading of the gospel, I noticed a small envelope fall from the baby's shawl. I bent to pick it up, unsure whether this was intentional, but the mother nudged the envelope towards me and nodded her head. All then sat down and the mass continued. I placed the envelope in the pocket of my dress.

While the final blessing was being said, I left the pew and slipped unnoticed into the confessional booth behind it. Here I opened the envelope and read its contents.

You must find a way into his bed, then you will be safe and above suspicion. Your guests must be supplied with food and water but you should be ready to help move them to safety elsewhere and to welcome others. For the moment we will only communicate with you at the church but this may change.

Through a crack in the door, I watched the congregation leave the church. The old woman was there, this time with a uniformed *gendarme*; she was leaning on his arm and talking to him. I had no doubt that he was her son. I hid the envelope and letter in my bodice and made my way back to the château. The cooking range would be lit by now and I could dispose of it there. As regards its contents, I understood what I had been asked to do but whether I would be capable of achieving this was another matter. I must first find out what kind of man Karl von Werstein was; all I knew of him at present was that he was the feared enemy of those I had to protect.

37

I did not sleep that night. I waited until I was certain that the household had settled in their various rooms. I had noted that the guards changed over at 10 p.m. and that those who took their place settled on the ground by the gates to smoke and enjoy the warm summer's evening. I left my bedside light on and locked the bedroom door behind me. I crept down the rear staircase to the kitchen and out, through the kitchen gardens, past the ruin of the gardener's cottage and into the woods beyond.

The cook had returned to Caen after preparing the evening meal. It seemed from my conversation with the secretaries, Lotti and Emilia, that he had found a woman to keep him company in the evenings. Both girls spoke French. Lotti explained that her parents were from Alsace and of German descent. She had spoken French and German as a child. Her parents had moved to Berlin in 1932 and the rise of the Führer as the saviour of the German people had caused her father to insist that only German was spoken at home. Both young women were slightly older than me – they were pleasant enough and clearly efficient in their work, but I did not think that the *Kommandant* would find either of them attractive. I despised myself for making such a judgement but realised its importance if I was to do as I had been instructed.

Once in the woods, I followed a track to the glade and the hidden trapdoor. There, I eased my way inside, pulling the brushwood behind me to cover the entrance and made my way to the hidden room.

They were pleased to see me but very anxious. Leah was desperate for news of her husband and son-in-law. In this, I could offer no comfort. I explained how difficult it would now be to make visits to the shop but promised to do my best. They had recently been brought food and drinking water, which had been left inside the trapdoor to the woods. They were warm enough but the toilet buckets were full and they were running out of water to wash themselves. Ruth had a fever and had been vomiting and Leah was worried about disease due to the close confinement and lack of sanitation. I knew enough about medical matters to realise that the living conditions in the room, with limited access to fresh water for drinking and for washing plus the close proximity of the toilet buckets, could lead to dysentery or worse still, cholera. I took the buckets one by one up to the trapdoor and emptied them behind bushes in the woods. There was no way of rinsing them clean. I promised to bring more fresh water the following night although I was at a loss as to how to achieve this. Leah knew that her granddaughter must be given plenty of fresh water and be kept warm, but asked if aspirin could be brought to her to help with the fever. Again, I promised to do my best.

I returned to the château the same way I had left it. As I made my way through the woods, I realised that these too could soon be under guard. The future seemed very bleak indeed.

The following morning, I approached the cook to ask if he needed any grocery shopping in the town. It was market day and I persuaded him that I knew the best places to buy good meat and vegetables. He agreed that this was an excellent idea. I found that he too spoke good French. It seemed that the staff had been hired because of their proficiency in the language. He told me that his mother was French and had married a German soldier in Lorraine in 1898. After the Treaty of Versailles in 1918, the couple moved to Germany. There had been much ill feeling towards French women who had married German soldiers.

He handed me a packet containing German marks and explained their value in the French shops and markets.

I went immediately to the *boucherie* owned by Leah's family, where I was shocked to find that a crude Star of David had been drawn on the glass window, part of which was broken. Also, on the window were the words *"Enterprise Juive"*.

Of Leah's husband, there was no sign but I saw the son-in-law inside the shop sweeping up glass and debris. I walked down the street, turned into the alleyway behind the shop to the back door of the shop and knocked on it. To my relief, Leah's husband appeared. I expressed my shock at what had happened to the business and gave him news of the family. I decided I would not tell Leah what I had seen. I handed him some of the marks from the envelope and accepted four chickens in return, promising to return as soon as I could. I then went to the pharmacy and bought aspirin and vitamins for Leah and her family. Again, I used the German marks reasoning that it would be safer now to be considered as being in the employment of the Germans. This would cause me to be despised but also feared, and enable me to protect Leah and her family. I shopped for fresh fruit and vegetables in the market, where I found long queues at all the stalls and people complaining that the Germans were taking the best of everything. I approached a group of soldiers who were sauntering around the market. After I explained who my employer was, they immediately set to helping me to the front of the queue, where miraculously a large supply of fresh vegetables – including asparagus and endive – was made available for me to buy. The soldiers carried the parcels for me. As I passed the queue, a glob of spit hit my shoe and I heard the word *"Putain"* levelled at me. I held my head high and directed the soldiers to the dairy stalls, where again I was able to purchase the best of everything – fresh butter and cheeses – all of which were doubtless denied to the local people. The soldiers carried the wares to the château for me. They attempted to speak French with me and were charmed by my smiles of encouragement. Despite the knowledge that I was now regarded as a loathsome collaborator by the people in the town, I felt pleased with myself; perhaps this would be easier than I had feared.

The cook was delighted with my purchases and even asked my advice on the local way of cooking some of the items. My hours in the kitchen with Leah had been well spent. I also engaged with the valet in the need for extra bedding and linen for the château. I drew up lists and suggested the best places in Caen to shop for these. I made the calls to the shops and the items were delivered that afternoon. I asked the secretaries to set up a desk for me in the corner of the library where I could organise the household accounts. This would make me more visible to the *Kommandant* and highlight my useful role in the running of the château.

38

The following day, I recommended a nearby dairy farm where the farmer could be persuaded to supply fresh milk as well as homemade cider and Calvados brandy. The cook was amenable to the idea and suggested that I go with two of the guards to requisition this and ensure regular supplies. I made a show of considering his proposal and the offer of transport, but then demurred.

'It is a beautiful day and I would like some country air. I will cycle to the farm. It is not far. *Madame* Abramsky-Erhart ordered from there and I had to collect what she wanted.'

And it was a beautiful day. June had melted into a sultry July. There were frequent thunderstorms at night which cleared the air by morning and the heat of the sun was tempered by light breezes. I wore a light sleeveless summer dress and cycled briskly out of the town and onto one of the narrow country roads that led to Sainte-Honorine-de-Ducy. At one point, I had to pull over as a truck full of young soldiers sped past. I was hailed with cheers and whistles of admiration from them. This both embarrassed and emboldened me. If I was going to do as instructed, I would have to learn how to accept compliments – even such as these.

I arrived at the farm and put my bicycle against the wall of the milking parlour. Amélie was inside the parlour, scrubbing it down in preparation for the later milking. At first, she did not recognise me – the blonde hair confused her – but as soon as I fell into her arms, she held me close, stroking my head.

'My darling Helen! How worried we have been. We know that the château is now in the hands of the Germans. We could get no news and dared not ask after you.'

I hugged my aunt closer. 'I am well but now it is very dangerous.'

'And they are still safe, the family of Jews?'

'Yes, but it will not be easy for them, nor their men.'

I told Amélie of the damage to their shop in Caen, how difficult it was for them in the underground room and my fears for their health. I then told her of my role at the château and my enterprise in suggesting that their farm be used to supply milk as well as cider and Calvados.

'Of course, it must seem to be under duress. The Germans will not pay the true value of these things and it must appear that Damian is afraid to resist their demands. It will also mean that I can communicate with you and Damian when the deliveries are made.'

Amélie nodded.

'And I am no longer Helen Douglas. She departed with *Madame* Abramsky-Erhart and the children before the Germans arrived. Perhaps she is in Switzerland. I am Gabrielle Doucet from Lisieux. I and my parents died in an automobile accident and are buried in the cemetery there. I was employed by *Madame* to care for the château when she left. I am most aggrieved that she never paid me.'

At this, I started to giggle and then both of us were laughing hysterically.

With tears of amusement running down her cheeks, Amélie said, 'What stories we will have to tell when this war is over.'

We were silent for a few moments; both of us realising that this could be a very long time indeed. And that it may be that Germany would prevail.

I then spoke, 'Aunt Amélie, *Maman* cannot be told of this. Letters and phone calls can be intercepted and I must maintain my cover; it is important to Leah and her family, and perhaps others will be sent to me. And in order to continue in this, Gabrielle Doucet must become the mistress of *Feldkommandur* Karl von Werstein.'

Amélie gasped.

'Helen, are you sure you can do this? Yes, you are beautiful and clever, but it is more dangerous than you think. If he discovers the truth, you will be killed. There is no doubt of this. If he discovers you are hiding Jews, you will be killed. That is what is happening in other countries the Germans have conquered. They will torture you until you reveal your contacts and your Jews will suffer the same. And, I have to ask this, have you ever been with a man?'

I felt myself blush and admitted that I had not but did at least know the technicalities of what would be required of me.

The green book had shown some useful diagrams and my peers at school had occasionally and clandestinely brought salacious paperback books on their return from school holidays. These were giggled over by torchlight in the dormitory and I had been invited to join in the merriment. Pictures of young women with large bosoms which threatened to tumble from their low-cut bodices were pictured in the arms of muscular men.

'I will do what I can. I may fail. I believe he is married, with a wife and children in Germany. I have only seen him twice and have not looked at him closely. You can imagine how afraid I was when he arrived, and how afraid I now am.'

Amélie also cautioned, 'You will be despised by those who do not know who you really are and why you are doing this. You will be spat upon in the streets and punished as a collaborator if and when the Germans leave.'

'I know this, Aunt Amélie, but I feel I must at least try. For me, there is no question of refusing. I am already too deeply into this to stop now. Leah and her family need me and I have already killed to protect them.'

I told my aunt about the gardener and his friend.

'You are an incredible young woman.'

It was only while cycling back to the château that I realised that my aunt had known that Leah and her family were hidden at the château.

Amélie had loaded up the basket on my bicycle with fresh eggs and homemade cheese. I was able to promise the cook daily milk deliveries as well as a consignment of cider and Calvados.

The cook was impressed by my enterprise and most appreciative of the eggs and cheese.

That night, I retired early to my room to rest, refusing the offer of a meal with the secretaries and adjutant.

As soon as I was certain all in the household were in bed, I lit my bedside light and left the room, locking the door behind me. The kitchen door was locked but I had kept spare keys for all the doors to the château. This time, I crept to the rose garden. Heavy clouds covered the moon and there was a distant rumble of thunder. I had to feel my way along the wall and into the ruined tower. Once inside, I turned on my torch and made my way through the trap door and into the underground room.

They were relieved to see me and I immediately checked on Ruth. The vomiting had subsided but now she had diarrhoea. She felt feverish, so I gave her two of the aspirin tablets and instructed Leah that she should give her two every four hours until the fever subsided. I handed out vitamins to all four of them and gave the rest to Leah to administer as she thought necessary. I told them of my meeting with their two men but omitted the details of the damage to their shop.

Leah told me that fresh water for drinking and washing had been provided in the early hours of the morning. I explained that these supplies may become difficult once the *Kommandant* stationed soldiers in the woods, as well he might. I took the waste buckets and emptied them outside behind a pile of rubble. Leah requested some books and playing cards. She missed the wireless and time passed very slowly in the room. I assured her that I would return with these the following night.

As I returned to the château, I realised that I had not listened to the news on the wireless for some time now. I resolved to listen in to Radio Londres, which was now broadcast at 9 p.m. every night.

I needed to know what was happening outside of the Château des Tilleuls – in the rest of the world.

39

The *Kommandant* left the château early the following morning. The secretaries informed me that he was travelling to Berlin to celebrate his wife's birthday and would return in three days.

His absence created an atmosphere of holiday in the château. I watched the guards smoking at their posts by the gates and engaging local girls in conversation. There were no guards in the woods so far. The cook left after serving supper and informed us that he would not be returning until the following morning. It was six o'clock in the evening and I realised that *Père* François would soon be beginning the evening mass. I told the secretaries that I wished to attend the mass in memory of my parents, the anniversary of whose death was approaching. I pretended to wipe tears from my eyes as I told them this and they both expressed sympathy.; to my relief, neither offered to accompany me.

I sat at the back of the church, anticipating that a member of the group might approach me, but mass neared its end without any contact.

Before the final blessing, I slipped quietly out of the church and went to the door of the sacristy, where I waited for *Père* François to return. He was pleased to see me. He took me through to the small kitchen in the presbytery and made two cups of tea, which he poured from an English teapot.

'A souvenir from my days in Durham,' he explained with a smile.

'I know of your exploits, my dear. You are brave and resourceful. I must now tell you about your employer. The *Feldkommandur*, Karl

Johannes Franz von Werstein, is thirty-seven years old and has the rank of general in the *Wehrmacht*. His family are Junkers – Prussian nobility – and they own estates in the north-east of Germany. As the first born son he inherited responsibility for the estates on the death of his father in the Great War but, as he had already decided on a military career, he left the management of the estates to his younger brother Frederic. He joined the German army as a cavalry officer cadet at the age of sixteen and in June 1918, became the youngest lieutenant in the army, earning the Iron Cross in the Second Battle of the Marne. After the war, he studied Law at the Friedrich Wilhelm University in Berlin. He is well-travelled and has visited Britain many times. He speaks both English and French. In 1928, he married Countess Sophia von Karstein, whose family also have a long-standing military tradition. He returned to military service following the marriage and was sponsored by no less of a figure than General Paul von Hindenburg. According to our contacts, he is not a typical Prussian officer. He dislikes the regimentation and ostentation of the army. But he is a loyal German and will follow no doubt the orders of the High Command – whatever those orders are, and however brutal.

'He is an accomplished cellist and is particularly fond of the works of Brahms, Beethoven and Schubert – the *Arpeggione Sonata* is a particular favourite of his.

'He and his wife have three children: two boys and a girl. Following the birth of the youngest child, his wife suffered a serious nervous breakdown. She is in a clinic outside of Berlin and is visited regularly by her husband, but it seems that she no longer recognises him and there are fears for her physical health.'

I was astonished that *Père* François knew so much about my employer, but knew better than to ask how he had come by this information.

He continued, 'It is for you to decide how best to use this information. The other members of your new household are loyal Germans and cannot be trusted, but the cook's new lady friend is one of us. Should he have any suspicions about you, we will be informed. At the moment, it seems you are proving indispensable in the running of the château.'

I smiled at this. 'I am doing my best to be so.'

I then went on to explain the main reason for my visit.

'I am worried for the granddaughters of Leah. Ruth is very sick. I think the conditions in the chamber – with toilet buckets and shortages of clean water – are affecting her health. Leah is anxious that she will not survive. Is there any way we can get her out safely and to another place of refuge?'

The priest promised to do what he could. He advised me to attend confession weekly but to come at the end of the session and leave while mass was in progress. In that way, my presence would be less likely to be noted. He was aware of my anxiety with regard to the old lady and agreed that she could be dangerous, particularly as her son had accepted the role of *Chef* of the local *gendarmerie* following the resignation on principle of the previous incumbent. He told me to listen as often as I could to Radio Londres as there may be important information for me. His face was inscrutable when he said this.

I returned to the château where I found the secretaries listening to dance music in their bedroom. The other staff members were at the garrison and the only military presence – the guards at the gate – had been half asleep when I passed them.

I went up to the tower and removed the wireless from its alcove. At 9 p.m., I found the station BBC Radio Londres. The first few chords of Beethoven's *Fifth Symphony* were followed by the announcement:

'*Ici Londres. Les Français parlent aux Français.*'

I realised that this was the voice of the Free French Forces under General De Gaulle. It would be illegal to listen to the broadcasts, but I would take my chance along with other French people: those who hoped for the defeat of the Germans and would play a part in participating in that defeat.

After shutting down the wireless and replacing it in its alcove, I went to visit Leah and her family. Ruth's condition was deteriorating. Her diarrhoea was worse and although aspirin was keeping her fever in check, her sunken eyes and drowsiness told me that she would not survive without medical intervention.

As I emptied the buckets, I thought of a plan – it was dangerous but just might save Ruth's life. I knew of a Jewish doctor in Caen, a Dr Raphael, who had been to the château to treat Stefan. He had beds at the Saint Pierre Hospital in Caen. It was possible that I could get Ruth to the hospital and from there, to a more suitable place than the underground room to convalesce. I remembered where he lived, as Stefan had once asked me to go there to settle his medical bill.

The château was in darkness. I crept through the back door and collected my bicycle. I could not risk going through the front gates but went through the woods and onto the narrow cart track that linked up with one of the minor roads into Caen.

I cycled through the dark streets. There were few people around at this time of night. The 11 p.m. curfew was strictly enforced and people preferred to be in their homes long before it began. I found the doctor's house, went to the back door and rang the bell. The doctor himself answered the door. I stayed in the shadows of the doorway, hoping that the doctor would not recognise me. I explained that I had a young friend, a Jewish girl, who needed urgent medical care. As it was too late for the doctor to attend to her now, I could bring her to the hospital the following day, if he agreed to this. Meanwhile, I could take some medicine for the girl, if the doctor would be so kind. I described the nature of the illness and my own assessment of the gravity of the girl's condition.

The doctor was reluctant to prescribe medicine without seeing the patient, but I insisted that I had medical experience and that I would bring the girl to the hospital at 6 a.m. the following morning. He invited me to come into his surgery but I demurred, using the imminence of the curfew as an excuse. He returned with a piece of paper and a small jar containing three capsules.

'Make sure your friend has plenty of water to drink, keep her warm and as clean as possible. Give her two of these capsules tonight and another before you leave for the hospital tomorrow. Now go, *mademoiselle*, it would not do for you to be found on the streets after curfew.'

It was midnight when I got back to the family. Ruth swallowed the capsules. On the piece of paper was written the word "Sulphonamide M&B 693". Raisa promised to give Ruth as much water as she could take and to give her the third capsule at dawn. I instructed her that after this, they should wrap Ruth up in as many clothes as possible and be ready to help her through the tunnel to the trapdoor in the woods.

At 5.30 a.m., I was waiting for them by the trapdoor. I had left my bicycle on the track outside the woods – it was raining hard and I wondered how I would manage with Ruth on the bicycle on the muddy track. I heard them push at the trapdoor and with their help, I hauled Ruth through. Leah told me that Ruth had managed to sleep after the tablets and that her diarrhoea was already improving.

But the girl was too weak to stand up and I struggled to hold her. I covered the trapdoor as usual and used brushwood to cover our footprints and then half-carried, half-dragged Ruth to the bicycle.

We reached the hospital just after 6 a.m. A young nurse was waiting by the entrance. She gestured to me to be silent and taking some of Ruth's weight, led us along a corridor and down a staircase to a door, which opened into a small room containing a bed with a stand attached to it. The nurse helped me to undress Ruth and left the room. She returned with a bottle of liquid, which she hung on the stand, and a large needle and tubing. She asked me to hold Ruth's arm steady while she pierced her hand with the needle, quickly attached the tubing to the end of the needle and connected it to the bottle on the stand. She secured the needle with bandaging and instructed me to ensure that Ruth did not move her arm. The liquid in the bottle slowly dripped through the tubing.

'This is a saline infusion which will replace the fluids she has lost. In a while, the doctor will come and give her some medication. Please stay until then.'

She left the room. Ruth was drowsy and feverish again and I worried that I would be missed at the château if I stayed much longer. But the doctor arrived soon after. He explained that Ruth would stay in this room until she had fully recovered. She would then be collected by friends and taken to a place of safety. I should now return to my home, where a message would be sent to me.

His final words surprised me, 'I understand that the milk is delivered on this day.'

I guessed who would deliver the message.

40

Damian arrived early the following morning. As I helped him unload the churns from the cart, he put a note into my hand, which I slipped into the pocket of my dress while calling for the cook to help me carry the churns into the larder. With the cook at my side, I bade Damian a curt farewell and instructed him to provide the same every other day. I made an excuse to return to my room where I read the note. It informed me that Ruth would be transferred to the farm as soon as she was well enough. Ellana was to leave the underground room that night, to take advantage of the more relaxed security during the *Feldkommandur's* absence. She too would now be hidden at the farm. I felt a huge sense of relief. I knew better than to ask questions regarding Ruth's care at the hospital, but I was certain that the mysterious group were involved in this and equally certain that *Père* François was a pivotal member of this group.

I made my late-night visit to the underground room and was able to inform Leah and Raisa of the good news about Ruth and the plan for Ellana. I had no idea how Ellana's escape was to be achieved. I found that they had food and water supplies, but there was the inevitable task of emptying the waste buckets. I had just finished this when a figure appeared in the doorway leading to the other exit. It was the young man I had met at the church.

He urged Ellana to dress in as many clothes as possible, despite the warmth of the August evening and told both of us to follow him. We made our way to the trapdoor and out into the forest, where the young man instructed me to follow him and Ellana, covering their tracks with brushwood, and then to return at once to the château by the kitchen door.

'We have news that the *Kommandant* is returning sooner than expected. Your absence must not be noted, nor should you be caught in the gardens.'

I kissed Ellana farewell and asked the young man, 'Can you assure me that Ruth is safe in that room? I have learned that the Germans are not permitting Jewish patients to be treated in the hospital in Paris. Perhaps it is the same here.'

'Do not fear. The nurse is one of us. The room has been removed from the hospital. It does not exist.'

With that, he took Ellana's hand and led her away.

I did as I was instructed, covered their tracks and then returned to the château. Sure enough, the *Kommandant's* car was coming up the drive. I waited until he and his entourage had entered the hall and went to welcome him.

'Good evening, *Herr Kommandant*. It is good to have you back here. I hope your wife enjoyed her birthday. May I make you something to eat, or drink?'

'That is not necessary. The cook can prepare something for me.'

I was aware that the cook was still in the arms of his mistress in the town. It would not do to make an enemy of him by revealing his absence.

'Unfortunately, the cook is indisposed. He had to retire early to bed due to a mild fever and stomach pain. Do not worry. I have treated him with some medicine for this and I am sure he will be recovered by the morning.'

'You are indeed a young woman of many abilities. Yes, if you would prepare me an omelette with salad, with perhaps some of the excellent wine we have here. That would be most welcome.'

I lit the cooking range and prepared the omelette. I set up a tray with the best linen and made a salad with a vinaigrette dressing. I placed a crystal glass and half a bottle of red wine on the tray and carried the tray into the *Kommandant's* office in the library, where he was at his desk opening the pile of letters that his secretaries had left for him. As I placed the tray on the desk, I noted that some of the letters were marked in red as confidential. I was sure this meant that even the secretaries were not permitted to know the contents of these letters. I wondered how useful it would be to know what they were about.

I returned to the kitchen and made omelettes for the *Kommandant's* adjutant and driver. They had just finished their meal and left the kitchen when the cook came through the back door. No doubt he had received news of the *Kommandant's* early return.

'Do not worry. You are in bed with a stomach malady which the *Kommandant* will no doubt attribute to the rich Normandy food.' His relief and gratitude were palpable.

It was now 2 a.m. but I waited until I heard the *Kommandant* open the library door and then went to collect the tray. The vague thought that he might forget to lock away the letters crossed my mind. But he waited by the door until I had picked up the tray. Once again, I felt his eyes on me and that curious feeling of nakedness and vulnerability that this gave me. Perhaps he could see into my soul and read my thoughts, and my lies. This caused me to shiver and I stumbled with the tray. He was there immediately and caught my arm, steadying the tray and taking it from me.

'Allow me to help you, *Fräulein*. You are tired. The omelette was excellent; another tribute to your wondrous talents.'

This was said with no apparent irony on his part. His smile was warm and the pressure of his arm on mine felt comforting. I felt myself blush and tried to make light of the incident. But he took the tray into the kitchen and waited while I turned down the cooking range.

He then bade me goodnight and went to his room.

Once in bed, I fell into a deep sleep in which images of myself naked in his arms were recurring themes. There was pleasure as well as fear in these images. I awoke detesting myself for the dreams and was determined to loathe the man regardless of what I had been instructed to do.

41

My relief that Ruth and Ellana were now safely away from the château was tempered by the arrival of two young British soldiers. Damian slipped a note into my hand one morning in early September informing me of their arrival by way of the woods that night.

Despite the constant presence of the *Kommandant* and the German military coming and going between the château and the town, I had been able to continue my night time visits to the underground room. Leah and Raisa found the lack of sunlight and fresh air difficult to bear. They looked pale and complained of muscle pains. I gave them vitamins regularly and they had enough fresh food and water. The cook allowed me free access to the pantry and did not appear to miss the remains of casseroles and joints of meat which I took with me on my visits. He no doubt assumed that the soldiers helped themselves.

There was no shortage of food for the château or for Germans anywhere in France. The Germans used the devaluation of the Franc against the Reichsmark to buy up most of the meat and produce in the markets. It was no different in Caen, where long queues of angry women lined the stalls in the market complaining of hunger and that their children were starving. I no longer shopped there personally but sent a driver with a list of what we required for the château.

Leah and Raisa's confinement to the underground room could seem premature as their fellow Jews were still to be seen around the town. Their *boucherie* still traded despite the presence of the aggressive young "guards". And the crude Star of David remained on the broken window. But Leah was adamant.

'No, we are not and will not be safe until the Germans are defeated. My husband and son-in-law should join us but I know how stubborn they both are. If things get worse for Jews, then they may reconsider.'

At midnight I left the château and went into the woods. I waited by the trapdoor and within a few minutes, two young men appeared. I opened the trapdoor and helped them inside. The exhausted young men were greeted warmly by Leah and Raisa.

To my amazement and delight, I found they were both members of a Scots Guard regiment that had been part of the British Expeditionary Force. The young men, Iain and Fraser, were equally delighted to find a Scots girl to speak to. But the story they had to tell was a terrible one. I translated it into French as they told it and Leah and Raisa were as horrified as I was by the brutality. Following the fall back to the beach at Dunkirk, they and others had become separated from their regiment but had joined the 2nd Battalion Royal Norfolks to protect the flanks of the Dunkirk evacuation. On the 25th of May, they and the Norfolk regiment had retreated to a farmhouse in a village called Le Paradis and held out against an SS unit for two days before running out of ammunition and surrendering.

They had come out of the farmhouse holding a white flag but, nevertheless, the SS commanding officer marched the men, many of whom were injured, to a nearby cowshed where they were lined up against a wall and machine-gunned. They had watched as their comrades fell to the ground around them. They pretended to be dead but watched as the Germans went around systematically bayonetting any they thought might still be alive. By chance, they escaped this second round of the massacre and after hearing the unit leave the village, had crept out and been given shelter in a nearby barn.

Now they were determined to evade capture and make their way back to Britain to re-join their regiment. This act of cowardly brutality had made them more determined to defeat the Germans.

I made sure that they had bedding and warm clothing and they ate the remains of a joint of beef with gusto. I promised to return the following night but urged them to be ready to be moved on at any time. I was sure Damian would have a plan in hand but did not share their optimism. I knew that all border crossings to Spain were heavily guarded, and escape by boat from the coast was fraught with danger.

I returned to the château by way of the trapdoor in the woods. I spent some time covering the soldiers' footprints. While doing so, I was shocked to find two cigarette stubs quite close to the entrance. I picked them up and looked carefully at them. They were German cigarettes. This could only mean that the soldiers were now patrolling the woods. I looked around and listened. Only the hoot of an owl broke the silence. I must find out if and when patrols were around the woods. Everything was now more dangerous than ever.

42

I used my desk in the library regularly now. It gave me the opportunity to show how necessary I was in the smooth running of the château. I kept a book of invoices and sent accounts to the adjutant for authorisation. I ensured that a laundry service took care of all the bed linen and personal clothing of the residents in the château. It also gave me an opportunity to observe the mail that arrived for the *Kommandant* and to listen in to phone calls. I could now understand some of the German language. I had heard it spoken when Odette and the family had lived at the château and much of it seemed similar to English. It appeared that the German air force planes were bombing British towns and cities. The war had come to Britain. How long could they withstand the might of the *Luftwaffe* and the blockade of ports? I felt as though a cold hand gripped my heart; I might never see my parents again.

Stefan's cellos remained in a corner of the room. The magnificent Bösendorfer piano still had its place in the bay of the window. While the *Kommandant* was having lunch in the dining room with his staff officers, I went through the cabinet where Stefan kept his music scores. As all were arranged alphabetically, I soon found the works of Schubert, including the piano accompaniment to the *Arpeggione Sonata*. I knew the piece well, as it was one *Maman* loved. I took out the music – the piano accompaniment was well within my range of proficiency. I went to the piano and started to sight read.

Normally, the *Kommandant* spent an hour at lunch and then strolled for some time in the grounds, so I was startled when I came to the end of the score and heard a faint applause from the other side of the room. It was the *Kommandant*. He reached over to where the cellos stood and selected one. I recognised it as Stefan's favourite, the 1749 Guadagnini which he always took to private recitals. He drew a bow from the case next to the cellos and tightened the hairs. He looked around for rosin and applied it. He then pulled up a chair alongside the piano and competently tuned the cello.

'So, we shall begin, shall we not, *Fräulein*?'

I stumbled at first with the notes but he played on and my confidence grew with each of the movements. He raised his bow after the final chord and stood up to bow.

'To do this correctly, I must also invite you to take a bow.' He said this with laughter in his voice. He took my arm and raised me from the piano stool. I stood beside him and took as graceful a bow as I could and felt my face blush.

'I have embarrassed you, *Fräulein*. You remind me of my cousin's daughter. She blushes as you do. She has red-gold hair and very pale skin. Your skin is like hers. I notice how pale your arms are. Blondes in my country go golden brown in the sun. Perhaps it is not so in France.'

Again, I felt his eyes scrutinising me. I blushed even more but tried to keep my voice steady, 'It is perhaps that I do not wish to be in the sun. I do not wish to be burned by it.'

'You play well, *Fräulein*, another of your many talents. Perhaps we should have a concert together. My fellow officers would enjoy such a performance. A good example of how our people can work together. Now, I must leave you. I have business to attend to in the town.'

With that, he abruptly left the room. I started to shake and a tumult of emotion made me feel faint. I had enjoyed playing with him but his sharp eyes had already found a flaw in my disguise. And the thought of playing before an audience of the enemy added to my torment. I had no idea how I could continue in this role and protect those in my care.

I then realised that again he had not made the Nazi salute.

43

After two nights, Iain and Fraser were moved from the underground room. I was alerted to the plan during a milk delivery that morning. Damian also informed me that Ruth was now fully recovered and safely at the farm in Sainte-Honorine. False identity papers had been obtained for her and Ellana, which verified that they were the *filleules* of Damian and Amélie and had left their homes in Paris as the German army approached in June of that year. They had decided to stay in the countryside to help with the harvest.

There was no possibility of alerting Iain and Fraser to their departure during the day, but as soon as I was sure that all in the château were in their beds – or otherwise, with respect to the cook – I went through the kitchen garden and into the woods. They had already settled to sleep when I reached the room but were soon awake and ready to make their onward journey. I had gathered more of Stefan's winter clothing and brought it to them. It could be close to winter before they reached safety.

By torchlight we reached the edge of the woods, where we found Damian with a cart of barrels of Calvados and cider. I hugged both men and wished them good luck for their journey, but also warned them that they must not give details of their refuge with me. I was tempted to request that they contact my parents to reassure them that I was alive and well but knew this was too dangerous – for the group and me.

Damian helped them into a secret compartment under the barrels.

'Where will they go from here?' I asked.

'I cannot tell you. You know how it is; the fewer that know, the better.'

I remembered the code: "them that ask no questions isn't told a lie".

Damian did not use those words but I understood.

44

From the summer of 1940, the first orders from the Vichy Government aimed at excluding Jews from French society came into force in the Occupied Zone as well as the Zone Libre. On the 3rd of October, the Law on the Statute of Jews defined who were considered to be Jews and ordered those who met the definition to register with the local *sous-préfecture*. The speed at which these laws were enforced by the French bureaucrats, at the bidding of their German masters, left no doubt in the minds of Jews that these edicts were not only welcomed but had been planned for even before the country was occupied.

The order ruled that a person who had two or more Jewish grandparents of the Jewish faith and those who practised the Jewish religion were considered to be Jews. This took many French citizens by surprise, as the fact of their Jewish origins had no bearing on their everyday lives. They did not adhere to any faith and many French-born and immigrant Jews had married Catholics or Protestants. Religion played no part in their lives. French officials in government offices throughout France, both in the Occupied Zone and the Zone Libre, poured over records and files to identify which of their citizens fulfilled these criteria.

The same orders forbade Jews who had fled the Occupied Zone to the Zone Libre from returning. Many Jews had fled to the Zone Libre following the Occupation only to find the Vichy Regime under Marshal Pétain and Pierre Laval an increasingly dangerous place to live. Although unoccupied by Germans, Vichy was no more than a vassal state of Nazi Germany and the Jews who had thought to find refuge there and wished to return to their families in the Occupied Zone, now found that they were trapped.

Jews were now banned from the professions, from owning businesses and from the universities. They were forbidden entry to places of entertainment, parks, swimming pools and restaurants. Their bicycles and wirelesses were confiscated and the telephone service was denied to them. They could not move addresses without informing the authorities. The orders demanded that all Jews were to present themselves at the local *sous-préfecture* by the 18th of October, where their addresses would be placed on a special register and their identity cards would be stamped in red with *Juif* or *Juive* written on them.

'This is being done in order to find us when the time comes,' said Leah. 'Please warn our men not to do this. Many will obey this order because they hope that by doing so they will be safe. But this will not be so. None of us will be safe.'

I tried to comfort her but I also felt that this was the first stage in the oppression of Jews in France.

'They will force my family to sell the *boucherie* cheaply to one of their collaborators. How will we live?' Leah sobbed.

I promised to do what I could to ensure that her husband and son-in-law did not starve. This was all I could do in the circumstances, but I could not go to the *sous-préfecture* to plead for them, as to do so would raise suspicion.

It was now over a month since Iain and Fraser had left and there had been no news of them. Damian managed to speak to me a couple of weeks later. He advised me to listen to Radio Londres whenever possible, as they may communicate with me that way.

'But how will I know there is a message?' I asked

'You will know,' he said and urged the horse on. He was now making all the deliveries using one of Michel's farm wagons, as gasoline was rationed. France had no oil production and all imports had stopped due to the Allied blockade. It was a private joke between us that Michel's conviction that horses would depose the motor car had proved correct – at least for the present time.

The *Kommandant* did not forget his proposal regarding the recital and now wished me to rehearse every evening after he had dined with his staff officers. I had no alternative other than to acquiesce in this, but as time went by I found that I enjoyed playing with him. He was very patient when I made mistakes or mistimed an entry, and his choice of music pleased me. The *Arpeggione Sonata* reminded me of *Maman* and home and Brahms' *Cello Sonata* moved me to tears.

One evening, I was late arriving for our rehearsal as the cook had scalded his hand. I stayed with him to cool the hand with cold water and dress it in ointment and bandages. He would need help in the kitchen until the hand healed. As I approached the library door, I was astonished to hear the plaintive sound of Bruch's *Kol Nidrei*. I was sure this work would be forbidden by the Nazis.

He did not stop playing when I entered the room and I waited by the door until he had finished. He smiled and gestured for me to take my seat at the piano. He gave no indication that he was embarrassed to have been heard playing the piece. I explained my late arrival and the need for me to help the cook for a while at least. I did not wish for another cook to be brought into the château, as that could compromise my activities.

To my relief, he agreed to this and we settled down to rehearse. As he packed away the cello, he informed me that he had arranged for a recital at the château in Caen in front of the *Oberfeldkommandur* and other military officers the evening after next.

I was appalled by this and stuttered, 'But I am not ready for this. Please could it not wait until we have had more practice?'

I was terrified at the thought of being in the company of more such as the *Kommandant*. Perhaps one or the other might guess at my deception. I felt vulnerable enough in the company of the *Kommandant*.

'And I have nothing suitable to wear.'

I despised myself for such a lame and shallow excuse. It was the sort that my peers at school no doubt made during their "season" in London in order to extract more frocks and jewellery from their doting parents.

'Well, *Fräulein*, we shall ensure that you have something appropriate for the occasion. We will meet tomorrow and visit the best couturier in Caen.'

45

The following morning, the *Kommandant* came to the kitchen where I was helping the cook. He instructed me to collect my coat from my room – I would require it as there was an early autumn frost. His adjutant was waiting by the staff car and his driver at the wheel. The door was held open for me to take my seat and the *Kommandant* sat next to me. Two armed guards sat behind us in the rear seat.

We drove into Caen. I could see and feel the hatred of the people we passed on the road and in the streets of the city. There would be no doubt in their minds that I was a collaborator and a whore.

The car stopped at a shop in a wealthy district of the city. The shop windows were filled with exquisite gowns, leather goods, hats and chocolates. A *parfumerie* displayed crystal dispensers and boasted *Joie* by Jean Patou and *Je Reviens* by Worth.

The couturier herself was at the door, clearly in anticipation of our arrival. She took me into a dressing room where a selection of gowns was on display and instructed me to undress to my underwear. I felt very uncomfortable under her gaze as she looked me over and expressed approval, saying that she knew which gowns would show my figure to its best advantage. Three were selected and I was made to wear each one in turn for the *Kommandant* to consider. I felt utterly humiliated and embarrassed. In my mind, I likened it to the Berwickshire County Show in Duns which I used to attend with my parents, where prize cows were trotted out to be valued and sold.

The *Kommandant* selected two gowns. One was in green silk – he noted how well the green matched the colour of my eyes. The other was rich blue velvet, cut low enough to show most of my breasts. I was determined not to be seen in public in such an immodest garment. I wrinkled my nose in displeasure as I turned around the room in front of the *Kommandant* and the couturier. Both laughed at this.

'I see this one does not please you. That is a pity as it becomes you well, but yes I agree, with your colouring, the green is better, nevertheless, we will take both.'

He then turned to the woman and requested that the gowns and a selection of lingerie be delivered to the Château des Tilleuls that evening.

We drove back to the château in silence. The *Kommandant* seemed preoccupied. He got out of the car before the adjutant had opened it, leaving me unsure of my situation. Should I just step out of the car and make my way into the château or wait until I was invited to do so by the adjutant? I noted that the guards stayed where they were in the rear of the vehicle. I felt a sudden terror that this was a trap set by the *Kommandant*. Perhaps there had been a betrayal. I feared for Leah and Raisa and all of those in my care. A wave of nausea made me put my head down between my legs. But the adjutant was opening the door for me and the guards were lowering their guns and talking amongst themselves. The moment passed. I stepped out and into the château.

That evening we had the final rehearsal before the recital. When it was over and he congratulated me on my accompaniment, he told me that he had to go into Caen to check on the security detail for the recital. I understood why this should be so, as it could be the perfect opportunity for a resistance attack on a high echelon of the occupying force. I had no fear for my own safety, but should I be killed, who would care for Leah and Raisa and others who might seek shelter?

I took the opportunity of his absence to visit Leah and Raisa. They were already feeling cold in the underground room. The benefit of the ventilation during the summer months also meant that cold air seeped into the room – and this autumn was unseasonably cold. They had plenty of warm bedding and clothing but missed the comfort of a warm fire. I emptied the toilet buckets and promised to bring more bedding but could not help in any other way. I told them of my experience today and my fears for the following evening. They were unable to offer advice save that this was something I had to manage with my own resources of courage and intelligence.

46

The following evening, dressed in the green silk gown, I followed the *Kommandant* into the staff car. Stefan's cello was carefully packed in its travelling case. There was an air of festivity amongst the entourage, with the guards laughing and joking with the *Kommandant*. He remonstrated with me when I appeared in my shabby coat over the beautiful gown, but acquiesced when I explained that the coat was warm and that I had no other.

Coloured light bulbs led the way into the castle. Our guards saluted those at the massive gates as we passed through. We were taken into a reception hall where uniformed officers and elegantly dressed women were sipping champagne. They looked up when the *Kommandant* entered and I was aware of the appraising glances of the women – and those of the men. I refused champagne and asked for a mineral water. I was introduced to the *Oberfeldkommandur* and his officers and responded to their well-intentioned but grammatically incorrect attempts to speak French with grace and apparent humour. Then it was time to begin the performance. The *Kommandant* tuned the cello to the piano and we began with the *Arpeggione Sonata*. My hands were shaking but found the keys and once we were playing, all that mattered was the music. The applause at the end came as a surprise; I was so lost in the complexities of this most eloquent of sonatas. He raised me up to take my bow and again that reassuring arm on mine confused me. The Brahms was equally well received, but for me, it was the *Arpeggione* that was important.

The audience called for an encore and after a quick nod between us, we reprised the final movement of the *Arpeggione*. I felt *Maman* behind me, encouraging me and suddenly a feeling of loss for a past that could never be retrieved, and also a profound fear for the future, overwhelmed me. The clapping became a dull ringing in my ears and then darkness surrounded me. I had fainted on the stage.

I had the impression of strong arms carrying me from the stage and into the car, and then a drive through the darkness and the same arms carrying me through corridors and into bed. I was dimly aware of my clothing being removed and a brief intense gaze.

I awoke in the dark in the early hours of the morning to find my clothing neatly arranged on the chair next to my bed. I was wearing my nightdress and a glass of water had been placed by the bed. I moved it away from my reach, as *Maman* had taught me.

47

The following morning the *Kommandant* was not at breakfast. After helping the cook, I took my place at my desk in the library. The two secretaries were curious to learn about the recital. They had heard how wonderfully the *Kommandant* had played and congratulated me on my accompaniment but were also concerned about my health. I had fainted and no one had been allowed to help the *Kommandant* when he brought me home. The rumour was that I had a fever.

I reassured them that I had merely been very tired and overcome by the honour of playing in such august circumstances. I was anxious that I may have given away some secrets while I was in the semi-conscious state. I knew from helping Papa that unconscious patients sometimes become indiscreet. This anxiety made the morning pass slowly and I was pleased to be needed to help the cook in the kitchen with the midday meal. The *Kommandant* returned for this with two elegant young women and another officer. The women were French but spoke German throughout the meal. I was told that they were from Alsace, which I knew was a part of France that had passed many times between French and German control and the people there were normally fluent in both languages.

The women addressed me in French as I served them. Something in the inflection of their speech reminded me of Odette. I knew that I shared with most musicians the ability to detect cadences in a voice that could tell me approximately where a person was born and raised. The people in Berwick spoke with an accent that owed as much to the Geordies of Newcastle as to the Scots of the lowlands. This observation perplexed me, as I was certain that Odette had been born in Caen. And then I found myself wondering how it was that Odette had also spoken German with Stefan and his parents. I had never questioned this before, but listening to these women now made me wonder why I had not.

After the party left, the *Kommandant* worked for a while at his desk. I went into the kitchen to help the cook. His hand remained painful but the scalded skin had sloughed off and new skin was forming over the tissues beneath. He was very grateful for my care.

I spent some time organising the laundry for collection and ordering food and wine for the château. The young soldier who had been delegated to do the shopping in the market politely deferred to my orders. I was not comfortable with this deference but realised it was to the advantage of Leah and Raisa.

The *Kommandant* left the château in the evening after informing the cook that he would not be requiring an evening meal. I was surprised by my feeling of disappointment when I learned of this – with the thought that he would be spending the evening with one of the young women who had been at the lunch that day.

His absence gave me the opportunity to visit Leah and Raisa, who were eager to find out about the recital. I told them as much as I could about those who attended and that the recital had been well received. But I did not tell them about my humiliating faint onstage or the circumstances of my care afterwards.

I went up to the tower to set up the radio. At 9 p.m. came the familiar opening to Beethoven's *5th symphony*; the first four notes "dot dot dot dash" indicating the Morse code V for victory and then the instruction:

'Before we begin, please listen to some personal messages.'

What followed were a series of apparently bizarre and inexplicable phrases, such as, "Aunt Dolly's parrot is unwell". I giggled over some of the most flamboyant, but then came:

'"Trusty's here, and Pincher's here, and see how dumb they lie."'

I found myself replying into the void, '"They don't fret to follow when the Gentlemen go by."'

So, Iain and Fraser must be in Britain. I wondered if Damian knew this and also how often this message had been broadcast for me. I had no way of telling them how happy I was for their safe arrival.

In this state of euphoria, I left the tower and returned to my room to prepare for bed. Then I remembered that the cook had asked me to add more fuel to the oven, as he had a pass to be in town for the night. No doubt in the arms of his accommodating and long-suffering mistress, I smiled to myself.

I was leaving the kitchen when the *Kommandant* appeared. The shock of his sudden presence and the memory of my resentment that he had been with one of the young women from the lunch party caused me to shy away from him, but he caught my arm gently and drew me towards him. In a moment, I was clinging to him and sobbing – the elation of the radio message and the feeling of longing to be held merged into a desperate need to be loved by this man, whatever would come of it.

He carried me to his room and placed me gently on the bed. Slowly and carefully he removed my clothing. He smiled when I instinctively and protectively placed my hand over my underwear.

'My dear *Fräulein*, I already have experience of this with you.'

I watched as he removed his clothing and then the maddening and embarrassing blush that I so despised; I had never seen a man entirely naked before.

I found myself responding to his every caress and touch, my body eager for more of what this man could give me. He stroked my breasts and suckled gently on my nipples, his hands probed my body expertly, exploring me and finding what gave me the most pleasure. And then a sharp pain as he entered me and I found my hips moving in time with the thrusts of his, each one bringing more pleasure than I could have imagined possible. And then a wave of pleasure that made me cry out, and for a while we were both locked together in silence. I wept and he kissed the tears as they flowed down my cheeks.

'Now you are a woman,' he said smiling.

The absurd thought that the green book had not said anything about pleasure made me laugh.

When he asked why I smiled.

'The green book.' Without thinking, I said it in English.

He looked at me and said in English, 'You never told me you spoke English.'

'You never asked me,' I replied, in French.

48

The *Kommandant* left for Paris the following day. I had left his bed early in the morning in order to bathe and prepare breakfast for the household. He gave no indication as to what had passed between us as I served breakfast to him and his adjutant. But before he left, he came into the kitchen and noting that the cook was not in the room, kissed me gently on the lips. My instinct was to lean into him, to keep him with me, but he abruptly turned and left.

Later that morning, I managed to visit Leah and Raisa.

Leah looked at me and remarked, 'So it has happened.'

I realised that this was not a question.

'Yes. And I think I am in love with him.'

Leah sighed. 'I thought this could happen and I do not judge you for it. You cannot choose who to love and sometimes it is not the wisest choice. But I trust your judgement. It could be that this man is not like the others. He is a soldier and he loves his country, so he will fight for it. That is an honourable thing. I would imagine there are many such as him: loyal Germans but who regard the Nazi regime as abominable. But, Helen, you must be careful. What would happen if you became pregnant? Did the *Kommandant* use anything?'

I blushed and admitted, 'I'm not sure what you mean.'

'Did he put something on his male part before he entered you?'

'I don't think so.'

Leah sighed. She clearly had not realised how naïve I was in these matters.

'Then you must go to the pharmacy and ask for something. It is forbidden by law but the woman who serves there will know what to give you. Men do not like putting things on so it is often we women who have to take the responsibility. I and my daughter have done the same; otherwise, we would have more children than we could afford to feed. As for last night, when was your last monthly course.'

'It finished three days ago.'

'That is good. The most dangerous time is in the middle of your courses. But you cannot be sure. You must talk to him about this.'

I could feel myself blushing again. While I was grateful for Leah's advice, I could not imagine how I could begin to have such a discussion with the *Kommandant*.

'And he knows I speak English.'

Leah sighed again.

'Well, it seems he knows more about you than just your body. This could be dangerous. But you can explain to him that English was part of your training to be *Institutrice*.'

I left them and promised to return later with some roast chicken that I had hidden in the pantry.

I had not dared to tell Leah that I neglected to apply the peroxide to my pubic area.

The *Kommandant* returned late in the evening. The cook had been granted another evening pass and the secretaries and adjutant were in Caen at a social evening with members of the garrison. Apart from the guards at the gate, we were alone in the château. I immediately offered to make him a meal and he accepted.

'But only if you permit me to help you.'

And he did. He asked me to show him where all the cooking utensils were kept, as well as the eggs, butter and ham. He instructed me to sit at the table in the kitchen, poured me a glass of wine and proceeded to prepare the meal. During this time, I found making conversation with him difficult. It seemed that our relationship had veered too quickly from that of master and servant to lovers, if that was what we were. Self-doubt and self-deprecation made me shy and

I found it difficult to meet his gaze. When we had finished eating, he took my hand and led me to his room. He undressed me slowly as before, but this time there was less urgency in his taking of me. He took his time, teasing me with gentle fondling and caressing, until I begged him to enter me. When it was over, we lay quietly in each other's arms. I had never felt such joy, but with that came fear for the future, for the fact that I was not the woman he thought me to be.

After a while, he took me again in his arms. He invited me to mount him and showed me how best to do this for my enjoyment. I found the position uncomfortable at first as I was still unaccustomed to his size inside me, but as we moved together, I could not believe the pleasure this gave me, and looking down at his face, I could see it was the same for him.

We stayed together all night and as before, I rose early to bathe and prepare food for the household. The cook was almost fully recovered, but I guessed he was enjoying his convalescence, as this gave him more time with his lover in the town. I reflected on this: could it be that the relationship was now reciprocated? Perhaps the woman was enjoying his attention and falling in love with him. It seemed possible; I had been determined to loathe the *Kommandant* and now I could not bear to be parted from him. What had seemed would be dangerous but simple, was now dangerous and extremely complicated. The fact that both men were part of an enemy army did not alter the men they were; I would have loved Karl von Werstein, with his love of the *Arpeggione Sonata*, his ironic humour, his gentle teasing and his love-making, wherever and whenever I had met him.

The problem was how to reconcile this love with my duties to Leah and Raisa. It would be difficult to make midnight visits to the secret chamber and be in the bed of the *Kommandant*.

As it happened, he made it very simple for me, but not before making the observation that I had been so afraid of.

As I lay in his arms on the third night, he enquired, 'So, my dear *Fräulein*, why is it that you disguise your lovely hair with peroxide?'

I had my answer at once. 'All young women wish to be blonde, as in Hollywood. It is no different for me. I never thought it would be questioned.'

'Well, I would like to request that you throw away the peroxide. It is not good for the hair and it does not suit you.'

At least he had not questioned me regarding my English language proficiency.

He informed me that he would be required to stay in Caen for a number of nights each week, as the *Oberfeldkommandur* had requested this. It was acknowledged by the Military Command that Château des Tilleuls was not a prestigious posting for an officer of the *Kommandant's* experience and rank. It did not, therefore, merit the levels of security afforded to the château in Caen, with a large number of guards posted around the building. Though older, the *Oberfeldkommandur* was of lower military rank than the *Kommandant* and felt unequal at times to the responsibilities of his post, and had requested the *Kommandant's* advice and support.

He explained this to me as we finished practising for another recital that he was planning.

'Of course, I would like you to join me, but that would not be appropriate. And I do not think that you would wish it.'

Again the inscrutable face, and the gently ironic way of speaking to me.

I wondered whether by inappropriate he was referring to the fact that he was married.

He must have read my thoughts for he said, 'It is not because I am married. It is considered usual that soldiers far from home will have love affairs with available women. We call it the spoils of war. But before your face goes as red as the apples in the pantry and you feel you wish to hit me with the cello, let me assure you that I do not regard you as such.'

I laughed, 'How did you guess?'

'My dear *Fräulein*, you are no mystery to me.'

I reflected on this later. Surely, this was just his manner with me and not an allusion to my activities. Of course, it could not be. How could he know? But it was a relief to know that I would be able to continue to protect Leah and Raisa without the risk of detection.

If the rest of the household were aware of my change in status, they did not show it. The secretaries still engaged me in conversation, confiding their love affairs and flirtations, and the guards and adjutant afforded me the same deference and consideration.

49

The winter of 1940 was the longest and coldest since records began in France. I feared for Leah and Raisa in the unheated room. I took in sacks that had held potatoes and carrots and together, we blocked and filled the gaps in the two doors into the room. What had provided excellent ventilation in the summer now permitted cold air to permeate the room.

I was able to bring news of Ruth and Ellana: both girls were enjoying farm life and had learned how to milk the cows and kill chickens. Damian brought a chicken they had prepared and cooked, and I took it to them that night as well as clean clothing and more blankets. I emptied the waste buckets as usual. There was plenty of fresh water for drinking and washing. Damian had devised a new system using milk churns, which were replaced whenever I told him they were low on supplies. The women knew to wait under the trapdoor for a signal and the empty churns were replaced by full ones. Neither minded washing in cold water. Leah and Raisa had endured worse in Odesa.

The nights the *Kommandant* was in Caen were both a torment and a blessing for me. I was free – although very cautious in doing so – to visit Leah and Raisa but found his absence hard to bear. I needed to be close to him. It was difficult enough during the day when he was at work in the library or when I was serving meals to him and his staff officers. My instinct was to reach out to him and I craved to touch him, to feel his hard body next to mine, but I knew this was not possible. I felt sick with longing for him when he was not there and could neither eat nor sleep.

There remained the issue of the risk of pregnancy. I had not had the courage to go to the pharmacy or talk to him about this. He had been away during the nights that Leah had warned me would be the most dangerous to risk a pregnancy, but inevitably there came a night when I realised that I was at the peak of my fertility – Leah had described how I would know this.

As he undressed me, I found the courage to ask him, 'Should I worry about a baby coming from this?'

He did not answer immediately but waited until he was beside me.

'No, *liebchen*, you need not worry, although there are times when I wish it were not so. My wife became very ill after her last pregnancy, the birth of our daughter. She never recovered and is in a clinic in Berlin. The doctor told me that she should never have another child but also that it would be dangerous to remove her womb. I decided to have a procedure that removed the possibility of further children. As it is, my wife's condition has not improved; in fact, she is dying slowly and no longer recognises me.'

'I know nothing of these things but...'

'You wish to know how I am able to make love to you in this way.'

I blushed, 'Yes, it seems there is no difference. I would not have known.'

'The procedure only blocks what would join with your eggs to make a child. It does not stop my virility. But for other reasons, I am glad it is done.'

'Why? Perhaps if your wife recovered you would wish for more children.'

'I would not wish for more of my children to be brought up in Hitler's Reich. It is enough that my sons are dressed as soldiers to play war games and are taught to hate the very people who taught me music. Barbarians now rule my country but I am a soldier. I will fight to the death and kill for the Fatherland. But there has been no honour in this war. We are in your country because of our wickedness.'

I had no words in response to this. I moved on top of him and slowly covered every part of his body with my kisses and tears.

The following afternoon, he invited me to walk with him in the grounds. I hesitated before asking the question but needed reassurance.

'Are the guards and others suspicious of my position here?'

'My dear *Fräulein*, we have had this discussion, have we not? They will assume correctly that we are lovers and they will equally assume, but incorrectly, that you are, as we say, part of the spoils of war; a temporary diversion which is easily displaced. The guards are enjoying the attentions of some of the prettiest girls in the city. Who knows what this war will bring? They may be killed in battle before they return to their wives and girlfriends or murdered by saboteurs in Normandy. It is happening every day. But these are my men. They fought with me in Poland and through Belgium, into France. They will follow me into battle again, of that I have no doubt.'

He reached into his pocket and removed a slim silver cigarette case and lighter.

'I did not know you smoke.'

'Only rarely and in nature. Sometimes it is pleasant to walk in the woods with a cigarette and listen to birdsong. They are beautiful the woods here, are they not?'

I felt a return of the fear and vulnerability that had beset me during the early days of the *Kommandant's* residence at the château. Surely he could not have found the entrance to the tunnel on his strolls through the woods. I needed to see the cigarette.

'May I try it?'

'Of course, but I do not think smoking is good for young women. It changes their skin and I do not like to smell it on them.'

He passed it to me. I looked at the end of the cigarette and saw a German letter. It was identical to the stubs I had found in the glade near the trapdoor. I put it in my mouth and withdrew it immediately.

'No, it is not for me. But thank you.'

He smoked the cigarette and when it was finished, threw it to the ground.

He turned to me with the cool analytical gaze that used to make me feel so exposed, and said, 'And now, my dear *Fräulein*, tell me who you really are.'

I felt faint and started to shake. So this was a game for him. How could I have been so foolish to believe I could continue to care for my friends without detection? He had known of my activities all along. I did not fear for myself at that moment, only for my friends.

He did not wait for my reply, but instead took me gently by the arm and led me behind the château, past the ruin of the gardener's cottage and into the woods. He did not take me to the glade but sat me down on a fallen tree.

'Tell me the truth.'

'No, I will not. You can do as you wish with me. You can send me to your police in Caen and torture me, but I will never tell you.'

He started to laugh and put his arm around me.

'Your face is the colour of those apples in the pantry and fortunately for me, there is no cello available for you to hit me with. All I want to know is who the young woman I love really is. I am sure that she is not Gabrielle Doucet. I made discreet enquiries and a young woman of that name died along with her parents in a motor accident some time ago. Of course, it is entirely possible that there are, or were, two Gabrielle Doucets at one time. Tell me and I will ask no further questions of this.'

I knew then that there was no denying the truth, that part of it anyway.

In English and my Scots lilt, I told him, 'I am Helen Douglas. My home is in Scotland, on the Borders close to England. My mother is French and my father is Scottish. My father is a doctor and my mother studied music at the Paris Conservatoire. They met at a field hospital during the Great War, *La Guerre Quatorze*, and were married here in Normandy. I came to the château in 1938 to care for the children of *Madame* Abramsky-Erhart, but she left with the children when the Germans invaded France. I do not know where she is. Her husband, Stefan, is German but he and his family left Berlin to escape persecution by the Nazis. They are Jews. He left Normandy to find his sister in Berlin and was arrested and imprisoned in a place called Sachsenhausen.'

'And it is his cello that I play?'

'Yes, he was first desk in the Paris Opera Orchestra.'

'I hope I do his cello justice,' he said with that familiar ironic smile.

'No less than I the beautiful piano.'

'Then, we make quite a pair, we less than perfect musicians, do we not?'

'And I am your enemy, am I not?'

He took me in his arms and kissed me slowly and with infinite tenderness.

After a while, he took my hand and said, 'You are as brave as you are beautiful. But you must be careful. We must not speak English together and I do not wish to know anything about your activities. I would not knowingly betray my country. I have instructed my guards that the woods are of no consequence. It is more than sufficient to place the guards at the gates. Besides, the woods are haunted as is the tower, or so my secretaries tell me.'

I laughed. 'I am sorry. I never thought this would happen. I am supposed to despise you.'

'And I should arrest you and have you sent to one of the camps my country is so fond of constructing.'

He took my arm. 'We must return to the château. My guards will believe I am ravishing you in the woods but may fear for my safety.'

That night we had the final rehearsal for the recital the following evening in Caen. We had chosen to play the Beethoven variations for cello and piano. *The Ein Mädchen Oder Weibchen* would be very popular, as would their arrangement for the cello and piano of Schubert's piano quintet *Die Forelle*. We would play the fourth movement as an encore.

'It may encourage them to sing along.' I said this with a smile.

50

'And, so, he knows everything?' asked Leah the following day.

'No, not everything; I believe he does not want to know. I am certain he feels it would be a betrayal of his country – to know and do nothing. So, I must continue to be as careful as before. There is always the possibility of betrayal by guards or others. We cannot trust French citizens either; many have welcomed the Germans and are content to witness the persecution of their Jewish neighbours.'

I left to prepare for the recital that evening. As on the previous occasion, the castle was ablaze with coloured lights. In the reception hall, we handed our coats to waiting staff and took the music and cello onto the stage. The *Kommandant* prepared his chair and set the cello on the floor in front of it. I arranged the music on the piano. The recital was to open with the *Kommandant* playing the Bach *Cello Suite in G minor*. As this was unaccompanied, it was agreed that I should sit in the front row and after the applause, mount the stage to accompany him in the Beethoven *Variations*. There would not be an interval and we would go immediately into the Schubert.

The audience were taking their seats as I arranged the music on the piano. As well as Germans in uniform, there were also a number of French *gendarmes*. To my great dismay, among them was the *gendarme* I had seen holding the arm of the woman who had questioned my identity. My dismay turned to alarm when I saw that my seat – at the end of the front row – was next to that *gendarme*. We had been told to stay on the stage while the *Oberfeldkommandur* made a short speech. He spoke in French, welcoming the audience and extending a special welcome to the *gendarmes* of the city, who were proving indispensable to the smooth running of the new administration in the *Frank Reich*. He asked them to stand up and take a bow, which to a man they did. He then turned to the *Kommandant* and myself and used the same theme of cooperation between the two nations to present us to the audience. We both bowed and I was invited to take my seat.

As I sat down, the *gendarme* whispered, 'Well done, *mademoiselle*. I have seen you at the church many times. My dear mother thinks she knows you. We must meet and talk about your employment.'

I tried to stop my hands from trembling and control my breathing. I could not permit this man to know that I was afraid of him.

I kept my voice as steady as possible as I replied, 'You are correct. I am regularly at mass, but your mother was mistaken. I corrected her on that day. It is no doubt an issue with her eyes. Perhaps you could help her with some eyeglasses. My own grandmother found them very effective.'

'A good idea, I will think about it.'

The *Kommandant* took the applause after the Bach suite and I left my seat to go to the piano. At that moment, came the thud of an explosion. The rear of the hall filled with smoke, debris from the ceiling fell onto the people below and gunfire could be heard coming towards them. For a moment I was transfixed with terror. I saw the *Kommandant* leave the stage and rush towards the scene of the explosion. The *gendarmes* were drawing their pistols and heading the same way. There was utter confusion among the guests of the military. Many of the women were screaming and I could see injured soldiers and women desperately trying to escape from the smoke and gunfire. I grabbed the cello and its case, thrust the music into the case with the cello and placed it behind a screen.

I then went down to do what I could to help the injured, two of whom were haemorrhaging from their wounds. I knew what to do, as I had seen my father do the same for injured cowhands. I ripped up the bottom of my gown to use as a makeshift tourniquet on a *gendarme* who was bleeding from an injury to his lower leg and did the same for a young soldier whose arm was badly injured. For two of the women I could do nothing as both were dead, but for others, I was able to calm and lead them away from the dead and wounded. I went back to check on the two with tourniquets, keeping them warm with clothing I found around the hall, feeling for their pulse and doing my best to reassure them that the doctors would soon be with them

The fire was contained and an army medical team arrived. They took the men away from my care but I continued to do what I could for those still in the hall. It was after midnight before the *Kommandant* appeared. His uniform was bloodied and covered in dust. He came straight to me and took me in his arms.

I kissed him. 'I was concerned for you. And the cello is safe.'

One of the medical team thanked me for what I had done and described to the *Kommandant* how expertly I had applied the tourniquets that had saved the lives and limbs of two of the men.

The *Kommandant* smiled and said, 'There is no end to this young woman's accomplishments.'

We collected the cello and left the hall. The car was waiting for us.

As we drove out of the town, he turned to me and said, 'There will be reprisals. This was the action of a group we have been watching for some time now, but we did not imagine that they were ready to undertake such an act of sabotage '

'What do you mean by reprisals?'

'The *Oberfeldkommandur* will decree that ten hostages be taken for each person killed tonight. The saboteurs will have twenty-four hours to surrender and if none are forthcoming, the hostages will be shot.'

'Who will be taken as hostage?'

'There will be a random selection of men and boys over the age of fifteen. Of course, it could be that the saboteurs will be denounced by others. There is always that hope. The innocent should not die for the crimes of others. And a crime it is; people should know when they are defeated.'

I shrank from him in my seat. I could not believe the cold indifference in his voice.

'How can you speak in such a way, of taking lives?

'It is war.'

That night I slept alone having locked my bedroom door. I did not want him close to me. The *Kommandant* had returned to Caen after delivering me to the château. I did not dare to visit Leah and Raisa as there could be extra guards around the grounds.

Damian arrived with the milk delivery and news from the town. Fifty men and boys had been taken as hostages to the gaol. Their families were desperate for news. One of the hostages was only fifteen years old.

I had to ask the question, 'Were any of the group, our group, involved?'

'As far as I am aware, no, but that will not help the hostages. Unless the saboteurs surrender, or are denounced, the hostages will be shot tomorrow morning. All the roads out of Caen are blocked. It will be difficult for them to escape.'

I did my best to be calm and kept busy in the kitchen. The secretaries were desperate to learn the details of the attack and I told them what I had seen. They, in turn, were able to tell me that five people had died: a *gendarme* was shot by the saboteurs as he left the hall, two young women died in the explosion and two guards were shot and killed at the entrance to the château. One of the guards of this château had a serious arm injury, but his life had been saved due to someone applying a tourniquet.

I said nothing but was pleased that none of the *Kommandant's* men had been killed.

He did not return the second night. I made a quick visit to Leah and Raisa but decided not to tell them about the attack and the hostages. They would worry for their own family.

I went to bed but was awoken in the early hours by the *Kommandant*. He came into my room and sat on the side of my bed. His face was ashen in the morning light and it was clear that he had neither washed nor shaved since the night of the recital.

'They will not be shot,' was all he said before falling onto the bed and into a deep sleep.'

I carefully removed his boots and outer clothing and left the room.

Damian brought news later that morning. The cook had not returned from Caen the previous evening – no doubt due to the roadblocks – so we were free to talk. Damian had learned that the saboteurs were part of a resistance group from Paris and it was believed that it was an assassination attempt on the life of the *Oberfeldkommandur*. Two of the Resistance group had been killed during the attack and two had escaped: one was caught leaving Caen soon after the explosion and the other, a young woman, had been denounced by a local lady with whom she had sought refuge. She had been taken for questioning to the new police office, where she was interrogated by a German intelligence unit. She had been given a cyanide pill by someone and died before they could torture her further. All the hostages had been released.

At midday, I took some food and drink to the bedroom. He was still asleep but awoke as I placed the tray on the night table. I waited while he drank the wine and ate some of the food. He appeared famished. I offered to help him bathe but he held my arm and asked me to lie with him on the bed.

He turned to me and said, 'She was so young. I thought of you. They had stripped her naked and tied her to a chair. They had started on her face, her beautiful young face, and they broke it. But she would not talk, they said. They told me they took her to the bath and tried the drowning torture. But, still, she would not talk. Then they whipped her until her young body was covered in blood. But she would not talk. I had heard too much and told them they must leave her for a few hours. Believe me, *liebchen*, I have never been part of such as this young woman had to suffer. Promise me that this will not be your fate. It is not for this that I became a soldier. They enjoyed her suffering. They are sadists, not police officers. So I killed her. I waited until they were drinking and planning what else they could do to her and went to her cell. I gave her a cyanide capsule. She knew what it was and thanked me. I waited with her until she was dead and then left.'

I held him in my arms as he wept.

'I see that young woman in you. I see how they would do the same to you. Please, you must promise not to be that young woman.'

I held him close and eventually, we both slept.

51

The body of the young man was hung from the ramparts of the castle. A notice testifying to his guilt and warning others of the same fate was posted under the body. I could not believe the medieval brutality of this. His body bore the marks of torture. I did not ask whether he had given any information about accomplices. I did not want to know.

There would be no further recitals at the château in Caen, but it was hoped that the cathedral in Bayeux could be used in the future; as a centre for religious observation, it was considered a safer place for such an event.

I enquired after the injured guard and *gendarme* and was told that both were recovering well. The guard would be sent home to Germany to recover, as it was unlikely he would be able to fight again. I imagined the relief of his family that he would play no further part in a war that had already cost the lives of so many of his friends and comrades.

But the news was not all good. Damian whispered a message as he delivered the milk urns a few days later. The young man had disclosed the involvement of a local Resistance group in the attack.

'How else would the saboteurs have known that so many high-ranking officers would be where they were that night?'

The secretaries had more information. Agents from the *Sicherheitsdienst* or SD were now in charge of the investigation. I had not heard of this organisation and they explained to me that it was the intelligence branch of *Reichsführer* Heinrich Himmler's elite protection squadron, the SS. They told me that Reinhard Heydrich, the head of the SD, was coming to Caen with his own agents to investigate the crime.

Lotti explained, 'The *Oberfeldkommandur* is his cousin. He is determined to identify and punish those who tried to kill him. He will find them without doubt. They say his methods are brutal but effective and he is the most feared of all in the security services. He was put in command in Poland in 1939, but because of his actions there, the generals did not want him here in France. He is known as the man with the iron heart, as he has no mercy towards those who challenge his authority and the *Reich*. He is very handsome; no woman can resist him and he knows that to be so.'

I was shaken by this. The thought that this man would be coming to Caen, and the risk this posed to all who resisted the occupation, in whatever capacity, made me realise more than ever before how dangerous life now was.

The *Kommandant* did nothing to allay my fears.

'I know this man well. He has a fanatic's devotion to Hitler and the party, but he is also cultured and highly intelligent. He is not a man I like or admire. I met him several times at the home of Admiral Wilhelm Canaris, whose wife is a violinist. Heydrich plays the violin exceptionally well. He is Prussian, as I am, but not of a military family; his parents are musicians. I will be obliged to do what I can to assist in his enquiries. We are to have a recital in his honour. You must be calm; if he believes you have nothing to conceal from him, you will have nothing to fear.'

His words did not reassure me. He continued, 'And I must inform you, the *Chef de Gendarmerie* tells me that your grandparents will also be at the recital. He has been very busy looking for them in Lisieux, but now he is happy to say that he has found them. Naturally, he has invited them to the recital. They are eager to meet you after so many years. They have missed their dear Gabrielle it would seem.'

My heart skipped a beat and I looked at him. The ironic tone of his voice and inscrutable expression made me once again feel uncertain, and very afraid.

'Come, *liebchen*, we will now prepare for the recital. Our guest of honour, *Herr* Heydrich, must be entertained. He may well request that you accompany him, as he will bring his violin, of that I have no doubt. When he is not protecting the *Reich* from its enemies or seducing the ladies, he plays the violin. Perhaps we Prussians are all the same: music and ladies. Or perhaps not; Prussians are soldiers, not inquisitors.'

He said this with his familiar enigmatic face and mocking manner and continued, 'I understand you are to be honoured for saving the life of one of my soldiers. I shall miss him but now he returns to his mother and girlfriend and all are happy that he will be well.'

After the rehearsal, he told me he had to be in town for the night. This confused me. The saboteurs were dead and Heydrich was not yet in Caen. Why was he leaving me that night? Not only did it break my heart but it also made me very afraid. Perhaps he had decided that as a loyal German, he could not continue to keep an enemy of his country as his mistress. I remembered the young women at the lunch party. Perhaps he was with one of them. The pain this caused me was beyond any fear I felt for my life. At that moment, I did not care if the *gendarme* revealed me to be an imposter and arrested me as a conspirator and enemy agent. All that mattered was the thought that he did not love me and had never loved me, that I was no more than a diversion, the spoils of war.

I did not dare to go to Leah and Raisa. He could have set a trap there too. I could do nothing but get through that night and take whatever the following day held for me.

When I awoke, I saw the staff car parked in front of the château. He had returned during the night but this was no comfort. He had not come to me. I helped the cook in the kitchen. His scalded hand was now fully healed. Since the time of my intervention to conceal his absence and treat his injury, he had appeared to regard me as both a valued assistant and his saviour. Today, he seemed unusually subdued and indifferent to my presence. But I continued with my routine: serving the *Kommandant* and his officers their breakfast and dealing with the usual household responsibilities.

In the middle of the morning, the *Kommandant* came into the library where I was filing invoices. He asked me to follow him into the salon. On the sofa was the blue gown I had so disdained at the couturier.

'Your gown could not be repaired. I took it to the couturier but it was not possible. So, tonight, you will wear this. It becomes you well and it will be appreciated by those in the audience.'

'You know I will not wear this. It is something a whore would wear, one of your spoils of war perhaps.'

I no longer cared what he thought of me but at least I had my pride.

He said nothing in reply and made to leave the room.

I threw the gown after him and then fell crying onto the sofa, weak with anger, humiliation and the pain of loss.

Lotti came into the room and put her arm around me.

'Gabrielle, please be calm. There is much you may not understand. This night is very important for the *Kommandant*, he cannot risk any mistakes. Wear the gown and play for him tonight.'

52

At 7 p.m. I was dressed and waiting in the car. He joined me a few minutes later. He was wearing what I recognised to be the military dress coat of a general of the *Wehrmacht*, with silver braid to the right shoulder and medals on the left. He handed the cello to his adjutant and sat beside me. I wrapped a shawl tightly around my shoulders and pulled the dress up as high as I could. We drove to Bayeux in silence. When I saw the spires of Notre-Dame Cathedral, I recalled the occasion of my last visit there: my grandmother's birthday lunch. How simple life had been then; now I felt like a fly caught in a spider's web of deception and fear.

The cathedral was surrounded by a great number of soldiers. A Mercedes car decked with swastikas and the German flag stood outside the door to the main altar. The vestibule was a reception area, where uniformed officers and their guests were drinking champagne. There was an inner circle which parted when we entered. A tall slim man stepped from the circle. He was handsome and about the same age as the *Kommandant* – his hair was more blonde, and his eyes more blue than the grey blue of the *Kommandant's*, and his oval face was dominated by a large nose.

The *Kommandant* bowed slightly and gave the salute, '*Heil Hitler, Obergruppenführer* Heydrich.'

To which the other replied, '*Heil Hitler*, General von Werstein. And who is the lovely lady at your side?'

'Allow me to introduce *Mademoiselle* Gabrielle Doucet, my accompanist for this evening.'

Heydrich clicked his heels and bowed, taking my hand and kissing it slowly while looking into my eyes. I suppressed a shudder. The eyes of this man were cold and calculating and would inculcate fear in those caught in his gaze. He reminded me of a snake.

'I am sure she plays as beautifully as she looks. Perhaps she will do me the honour of accompanying me also. I have brought my violin. It will be like old times with our friends Wilhelm and Erika.'

'I am sure she will be honoured,' said the *Kommandant*. 'But now we must prepare for tonight's recital.'

He bowed again, gave the salute, and gestured to me to follow him.

I followed him into the nave of the cathedral, and there was the *gendarme* and with him an elderly couple. I stopped; a feeling of terror gripped me, so much so, that I thought I would faint again. But the couple advanced towards me with their arms outstretched.'

'My darling, Gabrielle, it is so good to see you after so many years. We have missed you and now we are honoured to be here tonight.'

The woman kissed me twice on both cheeks and, turning to the *gendarme*, said, 'We are so happy to find her well. You know, it was me, her grandmother, who first taught her to play and now she is here in such surroundings. Thank you, monsieur.' She continued, 'My darling granddaughter, we must leave you to prepare for your performance. *Monsieur le Chef des Gendarmes* has kindly paid for us to stay at the Hôtel de Fresnes tonight after the recital and then we will continue home to Lisieux in the morning.'

She kissed me farewell as did her companion, *"Grandpère" Norbert* and they left. The *gendarme* looked uncomfortable but did his best to compose himself. He then took his leave, wishing us both a successful recital.

We went onto the main altar which had been arranged with a grand piano and chair for the *Kommandant*.

As I arranged the music, he whispered in my ear, 'A life for a life; you saved my man.'

'So, it was my reward? Part of a deal, a transaction if you like? You led me into a trap. It could have ended badly for me if I had not been able to keep up with the ridiculous charade.'

'And if I had warned you, how would you have been with this meeting? The surprise showed on your face and our so-diligent *Chef des Gendarmes* was disarmed. Now he is assured that you are a beloved granddaughter. By the way, they have been instructed to enjoy the food and wine offered at the hotel, all of course at the expense of the *gendarmerie*.'

'You knew those people were not my grandparents and you made me fear this night. I hate you. I do not care what you do now. You can kill me and I will die happy. Who were they?'

'That is for later.'

'And why the horrible gown?'

'I thought to impress our honoured guest.'

'By making me look like your whore.'

'It suits you well as my accompanist. You know what you are to me. And, please, do not become so enraged. The colour does not suit a red face.'

He calmly took the cello from its case and tuned it. The audience took their seats. Heydrich sat in the middle of the front row. I could feel his eyes on me but a feeling of elation ran through me. There were still questions I needed to ask him, but I no longer felt vulnerable.

All three Beethoven variations went well; the audience particularly enjoyed the second and third variations which they could recognise as popular arias from *The Magic Flute*.

We took our bow and prepared to commence our arrangement of the Schubert Piano Quintet, *Die Forelle*. At that moment, Heydrich stood up, picked up his violin, and stepped onto the stage.

'I will join you in this. I know the piece well and it will be my pleasure to take part in this excellent recital.'

He nodded to me, I played the introduction and we began. He was a superb violinist and had no trouble adapting to the arrangement. We did a reprise of the *fourth movement, Andantino Theme* and *Variations,* to the enthusiastic applause of the audience.

At the end, we took several bows, with Heydrich ostentatiously taking my hand to kiss it. He then invited us to play an encore of our choice.

A nod passed between the *Kommandant* and me; we would play the *second movement, Adagio,* of the *Arpeggione Sonata.*

As we played, I felt an unbearable intensity of emotion. The slow and wistful melody evoked memories of our love. We played as one, his eyes meeting mine, acknowledging each other through the music and understanding what this meant.

We took our final bow. Heydrich mounted the stage again, this time to congratulate me on saving the lives of the two men. He reminded the audience of my actions on that night and to my dismay, produced a medal. He announced that my actions were an outstanding contribution to the war effort and that the War Merit Medal was my reward. He pinned the medal over my left breast. I felt his lascivious eyes lingering on me and felt a brief surge of anger that I had been forced to wear such a revealing gown for this occasion. I managed to find the words to thank him but before I could, he raised his arm in the *Heil Hitler* salute and the audience stood to attention to do the same. I was determined to avoid doing so. I made a move to adjust the medal and pretended that it had become loose from its fastening. This caused me to appear flustered and by the time I had apparently secured the medal, the audience were leaving the cathedral to attend the formal dinner that was to be held in honour of SS *Gruppenführer* Heydrich.

The *Kommandant* told me that he had to attend the dinner but would return that night. He helped me into his staff car and gave the cello to my care.

Once back at the château, I ripped off the gown and threw it into a bag of laundry. With luck, it would be destroyed in the wash. I did not remove the medal before doing so, willing it the same fate. I dressed and, noting that members of the household were either out for the evening or settled in their rooms, I set off to visit Leah and Raisa. They were relieved to see me as they had been worried by my absence. The waste buckets were full and fresh water had not been brought to them that day. I could not help with the water supply – there was enough to drink at least– but the waste buckets took over an hour to haul up to the woods to empty and disperse their contents.

Once this was done, I proceeded to tell Leah and Raisa about the events over the past two days. They were terrified that a man such as Heydrich was in Caen and directing the investigation, and amused and appalled that I had been awarded a medal. But when I told of my disposal of the medal and the gown, they could not help but laugh. While they were laughing, I heard a commotion outside the room. For a moment we were paralysed with terror; surely this meant that the refuge had been betrayed. I told Leah and Raisa to leave by the door to the woodland exit and promised to hold the intruders at bay until they were outside. They remonstrated with me to accompany them but I refused.

The door to the room opened and three young women entered. I recognised one as the young woman who had met me in the church. I greeted them and told them to wait while I hastened to call Leah and Raisa back to the room. They should not leave; it would be dangerous for them to be caught in the woods.

The young woman explained in English that her two companions were British agents who were part of the Resistance group in Paris who had masterminded the plot to kill the *Oberfeldkommandur*. They were now trying to evade arrest by the intelligence agents who were doing house-to-house searches in the city. They knew what had happened to their comrades but did not know what information had been divulged to their interrogators. Leah was watching me from the other side of the room while they were recounting this. I happened to turn my head and caught a warning glance from Leah and understood. Leah did not speak English but was shrewd enough to guess what the conversation was about. The glance was a warning to be careful what I said; they must not know of the *Kommandant's* part in the girl's death.

The two agents would stay until a message was sent concerning their rescue or escape. I asked them how they had found their way to the tunnels and they explained that they had used a tunnel from the ruined chapel. The guards had been distracted by four dogs running loose close to the gates, which had given the three women the chance to climb over the outside walls of the château and make their way to the chapel.

'We released them from their chains outside the *gendarmerie* and brought them with us. The *gendarmerie* was very quiet and we knew most of them would be in Bayeux tonight. It was an opportunity for us to get here. We threw meat over the walls and then let the dogs go free. It was most amusing watching the guards trying to catch them.'

I showed them where bedding could be found and left them with Leah and Raisa. The young woman from the group accompanied me to the trapdoor in the woods and then set off to follow the track to the fields and onto the road back to Caen.

The *Kommandant* returned at dawn, explaining that the dinner had gone on into the early hours of the morning. Heydrich had been very disappointed that I had not stayed.

'He is most enamoured of you and proposed to visit here tonight to further the acquaintance. Unfortunately, he received a call from Paris, where it seems the conspirators have returned. He and his agents departed soon after the meal to intercept them. And what of these dogs that are running loose around the grounds?'

'I have no idea. Perhaps the *gendarmes* will have to come and take them away.'

'See how easily you lie.'

But he smiled and undressed. Once in bed, he took my face in his hands and said, 'All I ask is that you are careful. I will not ask any questions of you, as I will not knowingly betray my country.'

I wrapped my arms around him and pulled him to me. I had no words, just the desperate need to be close to him, to feel his body next to mine and be filled by him.

Later, we lay in each other's arms. I asked him about the elderly couple of the previous night.

'You may thank the cook for that, or at least his mistress. She has family in Lisieux and saw the notices that the *gendarme* had placed around the town. Their family name is Doucet but it seems that many have that name in the town. Let us say that a tank full of gasoline for their motorcar, a large piece of the best beef, together with coffee and cigarettes can be very persuasive. But they do not like the *gendarme,* who has a reputation for dishonesty, and they are good friends of the mistress. You may have noticed how preoccupied our cook was yesterday. He was anxious that their plan would not work. He did not dare to warn you.'

'So, the cook knows about me?'

'Enough but not too much, he admires you greatly.'

'And you?'

'My dear *Fräulein*, surely you know by now that I love you.'

'And I you.'

He pulled me closer to him and slowly kissed me, not neglecting any part of my body. He lingered with his tongue around that most sensitive place of all, of which I had not yet been fully aware. He gently raised my legs over his shoulders, smiled at me and went down to me again, expertly teasing me with his tongue and using his fingers to caress me. The pleasure was almost too intense. I wanted to cry out to make him stop, and yet that was not what I wanted. An immense wave of pleasure shot through me, my body felt on fire and I could hear my voice begging him for more, then another wave and I was sobbing in his arms. He held me for a while and then gently entered me, his eyes never leaving my face. We moved together as one and I could feel him in my womb as he reached his climax.

The noon sun was shining through the curtains when we finally rose. I bathed and went to help the cook in the kitchen. The

Kommandant worked in the library for a few hours and then took his leave to return to Caen, but assured me that he would return that night.

After the household had been served their evening meal and the cook had departed to his mistress, I returned to the underground room. Fresh water had been delivered after I had left the previous night and I brought food and wine for my new guests. They were in good spirits, thanking me for what I had done for them. I returned to them later with clean underwear and clothing. The weather was now warmer with the approach of summer and this gave me hope. At least, Leah and Raisa had survived the winter.

53

He left for Caen the following day, informing me that he would not return that night. As usual, I kept busy in the kitchen as well as organising the laundry and supervising the cleaning of the château. I had been obliged to employ local women to help with cleaning and bed changing. This had been a difficult decision, as I did not wish for others to be in the château. I was concerned about the possibility of one of them discovering the secret room and informing the increasingly menacing *gendarmes*. To avoid this, I ensured that the women were only employed between the hours of 10 a.m. to 8 p.m. I did not wish them to know that I slept with the *Kommandant* and equally I did not want them around after dark to be witness to my nocturnal activities. Lest they discovered the wireless, I told them that it would be unwise to enter the tower, as the floors were rotted and they risked falling to their deaths. I did not think they would believe the tower to be haunted.

Damian arrived late in the morning. Along with the milk supply, he had a message to say that there would be a collection that night and that I must be in the woods at 2 a.m. with the cargo. I understood what was required of me.

At midnight, I crept through the rose garden to the ruin and into the underground room. I brought food, wine and clothing with me. I awakened the young women and told them of the plan. After their meal, they followed me by torchlight up the staircase, through the trapdoor and out into the woods. The glade was lit up in the full moon and the air smelled of moss and the first awakening of spring.

Clumps of primroses had replaced the bowed heads of the snowdrops and a few early muscari added a faint perfume to the glade.

After a short time, a beam of light appeared through the trees. A figure in a balaclava beckoned to us to follow. Once out of the woods, we followed the figure along a track through the fields until we came to a freshly ploughed field surrounded by steep hedgerows. The sound of an aircraft could be heard, and at the same time we noticed lights flashing from within the hedgerows. The noise of the plane grew louder and then it appeared over the fields to the left of where we stood. It passed over once and then turned and began a sharp descent; the engines roaring as it did so. It landed with a thud, which sent a spray of turf in all directions before coming to rest in the middle of the field. The figure in the balaclava raced towards it, pulling the two women with him. A door on the plane opened, steps were lowered and the two clambered up. Someone threw large packages out of the plane, which were immediately gathered up by figures that appeared from the hedgerows. The two women waved a quick farewell, the door of the plane closed and the engines roared to life. The plane turned and slowly ascended into the moonlight. The balaclava did not speak to me but gestured a farewell. I made my way back to the woods and the château.

To my dismay, I saw the *Kommandant's* car in the drive. I hurried in through the kitchen door and into the library. He was there, gathering papers and letters from the desk and packing them into cabinets. His adjutant stood by the door with suitcases. He asked the adjutant to place the cases in his car and, once we were alone, took me in his arms.

'I will not ask where you have been but I have to tell you that I must return to Berlin. They say my wife is dying. I do not know whether this is the natural course of her illness or whether she is the victim of those who wish all who cannot be productive to die.'

'I do not understand.'

'It is not in the *Reichsführer's* interest to keep alive those who are unable to be a part of the glorious new Germany that will arise from this war. They have been murdering – though they do not call it such – those who are frail mentally or physically. If I do not go to her, she will certainly die.'

I felt at once a profound sympathy for the plight of this woman, but also, to my shame, one of jealousy towards her. It had been easy to forget that he was married and with children.

'Go to her and stay as long as is necessary.'

I took him in my arms, kissed him and added, 'Know that I will always love you'

He held me close to him.

'All I ask is that you are safe and do not become as that girl.'

He kissed me once more and then turned to leave the room. I stood at the window and watched as the car sped off into the night.

54

For a short time following the departure of the *Kommandant*, I was hopeful that life at the château would continue as before. The cook appeared oblivious to the disappearance of meat and other foodstuffs from the larder, the guards treated me with the same respect and consideration and the secretaries made it clear that they were sympathetic to my sadness at the absence of the *Kommandant*.

Leah and Raisa were surviving confinement in the underground room, and the warm May breezes brought the scent of blossom and took away the chill that had seeped into the walls through the long winter months. I was able to visit their husbands and pass messages between them. The men still refused to go into hiding despite the fact that their business had now been taken from them. The rationing of food and heating materials meant that they were only surviving with the help of kindly neighbours.

The Germans were seizing the food produced on farms and either exporting it to Germany or consuming it themselves. People could no longer buy leather shoes, and wooden soles replaced leather ones when they wore out. Soap was now rare and households were making their own from fats and caustic soda. Coffee was impossible to buy except at extortionate prices on the black market. An ersatz coffee was made from toasted barley mixed with chicory, and saccharin replaced sugar. Those with families in the countryside were able to get clandestine supplies of fresh vegetables as well as rabbit meat and chicken, but many in the towns and cities were starving. As well as the curfew, they now had to close their shutters and windows and turn off all lights to prevent enemy aircraft from using the lights for navigation.

Two nights after the *Kommandant* left, I tuned into Radio Londres.

After the usual Beethoven 5th chords, I listened to the usual bizarre messages, until I heard:

'You'll be given a dainty doll all the way from France.'

I knew the two agents had arrived safely.

Early in June, an open-top Mercedes car decorated with swastikas pulled up in front of the château. Behind the driver sat an overweight man in a military uniform. One of the accompanying officers opened the door and he stepped out onto the driveway. I was in the library with the secretaries at the time and asked Lotti who the arrival was.

'He is *Oberstleutnant* Otto Mueller. He is here to replace the *Feldkommandur*, for a while at least.'

My dismay must have shown on my face for Lotti took my hand.

'But he will return, I am sure of it,' she said. 'Meanwhile, we must all do what we can to be useful. This man is not of the same rank as the *Feldkommandur*. I believe he will want to prove himself as an effective administrator.'

Lotti's prediction proved to be correct. Mueller appeared determined to rule the household and his area of command in an increasingly oppressive and ruthless manner. He increased the guards around the gates of the château and organised patrol details in the woods. The soldiers were authorised to shoot on sight any intruders found within the château grounds and in the surrounding woodland.

Within days of his arrival, a local farmer was arrested for selling meat on the black market. As his punishment, he was deported to Germany to join thousands of other French men as forced labour for the German war effort. This, as Damian informed me, had left his wife with seven children to feed and no man to help her with the farm. Mueller was now sending soldiers to all the surrounding farms to ensure that what was produced went directly under German control, either to feed the occupying troops or to be exported to

Germany. The soldiers were also instructed to search farms for anyone suspected of evading the *Service de Travail Obligatoire* – the compulsory labour scheme that had been imposed on France as part of the Armistice treaty, by which men between the ages of 18 and 50 were transported to Germany to work in factories to supply the German war machine. They were also instructed to find Jews who may be avoiding the registration required since October 1940.

I could see no way in which I now could visit and care for Leah and Raisa. I needed to speak to *Père* François. This would not be easy, as first I would have to ask for permission from Mueller to leave the château. We had not been formally introduced, as I had kept to the kitchen, where the cook – who I now felt to be an ally – ensured that I had enough to do to avoid him. I no longer occupied the desk in the library and it therefore took all my courage to go to the library where Mueller was attending to correspondence and make the request. I chose a time when both Lotti and Emilia were also at work there.

'I wish to attend mass and confession in Caen. It is the anniversary of the death of my grandmother and it is usual for me to attend a special mass for her.'

'And may I ask who you are, *Fräulein*?'

'I am Gabrielle Doucet. I have been employed here since the arrival of the *Feldkommandur* Von Werstein.'

Turning to Lotti and Emilia, Mueller asked, 'Do you know this young woman?'

'Yes, *Herr Oberstleutnant*. She is most trustworthy and efficient. That she is French is very useful, as she helps with all the translations.'

'Does she speak German?'

'No, *Herr Oberstleutnant*, but that is not necessary. Emilia and I speak French but not this dialect. It is useful to have a local girl to explain differences in the language.'

I was overwhelmed by gratitude to the two secretaries. Whatever their motives, they were not going to betray my relationship with the *Kommandant*.

Mueller agreed to my request but insisted that I report back to the library on my return. I thanked him and made to leave the room, but not without noticing how his eyes roved over my body, and Lotti's concerned face as he did so.

Once at the church, I waited my turn by *Père* François's confessional. Speaking in whispers, I told him of my predicament. I had not been able to visit Leah and Raisa since the arrival of Mueller and was desperately worried for their health and safety and that of others who may join them in the underground room.

To my relief, *Père* François was able to assure me that at least for the moment, they were well. He also explained that the entrance to the room from the ruined chapel could be reached by a tunnel from a safe location within Caen and one nearby. He reminded me that the city and locality rested on limestone which enabled both natural and manmade tunnels and caves to be used in times such as these.

'We are not the first to seek shelter from enemies. Our group have been preparing for this since the occupation by the Germans. For the moment, you need not be concerned for your friends; we will do all we can. But we must ask you to be vigilant. Your new employer is not a man of honour. His unit was responsible for the killing of hundreds of civilians in Pas-de-Calais as well as in Belgium.'

'I had no idea. And his men are now with him. The soldiers who were at the château when the *Kommandant* was in charge have now left.'

'This is only the beginning of his rule and worse will follow. He will bide his time and you must be careful. But you must also do what you can to resist.'

'In what way, as I am unable to visit Leah and Raisa or help anyone seeking shelter?'

'You can listen, learn what you can and appear to collaborate.'

'Collaborate?'

'Now go, my child. Appear to do your penance and leave.'

I was shaken by the priest's words. I knelt for a short time in the pew, appearing to pray, but all the while attempting to decipher the instruction the priest had given me.

As I left the church, I felt an arm on my elbow. I turned and saw the young woman who had brought the two agents to the underground room. She pressed a small package into my hands.

'Take this. Inside is what may be necessary for you. There are instructions.'

I placed the package in my pocket and cycled back to the château. Before I entered the gates, I dismounted and gave the appearance of checking the wheel. As I did so, I opened the package. Inside were two items: one was a capsule marked "cyanide" and the other was a cup-shaped piece of rubber with instructions on its use on a piece of paper.

I reported to the library as instructed and was relieved to see both Lotti and Emilia at work there. Mueller looked up from his desk and greeted me.

'So, *mademoiselle,* you are returned. Now you may go to help the cook prepare my evening meal. I will dine alone but would be pleased to have you serve me.'

I did as he instructed and served Mueller his evening meal. I could feel his eyes on me as I did so and recognised the threat he posed to me. With that came the determination not to allow this man to use his position to abuse me. Nor would I do as my contacts clearly wished, which was to seduce him. The anger I felt at this exploitation of my body overcame my allegiance to them. Would any of those young women willingly submit to a man such as Mueller? Of course, they would not. I felt debased and that my love of the *Kommandant* was regarded as prostitution by them. My only duty was to Leah, her family and others who may be put into my care.

Later that night, I considered the plot against the *Oberfeldkommandur.* He had been kind to me and gave every appearance of being an honest man in a situation that was not of his choosing. Those who wished to kill him could have caused the deaths of fifty innocent men and boys as well as being responsible for the torture and deaths of the two agents. The distinction between good and evil – a war that the nuns had taught could be righteous in the eyes of God as opposed to unrighteous – was blurred. It was clear to me that Hitler's war fell into the latter category, but for those who had no choice but to fight, where did they fall in this scale of righteousness? I was tired of all the subterfuge and intrigue. I would do as my conscience truly felt was best for my friends and countrymen. I would not prostitute myself in any way whatsoever.

The following night, I locked my bedroom door as soon as I entered. As far as I was aware, only I had duplicate keys to the rooms of the château, but nevertheless, I feared that Mueller may have some way of obtaining a skeleton key and be able to unlock the door from outside the room. To avoid this, I left my key in the lock and as an extra precaution, moved a chest of drawers against the door. As I did this, an envelope fell from behind the chest. Inside the envelope were two photographs – the sepia print had faded with age but I could clearly see the smiling faces of three young women in each photograph.

With astonishment, I recognised one of the young women as my mother. She was seated on a chair in a room I recognised as the apartment where Stefan's parents lived. The other two young women were leaning over the back of the chair. On the wrist of one was the bracelet I recognised as the one I had found in the cavity above the cistern in the apartment – the Star of David was discernible despite the age of the photograph. The young woman was wearing it on her left wrist. The other young woman I recognised was Odette, but most confusing was the fact that the two young women looked so very alike. They could be twins. But Odette had been an only child, *une fille unique* as *Maman* had explained, so this was extremely puzzling. The other photograph provided no clues. In that one, all three young women were standing with their backs to the massive fireplace that dominated the salon in the apartment. *Maman* was in the middle, the "twins" were on either side of her and, again, the Star of David bracelet was visible on the left arm of one.

I thought again about the bracelet, wondering why it been hidden away and the identity of the mysterious twin. I remembered then that I had hidden the bracelet in Stefan's desk, the very desk that first the *Kommandant* and now Mueller used. I needed to retrieve it as soon as possible.

I slept badly, dimly aware of footsteps outside the room and a possible turning of the door knob, but if it had been Mueller attempting to get in, he gave up after a while.

I waited until Mueller was enjoying his usual hearty breakfast to gain access to the library. Lotti and Emilia were still in their rooms and none of the guards were yet on duty inside the château. Using my duplicate key, I unlocked the door and went to the desk. It was unlocked. I remembered that I had placed the bracelet in a small compartment at the back of the top drawer so that was where I looked first. The drawer was full of correspondence dating from the time of the *Kommandant*. At first, it seemed it was not to be found, but then I noticed the small inner tray at the very back of the drawer and remembered how I had placed the bracelet in that. It was still there, hidden by the weight of letters and papers. I slipped the bracelet into my pocket and was about to make my exit when I noticed a document marked *Juif non-assimiles/non-naturalises* on top of the desk. The document was addressed to the *Kommandant* and dated from October of the previous year. I wondered why it was now on the desk of Mueller and what its purpose was.

Locking the door behind me, I ran up the stairs to my room. There I took out the photograph and compared the bracelet on the woman's wrist with the one in my hand. They were identical.

I now needed to determine the purpose of the list. I began with Lotti.

'Thank you for speaking on my behalf to the *Oberstleutnant*. It is important to me that I stay here. I hope for the return of the *Feldkommandur* one day. How is Herr Mueller managing his administration here? It seems his methods are very different.'

'I can only speak from what I know of the man. He had a reputation for showing no mercy to those who resisted as he led his infantry through the North of France. I understand he will be equally so here.'

She went on to say, 'Gabrielle, I have seen how he looks at you. You must take care not to be alone with him. He will not consider you in the way of the *Feldkommandur* and will treat you as no more than ...' Here she stopped and looked down.

'You mean a whore?' I felt my face suffuse with anger and embarrassment.

'I am sorry, that is not the correct word. We all know you shared the *Feldkommandur's* bed.'

'That does not make me a whore.'

I was about to rush from the room but Lotti held my arm.

'I mean you no disrespect. I am only trying to warn you.'

I met Emilia the following day as she was collecting the mail from the hallway. I offered to help her carry it into the library as Lotti was still in her room. I asked her the same question.

She replied, 'He is very thorough. It has been found that the *Feldkommandur* did not always follow instructions. I myself have to find the lists that were ordered by your Marshal Pétain. They had not been acted on. Perhaps the *Feldkommandur* was too busy with other activities.'

But she smiled as she said this and there was no malice in her voice.

'Lists? What lists? I was very careful to provide all the invoices for the household to the officer in charge of these things.'

I pretended indignation that my responsibilities had been found inadequate.

'No, not at all. These are the lists that have to be made of Jews who are not considered truly French. Perhaps they were born in another country and have no right to be considered as citizens of the Frank Reich, or France.'

'I do not understand.'

'I shall explain. Your Marshal Pétain signed the Armistice when France surrendered. The French people remembered him as a hero of the Great War and they saw him as the saviour of France, as they still do. For that reason, he could form his government with the help of his German allies. He appeals to the values of those who wish for a better France, with Work, Family and Homeland as its principles. He wishes to give France back to the French and to do that, he needs to limit the influence of foreigners including Jews and refugees, and send them to places where they cannot have such influence. We in Germany have done the same. We have sent people who do not support the *Führer* to countries where they may be kept away from loyal Germans. There were towns in Germany where people had to leave their homes and come to France because they could not be trusted to support the *Führer's* vision, or because they were Jewish.'

'And where are these people now?'

'They are in camps. There are camps in France – in the Zone Libre and here. More will be built to accommodate them. Many Jews chose to come to France when the *Führer* came to power. It was their choice but before them, many also came from Poland, Russia and other countries. Marshal Pétain makes the distinction between those Jews who are true citizens of France and those who are foreign Jews.'

'And what of those Jews who came to escape from the pogroms of Odesa?'

'They are not desirable in the new order of France unless, of course, they have been awarded special protection. It is the immigrant Jews who are on the list. It is necessary for security. For what comes later to those with true citizenship, I cannot say. Who can?'

Emilia turned her head away as she said those words.

'Emilia, you truly cannot say these words and believe that this is just. These are people who came to France to find safety and who have been good citizens. They have trades, they are doctors and they are teachers. They have families. It cannot be right to send them to a camp.'

'I don't make the rules,' she replied.

And I remembered the words of Leah. "Our safety depends on who makes the rules." The family of my friend, Leah, would be on that list.

56

Mueller took advantage of a quiet Sunday afternoon in the early autumn to assault me. I had received no news from the *Kommandant* since his departure and I was increasingly agitated regarding the silence.

Hitler had now conquered the whole of Europe and it had been expected that he would launch a full-scale invasion of Britain. The *Luftwaffe* had suffered heavy losses in the air battles with the Royal Air Force but a sea invasion was still possible. Lotti and Emilia were convinced this would be so. But in June of that year, Hitler declared war on his former ally, Josef Stalin's Soviet Union. In this way, he aimed to wreak violence on the country that, in his opinion, represented his two most despised enemies: Jews and Communists. I feared that my lover had been sent to the Russian Front. I remembered from my childhood history lessons that Napoleon had embarked on such a campaign, only to become trapped in the vicious Russian winter. The French army had been decimated – starved and frozen to death – as they crossed the Berezina River in the retreat from Moscow in 1812. The name of the river had become the word for disaster in the French language. That this could be my lover's fate was a constant anxiety.

The cook had been granted a pass to the town, as had the secretaries, and the guards paced the grounds and woods, out of sight and sound of what was happening in the château.

I was about to return to my room after clearing the midday meal dishes when he came into the kitchen. He grabbed my arm and threw me to the floor. I was quickly on my feet and ran to the door. He caught the hem of my dress and pulled me to the floor again. I felt it tear in his hands but I made my escape again. I ran up the stairs and into my room. I looked for the key but it was not in the lock. I realised that he had planned this, that there was no key. And then he was in the room, his face florid from the wine he had drunk, and anger that I was making this so difficult for him. I kicked him in the groin, but he was too strong for me and, in an instant, he had me on the bed and was tearing the clothes off me, his foul breath and angry grunts filling my senses.

When it was over, he lay panting and sweating beside me. For a while, I was completely still with tears flowing down my cheeks. My body was bruised from the violence of his attack but it was my mind that had abandoned me. I felt dispossessed of the woman I was before and now there only remained the woman of after. He had fallen asleep, snoring loudly. I crept from the bed and went to the bathroom. I counted the days since my last monthly bleed and realised that there could not have been a worse time for this to have occurred.

The woman I now was went into the drawer in her bedroom and removed the cyanide capsule.

57

I poured Calvados brandy around his mouth to disguise the almond aroma of the cyanide. I washed the tears from my face, wrapped a dressing gown around me and went down to the garden. There I screamed hysterically until the guards came running. I led them to the bedroom where they found their *Oberstleutnant* in a state of undress and apparently dead. One of them produced a mirror to check for the condensation of breath, while another checked his wrist for a pulse. It seemed to all that Mueller had died, intoxicated, in my arms.

The medical officer from the Caen garrison was called to certify the death. The following day, I was questioned by the police at the garrison and I related that Mueller had forced himself on me after drinking heavily at midday and that he was not a healthy man by all accounts. I was then interviewed by the *Oberfeldkommandur*.

'Did you submit willingly to him, *mademoiselle*?'

'No, I did not. I had no choice. He violated me.'

'Accept my apologies, *mademoiselle*. This was not conduct becoming an officer.'

Later that night, I slipped unseen through the rose garden and into the underground room. Leah held me while I related the events at the château.

'You mean you gave him the cyanide capsule? That was meant for you in the event of torture. It was too easy a death for him.'

'It was the only way I could kill him and escape detection. The doctor would find no trace of it in him; it would appear that his heart had stopped. He was snoring with his mouth open. I placed the capsule between his teeth and clamped his jaws together. He never woke up.'

I wept again as I told Leah of my fears that I could have been impregnated. Leah consoled me.

'We shall have to wait. If your monthly does not come, then we can arrange something for you. Do not worry.'

58

Mueller's guards left a month after his death. They were to be posted to the Eastern Front to support supply lines behind the advancing German army. The front line had apparently advanced far enough into Soviet territory that the spires of the Kremlin could be seen. Their progress had been slowed by the late summer rains which had mired panzer divisions in mud, but now the ground had hardened and they were confident that Moscow could be taken. Lotti and Emilia were full of enthusiasm for what they considered to be another triumph.

'The invasion is called Operation Barbarossa after a Holy Roman Emperor of that name. Our legend has it that Frederick Barbarossa and his Knights sleep in a cave in our mountains and will awaken to help the *Führer* restore Germany to its former glory in the Thousand Year Reich.'

'Do you truly believe that?' I asked. 'Do you believe that invading a country and killing thousands of people, or millions, will fulfil a legend?'

'It is to provide the German people with *Lebensraum*: more land for our people to live and to grow food.'

'And of those people who live there now?'

'They are to starve.'

I could see no point in continuing the conversation. I was shocked by their callous disregard for the fate of the people whose counties were conquered. I had long since realised that the two girls had been educated from a young age to believe in the righteousness of Hitler's oppression of Jews and those he considered undesirable. They were thoroughly conditioned to believe that Hitler's wars were in response to threats of aggression from other countries and therefore entirely justified. I had learned from William Shirer's broadcasts how effective the propaganda of Goebbels could be.

Sensing my discomfort with the conversation, Lotti changed the subject. Since the death of Mueller and the knowledge that I had been raped by him, Lotti had been very gentle with me. She knew that no letter had come to the château from the *Feldkommandur* and understood how painful this must be for me.

No replacement for Mueller had arrived and the guards were now those who had been under the command of the *Kommandant*. Lotti hoped that this was a sign that the *Kommandant* would be returning. When she enquired, Lotti was informed that in the short term at least, the *Oberfeldkommandur* would be in command of both *Feldkommandanturen*. She and Emilia would take orders from him but live and work at the château where the cook would also continue to work with my help. They were to pay me a sum of money every week for this.

So, I was to continue in my role as housekeeper of the château. This was a great relief, as I had feared that the château would be closed – at least now I could continue to protect my friends. I no longer slept in my bedroom but had moved into the nursery. No one questioned this and understood my aversion to sleeping in the bed where I had suffered a violent rape and a man had died. At midnight, I left the room, leaving my night table lamp on and locked the door behind me. I saw the guards by the gates smoking and talking amongst themselves. During the day, I had gone for a walk in the woods. It seemed that no patrols were now stationed there.

Leah and Raisa were happy to see me. They had been joined by two Jewish girls from Belgium. They explained to me that the girls, Noemi and Raquel, were from a family of five who were trying to get to Spain where they had relatives. They had been travelling for over a month with the help of *passeurs* and would be moved on as soon as possible. The family had been split into two groups, but the girls, who were aged sixteen and eighteen, hoped that the rest of the family would be with them the following day.

'How did you get here?' I asked.

'We had false papers for the train from Paris. Before that, we were hidden in farm carts. We were met at the station in Caen and taken to a church. Under the church was a cave and from there, we were led through tunnels to this room.

'Do you know where you will go next?'

'No, we are just told to wait and ask no questions.'

'That is how it must be.'

I promised to return the following night with food and clothing. I emptied the waste buckets in the woods. It was getting colder now. Winter was approaching and with that the need to keep Leah and Raisa, and now the two girls, warm and alive.

59

When Damian arrived with the milk delivery the following morning, his face was ashen. The cook, sensing something was amiss, discreetly left us alone.

'There has been a betrayal. One of the *passeurs* was an informer. The parents and brother of the girls were arrested close to the church. One of our group was also taken. The family have been taken to the camp at Drancy, close to Paris. They are holding Jews and resistants there.'

'And the other?'

'She will not talk. She has a cyanide capsule.'

'And the *passeurs*, do they know of the underground room?'

'No, they do not. We do not allow them to know where the next place of refuge will be.'

'But if they found the cave, they will find the tunnels.'

'That has been dealt with. One of our group entered this morning and used dynamite to collapse the tunnel and seal the entrances.'

'Who will tell the girls of the fate of their family?'

'That will have to be you.'

'And will the girls be moved tonight?'

'No, it is too dangerous. The Germans and the *gendarmes* will be looking for others. They will have to stay with you.'

'And the *passeur*, the one who betrayed them, what of him?'

'He will not be found. His body lies under the rubble.'

I was not reassured by this. There would be others willing to betray and inform. Meanwhile, I had to break the sad news to the girls.

That night, I took them food and clothing and then, with Leah, we sat with our arms around the two girls and broke the news of their family's arrest. There was nothing we could say to comfort them or to give them hope of being united with their parents and brother. I had to leave them sobbing in Leah's arms. They had heard the explosion despite it being some distance away. I explained that the entry from the church could no longer be used. There was now only the trapdoor in the woods.

60

At the end of November, I was informed of another arrival. It was late at night when the message was dropped through the grating of the trapdoor. Leah and I were filling up the cracks in the walls and doors of the room using the potato sacks that had been so effective against the cold and draughts the previous winter. The note instructed me to be waiting at the edge of the woods as soon as I was able.

I took my torch and went out through the trapdoor. I made my way to the edge of the woods. After a while, lights appeared in the hedgerows and a figure approached me. I kept the torch low as I guided him – by his height and clothing I knew him to be male – through the woods. I opened the trapdoor and gestured to him to enter. Once he was inside, I pulled some brushwood over the trapdoor and covered it as I went through. I attached the metal loop to secure the trapdoor and guided him down the winding staircase and into the underground room.

Leah was ready to greet the new arrival with wine and food. I introduced him to Leah and Raisa and the two girls in French. He became very embarrassed and stuttered with words of apology for his lack of the French language. I immediately put him at ease with my Scots-accented English. He introduced himself as George Vartis and explained that he was an RAF pilot who had been sent to pick up agents to return to London. His plane had crashed on take-off from a nearby field and the two agents had been injured. They were now in the care of a local Resistance group and he had been told to wait for rescue, which was why he was now here. I translated this for the benefit of the others. The two girls from Belgium spoke German and George was able to speak in what he described as schoolboy German with them.

The arrival of George seemed to enliven the two girls. They had been very withdrawn and tearful since the news about their family, but in his company they became animated. It was as though he brought them hope that they and their people were not alone in the battle against Hitler and his war.

Leah promised to take care of him overnight and I returned to the château.

The following morning I awoke feeling queasy. I had slept for a short time only after the arrival of George and felt sure that exhaustion and lack of sleep were the cause of this. I went into the kitchen and made coffee. The smell of the roasted beans brought on another bout of nausea and I vomited into the sink. The cook arrived just as I was rinsing my mouth. He made me sit down and told me he would bring Lotti. As I sat there, I thought about other symptoms I had recently noticed: a feeling of bloating in my stomach and pain and tingling in my breasts. And then I remembered that I had not bled since the rape. Lotti came into the kitchen and put her arms around me.

'Gabrielle, when was your last monthly?'

'I have not bled since that day. I have been too occupied to notice.'

And I wept tears of bitterness and anger that the father of this child was the loathsome man who had raped me, that the father of this child was not the man I loved, and also pity for the child inside me that I did not want.

'I cannot have this child,' I said.

61

I went to the nursery and wrote a letter to *Maman*. I would give this to George in the hope that he would get back to Britain safely and get it to her. With the letter, I placed two photographs: the one taken by Stefan at *Hanoucca* in 1938 and one of the two photographs I had found behind the chest of drawers. I kept the letter as brief as possible. I did not mention the rape or my fears that I may be pregnant. I sealed the envelope, kissing it as I did so. I imagined *Maman's* dear hands opening the letter and wept again.

That night I returned to the underground room. I was greeted by George who had been joined by two other men. I knew not to ask their names. Both were English but spoke fluent French. George explained that they were the two injured "passengers" but that their injuries had not proved serious. I ensured that they had enough bedding and food for the night.

As I left, George touched my arm.

'Are you all right? You look very pale. You are doing a fine job here, you know. It is both dangerous and extremely difficult.'

'I am well. Please do not worry. But you can do something for me. I have a letter and two photographs for my mother. I would very much like you to take these to her. I will write her name and address on the envelope. There is some mystery about the photographs that perhaps *Maman* can explain. It means much to me that *Maman* gets my letter and the photographs.'

'Of course, assuming that I make it safely to Britain.'

'And if you are caught and the Germans find the letter on you?'

'They will not get the letter, be assured of that.'

The following morning I vomited again. I was now certain I was pregnant; it was over two months since my last bleed. When Damian arrived with the milk delivery, he informed me that the three men would be moved on that night. He gave me a parcel which he explained contained warm clothing and waterproofing and asked me to provide food for their journey. I should be at the edge of the woodland at midnight and from there they would be collected.

I was able to leave the château at 11 p.m. The cook was as usual in Caen and the secretaries were attending a dance at the garrison. Only the guards at the gates were on duty and I knew how to avoid them.

I told the men that they were to leave within the hour. They dressed in the clothes I had brought for them and took the food parcels. I gave the envelope to George.

'Please tell *Maman* not to worry about me. Assure her that I am well and not in danger.'

My voice shook as I said the words. George took the envelope and gently kissed me on both cheeks. For the first time in months, I felt something akin to emotion, to love.

When we reached the edge of the woods, Damian was already waiting there with his cart. This was much larger than the usual one he used for Calvados and wine deliveries and could easily accommodate the three men. I bade them farewell and good luck and returned to the château.

I waited until Lotti and Emilia returned from the dance and went to their room.

Lotti took me gently by the arm and sat me on the bed, and with her arm around me asked, 'So, you are sure?'

'As sure as it is possible to be.'

'And you need to have it removed?'

'Yes.'

'In our situation, an arrangement would be made for a special clinic in Switzerland. This has already happened to some of our friends in Caen. But, for you, this is not possible. Do you have friends in Caen who could help you?'

I thought of *Père* François and how shocked he would be at the killing of an unbaptized infant, as he would view it.

I shook my head.

'And my family are Catholics, so this is unthinkable for them. It would be considered a Mortal Sin.'

Lotti shrugged her shoulders at that.

'If they have never been in such a situation, how would they know what they would do?'

'It is not so in my family.' I thought of *Maman* and how distressed she would be and broke down weeping.

Emilia spoke up, 'I have heard of a woman in the town. One of our soldiers got a local girl pregnant and she had the baby removed. Tomorrow, I will ask him, discreetly, of course. It is illegal and she will need to be paid.'

'I have money,' I said.

I thanked them both and left for my room. I thought of George carrying the precious envelope and said a prayer for his safe return to Britain.

62

After the midday meal the following day, Emilia informed me that the woman would come to the château at 9 p.m. that night. I tried to put the thought of the ordeal ahead of me and the guilt associated with it out of my mind as I went about my daily tasks. I managed to visit Leah during the early evening and informed her of my decision. Leah agreed that it was for the best. An unwanted child, the result of a brutal rape, would burden me for the rest of my life; it could even cost me my life.

'But does this woman have experience? This is a very dangerous procedure for a woman. I know of women who died after this.'

'I have to trust her. I have no choice.' And I cried in Leah's arms.

I had brought extra food and clean clothing, explaining that I may not be able to return for a day or two. I then kissed all four women and left.

As arranged, Emilia answered the door to the woman and brought her to my room. The woman told me to lie flat on the bed while she examined my stomach.

'You are nearly three months into this pregnancy. Why did you not ask before now? It is more dangerous at this stage. I will do it but first you must pay me.'

I counted out the 100 Reichsmarks into the woman's hands. I noticed that they were far from clean. I compared this to Papa's meticulous hand washing in his surgery before and after each patient.

The woman instructed Emilia to get a jug of warm water from the kitchen and opened her bag. From the bag, she took a bar of soap, a cheese grater, some rubber tubing and a funnel. When Emilia returned with the jug, the woman used the grater to scrape the soap into the jug where it dissolved. She then instructed me to lie with my knees raised and parted. Emilia was kind enough to take my hand throughout the painful procedure. I felt an intense burning pain in my pelvis and then excruciating cramps; the woman appeared indifferent to the pain I was suffering. When she had finished, the woman instructed me to stay in bed for a half hour. She then packed her bag and left. Emilia escorted her out of the château and returned.

'We will take it in turns to sit with you tonight, Gabrielle. I have heard that the pain will be bad and at some time, the... what is there will come out. You will need someone to help you to the lavatory. I will make some tisane and then Lotti will come to you for a while.'

I thanked her. It was extraordinary, the paradox, that these young women were capable of such kindness to me and yet had no compassion for the millions being slaughtered in Hitler's war.

An hour later, I felt the first gush of blood. With Lotti's help, I got to the bathroom. The cramping pains were unbearable; I wanted to scream with the agony of it. I stayed on the lavatory and, after a while, felt what seemed to be large clots falling from me. The cramping pains continued so I told Lotti to go to rest in her room; it would be better for me to stay on the lavatory. After some time, as she told me later, Lotti became concerned and came to the bathroom, where she found me collapsed and unconscious on the floor in a pool of blood. She ran to call Emilia and together they carried me to the bed. Lotti had changed the sheets but, as they laid me there, more blood was staining them. Emilia checked the lavatory; the woman's work had been effective from what she could see in the bowl. She pulled the chain on the cistern and it was washed away. They needed to get help for me. To call a doctor was unthinkable. A crime had been committed here in the eyes of the law.

It was Lotti who thought of the cook. She went to his room where, unusually for him, he was in his own bed and sleeping. She told him of my condition as briefly as possible. But he understood;

he told her that he had witnessed me vomiting and noted my pale face and tiredness. He told Lotti to go to the kitchen and make a tisane and he would follow, which he did almost immediately. In his hand he had a small flask containing a greyish powder; he carefully measured an amount of this into the tisane. The powder smelled of mould.

'What is this?' she asked.

'It is ergot, a fungus that grows on crops. It has many uses but this is the most important. My mother was the village midwife. I learned of this from her. It will stop the bleeding.'

They went to my room where I was unconscious and lying in a pool of blood. He told Lotti and Emilia to hold my head while he poured the liquid down my throat. I had gagged slightly, which the cook said was a good sign. He had then lifted my nightdress and placed one hand over my lower pelvis and the other slightly above, and gently rotating his hands had massaged the area.

'What are you doing?' asked Lotti.

'This will help her womb to contact and stop the bleeding. The tisane contains ergot which will be effective very soon. One of you must stay with her. When she awakens, she must drink plenty of tisanes. She has lost a lot of blood and needs liquids.'

He had continued massaging my abdomen and, after a while, the bleeding slowed and then stopped.

The cook left the room but asked to be called if the bleeding started again.

'With red hair, they can bleed more than others.'

Lotti and Emilia took turns to watch over me throughout the night. In the morning, I had appeared much improved. I was very weak but able to ask the girls what had happened.

'It was the cook. He knew what to do. Without him, you would have surely bled to death. He says you must stay in bed for two days. We are to give you tisanes and red wine. He will bring you food now that you are awake.'

I thanked them. I owed my life to them and particularly to the cook. The girls left but promised to return regularly as I would need help to the bathroom.

I dozed for a while but woke up when the cook brought in a tray of food.

'I understand from Lotti and Emilia that I owe my life to you. How can I thank you enough?'

'There is no need, *Fräulein*. I am indebted to you too, as you may remember. Now, eat this omelette and drink the wine. Both are good for the blood. You will need more of this.'

He made to leave the room but before he did, turned to me and said to my utter astonishment:

'And I will make sure that the guests are fed.'

63

Three days later I felt well enough to take a walk in the woods. The December air was cold and a downy flake of snow touched my lips. I felt it melt and saw this as a sign that I still had some warmth in my body; but my soul, my sense of self, remained as cold as the grave. I stopped at the trapdoor and, on an impulse, went down to visit Leah and the others. Leah was shocked by my appearance. I had lost weight and my sickly pallor worried her.

'You should still be resting. I have learned of what happened.'

'Who told you? Only the cook and the secretaries were with me.'

'It seems that your cook admires you greatly, and he has a mistress to guide him to a better understanding of the situation. Also, he has been bringing food for us.'

'But no one must know of this. If my priest were to find out, he would not approve – worse than that.'

'Do not worry. It will be our secret. Now, you must get better. When you are well enough, I will ask you to visit our men. I have had no news of them for some time.' I promised she would do that.

That night, I felt a sharp pain in my abdomen; it was as though the blade of a heated knife was twisting deep inside me. I felt around the site of the pain and found it to be hard and hot to touch. My head was aching and my mouth was dry. I got out of bed to get some water and noticed a foul-smelling discharge running down my thighs. I cleaned myself as best I could and, not wanting to disturb the household, I returned to bed.

I awoke to find Lotti and Emilia with me. It was dark outside but I knew I had not gone to their rooms to awaken them. It was all very confusing. I felt cold and shivered despite the weight of blankets on me. My head hurt so much that I imagined a hammer smashing it from inside.

I managed to speak, 'Why are you here? I did not wish to disturb you. But I feel so cold. What is happening to me?'

Lotti took my hand.

'Gabrielle, you are very sick. You have an infection in your womb. This can happen after the procedure you had. We are giving you aspirin and tisanes and bathing you, but it is not helping. May we contact your grandparents? Your family should be made aware.'

'No, not those people, only *Maman* and Papa and...'

Then there was only darkness and vague elusive sounds. A car arriving. Was it day or night? And voices, and then a presence in the room, arms around me that gave comfort, washed me and made me drink. The voice spoke to me in a language from long ago, far away. The voice called me Helen. But it was not the voice of *Maman* or Papa. My head no longer hurt but my eyes could not open, all was dark; only the arms around me and the voice existed. Time had no meaning; I floated above the world and saw myself as a child. I could smell the fields, Papa's clinic and the apples as they ripened in the orchard. I saw *Maman's* hands showing me the notes on the piano and felt her caress. I heard the cries of the geese as they flew over my home, the peep-ing call of the oystercatchers on the beach at Cocklawburn as they took flight and saw the puffins on the Farnes. After a while I felt the sharpness of a needle in my thigh, the voice that demanded that this should be done here and that he and no other would care for me.

I awoke to the sound of a cello, the *Arpeggione Sonata*. My eyes could not focus immediately; they had been closed to the world for so long. But my ears were awake and I slowly moved to where they took me. I must have made a sound, because the music, so familiar, but from so far away a time that I could not at once place it in my memory, stopped. But then my eyes opened and I saw him. I tried to speak but no words came. Then the arms lifted me gently from where I had been lost for so long.

'You are back, *meine liebchen*. I have waited for you.'

'And I for you,' I whispered.

I fell asleep, but this time there was peace and no pain.

64

Lotti and Emilia helped me to the bathroom when it was light. I had lost all sense of time and asked them how long I had been asleep. I had no recollection of when I had last been awake. It seemed so long ago.

It was Lotti who explained what had happened.

'Gabrielle, you were very sick. We thought you would die. We did all we could for you. It was late in December and the roads were blocked with snow. We decided that no more could be done. But the *Feldkommandur* returned. This was not expected. He had been wounded in Russia and was sent back to recover and to retake his command here. We told him about you. He never left your side. The doctors from the garrison came. They wanted to take you to the hospital in Caen but he refused. He would have no one care for you but himself. He is resting now that you are awake but will come to you later.'

I had to ask, 'Lotti, when I was asleep, as you say, did I speak?'

'You asked for him, in your language. Do not worry, that is between us. But please tell me: what is an "oystercatcher" and a "puffin"?'

He came to me later. He took me in his arms and kissed me.

'What happened to me? And how is it that you are here?'

'As for why I am here, that is for later. But I can tell you that I came here in the snow. If the Resistance had not blown up roads and train lines, the snow was equally determined to keep me from you. You had an infection in your womb which I have learned came about because of a procedure, an abortion. That you had to endure this I am angrier than you will ever know. I should have left you protected from such a man. The infection was very severe. You were on the point of death when I arrived, despite the valiant efforts of Lotti and Emilia.'

'And the cook,' I interjected.

'Ah, yes, the cook; he is an interesting man, I understand.' He smiled as he said this.

'So, I kept you warm and gave you to drink and summoned the doctors from Caen. They wanted to take you away but I refused. But our German doctors have the penicillin and this was given to you with my authority.'

'I felt it.'

'And you had to receive the injection three times a day for a week and after three days, you started to improve; your fever was better and your womb ceased to discharge the pus.'

'Did the doctor say I would recover fully? I mean, my womb.'

'He said it would take time to know this, but if you have a normal bleed in a few weeks he is sure that all will be well.'

He took me in his arms again.

'*Liebchen*, how could I have left you? There is so much I have to tell you. I will not speak of it all now. You must rest. But, first, the cook has asked to speak with you.'

He left the room.

After a while, the cook came in. I took his hand and thanked him.

'Not only did you save my life but also those of my friends.'

'This must not be spoken of, but for as long as I am here, I will do what I can. We cannot compromise the position of the *Kommandant* but, and now please forgive my English, "them that ask no questions, isn't told a lie".'

I laughed. '"Watch the wall my darling while the Gentlemen go by".'

He added, 'My father's parents were Jews. The *Kommandant* ensured my parents' safe passage to Switzerland and that my ancestry was not revealed.'

PART FOUR

Marie-Claude

65

The Flying Scotsman shrieked to a halt at Berwick-upon-Tweed train station, the steam of the engines melting the ice that glazed the platform of England's most northerly train station. Passengers waiting to board the northbound train huddled together for warmth. It was March 1942 and the war was now in its third year. Food rationing and war weariness were testing the resilience of the Borders people to their limits. They were inured to the harsh conditions of life in this remote part of the British Isles. The cold north-east winds, which blew icy brine onto the houses hugging the cliff tops of the rugged coastline, left in their wake the brackish *haar*, the cold sea fog that could linger for days at a time. The south-westerly winds in their turn, swept snow from the high Cheviots that lingered for weeks during the long dark winter months. It settled as ice in the gullies along the narrow country roads and in the deep ploughed furrows, but it would hopefully yield to the spring rains and, with enough sunshine during the short summer, the fields would turn yellow with ripe crops for harvesting. During this time of war, the people of Britain were dependent on the crops of the eastern Borders and the cattle that grazed on its rich pasture land.

Among those on the platform was a petite middle-aged woman, her dark hair neatly arranged in a chignon; elegant despite the unfashionable coat and hat. Marie-Claude Douglas had today received a vague, somewhat ambiguous letter posted from London three days previously. In the letter, she was instructed to await the arrival of the midday train from Kings Cross, as there was important information regarding a governess which would be given to her by a passenger on the train. Marie-Claude guessed that this was some kind of coded message, but could not imagine why there should be any reason for subterfuge. Surely, if there was news from Helen, it would be a simple enough matter to put a letter directly in the mail.

It was nearly two years since Marie-Claude had received any news of her daughter. Following Hitler's invasion of Poland, they had been desperate for their daughter to return to the safety of their Berwickshire home while there was still time for her to do so, but she had refused, citing the needs of the children in her care and other obligations which she had not elaborated on.

The invasion and occupation of France in June 1940 by Hitler's armies had ended all communication with their daughter. Marie-Claude's life since then had been a maelstrom of intense anxiety punctuated by bouts of weeping. She had tried to contact her elderly parents in Normandy but it had been her cousin Damian who answered the telephone. She heard a click on the line as he spoke and when he told her abruptly that she had misdialled, she terminated the call immediately. She intuited that there must be some risk to him by continuing the conversation.

The doors of the train opened and passengers stepped cautiously from the carriages onto the icy platform and into the arms of welcoming family and friends. Many were young soldiers returning on leave, their hair cropped close above their ears revealing the rawness of their youth. She thought fleetingly of those young men at the hospital in Cambrai, the memories of that time she and Jamie tried so hard to repress: the devastating wounds and the desperate pleas to be allowed to die, as all that made them the men they had been was now destroyed. This could be the fate of these young men and that of her son, had he lived. The war that was to end all wars had brought them to the same battlefields.

The train was preparing to depart for its next destination and Marie-Claude had no indication as to the identity of the mysterious messenger. Nobody had looked in her direction and the platform was emptying. The guard blew his whistle and with a massive hiss of steam and a thunderous roar, the Flying Scotsman made its way north. Through the steam, Marie-Claude detected a tall figure approaching her. He must have been at the end of the train, furthest from the exit area where she was waiting and, as he came closer, he was revealed to be a young man, dressed in the grey-blue uniform of an RAF officer. He was carrying a canvas satchel.

'Madam Douglas? Am I correct? I am George Vartis.'

He shook her hand formally.

'Thank you for meeting me. Is there somewhere we can sit and talk? I have to return to London later. Perhaps there is a café or bar close by where we can go.'

It was clear to Marie-Claude that there would be no time to take George to her home in Foulden, so she suggested that they go across to the Castle Hotel, an imposing building with a popular bar which faced the station.

Once they had found a quiet seating area, George ordered two gin and tonics.

'Make them doubles,' he requested of the genial barman, who was clearly impressed by George's uniform and medals.

Marie-Claude's hands were shaking and she could not form the questions that she so very much needed to ask. She folded her hands in her lap in an attempt to control her trembling – her desperate need to have some indication that her daughter was alive, safe and would return to her soon, unharmed.

'So, George, you are a pilot. Have you flown many missions?'

'My squadron covered the evacuation of the British Expeditionary Force from Dunkirk and we flew Spitfires during the Battle of Britain.'

'So, it is men such as you that we must thank. We feared that Mr Hitler would invade Britain, as he did my own country. Your courage has saved us from such a terrible fate. As Mr Churchill said, "Never in the field of human conflict was so much owed by so many to so few". You are so very brave.'

'We lost many of our best pilots. We say it was the brave who died and the lucky who survived. I am here because of your daughter's courage. I owe my survival to her. We will talk of this later.'

At this, George opened the satchel and removed an envelope and a magnifying glass. He opened the envelope and took out two photographs which he placed on the table in front of Marie-Claude.

'I would like you to look closely at this first photograph and tell me if you recognise the people in it.'

Marie-Claude took her reading spectacles from her handbag and used them to examine the photograph. With a surge of emotion that brought tears coursing down her cheeks, she recognised her daughter, Helen. She was sitting on a *chaise longue* with two small girls on either side of her. Behind the seat stood a blonde lady whose hands were resting on the shoulders of the older of the two children.

'That is Helen. Please, tell me when this photograph was taken. I must know that she is alive and safe.'

'The photograph was taken in December 1938 at the time of *Hanoucca*, as is written on the back of the photograph. It was taken by Stefan, the husband of your friend, Odette. As you can see, Odette is in the photograph. We understand that Stefan was arrested in Germany in June 1939 and imprisoned in Sachsenhausen, a prison camp north of Berlin. He left France to return to Berlin to rescue his sister, Gisela, who he knew was in danger of arrest and worse. Gisela's husband abandoned her for another woman following the Nuremberg Race Laws in 1935. These laws prohibit marriage between Jews and non-Jews. It is part of the Nazi theory of racial purity. The laws also removed German citizenship from Jews. Gisela managed to get the two children of the marriage onto a rescue train to England, the *Kindertransport* as it is called. They are now in London with Stefan's cousins. Of Gisela, sadly, we have no news at the present time.'

Marie-Claude looked thoughtful and replied, 'Of course, the children would be Jewish. Odette explained to me many times that their religion is through the mother. Gisela's husband and new wife would not wish to have Jewish children in the family. How can such terrible laws exist? In France, Jews are considered citizens of the Republic and as such, have the same rights as non-Jews.'

'I am sorry to say that is no longer the situation in France. I will tell you more of this later, but for now, I would like you to use the magnifying glass and look more closely at the photograph of the lady you call Odette and tell me what you see.'

Marie-Claude took the magnifier and held it over the photograph of Odette. The hair and eyes were those of her friend, surely, also the nose and mouth. Holding the photograph closer, she noted a small mole above the left eye of the woman. This puzzled her and provoked a vague memory. But it was when she lowered the magnifying glass over the arms of the woman that she exclaimed:

'That is not Odette.'

George gently removed the photograph and magnifier from her trembling hands.

'Can you explain why you believe that this woman is not your friend?'

'It is the bracelet. It is not there. Odette would never remove it. Even when she was so ill with fevers and in the hospital for days, she would not permit it to be taken from her. It was always on her left wrist as a charm against ill-fortune. It had been in her family for generations. It had the Star of David as a charm on the gold band. Please let me look again at the photograph.'

Marie-Claude now noted that although there was a simple wristwatch on the woman's left wrist, on the right wrist was the gold bracelet inlaid with diamonds that Auriole had so coveted that day so many years ago. This triggered another memory: that of the mole above the left eye. Auriole used to joke about it, referring to it as her *La Passionée,* a beauty spot. She explained this to George.

'Now, may I see the second photograph?'

George placed the second photograph on the table.

'There we are, all three of us in the apartment of Odette's grandparents. I am seated on a chair and one side of me is Odette

– she is wearing the Star of David bracelet – and on the other side is Auriole.'

'Auriole?' questioned George

'The woman in the first photograph is not Odette Abramsky. She is Auriole Ritter. She was born in Alsace in 1893 and studied with Odette and myself at the Conservatoire in Paris. In June 1914, she disappeared. I remember the day well. It was the day of our final recitals at the Conservatoire, she did not arrive and I was sent to her room to look for her, to check that she was not ill. I went into the room, which she shared with me and, although all her belongings were there, she was not. After that time we had no news of her. Of course, there was the War; many people disappeared. We did not think to look for her. Why is she in the photograph and where is my Odette? And where is Helen now? Is she safe?'

George took hold of Marie-Claude's hands.

'I can only tell you that Helen was alive and well when I left France three weeks ago. But before I tell you the circumstances of that time, I need to ask you more questions about Auriole Ritter. It is clear that she is impersonating your friend and I need to know how that could be possible and for how long she has been using Odette's identity.'

'I will tell you all I know. Auriole and Odette had a remarkable resemblance. Many at the academy thought them to be twins, or sisters at least. We were all three of us pupils of Professor Diemer at the Conservatoire in Paris. Odette was by far the most gifted. After a few months, Auriole was visited by a man she introduced to us as her Uncle Heinrich. He seemed to be very impressed by Odette. Whether it was for that reason or another, but after he returned to Germany, Auriole began to copy Odette. At first, it was in small ways: arranging her hair as Odette did hers, wearing the same clothes or similar, but most of all, imitating her stage technique and playing the same programme at recitals. I have to say that I did not like Auriole. At first, I accused myself of jealousy. Odette had been my friend since childhood. I stayed at her château many times and she often came to my parents' farm in Calvados. When we were in Paris, Auriole came with us to Odette's grandparents' apartment in Saint-Germain-des-Prés. She was not invited on these occasions but, somehow, Auriole always succeeded in accompanying us. I resented her presence, I must confess.'

'Can you remember anything else from those times?' asked George as gently as he could.

'Yes, the bracelets. Auriole questioned Odette about the Star of David bracelet. She was curious as to why she wore it on her left wrist. Odette told her that it was a family heirloom and never to be removed by the wearer. And that it should be worn on the left wrist. It was the other bracelet, the one in the first photograph, which Auriole wanted. And I see now that she got it.'

Marie-Claude went on to describe the look of avarice on Auriole's face when the grandmother had explained the history of the gold band with its inlay of diamonds. She described her own distaste when Auriole asked to put it on her own wrist and her apparent reluctance to remove it.

'This was not polite or respectful behaviour. I never spoke about it to Odette but I believe she felt the same.'

Both took time to take a few sips of their drinks.

Then Marie-Claude continued, 'And there were books under her bed. I told you that we shared the same room. I had to return to collect a music score and the maid was cleaning the room. When she turned the mattress, some books and pamphlets fell onto the floor and I helped the maid pick them up. They were horrible: cartoons of Jewish people and books that I know about, books saying bad things about Jews. And not only the books, I overheard Auriole using a very unpleasant phrase to describe Odette as a Jew. I was so shocked. She was pretending to be her friend.'

George posed another question, 'Did Odette speak German? I need to know this.'

'No, she did not, but her grandparents did. They were from Odesa and had spoken Russian and German at home there. Much of the fur trade of Odette's grandfather and great-grandfather had been with Germans who did not speak Russian. I remember her grandparents telling me this. Of course, by then they spoke excellent French. They also told me that the Russian word for German is *Nemetskiy,* which also means dumb, unable to speak. The Germans communicated with the Russians in sign language but were always pleased to find German-speaking furriers. Auriole spoke excellent German. At that time, Alsace belonged to Germany but also Auriole studied in Frankfurt before she came to Paris. The grandparents enjoyed speaking German with Auriole; she could be charming and they adored her. It was just me who had bad thoughts about her. I am sorry. You must think me a horrible person.'

'Not at all, dear lady, I am very grateful for all you have told me. My superiors in London will be equally so. Would you like some tea? I have only a short time before my train and I still have a lot to explain to you.'

He went up to the bar to request two cups of tea. As he waited for the order, he took time to reflect on what Marie-Claude had told him. He was as certain as he could be that Odette was dead and that her doppelganger was a person of interest to the intelligence service, and a threat to the SOE operatives and their Resistance comrades in France.

It was also clear that Helen's life could be in great danger.

He returned to the table with the tea. He looked around the room. The few customers who had been around the bar had departed, and none of the tables adjacent to theirs were occupied.

'What I am about to tell you, Madam Douglas, must be considered top secret. If we were in London you would be asked to sign the Official Secrets Act. But we are not in London and you must understand that should the information I am about to impart be divulged to, shall we say interested parties, the lives of many will be put at risk, including that of your daughter. It could even cost us the war. Do you understand this?'

Marie-Claude nodded in response to the question but her heart was racing and her hands shaking all the more. Whatever George was going to tell her, she was certain would do nothing to suppress her fears for her daughter.

'Following my service in the Battle of Britain, I was assigned as a pilot to the Royal Air Force Special Duties Service or SD161 as we know it. We provide air transport to support the Resistance movements in territories controlled by Axis powers: Germany, Italy and Japan as well as Bulgaria, Croatia, Hungary, Romania and Slovakia. My area of operation is occupied France, which includes much of Northern and Western France, and therefore your family's home and the place where your daughter was employed. We support the Resistance by flying in agents, wireless operators and supplies by parachute drop to the occupied territories, and on return flights, picking up agents, political leaders and special communications to bring back to England. This is confidential information at the highest level. We pilots are not told the identities of the agents we drop or that of those we pick up. Officially, the organisation, that is the training and the drops, does not exist. I must, therefore, request that you refrain from asking me any further questions about it.'

George paused to sip his tea, checked his wristwatch and continued, 'In December 1941, my plane crashed on take-off from a field in Normandy where I had picked up two agents for a return flight. The two agents were injured in the crash and were taken by the local Resistance to safe houses. I stayed to blow up the plane and, thereby, remove as much evidence of the operation as possible. I salvaged a flashlight and some blankets and made my way to nearby woodland, where I had been instructed someone would meet me. Thankfully, there was no snow and I made no tracks due to a hard frost. I kept walking and, after a short time in the woods, a young woman appeared with a flashlight and beckoned me to follow her. We came to a clearing, where she stopped to move a pile of brushwood and brambles which exposed a trapdoor in the ground. This she opened and instructed me to enter, she followed me though it and then guided me down some fiendishly difficult steps and into an underground room. In the room there were people sleeping on camp beds: four women, two of them young girls of around sixteen years of age. None of them spoke English, but the young woman who had brought me there introduced herself. She was your daughter, Helen Douglas.'

Marie-Claude started to cry. George gently placed his hand on hers.

'Madam, I do not have much time. The train south is in thirty minutes and there is much more to tell, so please try to be calm'

'I will try to be calm. Please continue.'

'Helen left us and promised to return the following day and the older ladies helped me make up a bed.'

'My schoolboy German came in useful as the two girls in the group spoke German. Through them, I discovered that the older ladies were a former cook and her daughter, who had been employed at the château. I asked them where I was and they explained that the room was a hidden chamber in the ruins of a former castle. It is situated in the grounds of the Château des Tilleuls, where your daughter had been employed as governess to the children of *Madame* Odette Abramsky and *Monsieur* Stefan Erhart. The girls translated and explained that the older women were Jews, as they themselves were, and that your daughter had discovered the room and made it into a refuge for them. Your daughter is trying to save the lives of these people. She has also cared for British soldiers evading capture following the evacuation of Dunkirk and others too, I believe.'

'I remember that ruin. Odette and I played there. Of course, her parents would not have approved. There was also a ruined chapel which we supposed had secret passageways.'

'Does Auriole know of the hidden chamber? This is very important.'

'I think not. She never visited the château with us. She knows the history of the château. She asked many questions of the grandparents whenever we were at their apartment. Yes, she knows that there was a room underground where the Huguenots were hidden, but the grandparents told us that the villagers destroyed the former château completely and I suppose they believed that would have included all the chambers. Odette and I only explored the ruin above ground. There seemed to be nothing else. I am certain that Auriole does not know of this hiding place.'

'So, this is good news. We have hope for the people your daughter is sheltering. Late the following day, Helen came with food, hot soup and water supplies for washing. Late the following night, she came back accompanied by the two agents who had been injured in the crash of my aircraft the night before; it transpired their injuries were not serious. Helen then explained that we were to escape from France and return to England but must be patient. She would bring news of our departure as soon as she could.

'But this is so dangerous. If the Germans find out, she will be arrested and worse. And how is it that she can live in the château? She is British. She would have been arrested by the Germans by now. And Auriole knows she is British. She will inform them. Now I am even more anxious for her.'

'I will explain to you more of this later. I regret to say that you may be surprised, even shocked by what you will learn.'

George checked his wristwatch again and continued, 'The following night, she came to inform us that we were leaving within the hour. She brought clothing for us – old trousers and thick wool jumpers, as well as some old jackets and shoes – and waited while we changed into them. She told me she would burn my uniform later. She then led us out through the trapdoor and into the woods. The frost had thawed somewhat during the night, so after we had helped her replace the brushwood and stones, we each took a fallen branch and used it to cover our tracks as we walked through the woods. There was little moonlight due to the cloud cover, but when we reached the edge of the woodland, I could see the dim outline of a horse and cart. Helen gave a flash of her torch, which was met by two from the cart. This was our signal to approach the cart. A middle-aged man shook our hands as Helen introduced us to him as her Uncle Damian. She explained that he would be taking us to a boat.'

Marie-Claude gasped in amazement and horror.

'That is why he had to stop my call. He too is in danger. Someone was listening to his telephone. The Germans must know of these activities.'

George took her hand again.

'Madam, it may not be so; resistants also listen to the telephone. We call it tapping, to make sure that the Resistance group is secure. Sadly, there are many infiltrations of Resistance groups by Germans and collaborators. Brave local people are helping those like myself who are evading capture, as well as hiding Jews, but there are many who betray their countrymen. This is sometimes done for money, or because of a grievance against a neighbour, but also out of fear of arrest and torture.'

He went on, 'Helen explained that Damian would be taking us to a small harbour in a secret compartment under a cart, which was carrying barrels of Calvados brandy for the market. She told us that she did not know where this harbour was or where we would go from there, as it was important to keep each stage of the journey a secret. She bade us farewell and good luck but before we left, she handed me an envelope containing the photographs you have just seen. She told me to give it to you with all her love. I also have a letter to give you before I leave for London.

When we arrived at the port, which we found to be Port-en-Bessin, Damian explained that the port was not considered important to the German military and, therefore, not guarded by German soldiers but by the local *gendarmerie*, a few of whom are sympathetic to the Resistance. At the port, a fishing boat was waiting, ready to commence its regular fishing trip in waters around the Brittany coast at dawn. We were boarded onto this boat before dawn. Damian took his leave and wished us luck.

After we set sail, the captain told us we were to be taken to a beach in Brittany to await rescue. He explained that many rescues had taken days to effect, as the voyage was long and the coast heavily guarded by the Germans. We would have to be patient. After six hours of rough seas, we approached the coast of Brittany. The captain explained that the boat would hug the coastline close to the cliffs and at low tide we would leave the boat to wade through shallows and across rocks at the base of the cliff to a beach called Bonaparte Beach. Here, we would be met by the local Resistance group from a village called Plouha.

We got to the beach safely, all the time aware that above us were German artillery units. The beach was just a narrow stretch of sand between two cliffs. After dark, a group of four men arrived. The leader of the group was the local butcher, François Le Cornec. He explained that a Royal Navy Gunboat would be anchored off shore and when conditions were favourable, sailors would attempt to reach the beach in a rowing boat to collect us. We were given warm dry clothes, food and water, as well as a bottle of local brandy. The latter was most welcome.

After five nights on the beach, we heard the sound of oars approaching. It was still dark but we did not dare to use a flashlight for fear of alerting the Germans. We waited until we heard the splash of someone leaving the boat, before going to the water's edge. There, we were delighted to see a young man wearing a pea coat and fisherman's waders beckon us to follow him. We clambered aboard and let the tide take us before rowing hard out to sea. The gunboat was waiting for us and, soon, we were aboard and safe among fellow countrymen. We were fortunate as we learned that this escape route had failed many times with the deaths of agents and pilots, as well as the rescue crews.

We landed at Plymouth and were taken immediately to London for debriefing. It was there that I showed intelligence officers the photographs your daughter gave me. One officer – and I cannot reveal his name – was a double agent during the Great War, infiltrating the German *Abteilung* as well as the French *Deuxième Bureau*, all the while working for British wartime intelligence. He recognised the woman in the photograph as an agent known as "Elise". I was tasked with verifying this with you, Madam, as you knew your friend Odette so well. You have confirmed the officer's suspicions. We need to know where Ritter is and what activity she is engaged in. She may even be in Britain working for the *Abwehr*.'

Marie-Claude was astonished and utterly confused by the story George had just told her.

'But is Auriole not at the château? Surely she would not leave it, and what of her daughters?'

'According to Helen, Auriole Ritter, or Odette as Helen believes her to be, left the château in June 1940, soon after the fall of France and the occupation. She took the two girls with her. Helen has no idea where they are. She knows that their father is a prisoner in Sachsenhausen prison camp and is very anxious for the safety of the family, as Jews are being arrested and sent to camps in Poland. There are rumours that they are murdered on arrival there.'

'So, who lives in the château now? How is my daughter able to look after these people? What will become of her if Auriole betrays her?'

George looked again at his watch. He stood up and removed another envelope from his satchel.

'My train is due in five minutes. Before I leave you, here is the letter from your daughter. You will note that it has been opened and read by the intelligence officers. I think it will be easier for you to read it yourself. The contents may be hard for you to accept. If I have news of your daughter or of Ritter, I will return to Berwick. Meanwhile, Madam, have faith in your daughter. She is more resourceful and brave than you may have imagined.'

Marie-Claude took the letter and placed it deep in her handbag. She accompanied George to the platform and waited while he boarded the train. The icy wind that blew across the platform was matched by the cold grip of fear that she felt in her heart.

66

Chère Maman,

I send all my love to you and Papa.

By now you will have received the photograph of me with your friend, Odette, and the children. The photograph was taken in happy times, when all the family were together and we were hopeful that peace would prevail in Europe.

That was not to be, as you well know. Odette's husband, Stefan, went to Berlin to find his sister. He did not return. I now know he is a prisoner in one of Germany's terrible camps. And now my darling protégées have disappeared along with their mother. I fear for them.

After the Germans overcame the French army, they took over most of your country, including your beloved Normandy. Madame Odette departed with the two girls and I was left alone with the cook, Leah, and her daughter and granddaughters. They are Jews from Odesa and had already experienced the terrible persecution of their people. I tried to assure her that such things could not happen in France. But it is happening. In October, seven synagogues in Paris were bombed and there have been arrests of Jewish men since the summer. They are taken to a camp near Paris called Drancy. There are other camps elsewhere in France, where Jews from Germany and the Zone Libre are imprisoned. I am told they may be taken to camps in Poland from there. There are children in the camps, babies too. They are cold and hungry and their mothers have no way to care for them. There are rumours that soon the Jews in Normandy will suffer the same fate. The gendarmes are happy to obey the Germans; they rely on informers and are willing to arrest the Jews and have them sent to Drancy, the camp I told you about.

When the Germans arrived in Caen, I took Leah, her daughter and granddaughters to a hiding place I discovered in a ruin in the garden. They are kept safe there. My dear friend, Père François, told me how I must do all I can to protect Leah, her family and others. With the help of a group of resistants known to Père François, I was given a new identity. I was to be the housekeeper of the château in the absence of the family Abramsky-Erhart and to safeguard Leah, her family and others who would be sent to me for protection.

For a few months, this worked very well. There was plenty of food in the storerooms and I was able to visit the family freely. But soon after the Germans arrived in Caen, the château was requisitioned by the German army under the control of Feldcommandur Karl von Werstein.

There is much more on this that at the moment I cannot write. Just listen to the Arpeggione Sonata and think of me. One day I hope I can explain everything.

This is how it is as I write this letter that George, I hope, will put into your dear hands along with two photographs. As you see, one is of Odette and the family with me in happy times. The other, I am confused by. You are there with Odette, but the other woman in the photograph is wearing the bracelet that I found in a hidden cavity above the cistern in the apartment of Stefan's parents in Paris. The apartment belonged to Odette's grandparents, but following their deaths and the deaths of Odette's parents, they became tenants. I took Odette's children there for Hanoucca *in 1939 and during a game one of the children dislodged some tiles above the cistern. It was when I climbed up to replace the tiles, that I found the cavity and the bracelet. Stefan's parents, who are good people and I have no news of them since the Germans occupied the city, did not recognise the bracelet and advised me to return it to Odette. I have not had the opportunity to do this but I will keep it safe for her.*

I have another photograph of you with your two friends. I keep it under my pillow and treasure it.

One day, all this will end and I will sit with you in the orchard watching the apples ripen on the trees and listening to the geese flying overhead and the horses neighing in the field.

Your loving daughter,
Helen

Marie-Claude read the letter twice and then threw it into the fire. This was not done in judgement of her daughter but to protect her should the war be won by Germany. She would find the right moment to reveal its contents to her husband. But it was clear from the letter that Helen was unaware of the identity of the woman she believed to be Odette. The fact that her friend, Odette, had hidden the precious bracelet in the safe meant that she had done so in desperation and fear for her life.

One day, Auriole would return to the château and, without doubt, Helen's life would be in even greater peril.

PART FIVE

Odette & Auriole

67

My family suffered much ill fortune before they came to France and they still hold the superstitions from those days.

It was ill fortune that had brought Odette to the apartment in Saint-German-des-Prés. The Abramsky family were still in mourning for the deaths of her grandparents when they learned of the deaths of Odette's parents in a street accident. As the grandparents' executors, her parents had been at the apartment sorting out papers and administering the wills, as well as organising the rooms in preparation for Odette's occupation. She was much in demand for recitals in European capitals, but she also had a coterie of post-graduate pupils who would be taught at the apartment.

According to witnesses, the driver lost control of his car, which then mounted the pavement killing her father outright. Her mother had survived long enough to inform a neighbour of her wish that Odette should inherit both the château and the apartment. The driver had not stopped at the scene of the accident and no one had been able to give a clear account of either the make of the car or its registration number.

She had decided to spend the week following their funerals setting up a music studio area in the apartment, as well as emptying drawers of clothing and packing it up to be given to the poor of the city. The jewellery she placed in a safe at the bank, along with her grandmother's furs and a number of gold bars. The key to the safe she entrusted to the neighbour who had comforted her mother as she died of her injuries. The only piece of jewellery she kept back was the gold bracelet worn by her grandmother, the one so admired by her friend of long ago, Auriole. She placed this on the mantelpiece in the salon next to a photograph of herself with her parents and grandparents. In the natural course of events, it would have been her mother's. The cruelty of fate brought tears to her eyes again. She felt so alone. Her Abramsky cousins were now in America, where they had gone during the anti-Semitic riots that shadowed the Dreyfus Affair. They believed these riots were precursors of worse to come.

In 1930, France was still enjoying an economic boom, but her relatives were astute enough to realise that this was a bubble which would burst eventually and be followed by an economic depression, for which Jews would be blamed. Anti-Semitic propaganda in the form of posters and pamphlets handed out at metro stations had become commonplace already. Following the deaths of her elderly grandparents, they had tried to persuade Odette's parents to join them, but they had refused. Neither of her parents had felt pessimistic about their future in France. This was the country of their birth, the country of the Rights of Man and of the Citizen. They did not fear the thugs who were doubtless emulating their German counterparts, the supporters of the fanatic Adolf Hitler.

Placing the bracelet by the photograph, she remembered her friend, Auriole, and how enamoured she had been of it. Marie-Claude had been surprised by the girl's effrontery in requesting to try it on. She had long sensed that Marie-Claude did not like or trust Auriole, but even she, Odette, had caught the look of avarice in Auriole's eyes and her hesitation when returning the bracelet to her grandmother.

Memories of those days of happiness and laughter with her grandparents brought into focus the silence and emptiness of the flat as it now was. She shivered and the feeling of unease that had beset her on the few occasions she had left the apartment caused her to check that the door was locked. The kindly neighbour who had been such a comfort had left to care for her elderly relatives in Nice. Odette had the impression she was being followed whenever she went out. She couldn't determine whether her fears were warranted as whenever she looked behind her the street was either empty or peopled with families strolling towards the Jardin du Luxembourg.

The sharp ring of the doorbell startled her; she was not expecting any visitors. Her pupils had respected her need to recover from the shock of her parents' deaths and lessons had been paused indefinitely. She wiped her eyes on a handkerchief and went to answer the door. To her astonishment, she found Auriole Ritter standing in the doorway.

She hesitated and stammered a greeting, 'Auriole, it is so strange that you are here. I was thinking of you only moments ago. It has been such a long time. Why are you here? Please, forgive my ill manners, come in, you are most welcome.'

She stepped aside and allowed Auriole into the apartment. The resemblance to her that had so fascinated her grandparents was now even more remarkable. Auriole's hair was arranged in exactly the same style as her own and had lost none of its blonde. Furthermore, she was wearing an identical dress and jacket to the one that Odette herself had worn the previous day. Her sense of unease increased when Auriole did not sit in the chair as she was invited to and declined the offer of tea. Instead, she moved restlessly around the room, picking up objects and looking carefully at them, as though she were a buyer in a shop. Her eyes alighted on the bracelet on the mantelpiece and as she reached for it, a cruel smirk crossed her face.

Finally, Auriole spoke.

'You are wondering at my calling on you after so many years? In fact, dear Odette, I have been with you for quite some time. Your suspicions that you were being followed were correct. You are such an *ingénue*, my dear; to keep looking behind you, when most of the time I was ahead of you in every way. As for your parents, it was a pleasure to watch them die. Yes, I arranged all of it. What needs to be settled now is your death. Well, perhaps not your official death, as the life of Odette Abramsky will go on without you.'

With those words, Auriole drew a small pistol from her handbag and aimed it at Odette.

Odette could not believe what she had heard from the mouth of the girl she had believed to be her friend. With a mounting terror that caused her heart to pound in her chest and her body to shake, she understood the implication of Auriole's words. She was about to die and Auriole would take over her life.

She begged her former friend, 'Auriole, you can take all you want from here. I will sign the apartment over to you. Please do not kill me. The bracelet you so admired can be yours. Just take whatever you want. And why kill me? I have done nothing to hurt you. My family were kind to you; they welcomed you into their lives. What do you hope to gain from this?'

As she pleaded for her life, Odette realised how much Auriole stood to gain. She would have money, a great deal of it, and a position in society. The château would be hers and whatever her plans for the future, it would be a perfect cover for any activity she was involved in. And then she remembered the one item that she could not, ever, allow to fall into the possession of another: the gold bracelet with its rose gold Star of David which she wore on her left wrist.

Her heart hammering in her chest, Odette backed into a small side table on which lay her grandfather's lead crystal ashtray. With a courage and strength born of her desperate instinct to survive or at least to protect the one item that must be saved, she reached round and hurled the heavy sharp-edged ashtray at Auriole. It hit Auriole's lower arm, which was enough to make her drop the gun. Odette ran out of the room and into the bathroom, where, after locking the door behind her, she quickly removed the bracelet. She could hear Auriole cursing as she recovered the gun and approached the bathroom. Behind the cistern of the lavatory was a safe concealed by tiles. Her grandmother had revealed this to her many years ago.

Odette remembered her words, "My darling child, we have always lived with uncertainty and fear. It is part of our tradition to be prepared for misfortune. For that reason, there must always be a place in our homes for those things most precious and which must not fall into the wrong hands. Your Star of David bracelet is such a treasure."

Her grandmother had shown her how to remove the tiles and replace them in such a way that the entrance to the safe was invisible. Many years later, she had shown the secret hiding place to Marie-Claude, explaining that her grandmother had also counselled her to reveal it to one trusted friend. Marie-Claude was such a trusted friend.

Odette ran the bath taps to muffle the sound of her climbing up and removing the tiles. She quietly placed the bracelet in the safe and said a quick prayer "*Adonai dayan ha-emet*", God is the righteous judge.

After replacing the tiles, she jumped down and turned to face the bathroom door. There was no escape. The windows were high in the wall and locked. There was nothing she could use to defend herself. A bullet shattered the lock to the door and there was Auriole.

With the words "I have no use for Jews", she fired two shots into Odette's chest.

68

Auriole worked quickly before rigor mortis could set in. She emptied the large leather suitcase of the clothing belonging to Odette's parents and folded the body neatly into it, padding it carefully with towels. She cleaned the floor of the bathroom and waited until nightfall, when she dragged the suitcase across the hallway to the elevator. The apartment block was in darkness and she was certain that no one witnessed her exit the elevator and cross the courtyard to the doors of the building.

The agent was waiting for her in the shadows of the portico and together they carried the suitcase along a quiet back alley to the banks of the Seine, where a pile of stones and ropes had been prepared. They used the rope to anchor the stones to the case. The river was deep here and far from any bridges and potential onlookers. They pushed and then heaved the case over the smooth stones of the river bank and into the dark water, where the case sunk silently into the murky depths. With a smile of satisfaction, she pulled her coat closely around herself. It was an exceptionally cold night, which meant few people had ventured out – this was to her advantage. She reached inside the lining of her coat, removed the stiletto blade and swiftly slashed her accomplice's throat. Shock and pain registered briefly on his face as he raised his hands to his neck to staunch the flow of blood. It was now a simple matter for her to push him into the river, where, as with the suitcase, his body sank into the dark water.

Fräulein Doktor had taught her well. There is no honour in murder, only satisfaction.

PART SIX

Helen

69

My convalescence took time. When I stood up from my bed, I felt dizzy and weak. He explained to me that this was to be expected, considering the amount of blood I had lost and the seriousness of my infection. I still had no appetite and continued to lose weight, but one day I felt well enough to accept his invitation to take a walk around the grounds. It was a bitterly cold day and the grey clouds that massed over the château portended heavy snow by nightfall. He wrapped his army greatcoat around me when he discovered that all I had was the shabby coat I had worn the night of the recital. I took his arm and leaned into him as we walked – I felt all I wanted in my life was to be close to this man, never to be parted from him again.

After a while, I asked, 'And how was it with your wife?'

'I was too late; she died the day before I arrived. But it was not as I feared. My brother and his wife had been to the clinic and taken her to our estate. She was well cared for and the children were with her at the end. She was interred on her family estate.'

'And your children?'

'They will stay with my brother and his wife. They have children of the same age. It is a good arrangement. They are in the countryside and safe from the bombs that are now falling on German cities.'

'And what of Russia? Lotti and Emilia were most enthusiastic about Operation Barbarossa. And they say you were wounded. Please tell me how this happened.'

For a while, he was silent and took my arm gently from his. With a heavy sigh, he put his hands over his face. For a moment, I thought he would weep.

'The wounds are healed but I was in a field hospital for two weeks. Before then, we got within sight of Moscow. Others had reached there before us. But the Soviets will win this war. They have more men than we have ammunition, and their determination to survive and to defend their country surpasses ours as the aggressors – for that is what we are.

But it was the wickedness my unit discovered as we advanced along the front line. Whole villages are being deliberately destroyed and the people living there are murdered by killing groups – *Einsatzgruppen* they are called. This is not a war for soldiers but for sadists. They were hanging children in a village when we arrived. The parents are made to watch as their little ones die, and then they are killed. The little ones take a long time, they said, and they were laughing. We stopped them, but for one child it was too late. I shot the officer in charge of the unit and reported the crimes to General von Rundstedt but I received no response from him.

Our soldiers take drugs – stimulants – that can keep them awake for days. It is for that reason we were so successful in crossing Europe and into France; no other army was able to fight without sleep. But the same drug takes away any compassion that they may have. From what I witnessed, these men behaved like wolves among a flock of helpless sheep – there was never any compassion to be found in them. There was no mercy even for the smallest and weakest. I can still see the bodies of the women and children. It was not for this that I became a soldier.'

'All wars are terrible,' I said. 'The Great War was to be the war to end all wars. My parents met at the hospital in Cambrai. They never spoke of the things they saw. I was not encouraged to ask and I understood that it was too painful for them.'

'This war is far more brutal and I fear we will know of worse before there is peace. I have learned of the camps in Poland where they are killing Jews. This will happen here, I believe. They will be arrested and taken to internment camps and from there to Poland.'

'And you are certain of this?'

'I have no details but I believe it will come. My influence here is limited. I am under the command of the *Oberfeldkommandur* in Caen. He is an administrator, not a soldier as I am. I am sure he will follow orders from the High Command. When you are well, we will speak more of this. Now my mind is with my soldiers who are suffering in the Russian winter. I fear they will be dead before I return to them.'

'And you have to return?'

'Yes, but not yet, and also much depends on the war in Russia. It could be that it will be decided before they consider that I am ready to return to the battlefield.'

'I don't want you to leave.'

'I will have no choice when the time comes, but before then, I must make arrangements to ensure that you are safe. I think I should marry you.'

'Are you sure of this? You know how much I love you but you also know that I am helping those who are considered to be enemies of Germany.'

'I know nothing of these things. Now, *liebchen*, how are we going to marry? Will your priest do this for us? I was baptised a Catholic on account of my mother. She is Luisa von Blumenthal, and her family trace their ancestors to the Holy Roman Emperor. If your priest agrees, we will organise a small private ceremony with the cook and your friends, Lotti and Emilia, as witnesses. I will speak to the *Oberfeldkommandur* about the legal papers. Now your face is getting red. That is a good sign, but perhaps you are angry, that I am not on my knees with a diamond ring?'

I laughed, 'I do not like diamonds and would be happy with a ring from an old curtain.'

'Come now, *liebchen,* perhaps if you are not too tired or overwhelmed by my proposal, we can play the *Arpeggione Sonata* together.'

I slept in his bed for the first time since my illness. We did not make love – he said it was too soon, that I was not fully healed – but we slept peacefully in each other's arms.

70

I felt able to make the journey into Caen the following week. I was still too weak to cycle and accepted the offer of transport in one of the staff cars. I timed my visit to coincide with the confessional hour at the Église Saint-Pierre. I waited my turn by the confessional and once inside, spoke in English. He knew me at once.

'*Ma petite*, we have been so worried about you. I understand that you have been very ill. Are you well now?'

'Yes, almost, but I wish to be married and require a priest to perform the ceremony. Will you please be that priest?'

'And who is your future husband?'

'It is the *Feldkommandur*, Karl von Werstein.'

'But does he not have a wife?'

'She is dead. There is no obstacle to our marriage. We love each other and have loved for a long time. He is baptised a Catholic so I cannot see an impediment.'

'You do realise that this would not be regarded favourably by the British government or indeed their allies.'

'It is none of their business. He is a good and honourable man and I love him, as he loves me.'

'And regarding your other duties, will they continue?'

'Of course, but he does not wish to know.'

Père François chuckled and replied, 'So, he will watch the wall!'

I continued, 'But this must be a secret from the group. I worry that they would no longer trust me if they knew. My Uncle Damian must not be told, nor any of my family.'

'Your secret is safe with me. But I must hear your confession before the sacrament. You must be honest with me and before God before I can agree.'

I knew it would come to this but it had to be confessed.

'Bless me, Father, for I have sinned, it is many weeks since my last confession. In that time, I killed the man who violated me and aborted the foetus that was the result of the violation.'

'In the eyes of God, you have suffered enough on account of this. We will have a mass and prayers offered towards the release of the baby's soul from Limbo. You are absolved. Go in peace. Your penance has been paid in full. Come to me tomorrow and we will make the arrangements.'

I left the confessional and made my way to the car, where a young soldier was waiting for me. He gently helped me to my seat. I knew myself to be very unwell still. At that moment, the need for *Maman* to be beside me was overwhelming and I began to weep. This should have been a time of great joy for my parents. But how would it be if they knew I was marrying an enemy of their countries? The young soldier stopped the car and looked at me solicitously.

'It is war, *mademoiselle*. We are all the same. One day this will be over. We all wish for that time. I want to be at home with my mother and my brothers and sisters. They may not be alive, who knows. I was studying to be a doctor, like my father and my mother. Then I am given a gun and told to kill, not cure. Who knows what war will bring? I wish you well.'

It was only when I returned to the château that I realised he had spoken in English to me.

We were married at night in the Lady Chapel of Église Saint-Pierre. Lotti, as my bridesmaid, made bouquets of snowdrops and ferns from the woods. Despite my protestations that a curtain ring would suffice, he placed a simple gold band inlaid with garnets, my birthstone, on my finger. The cook and Emilia were witnesses to the marriage. The civil ceremony had been held by proxy in the *Mairie* earlier in the day, with the *Oberfeldkommandur* acting for the bridegroom and a young French woman, nominated by the cook, acting for the bride. The marriage was recorded in the register of marriages at the *Mairie* in Caen on the 20th of February 1942.

71

As my health improved, we regularly walked together around the château grounds. Spring was late in coming and on that March day, the ground was brittle with frost and the cold air stung my breath. I was careful not to take him to the ruins in the rose garden and avoided the area in the woods where the trapdoor was hidden. This was not because I did not trust him, but felt that he would be more comfortable not knowing. My monthly bleed had started the previous day. This was a sign that I would recover – of that I now felt confident. With this confidence was the sadness that I would never bear his child. But at least we would now be able to make love, something I was as desperate as he to resume.

While we were walking, he asked me about my parents and my home.

He had spent time in Britain as a young man and had visited Edinburgh. He had crossed the magnificent Royal Border Bridge on his journey. I was happy to share this part of my life with him. He asked if I had a photograph of my parents and I told him of the photographs I had found hidden behind the chest of drawers in my bedroom. When we returned to the château, I went to get the one I had kept.

'There is *Maman* between Odette and another woman. It is strange because the other woman looks very much like Odette. They must have been at the Conservatoire together. There was another photograph but it is not here. In that photograph, as in this one, the other woman is wearing the bracelet I found in the apartment in Paris where Stefan's parents were living. They rented the apartment from Odette when her parents died. If you look closely at this photograph, you will just see it on the other's left wrist. The photo is very faded but it is there.'

He looked at the photograph carefully, at the woman I had said was Odette.

'I know this woman. I met her many times at the house of Admiral Wilhelm Canaris. His wife, Erika, is a talented violinist. This woman played the piano at musical soirees we held there. Reinhard Heydrich was also often there. He and this woman were lovers, I believe. But her name was not Odette, but Auriole Ritter. She was from Alsace as I remember.'

I thought about this and the memory of the young woman who had attended the lunch party, whose intonation had reminded me of Odette.

'Are you sure of this? Perhaps you are confusing the two women; they are very alike.'

'I am certain that the woman you say is Odette is, in fact, Auriole Ritter. The other woman is a Jew; she is wearing the Star of David bracelet on her left wrist, which is traditional.'

'*Maman* has the other photographs, the ones I sent with my letter. That is if they safely returned to Britain.'

'I am not supposed to know of these things. But, *liebchen*, it would be very useful if this could be confirmed. More than useful; your life could be in danger and we need to know.'

'But why?'

'Because Auriole Ritter is a very dangerous woman.'

'And I have the bracelet that the other woman was wearing. It was hidden in the apartment where Stefan's parents are living. The apartment belonged to Odette's family. I found it in the wall of the bathroom. The other woman must have hidden it there.'

I struggled to reconcile the memories I had of the Odette I had known in the early days at Château des Tilleuls with the knowledge I now had, that it was likely, perhaps certain, that she was not Odette but a woman my husband described as dangerous, and therefore that the true Odette was dead.

That night, I went to the tower and got out the wireless. I tuned in for the first time in weeks to Radio Londres. After the opening chords of Beethoven's *5th symphony*, came the coded messages, including:

"Little barrels roped and tarred all full of brandy wine."

I had no idea how many times this message had been read, but the relief that George and his companions had made it safely to Britain was immense. *Maman* would have received my letter and, with it, the photographs. *Maman* would also be aware of the danger I was in.

Later, I told him of the time Odette/Auriole had reacted so angrily when I played *The Lorelei* on the piano.

He explained, 'The song was banned by the Nazis because the words were written by a Jew. It confirms my suspicions. The woman you knew was not Odette but Auriole Ritter. Her husband, I am certain, knew nothing of this. She will think you are dead or imprisoned at least. We must ensure that your identity remains a secret. We can trust Lotti, Emilia and the cook. No one else shall know.'

'But what about the register at the *Mairie;* surely it is my name on the marriage entry?'

'I gave your French name to the *Oberfeldkommandur*. I thought it to be safer. But we are married in the eyes of the church and this small detail can be resolved later.'

72

It was agreed that I should resume my duties as the housekeeper and that the domestic staff at the château be kept to a minimum; this would avoid any suspicion regarding my identity and position in the household. I kept my belongings in the nursery but slept with my husband at night.

I was more than happy to help the cook in the kitchen and he, in turn, was delighted to have me there.

I now ordered food from the market and arranged for it to be delivered by the stall holders, and paid them well above what they would achieve in the market place. I knew how bitterly the German soldiers were resented and that the sight of them shopping for food that was denied to ordinary citizens caused anger. I feared this could lead to rioting and worse.

While unpacking a sack of potatoes, I found a news sheet inside the sack entitled *J'accuse*. I took it up to the nursery to read and discovered that my worst fears were realised. Deportations of Jews from France to the East had begun at the end of March of this year. They were taken by train and promised resettlement in a homeland in Eastern Europe. But the editor of *J'accuse*, Adam Rayski, had learned of the true fate of those deported following contact with an escaped slave labourer from Poland. The Jews and all those who the German Nazis considered undesirable were taken to camps in Poland and murdered. The most notorious camp was one named Auschwitz. But before this, in May 1941, Jewish men in Paris had been ordered to report to the Paris police. More than five thousand had been arrested – most of these were Polish and Ukrainian immigrants who had been welcomed into France and had been hard-working citizens of the Republic.

What I found most shocking was that the camp at Drancy – where Jews from the Occupied Zone were interned in atrocious conditions of starvation and lack of sanitation – was run entirely by the French authorities. From there, the inmates were loaded onto French trains by French guards and taken to their deaths. The news sheet urged French people to protect their Jewish compatriots and to oppose as far as possible the deportations. It exhorted the readership to spread the truth about the collaboration of the French authorities in this exercise in mass murder.

My hands were shaking as I put the news sheet in a drawer. I had to speak with him; our pact of denial of my activities had to be tested.

I spoke with him that night as we lay together. The pleasure of being with him had not diminished. I loved him even more since my illness – his tenderness and devotion to me when all others had thought me lost to death. And now that I was well, my passion equalled his. I knew how to arouse him as he did me. Every moment I spent with him was a revelation: of my ability to receive and give pleasure, of our need for each other and, of course, our shared love of music. But this issue of his country's merciless indifference to suffering and its willingness to destroy life on the basis of race and religion could not go unchallenged. It could not have been possible without the complicity of the German population.

'My love, I have to ask you this. I know you have told me many times that you are a soldier, a loyal German and that as a soldier you must be prepared to die and kill for your country. This is war, and on this we are agreed, but I have read today that what you told me may happen is already happening in this country. It has been happening in Poland and in every country which Germany has invaded and conquered. And surely you were aware that this was also happening in Germany since the time Hitler and his Nazi party came to power. Have you been part of this?'

'You are asking me if I am a member of Hitler's Nazi party.'

'Yes, I am. From what I understand, the people of Germany were happy to follow the *Führer* and do his bidding. By that, I mean all people: soldiers and civilians alike.'

'I did not join the party and neither did my brothers. For a while it was difficult, as they wanted to take away my rank and commission, but also after a while, they forgot about this, shall we say omission. This happened with other Prussian officers. We despise Hitler and his barbarians as I have described them to you before now, but as soldiers we would not refuse to fight for our country. I do not fear death and it is certain that Hitler's thugs would be happy to have me killed had I refused to fight in this war. But they know that we Prussians value honour and courage above all else and we will fight to our deaths for the Fatherland. I am an excellent leader and my men respect me. I do not tolerate the brutality such as I described to you that day and I have learned of worse since. I have shot men under my command who have dishonoured the flag. Sadly, *Herr* Himmler, our chicken farmer *Reichsführer*, is now arrogating Prussian courage as an example to follow in the persecution and extermination of Jews. This is not what we are.'

'And how will it be when the Jews in your command here are arrested?'

'There will be no arrests. I will follow the lead of our interesting cook and my beloved wife to make sure that this is so, but of course I will not be aware of their activities.'

'We will do all we can to be discreet.'

'Now, *liebchen*, I wish you to be astride me in order that I may watch your beautiful face when I am deep inside you. Do you know your nipples will never become brown as in other women? Even when you have had a child or many children, they will stay the colour of a rose.'

'How do you know this?'

'"Them that ask no questions..."'

'"Isn't told a lie". How do you know this also?'

'I will not repeat what I said.'

His face still held the familiar mocking smile and he moved under me.

But the sadness that I would never bear him a child returned, along with the lingering uncertainty of who my husband truly was: whether he was aware of the mass murder of Jews in Germany and elsewhere by the Nazi regime or if he had been part of the invasion of Poland. The Polish Airmen – who had their own squadron in the RAF – had taken refuge in the underground room for two nights. They had described the brutality of the *Wehrmacht* in Poland in 1939 and the German occupation of their country.

the father died later. The mother and daughter were arrested and deported. I was appalled by this. The cleaning lady must surely have denounced them for the arrests to be made. Had she no compassion for these people? I was now very anxious for the two men.

'Did you register with the *sous-préfecture*?' I asked.

'We did not, but it has made no difference. When we had to buy the Yellow Star, they wrote down our address. There is no way we can escape identification.'

'Then, surely, now is the time to join Leah and Raisa.'

'We will wait. As long as we keep out of sight of the *gendarmes*, we should be safe for the moment.'

I promised to visit them again soon with food and wine. I was able to assure them that Ruth and Ellana were safe and well, which was a comfort to them.

He was playing the cello when I returned, the sublime melody of Saint-Saëns' *The Swan*. He invited me to accompany him on the piano. When we finished, I told him what I had heard and read.

'*Liebchen*, it will become worse for Jews. I did not inform you of this before; it was during the time of your recovery and I knew the distress it would cause you, but in January, our now departed friend, *Herr* Heydrich, and his equally fervent colleague, *Herr* Eichmann, presided over a conference in Berlin, the Wannsee Villa to be precise. Here, it was decided how best to eliminate the Jews in Europe. They have named this "The Final Solution" and for this, they have determined that they need the help of organisations in all the counties we have overcome. They have discovered that the citizens of those countries have been most willing to enable this elimination of Jews. Their bureaucratic systems facilitate the identification and location of Jews, and their populations are eager to deliver them up for slaughter. This, of course with exceptions, those I am not to be made aware of.'

He said this with his now so familiar slightly mocking tone, but his face showed no mirth.

He continued, 'I am certain your own countrymen would behave no differently in such circumstances. Your policemen, the "Bobbies", as I understand they are known, are equally supportive of this Final Solution in your Channel Islands. They are British subjects, are they not? Their Jews were taken away and are now in the camps in Poland, alive or dead, who knows?

Liebchen, this means that very soon, this will be a situation beyond your endeavour. In France, they have no need of our *Gestapo*, as the *gendarmes* are willing to serve their German masters. Those who protest the arrests and deportations will suffer the same fate.

Very soon, I will be ordered to take command of my division. At present, they are in Kharkov and seem victorious, but my superior, General Paulus, wishes me to return as soon as I am able. For that reason, I have asked my brother if you may travel to our estates to be safe there during this time. Also, my mother wishes to meet you. She spent time in Edinburgh as a child, as she has relatives in Scotland.'

'I will not go.'

'And if I demand it?'

'I will still refuse to go. I will hide from you until you have left. But I do not want you to go. I cannot live without you.'

'*Liebchen*, this is war, as you well understand, and so I must go. When my tutor taught me English, he insisted that there is a difference in your language between "I must" and "I have to". He explained that "have to" means an order from outside of the person, whereas "must" is an obligation from within. I learned on my travels in your country that your people do not always make this distinction.'

'What are you saying?'

'You understand perfectly well what I am saying. I do not require an order from another. I know that it is my duty to go and fight for my country. I must go. It is a question of honour, of what I know to be the honourable action.'

'You are talking about conscience?'

'Perhaps, but conscience can mean many things to different people. For some, as I have witnessed, it is a very imprecise concept, nebulous, and often floating free of restraint and humanity. For others, it has constraints which, also perhaps, can be defined in terms of compassion, empathy and even a desire to be above the norms of human frailty, to strive perhaps to be too perfect. Between the two is where most of us live.'

'As a child, I was taught by nuns. They placed great emphasis on what they defined as a perplexed conscience and a lax conscience. The nuns considered the former was preferable, although I am sure it would lead to obsessive self-doubt and self-deprecation. The latter was the road to Hell, as they explained. I am afraid my conscience would be consigned to the damned.'

'And what is on your conscience, *liebchen*?'

'I have already killed three men and...'

'Enough of "and"! It was not a matter of conscience but a necessary choice. And of the men?'

'There was a gardener here and his friend. They were a threat to my guests. And there was Mueller.'

'You truly are a remarkable woman. Now, enough of this philosophy of life and death. We will prepare for a recital in honour of our marriage and of my return to the Eastern Front. We shall invite the *Oberfeldkommandur* and his officers. He will be thanked in private for his services to our marriage and we will play an exceptional programme to reward him.

'And have you thought about this programme?'

'Of course, we shall begin with *Monsieur* Gabriel Fauré's *Élégie*. This will not be as a tribute to the Reich Protector, as they will believe, but a tribute to those who have suffered since. We will then play Beethoven's *Sonata Opus 69 in A major*. It is the most beautiful but also the longest and I have no doubt half of our audience will fall asleep at some point during its performance. Then we shall play *The Swan*. The composer as you know was Camille Saint-Saëns. There was always much discussion that he was a Jew. But this was not proved and we will play it. If they are discomforted by this music that is not our concern.'

'And as an encore?'

'The second movement of the *Arpeggione*, of course.'

74

The recital was to be held on the evening of the 15th of July in the salon of the château. The air was filled with the fragrance of roses and night-scented stocks which I placed in vases around the room.

The occasion would be formal, with the *Oberfeldkommandur* present together with his senior officers and their guests. My husband planned to wear his *Wehrmacht* officer's uniform and asked me what I would wear.

'I have not decided.'

'But have you not the blue gown you wore on the occasion of our recital in Bayeux?'

'No, I have not. It was destroyed in the laundry.'

'And the medal?'

'Alas, it too could not be saved.'

'It seems my wife will have to play in her undergarments following this laundry calamity.'

'As you wish.'

'I am sure the men in the audience will be delighted by such a vision of loveliness at the piano, but in the circumstances it would be a distraction. Perhaps another gown should be found for you.'

'I will not parade like a prize cow in that shop again.'

'Then I will see to it.'

The following evening, he returned from Caen with a white Grecian-styled gown, cut low at the bust and back, and with silk shoulder straps adorned with dusky pink roses. It was exquisite. I thanked him.

The guests started arriving at 7 p.m. The château was guarded by troops from the garrison; the Resistance was very active in Normandy and another assassination attempt was always possible. Together with the secretaries, I poured champagne for the guests as they arrived and once everyone was seated in the salon, took my place at the piano. The *Oberfeldkommandur* asked if he could say a few words before the recital and with our agreement, stood up to face the audience. With an attitude of enormous pride and satisfaction, he announced the progress made by the victorious German army as they advanced across Soviet territory. They were now within reach of the great oil fields of the Caucasus. This would cut off the enemy from the fuel they needed for the war and provide the German army with all they needed for victory. He clicked his heels together and the audience stood up in response, raising their right arms.

'*Heil* Hitler,' he proclaimed.

'*Heil* Hitler,' they responded.

I stayed seated at the piano and made much of arranging the music. My husband appeared to be having a problem with inserting the spike of his cello into its stop on the floor. When everyone had taken their seats, we began playing. As my husband had predicted, the *Oberfeldkommandur* and his officers fell asleep during the second movement of the Beethoven piece. We took our final bow after the encore and prepared to bid farewell to the guests. My husband became engaged in conversation with the *Oberfeldkommandur* and his guest, a very elegant lady.

'"To the victor belong the spoils" of war,' I muttered to myself. Then the cook was at my side.

'*Madame*, you are required urgently in the kitchen.'

I left the gathering and followed the cook into the kitchen. To my astonishment, Damian was there with another man.

'How did you get in here? There are guards everywhere.'

'It was not easy and we shall wait here until they have returned to Caen.'

'Why are you here tonight? It is very dangerous.'

Damian went on to tell me the shocking news that a *rafle* – a roundup – of Jews in Paris was planned early the following morning. Nine thousand *gendarmes* were poised to arrest as many foreign-born Jews as could be found in the city. The man with him was a *passeur,* who had driven from Paris to request my help in bringing an elderly Jewish couple – the parents of *Monsieur* Stefan Erhart – and others from their apartment to safety. They had been warned by a neighbour that the round-up would take place the following morning, but were too terrified to leave with him. They had asked him to bring me to Paris. They would only trust the *passeur* if I was with him.

The man spoke up, 'The neighbour is an old friend of the Abramsky family and known to me. She has the key to the bank deposit boxes of the family. It seems that Odette Abramsky gave the key to this neighbour for safekeeping. She will continue to guard the key for them but is anxious for their safety if they remain in the apartment.'

'How strange that Odette did not reclaim the key.'

And then I remembered, the "Odette" I knew would not have known about the key – at least she had not been able to misappropriate the family's money.

I did not disclose any of this to Damian and asked, 'So, what can I do? We have guests.'

'Helen, you will have to leave tonight. There is no time. The arrests will start at dawn.'

I waited until the guests had left, changed and went to speak to my husband.

'I am leaving for Paris.'

'May I ask why?'

'You would not wish to know.'

'If my wife tells me she is leaving me this night to travel, I wish to know why.'

'There are people who need my help.'

'Tell me what is happening.'

And I told him.

'I warned you that something of this kind was coming but I hoped that without Heydrich, it would not happen, or at least not for some time. I have to ask you not to make this journey, but I fear that whatever I say, you will do it.'

'I must do it.'

And he understood.

He took me in his arms and held me close.

'You are more precious to me than you will ever know. But I cannot be sure that I will be here when you return. Tonight, the *Oberfeldkommandur* informed me that I have to join my division. There is a battle ahead in a city called Stalingrad. It will not be for some weeks, I believe, but they need me within a few days to assemble our forces.'

'My love, I promise I will return.'

I waited until the *Oberfeldkommandur* and his guests had left. The cook promised to ensure the well-being of Leah and the others in my absence. I packed the car with food and blankets, and then I and the *passeur* – whose name I would never know – set off for Paris.

75

It was still dark when we arrived at the apartment. Two frail and visibly terrified elderly people opened the door.

'Helen, you have come. We did not dare to hope. Please enter; there are others here too.'

My heart sank when I saw around twenty people assembled in the salon. There was a family with three young children and a mother in an advanced stage of pregnancy. And others too; the boy who had played with Céleste and Séraphine was there with his parents and a younger brother. How could all these people get to safety and how could I care for them even if I succeeded in evacuating them from Paris?

'We will have to do this very carefully and in small groups. *Monsieur* and *Madame* Erhart should leave first in the car together with...'

I had no desire to make such a choice, but it had to be done.

I decided that the family I had met at *Hanoucca* should be first to go; the discovery of the bracelet following the boy's misadventure on the cistern had been fate and it was fate that would determine all their lives. I asked the *passeur* to leave immediately with the first group, but to return as soon as he was able and that he would be well paid. I told him to take the group to Église Saint-Pierre until I could arrange for an alternative place for them. He must not know of the underground room. It was too dangerous to reveal its presence.

'There will be road blocks and identity checks.'

'Do not worry; I have papers for all.'

They left and I counted how many remained. There were now fourteen. The men immediately offered to stay until last, for which I was grateful.

Dawn was breaking and the first light of the July sky filtered through the blinds. We could hear the sound of motor vehicles but none stopped by the apartment building. As it got lighter there was more noise, but again no vehicles came to our building. The neighbour came to the door, but I would not open it until I was certain of her identity. She brought hot chocolate for the children and coffee for the adults. She expressed concern for the pregnant mother who seemed to be in a lot of discomfort. I was grateful for her kindness and asked her to keep a lookout for the *gendarmes* and, if necessary, hide the group in her apartment.

I told the group I would leave for a short time to find out what was happening but instructed them to keep all curtains drawn, the lights off and not to answer the door. I left the building and walked along the river bank. I did not know my way around Paris so thought it safer to follow the river. It was not long before I encountered a group of *gendarmes*. They were standing on a street corner smoking.

I asked them why so many *gendarmes* were around the streets at such an early hour.

'We are hunting today.'

'Here, in Paris?'

'Where else are there so many Jews?'

'And what will happen to them?'

'They will find out soon enough.'

Then I heard the noise of motor vehicles: buses were approaching. It was 6 a.m. and long before people would normally be taking the bus to work, and yet I could see that these buses were full. As they passed me, I saw families: mothers with young children sitting on the floor with sheets apparently folded around household goods and other possessions. I could hear children crying. There were elderly people too.

'Who are these people and where are they going?'

'This lot is going to the *Vél d'Hiv.*'

'What is that?'

'The Winter Velodrome. They will be held there until we can move them on, to camps and then to the East.'

I heard the sound of clapping and saw that a group of people – some still in their night clothes – had emerged from surrounding buildings. To my revulsion, I realised that they had come out to celebrate the roundup. One woman was shouting "Well done! Well done!"

But then I heard a man's voice.

'The poor people, have you no shame? After them, it will be us.'

I returned to the apartment, where all were anxiously awaiting my return. There had been no raid by the *gendarmes*, but they had seen people taken out of an apartment in the adjacent building. They had also seen the concierge of that building enter the apartment and later emerge, clearly having looted the apartment of valuables.

At midday, the *passeur* returned. The first group were safely in the Église Saint-Pierre. I then arranged for the family with the pregnant mother to leave with her three children. The *passeur* informed me that Damian had arranged for them to be hidden at a farm in Foulognes, a village close to Sainte Honorine-de-Ducy. The woman would be passed off as his wife at the checkpoint, but the children would have to be hidden in the trunk of the car. The woman bade farewell to her husband and they left. There still remained four men: one with a wife and three teenage children.

The day passed slowly; each in the apartment alert for the sound of entry by the *gendarmes*. The neighbour brought food for them and offered refuge in her apartment should the worst happen and the apartment be raided. At 8 p.m., the *passeur* returned. He apologised for the delay, but he had been obliged to make a detour as the *gendarmes* had blocked most of the minor roads out of Paris. He feared he could only make one further journey as the roadblocks were increasing and he could not guarantee safe passage.

The men made it easy for me.

'We will leave before dawn and take our chance. Take the mother and her children.'

The father of the family kissed his wife and children.

'If you survive, tell the world what happened. Leave France and make a new life in a country where our people are not despised.'

The *passeur* promised to return for me and took them away.

The men left separately before dawn. I took their names and instructed them to make their way to Caen if possible. I could not risk giving them the name of the château. I suggested that they find a church and seek sanctuary there, either in Paris or in Caen, and promised to care for their families.

At first light I went out onto the streets. Buses were still passing, full of families. The frail and elderly could be seen lying in an open carriage. A young woman looked desperately out of the window of the bus. She was holding a tiny child.

As the bus slowed to allow an army truck to pass, the woman saw me and begged, 'Take my child, please take my child.'

Others on the bus were equally desperate, begging for help from those who stood silently and indifferently watching the lines of buses, crying to them to save their children. I reached up and tried to take the child from her arms. In an instant, a *gendarme* grabbed me by the waist and pulled me to the ground.

'Be careful, *mademoiselle*, or you will join them.'

I was badly shaken, but far worse was the memory of the anguish on the woman's face, her cries for help and the sweet trusting face of the child. This would haunt me forever.

I made my way back to the apartment. The neighbour was waiting there and told me what she had learned of the roundups. At first it had been thought that only the men were to be taken so many had gone into hiding, but when the *gendarmes* came, they were taking everybody. No one was given time to pack. Mothers had thrown themselves and their children from windows, preferring death to the fate that awaited them. My neighbour had heard of one mother pleading with the *gendarmes* as they pushed her onto a bus, that her six-month-old baby was still in the apartment and no one would be there to care for him. They had laughed in response. Neighbours had been entering the apartments of those arrested and looting whatever they could.

The neighbour had news from the *passeur*. He would be unable to return to Paris that night and advised that I should make my own way back to Caen. I had no papers on me and no idea how I could travel without them but I thanked the neighbour who in turn promised to look after the apartment and keep the key to the bank deposit box with her.

Before I left, I asked the neighbour, 'Did you meet *Madame* Abramsky-Erhart, Odette, at any time in recent years?'

'I last saw her immediately after the death of her parents. That is when she gave me the key. That night I received news that my parents in Nice were unwell, so I went to be with them, to help them in their old age. They died in 1940. I did not wish the apartment in Paris to be empty when the Germans arrived and risked that it would be taken by them. I was surprised when I found there to be tenants in the apartment. Odette had told me she would be teaching her students here. But, as it was, the Erharts were charming people. I was pleased to be able to help them.'

'What about the concierge? Did she ever meet Odette?'

'I am sure she would have met her many times. The Erharts told me that she and her husband, their son, Stefan, were regularly at the apartment. But our concierge does not take an interest in the people who live here. She keeps the hall and stairs clean and that is all. It was better that way for the Erharts; many in her position have made life difficult for Jews in their buildings since the Germans came. Why do you ask?'

'It is not important. But thank you again, *Madame*. I am grateful for what you have done for them and the others. Please keep the keys safely in your possession.'

I kissed the woman on both cheeks and left.

I decided to take my chance at the train station. It would not be easy to travel with neither a ticket nor identity papers, but I would have to try.

The Gare Saint-Lazare was full of soldiers checking identity papers and watching the crowds. I looked at the board, there was a train leaving for Caen in ten minutes. I approached the young soldier guarding the gate and started crying hysterically. People looked around to determine the source of the noise and were treated to the spectacle of a young woman on her knees in front of the guard, begging him to allow her to board the train, as thieves had stolen her purse and now she had neither ticket nor money, nor even papers. Everything had been stolen from her. The guard appeared flustered and started to pull me roughly to my feet. I shrieked in apparent pain and sobbed all the louder. This caused a large section of the crowd to protest at a young woman being abused in this way. There was a lot of shouting and pushing, and people began to move towards the guard. He ordered them to step back and waved his gun at them.

I reached up to the gun and pulled it towards me, 'Shoot me, if you must, for now I have nothing. All has been stolen from me.'

I could see that the young soldier was out of his depth in the situation; it appeared that he had a young woman who had lost her mind, and now it was likely he would have a major riot to deal with.

He tried to wrench the gun from my hands, but I held fast. Glancing around, I noticed a small group of people had sidled past the crowd and were boarding the third-class compartments of the train, no doubt in the same situation as myself. The train was about to leave.

'*Mademoiselle*, if you return my gun, you may board the train. Just go. I do not want to see you on this platform again.'

I ran to board the departing train. Once on board, I moved along to a first-class compartment and assumed a haughty manner when the guards came to check the tickets and papers. I informed them that Saint-Lazare was a den of thieves and vagabonds who had stolen everything from me and that the *Oberfeldkommandur* in Caen would vouch for me.

They did not believe me and threatened to put me off the train at Lisieux, the next stop. To my great surprise, a voice said:

'I know this lady and I can vouch for her. She is the housekeeper at the Château des Tilleuls. I was her guest two nights ago when she and the *Kommandant* gave us a wonderful recital.' A uniformed German officer was returning to the compartment.

The guards were full of apologies and left the compartment. I thanked the officer but repeated my lies about the theft.

'But why were you in Paris, *mademoiselle?*'

'I was shopping for a new gown.'

'But where is it? You say only your purse was stolen at the station.'

'They took the gown as well.'

'It was not a lucky day for you.'

'No, it was not. I shall not return.'

I closed my eyes and pretended to sleep but my heart was pounding in my chest. The strain of the past nights and days weighed heavily on me. Looking to the future, I had no idea how I could now care for so many, but I hoped that they were safe for today at least.

It was now dark outside and there were no lights to be seen as the train sped through the countryside. I fell asleep and was awakened by the officer shaking my arm.

'*Mademoiselle,* you are arrived. We are in Caen. Allow me to drive you to the château.'

The officer took my arm and helped me off the train. I felt weak with exhaustion. When we arrived at the château my husband was waiting for me.

He took me in his arms and thanked the officer, who said, 'It seems the *Fräulein* did not enjoy her shopping trip to Paris. She was robbed of all she had.'

'But she is now home so all is well.'

The officer bowed and saluted, '*Heil* Hitler.'

But we had both turned to enter the château.

When we lay quietly together, I told him all that had happened in Paris, omitting the destinations of those in the apartment. But I cried when I related the encounter with the mother desperate for me to take her child, and my own failure to help. I described the sight of the families on the buses and my fears for their fate.

He was quiet for a while and then said, '*Liebchen*, you cannot save all the world, but just to save one life of these people is to save a future for many. I did not tell you of my cello professor. He was also a Jew. They came for him at the Conservatory in Berlin. It was the 10th of November, 1938, *Kristallnacht*, the night of broken glass. They broke his cello into pieces and took him to Sachsenhausen. I tried to save him but the SS had already taken him and other professors who were Jews away in the trucks. I could do nothing that day but I went to the prison the next day and found that he was dead. They had beaten him to death. *Liebchen,* I cried. I am a soldier but I cried. He taught me all I know about the cello. But his wife and family were still in Berlin. I used my influence to get papers for them and now they are in Switzerland. They are safe.'

I moved closer to him. 'You are a remarkable man.'

'Then we are well matched.'

I told him of my performance at the train station.

'So, my wife is now entertaining the crowds at a train station as well as on the piano. And it would appear on the train. There is no end to her talents.'

'I would not be with you now without them.'

76

The following day I cycled to Caen, to Église Saint-Pierre, and waited my turn outside the confessional of *Père* François. As usual I spoke in English so he knew at once it was me. He gave me the good news that the Erharts were safe in Bayeux at the convent of the Notre-Dame nuns. The family who had arrived with them would be welcomed there that night; at the present time, they were hidden in the presbytery while the nuns made arrangements for their accommodation. As regards the other family, the expectant mother would be cared for along with her children with a family in Foulognes. But there remained the mother with the teenage children; no place had yet been found for them.

'It would not be suitable for them in the underground room,' I said. 'The weather is now very warm and eight people in such a small space without proper sanitation would be dangerous.'

I remembered how ill Ruth had become in such circumstances.

I continued, 'I will think about it. But where are they at the moment?'

'They are also here in the presbytery. It is getting somewhat crowded.' He chuckled as he said this.

'If they can stay a few more nights with you until I return with a plan.'

I told him how the men in the group had decided to leave and take their chance.

'We can only pray for them, but that may not be enough,' he said.

When I returned to the château, my husband was not there. Lotti told me that he had been summoned to Caen by the *Oberfeldkommandur*. I went to see Leah and the others and told them what had happened in Paris. They were shocked but not surprised.

Leah said, 'Now that Hitler has made war with Stalin, it will be worse for Jews. We Jews will be described as communists too; all the easier to hate us and have us arrested.'

I had witnessed the truth of this but said nothing.

The cook was getting regular supplies of food to them and they knew when to collect water from the trapdoor in the woods, but the waste buckets remained a problem. I knew how dangerous this was in the heat of the summer and promised to come twice a day to empty them. They had plenty of vitamins but the lack of opportunity to go out into the fresh air depressed them. I tried to encourage them to be patient and assured them that this could not last forever.

The fact of the danger to my friends was validated by the copy of *J'accuse* that I found in the potato sack two days later. The cook was preparing lunch for the *Kommandant* and officers from the garrison in Caen and I was helping him. My husband had not returned from Caen the previous evening but would be at the château for lunch.

The news sheet described the conditions in the Vél d'Hiv. The people I had seen on the buses that day had now endured five days of appalling conditions. There were no toilets or washing facilities for the thirteen thousand people who were interned there – this in the oppressive summer heat. Some had taken their own lives by throwing themselves off balconies and many were shot by the *gendarmes* who were guarding them. They were now leaving for transit camps in Drancy and Pithiviers, from where it was assumed they would be deported to Auschwitz. The news sheet emphasised that the roundups would not have been possible without the collaboration of the *gendarmerie*, as the Germans did not have the resources to carry out such operations in France.

It warned that the Germans aimed to exterminate the entire Jewish population of France, along with that of the rest of Europe. This murder of innocent people was facilitated by the collaboration of the *gendarmerie* as well as the bureaucratic systems that had been put in place by the Vichy government. No other country, it proclaimed, had been so active in collaboration, its citizens so abject in their obedience to this tyranny, so indifferent to the suffering of their fellow citizens, and how far had the Declaration of the Rights of Man been abrogated.

I thought of the woman and her child on the bus and wept, but I also knew that not all French people should be condemned for indifference and collaboration; many were risking their lives to resist and to save the lives of others.

Two staff cars appeared at the front of the château. The *Oberfeldkommandur* was in one, along with his adjutant and two other officers. Two guards sat in the rear seat. In the other car was the *Kommandant* with two fashionably dressed women and two of his guards. I recognised the women from the lunch party, now so long ago.

It had been arranged that Lotti and I would serve the food, while Emilia served the wine. I could not help but notice how the two women vied for my husband's attention. I could understand why this was so; he was very handsome and the uniform became him well. Not so the *Oberfeldkommandur*, whose stomach threatened to burst the buttons of his jacket. My husband's reserve and composure were in contrast to the joviality of the *Oberfeldkommandur*, who reminded me of a much-loved relative in Scotland. Perhaps when the war was over I could introduce them. "When the war was over" – how many others wondered as I did when that would be?

The *Kommandant* appeared to all as a gracious host whose slightly haughty manner added to his appeal to women such as those at the table. They were not to know, of course, that he was married and certainly not to the housekeeper, as they regarded me. I disliked the peremptory tone they used towards me when they required fresh napkins and complained that the glasses were not clean enough. I inwardly seethed, but the secret had to be kept. I felt a pang of gratitude towards the *Oberfeldkommandur*, the proxy husband, for his discretion. But the conversation I overheard made me very uneasy, as frequent references were made to the war in the East and a major new offensive there. On more than one occasion, the women expressed sadness about a departure.

The meal ended, I cleared the table and went to help the cook in the kitchen. After a while the guests left and I felt a pang of anxiety that perhaps my husband had left with them. But then I heard the sound of horses' hooves on the drive. I looked out of the window to see one of the guards approaching the château mounted on a beautiful black thoroughbred and behind him on a lead rein, a dainty chestnut Arab horse.

The *Kommandant* went out to greet him and then returned to speak to me, 'Do you ride?'

'I did in Scotland but that was many years ago.'

'Good, so we shall ride together, you and I.'

'But I have no riding clothes here.'

'You can ride as you are. The mare is well-schooled. I would not have bought her otherwise.'

'You bought her, for me?'

'Yes. I shall explain.'

With that, he took the thoroughbred from the guard and mounted. While I checked the girths on the mare's saddle, I watched him put the horse through its paces on the drive; he was a superb horseman. Once in the saddle, I patted the neck of the mare.

'What is her name?'

'Doucette. The name attracted me as I know a young woman of a similar name. She has a sweet nature but I hope not the fiery temper of that young woman.' At that, he cantered off towards the woods. I followed him.

We trotted through the woods and into the fields beyond. There he took off at a gallop and I followed. The summer evening was mellow with none of the oppressive heat of the July day. Blackbirds and thrushes flew in and out of the hedgerows and skylarks rose above them. We galloped towards a forested area, far from where I had ever ventured. The mare's gait was so smooth and she had such a light mouth that I had only to give a slight pressure of my bare knees for her to change gait or direction.

Once in the forest, he slowed to a walk and I followed. Woodpigeons cooed and hooted unseen in the dense foliage and far above a buzzard circled above its prey. He stopped by a stream and dismounted, leaving the horse to drink and then gently lifted me from the saddle.

He laid me down on the mossy bank of the stream and slowly removed my clothing. When I was completely naked, he lay beside me without undressing.

'I imagined you in my dreams in such a place. I was not fooled by the disdainful looks or by the peroxide hair, but I had to wait until I was sure, until that day when you came into my arms, then I knew that I wanted to be with you forever.'

I pulled him towards me.

'It was the same for me. I was instructed to seduce you, to get information to help the resistants. I never thought that it would be as it is between us.'

He entered me slowly and gently, caressing me, loosening the clasp that held my hair and letting it spill onto the forest floor. He cried as he came and I held him close to me.

Afterwards, we lay quietly and after a while, he told me, 'I leave tomorrow. The order came yesterday and my men need me. Only I can lead them. They are approaching a city called Stalingrad, which we have to take if we are to be victorious. But you will be safe here. The *Oberfeldkommandur* has put the château into your care. Lotti and Emilia will work in Caen but sleep at the château. The cook will stay with you. There will be no Mueller. Of that I have been promised.'

'Thank you, my love. I will wait for you.'

'I do not doubt that. Now, tell me, how it is that you are so excellent a horsewoman?'

'As a young child I had a Shetland pony called Meggie and later a Norwegian Fiord horse called Ulrike. My father enjoyed riding and together we rode the Common Ridings.'

'And what are these?'

'We ride on a certain day of the year to celebrate the Reivers of the Borders, those who robbed the cattle and sheep from the English during the times when the Borders were contested and Scotland was at war with the English kings. The Reivers were the raiders. It is an old Scottish word for raiders and thieves.'

'So, my wife is a thief *and* a resistant?'

'It is part of our history, as this will be one day.'

I drew him to me again.

It grew dark and owls hooted in the trees.

'How will I care for the horses while you are away?'

'Tonight the horses will be returned to the stables in Caen, but tomorrow the guards who are to remain here will begin the repair of the stables at the château. It is many years since they were occupied. Our horses will keep you engaged while I am not with you. You may ride mine if you wish, but he is strong so you should take care.'

'What is his name?'

'Bathory. It is an old name meaning hero.'

'I will care for both of them.'

Later that night, I asked him about his first wife.

'Yes, I loved her but it was a marriage of convenience between our families; both of us of Prussian noble blood. It was a different kind of love; we knew from childhood that we would marry and accepted that it was so, and that we should love. It is different with you.'

'In what way different?'

'"Them that asks no questions..."'

And he pulled me to him.

77

He left the following day. That night I listened to the BBC news. The battle for Stalingrad had begun. It was projected to be one of the most important and brutal battles of the war. If victorious, the Germans would be able to cut Soviet transport links to southern Russia and enable the German army to take the oil fields of the Caucasus. Hitler would then move his armies north to take Moscow. As a prize to the German war effort, a victory at Stalingrad would be immeasurable, and it would also be a huge propaganda boost to Hitler.

A few days later, Damian came to the château with the news that arrests were being made of foreign Jews in the city. He asked me to leave immediately to find Leah's husband and son-in-law. He warned me to be careful, as the *gendarmes* doing the arrests were threatening all those who intervened with the same. I left at once and made my way to the street where the family's butcher's shop had been. I hid my bicycle behind a wall and went round to the outbuilding at the back of the shop. It was empty but there was evidence that they had left in haste as there was a half-eaten meal on the table. I had no choice but to go into the shop to enquire about the men. They refused to give me any information, telling me that the men deserved no better and that they were glad to see the Jews taken away.

I went to retrieve my bicycle intending to go to the church. The family from Paris were still there as I had not found an alternative refuge for them. As I set off, a woman approached me.

Looking furtively around her, she told me, 'They are at the train station. I tried to get a message to you. One of our group informed their wives and they are leaving too.'

'But how can that be? Nobody but me should go to them.'

'It is too late. It was decided they should know immediately.'

I cycled as fast as I could to the train station. There, I saw a group of around thirty people – men, women and children – being herded out of trucks and onto trains by *gendarmes*. I pushed my way to the front of the crowd and, to my horror, recognised the *Chef des Gendarmes*. It was too late to hide, he had seen me.

'*Mademoiselle* Doucet, I am enchanted to see you again. May I ask why you are here?'

'I want to know where you are taking these people. Some of them are my friends.'

'You have friends who are Jews? Now, that is interesting. These Jews are going to Drancy and from there they will be resettled in the East.'

'You know that is not true. There is no resettlement.'

'Keep your voice down, *mademoiselle*; otherwise I shall have to arrest you too.'

At that moment I saw Leah and Raisa as they, along with their husbands, were being pushed out of a truck. I pushed past the *gendarme* and ran to Leah.

'You cannot leave, please do not leave. I will get some papers for you. All will be well.'

Leah put her arms around me and whispered, 'No, you have done all you could for us. We will stay with our men and share what fate is before us. You must go back so that others can be saved. Ruth and Ellana must survive. They are part of the future of our people.'

I continued to cling to my friend but was roughly thrust aside by the *Chef*. I fell to the ground crying Leah's name. The *gendarmes* pushed Leah and Raisa into a cattle truck on the train where they stood next to their husbands. Then the doors were slammed shut and the train began to leave.

I got to my feet and spat at the *gendarme.*

'You are a man of no principle or humanity. One day you will have to account for your actions and I will be there to point my finger at you in a court of law.'

'I shall look forward to that, *mademoiselle,* but before then, I shall be asking myself why this young woman wishes to save these people.'

'Ask all you like. The two women worked at the château before the Germans came. They were my friends.'

'And since the Germans came?'

'That I do not know. They left and went to hide.'

I realised the dangerous turn his questioning was taking. For the sake of the others I had to make sure he did not suspect me of hiding them.

'I believe that they were hidden in the *boucherie* with their husbands. Perhaps you should go there and look for more of them.'

'Perhaps I will.'

I hoped he and his men would now go and pull the shop apart to look for others. That gave me some satisfaction at least. But I could not imagine how Ruth and Ellana would take the terrible news of their parents' and grandparents' arrest.

I returned to the château. The world seemed a very bleak place. I would miss my dear friend and her good counsel. I remembered the happy times I had spent with her in the kitchen of the château before the war, before life became so tenuous.

The guards had almost finished the stables and promised to return the following day with the horses. Feed and bedding for them would be provided by a local farmer.

That night I went to confession at the church. *Père* François had learned of the arrests and tried to comfort me.

'My child, you must have faith. Some will survive, I am sure of that; how else will the world be told of the evil that is done to "God's people"? Stay for mass and after we will go to the presbytery to meet with the family from Paris. You will tell them that space has been found for the mother and the two daughters. For the son it will be more difficult to find a place, but he can stay here until we do.'

Late that night the family were brought to the woods. I guided them by torchlight to the trapdoor and there they joined the two girls from Alsace.

I listened to the BBC news. The battle for Stalingrad continued. The Soviet army had avoided encirclement by the German panzer divisions and Stalin had decreed that the city would "not take one step back, to fight to the last man". He also refused to evacuate civilians, stating that the army would fight all the harder for the city knowing they were defending its residents.

I thought of my parents, whether were they under attack by *Luftwaffe* bombers. Bombs had fallen in Liverpool and other cities. RAF planes were bombing cities in Germany. I learned that the USA had joined the Allied powers and that American troops were now in England. Singapore had fallen to the Japanese. In North Africa, the British forces prevailed over Rommel and his divisions. I learned of the failed landing of Canadian forces at Dieppe on the 19th of August.

And I realised that I had not bled since the end of June.

78

I decided that anxiety was the cause and took to riding every day, alternating between Doucette and Bathory. The latter was a more challenging mount; his size was intimidating as he was at least seventeen hands, but he had a sensitive mouth and was responsive to my commands. It was an afternoon in early September and the sun was low in the sky above the trees. We were approaching a spinney on the far side of the field when a flash of light hit my eyes. Bathory reared in terror as the flash hit him at the same time. He panicked and bolted and I could not hold him back. A tree seemed to come towards me and my last conscious thought was that this would be painful. There was a vague impression of someone kicking my body to one side and covering it with branches, and then darkness.

I awoke to lights; someone in white was shining a torch into my eyes. There were lights all around me and people in white moving around beds. I could hear a language I did not understand but which was familiar. The figure with the torch spoke to me in French and addressed me as *Frau* von Werstein.'

'You are back with us. I am Doctor Meyer.'

'Where am I? What happened to me?'

'As for what happened to you we are not certain, but you are in the military hospital in Caen.'

'How long have I been here?'

'For eight days now. We thought you would not wake up. Your cook found you. The horse you were riding came home without you so he went in search and found you buried in the forest. He thought you were dead but carried you to the château and the guards drove you here.'

'Am I injured?'

'You sustained an injury to your head from which you were unconscious until now. From that you have recovered, but sadly the baby is lost.'

'What baby? I cannot be pregnant.'

'*Madame*, you were at eight or nine weeks of pregnancy. It was very early and in other circumstances the baby would have grown as normal. But the accident was too severe. I am very sorry.'

'I still do not understand. My husband told me...'

'Yes, I have spoken to the General. He confirmed that he thought it to be so, but I explained to him that the operation he had is not perfect and this has happened many times in my experience.'

'Is he here, my husband?'

'Yes, we will allow him to see you now that you are awake. We had to contact him in Russia and it was some days before he could get here. But yes, he wants to see you very much.'

I closed my eyes. I had lost a child and this time a much-wanted child. Perhaps this would be my last chance to bear him a child. The thought of this lost child made me weep.

And then he was with me, holding my hand.

'*Liebchen*, how is it that I leave you and such things happen?'

Later, I was able to speak.

'I am so happy that you are now here. I cannot tell you much but I remember a flash of light from the trees and Bathory was frightened, spooked, we say in English. It was not the fault of the horse.'

'And the cook tells me that you were buried under branches.'

'I do not know of this, but... now I do remember. Someone was there. This person moved me with their foot under the branches. This person thought me to be dead, wanted me to be dead.'

'We will talk of this later. Now, *liebchen*, we have lost a child but we know we can have another. The doctor told me you are not damaged inside – your emotions are damaged, that is to be expected

– but our child could not survive such an accident. We will have other children, I promise you.'

'Do you have to return to Russia?'

'Yes, I must, but for now, I do not have to. General von Manstein is in charge of my divisions and I will join him as soon as you are recovered.'

'And the château?'

'All is well. Our excellent cook has more mouths to feed, I understand. Yes, I know about your friends. I am sorry. I can do nothing for them. But the cook has taken over all your other duties for the present time.'

'He is a remarkable man.'

'And soon to be married I understand. It is being arranged.'

'I had a problem with the *gendarme*, he who wanted to find my family.'

'We will talk about that later. Lotti and Emilia are also here to see you if you are not too tired.'

I was allowed home the following day. He carried me from the car to the bedroom and lay with me for that day and into the night, stroking my head gently and reassuring me of his love. I had no physical pain apart from occasional abdominal cramps which the doctor had explained was my womb evacuating the remains of the pregnancy and to expect these to continue for a week or more. The thought that this evacuation was the remains of our child was unbearable. I slept for short stretches of time, only to awake with a feeling of great sadness at the loss of a child who would have been so welcome, so loved. And then I was assailed by feelings of guilt for that earlier child who had not been welcome and whom I had asked to be taken from me. My Catholic faith had taught me that both babies would remain in "Limbo", the part of heaven allocated to those who died unbaptized. I had never truly believed this article of dogma; it had seemed such an unjust punishment for the innocent, for those untimely born and destined to die without the sacrament of baptism and therefore denied eternal life in heaven. Now, if the nuns were correct, there were two of mine in there. *Maybe they would comfort each other*, I thought dully.

We spoke more about my accident the following day.

'I rode Bathory to where you were found. I saw the bushes where you described the light. There could not be sunlight there. The foliage is too dense. I fear someone shone a strong light at you, perhaps a flare or even a strong flashlight. Such a light would startle a horse. Also, I looked at the branches. I took the cook with me to confirm this. It is certain that those branches were taken from the woods, the better to cover you.'

'Do you mean that someone carried those branches, to bury me under them so that I would not be found?'

'So it would seem.'

'I do not understand. Why should someone want to kill me?'

'For now, we will not talk to anyone of this. But before I leave, I will order that guards are to be with you when you ride and that there are always guards at the château.'

'But what about—'

'I know nothing of these things, but the guards understand that you are not to be disturbed unless you call for them. And the woods are not to be entered without your permission. There is a rare species of owl which inhabits the woods and you are anxious that it is not disturbed.'

For the first time in days, I laughed.

'And the *gendarme*?'

'He will be informed that the wife of General von Werstein is to be treated with respect.'

I wrapped my arms around him

'Please return to me as soon as you can.'

'I cannot promise when that will be. The Soviet Army is formidable and seemingly infinite in number. We will have to fight them street by street to win Stalingrad and I fear we will lose thousands of our men in doing so. It is not what we wish for but it is war.'

'I will follow the news on the wireless.'

'I do not know of any wireless. But be careful, *liebchen*.'

'"You be careful what you say, and mindful what is said",' I teased.

He smiled.

'He was an interesting man, your Mr Kipling. I visited his house, Batemans, in your East Sussex. Despite his sentiments regarding Jews and colonial subjects, I admire his work greatly, as did my first wife. He was a man of his time and suffered greatly from the death of his son. My children were schooled in his verse. Perhaps one day you will read to them.'

'I will be happy to do this.'

He left early the following morning. I bade him farewell and cried as his car disappeared through the avenue of lime trees.

79

Late in October, the cook and his mistress were married secretly by *Père* François. Lotti, Emilia and I were invited to be *demoiselles d'honneur* and witnesses to the marriage. The couple would now live together in the town but the cook would come to the château every day, ostensibly to work but in reality to provide company and protection for me by day.

Damian arrived with a letter. It was from George.

Dear Helen,

I hope this letter reaches you and finds you in good health. I was informed of your accident but understand that you had good care and have now recovered.

Our sources tell us that the woman you knew as Odette is in Normandy and that she was seen in the vicinity of Caen in September. I warn you to take every care. She will recognise you and she will suspect that you know her true identity. To avoid exposure and the impact this may have on her activities, she may try to harm you.

I met with your mother and gave her the letter and photographs. She too worries for your safety and hopes for your safe return home.

With my regards,
George Vartis

I placed the letter at the back of my wardrobe. I was certain now that someone had tried to kill me and that person probably knew I had survived. I was equally certain that Auriole was that person or someone employed by her. I checked in my drawer. The gun was there and five bullets remained. I would keep it with me at all times. But the question as to why Auriole would want to kill me was puzzling. She could just denounce me as British and hope I would be arrested and sent to Ravensbruck, although my marriage to a German general would surely afford me protection. Auriole would know that. But perhaps she was not aware of my marriage. George would have seen the photographs when he delivered my letter to *Maman* and no doubt *Maman* had identified the two women with her in the photograph: her friend Odette and the imposter, Auriole Ritter. They must both believe me to be in danger.

PART SEVEN

Auriole

80

Auriole returned to the apartment a few days later. The concierge was new to the building and it seemed had only met Odette's parents a few times and Odette only in passing. She greeted *Mademoiselle* Abramsky and expressed her condolences for her tragic loss. Auriole explained that she would be organising a tenancy for the apartment now she had packed up her grandparents' and parents' possessions.

On entering the apartment, her first act of possession was to place the gold diamond-studded bracelet on her wrist. She stood for a while, admiring how the light of the great chandelier in the salon made the bracelet shimmer on her slim wrist and the diamonds sparkle in its reflection.

It appeared that Odette had disposed of much of her family's clothing and possessions. She opened all the huge carved oak *armoires* and was disappointed to find that most were empty or held only Odette's clothing. She remembered the grandmother's furs and the boxes of jewellery she had seen on the walnut dressing table. She hunted frantically but found nothing. Neither could she find any details of bank accounts and safe deposit boxes. On a hunch, she knocked on the door of the neighbouring apartment but there was no reply. She did however find the keys to the château. They were in an envelope in the mahogany desk in the grandfather's study, along with an envelope containing a list of the domestic staff employed at the château. She sat down and wrote to them, giving each a week's notice to leave the château and find alternative employment. She would provide character references on the strict condition that they did not return to the château under any circumstances. She explained this drastic decision as a reaction to her grief and desire to start a new life for herself. The château was to be locked up and any keys in their possession sent to the apartment in Paris. She wrote similar letters to the Abramsky family. Most were now in America but a few very elderly aunts remained in France. There would be no problem eliminating them should it be necessary. She also wrote to the Conservatoire cancelling her private pupils. The need for a period of mourning would suffice as an excuse for that.

Her immediate problem was access to money. Himmler had promised to make arrangements for money to be sent to her if required, but that could compromise her present situation. The imperative was to find work and a wealthy husband.

Fortuitously, both did happen, in the form of a cellist at the Paris Opera. Stefan Erhart responded to an *annonce* she placed in *Paris-soir* offering a tenancy for the apartment. He came one evening following rehearsals and was clearly smitten by the attractive woman, unmarried and now bereaved of her parents. He explained that he and his parents had recently come to Paris from Berlin, where the rise of Adolf Hitler's Nazi party was making life for Jews increasingly difficult. Some of his family had gone to London but he had been offered the position as first cello in the Paris Opera Ballet Orchestra and had decided to accept. He had been first cello in the Berlin Philharmonic under the baton of Herbert von Karajan, who was also a family friend. He found the apartment perfect and promised to bring his parents the following day for their approval.

The tenancy contract was signed and with the deposit, Auriole made plans to take up residence at the Château des Tilleuls the following week. Stefan invited her to dinner with his parents. This was followed by an invitation to join him for a celebration with the orchestra after a performance. Stefan persuaded her to delay leaving for Caen for a few weeks; his family had time remaining on the tenancy of their current apartment and were in no rush to take up residence. After two weeks of walking together in the Luxembourg

Gardens and several meals *a deux*, Auriole was not in the least surprised to be offered marriage. A betrothal ceremony was held in the apartment. Auriole explained the absence of her relatives as due to them having emigrated to America. Her apparent stoicism and vulnerability quelled any suspicions that may have been raised by the Erhart family.

The marriage of Stefan Erhart to Odette Abramsky was an intimate affair with only twenty guests. It was blessed by the Chief Rabbi of Paris and legalised at the *Mairie* in Rue Bonaparte.

During their brief courtship, Stefan made enquiries at the Paris Opera Ballet and found that a position of pianist had become available. Auriole accepted the post immediately. She would need to be in Paris to make contact with agents. He also found a Jewish woman and her granddaughters in Caen who were looking for domestic work. Auriole employed them on the spot. Her cover was complete. She had a position in society, a wealthy Jewish husband and employment that would ensure time in Paris to make contact with other sleeper agents.

Auriole's life as Odette Abramsky-Erhart suited her very well. She appeared to all who met her as the perfect wife and mistress of the Château des Tilleuls. Fortunately, Stefan's approach to religious observance was fairly relaxed. His family was grateful to have been allowed to settle in France – a secular country – and felt an obligation to be citizens of France above religious orthodoxy. But this was in the security of knowing that freedom to practice their religion was enshrined in the constitution. Of course, Auriole had made a special study of the Jewish religion and traditions while in Germany as preparation for her new identity. She knew all the festivals and their historical context. She knew which foods were to be prepared and eaten on these occasions, as well as any Jewish matron would. Her knowledge of the history of the Abramsky family and of the château that was now her home was all garnered from her conversations in the grandparents' apartment, so many years ago.

In 1932, she gave birth to a daughter who they named Céleste. Another daughter, Séraphine, was born in 1934. The couple had agreed on a maximum of two children on account of "Odette's" age and the maternity risks associated with that. Stefan's disappointment that he did not have a son was matched by Auriole's secret delight. A boy would have been very inconvenient – circumcision and Bar Mitzvah unconscionable.

The girls were looked after by their *nounou* while Auriole and Stefan were at work in Paris. They spoke French with their mother and German with their father. Auriole maintained contact with Marie-Claude, having noted that Odette and Marie-Claude corresponded frequently by letter and by telephone. She continued the contact by letter only, explaining her reluctance to use the telephone as being due to damage to her throat following Diphtheria infection. Of course she was adept at forgery; *Fräulein Doktor* had taught her well.

When Céleste was six years old and Séraphine aged four, their *nounou* recommended a *gouvernante,* as the girls were too young to attend school but had outgrown her ministrations. And so it was that in 1938 Auriole wrote to her "dear friend" Marie-Claude, and both agreed that Helen should spend a year in France before taking up her place at Edinburgh University as a medical student.

Auriole realised there would be a substantial risk to this arrangement. Helen would wish to visit her mother's family in Calvados. But she reassured herself that as many years had passed since Marie-Claude's family had seen Odette or her for that matter, the risks were worth taking. It would be important for her daughters to be fluent in English. The ambitions of National Socialism for *Lebensraum* did not just extend to the east, but also to the west.

81

Her first contact in Paris was with Jacques Doriot, a former communist who had recently changed sides to found the right-wing *Parti Populaire Français*. Jacques was a fervent admirer of Adolf Hitler and wanted a system of government modelled on that of the Third Reich. His party emulated that of Hitler's Nazi party, using uniforms, salutes and a common enemy – the Jews – to validate its existence. It preyed upon the same prejudices and the need to find scapegoats for dissatisfaction and disaffection.

Through Doriot, Auriole met Stephanie Julienne Richter, whose title Princess Stephanie zu Waldenburg was by marriage to an Austrian prince. Stephanie was the same age as Auriole and had equally used her beauty and talents – in Stephanie's case as a ballet dancer – to attract powerful men.

Stephanie had moved to London in 1932 after the election of a centre-left government in France which accused her of spying for Germany. She settled at the Dorchester Hotel in London and continued to cultivate relationships with powerful and influential men. In 1935, Stephanie invited Auriole to her birthday party at the Dorchester and introduced her to Lord Rothermere, a newspaper tycoon who owned the widely read and, therefore, influential Daily Mail. Rothermere was an admirer of Hitler and supported an alliance of Britain and Germany. He aspired to be included in Nazi inner circles and paid Stephanie an annual retainer of £5,000 to promote support for Germany through her influential connections among the upper and ruling class of Britain. Auriole wrote to Hermann Göring and Heinrich Himmler recommending Stephanie as a useful agent in London. Her assignment would be to manipulate public opinion through the popular Daily Mail; a softening of the British public's innate antagonism towards its wartime enemy and a more benevolent attitude towards Germany should ensure that the political class would favour appeasement over war. If Rothermere's newspaper achieved this, he would be amply rewarded in Hitler's Reich.

In 1937, Auriole encouraged Stephanie to travel to Germany with her latest conquest, Lord Halifax, where she arranged a meeting for him with Hermann Göring. As the foreign secretary in Neville Chamberlain's Conservative government, Halifax became a major advocate of appeasement towards Hitler's aims and ambitions.

If Stefan ever questioned his wife's occasional absences from the home, she was able to assure him that a private pupil in Paris required home tuition. Her occasional trips to London could be explained as an opportunity to meet her "dear friend, Stephanie".

By 1938, Auriole had no further use for Stephanie whose relationship with Rothermere had broken down when he changed tack and supported the rearmament of Britain in the face of growing concern over Germany's military might.

82

The arrival of Helen Douglas to be the governess to her children enabled Auriole to set the scene for her inevitable return to Berlin. The girl was perfect for the role. Helen cared for her daughters well, teaching them English and encouraging their musical talents. She was beautiful – remarkably so – and Auriole had feared that she would attract male admirers and demand to spend her free time with them. But Helen did not seem aware in the slightest of her looks and the impact they could have on men. She was planning to study medicine and her free time was spent walking in nature, playing the piano or attending church.

She had anticipated problems with Helen's family in Normandy, whose grandparents and uncle had met Odette many times. The occasion of Helen's first weekend with her family had brought the uncle to the château for the first time in many years when he drove Helen home. She noted his hesitation and apparent confusion when greeting her. But clearly nothing had been said to Helen and she had made many subsequent visits to her family.

The departure of Stefan to look for his sister in Berlin was a godsend. She had been wondering how to be rid of him when the call to Berlin came. Of course, she made a great show of being averse to him leaving her, and it was certain that Helen believed her to be so, accepting the changes to the girls' routine without demur. The girl was too soft-hearted and trusting. She would be easy to dispose of when the time came. She was able to arrange for her husband's arrest in Berlin, along with his sister. His death followed shortly after that.

The war clouds gathered over Europe and Auriole bided her time. Without the possible intrusion of Stefan, she was able to speak freely to her contacts in Paris and spend time there. She disconnected the telephone line to the château and installed a private connection to her contacts in Paris and Himmler. When the inevitable war came, France would quickly fall to the might of the German army. She would be needed to ensure that troublemakers were rooted out, any resistance suppressed and be useful to the *Abwehr* as well as the SD.

She made arrangements for her daughters. They would be taken to her parents in Alsace. Meanwhile, she left the girls in the care of Helen for long periods of time. As soon as the *drôle de guerre* was broken by the invasion of France and the Low Countries, Auriole returned to the château to collect her daughters. The girl, Helen, had been delighted to see her, no doubt assuming that they would all leave together for a place of safety. It had been difficult not to laugh in the foolish creature's face. She would be arrested when the Germans came and sent to one of the camps – Ravensbruck perhaps – where she might meet up with Gisela. She allowed herself a brief moment of humour at the thought of this, and of the girl being beaten by the guards, her lovely face bruised and torn. There was also the gardener. He had been paid to ensure that the Jews in her home were disposed of – he might also enjoy himself with Helen. This made her reflect as to why she despised the girl so much. She did not envy her beauty; she herself was still very attractive to men and looked much younger than her age. But perhaps it was on account of the memory of Helen's mother, Marie-Claude Dubois, who she knew had seen through her façade of friendship with Odette and could be her enemy yet.

It was the *Abwehr* who approached her. This was done discreetly through her former friend, Erika Canaris, who, learning that she was in Berlin, invited her to a musical soiree at the family villa. In the course of the evening, Wilhelm Canaris, who remained the head of the *Abwehr*, requested her presence in his study. It was now the end of November 1940 and Auriole's frustration that she had yet to be given an assignment was growing.

Following the occupation of France, Hitler was considering plans to invade Britain but many of his advisers were opposed to the idea due to the risks of crossing the channel. Canaris held the rank of admiral in the German navy and was aware of these risks; many German Navy ships had been lost in Denmark and Norway and they could not afford to lose more. Hitler was still hoping for a negotiated peace deal and was aware that many in Churchill's war cabinet supported this. He saw an invasion as a last resort but preparations had begun in case an invasion became necessary. The *Abwehr* had sent a succession of spies over to Britain by parachute drops and boat landings. Their mission had been to determine British preparedness for an invasion and assess coastal defences, as well as to demoralise the population by causing explosions in public places. The operation, named "Lena", had been an abject failure due to the incompetence of the spies. Many spoke poor English and had no idea of English customs. Most had been swiftly arrested – one still munching on German sausage – and were either imprisoned or "turned" and were now working for British intelligence.

The only useful information that Canaris had received from the bungled operation was that an organisation had been created in Britain at the behest of Winston Churchill called Special Operations Executive or SOE. Churchill had tasked Hugh Dalton, a member of the War Cabinet, to form an organisation which would send specially trained operatives into Europe to help local Resistance groups and conduct espionage and sabotage there. Canaris's plan was to send Auriole over to Britain with a new identity and for her to be recruited by SOE. She would then work as a double agent in France with the aim of breaking up the Resistance groups and sabotaging their operations. It was a bold plan and Auriole would have to catch the eye of those on the lookout for potential agents.

83

At the end of December, Auriole was taken by a submarine across the channel and rowed ashore in a dinghy, landing under the cliffs of Beachy Head in East Sussex. She carried a passport in the name of Aurelie Anne Duncan, born in Hastings in 1905 to a French mother and English father. Her parents were now dead and she had lost contact with other family members. She had worked as a governess to a family who recently emigrated to the USA and was currently unemployed.

For two weeks, Auriole made journeys by train around England. On each occasion, she carried *The Times* and busied herself doing the cryptic crosswords. She was still a very attractive woman and frequently caught the eye of male passengers. She picked him out before he could her. He wore a nondescript grey suit and a bowler hat, and carried an umbrella and a copy of *The Times* newspaper. In other words, he was a man on a mission doing his best not to attract attention. She made a great show of filling in the squares rapidly. Crosswords were easy for her; encryption had been part of her training with *Fräulein Doktor*.

He initiated the conversation after only a few minutes, 'I see you enjoy crosswords. *The Times* is a difficult one. I struggled with todays; it is devilish.'

'For me it is easy. It is a little hobby of mine.'

She said this in perfect English but with an intonation that was distinctly French.

He then responded in French, which he spoke quite well for an Englishman.

He asked her how she came to speak French and about her family. She gave him the story of a French mother who had met her father while he was working as a fisherman. His boat had been wrecked off the Normandy coast and she had helped with the rescue of the boat. *It made a good story*, she thought, *romantic too*.

'And what of your parents now?'

'They are both dead. My father's fishing boat sank in a storm off Hastings many years ago when I was a child and my mother died of cancer.'

'And do you have family in Britain?'

'None that I know of as my father was an only child. After he died, my mother took me to live with her family in Normandy. I lived there for ten years and when she died, I returned to England to work in a family as a governess to teach the children French, but they emigrated to America. I would have returned to Normandy, but of course, the war makes that impossible.'

'So, you know Normandy well?'

'Of course, it was my home.'

He asked her about her current employment and was clearly satisfied by her story of the family emigrating to America. He apologised for appearing inquisitive but asked her if she would be interested in finding another employment. She admitted to being very short of money since the loss of her previous employment and, yes, she would like to find work. He then produced a card with an address in an area of London she had never heard of: Lee Green in Lewisham. He explained that he would be at that address on Tuesday the following week. If she was interested in work that could help their countries defeat the Nazis, she was welcome to be present. He left the train at the next station.

She stayed on the train for a further two stations and then alighted to take a train back to her lodgings in Eastbourne. Once there, she poured herself a glass of malt whisky and congratulated herself on an excellent day's work.

She took a train to Victoria Station and from there a bus to Lewisham. She walked from Lewisham to Lee Green along dirty snow-banked streets. It was bitterly cold and she cursed the threadbare coat and shabby shoes she had thought would be consistent with her respectable but impoverished persona. The address on the card proved to be an unassuming mid-terrace house of the Victorian era, with a front door of peeling green paint. She rang the bell and the door was opened by a woman of around her age – well, the age she really was.

'Miss Duncan? Please come in. Would you like tea?'

My first test, she thought to herself.

'Yes, thank you, with milk and one sugar.'

She was ushered into a small unprepossessing room, where a small coal fire struggled to raise the temperature above freezing. A single light bulb hung on a wire from the ceiling, casting a pool of yellow light onto the floor. The walls were papered in columns of straggly flowers of indefinable genus, and the ceiling and upper walls were stained with tobacco smoke. The chipped green skirting boards added to the general air of dilapidation. Whatever the outfit they were running from here, its aim was certainly not to impress applicants. She thought this as she checked her purse. Her papers were there with a passport consistent with her identity card, but she would need to be convincing with her back story. This did not worry her; most of her life had been a lie.

The tea was brought to her by a tall thin man with a prominent Adam's apple. He introduced himself as Archie Moore and began by thanking her for offering to help. He asked her whether she would prefer to speak in English or French and she replied "in French". He spoke the language quite well. He then asked her a question in German. *Another trap*; she looked confused.

He continued in French, explaining that she would have to undertake a period of training and she may be considered unsuitable, which would be the job of the experts to decide. He smiled as he said this and then asked to see her passport and identity card. She also gave him the reference from the eternally grateful Sinclair family for her excellent tuition of their daughters. He asked her a few questions about her childhood in Hastings. She convinced him with a few vague memories of playing "hide and seek" among the fish huts and visiting the smugglers' caves with her father. She gave a better account of her time in Normandy. He terminated the interview by telling her she would receive a letter to the address she had given them within the week, but that before she left, Miss Burrell, who met her earlier, would measure her for a uniform and there was a paper for her to sign.

He left the room and immediately "Miss Burrell" entered. She wondered if the woman had been eavesdropping on the conversation. Miss Burrell informed her that a uniform in the rank of an officer would be made for her and that she would be paid accordingly. After she had been measured up, Miss Burrell produced a form.

'This is the Official Secrets Act which I must ask you to sign. Everything you have spoken of today with Colonel Moore is secret, as well as this address. From now on, you must maintain utmost discretion in who you meet and what you say. The training will not be easy for a woman who is unused to combat or extreme physical exertion. You will find yourself tested to the limits. You will learn to do what you may find abhorrent.'

She means killing. Auriole struggled to maintain the façade of a willing and receptive recruit. She wanted to laugh in her face.

'This work requires very particular qualities, talents, if you like. If you fail, there is no disgrace.'

I won't fail.

She thanked Miss Burrell, who then ushered her out through the front door.

A week later, she boarded a train at Euston Station. Her ticket took her to a second-class compartment, where she found another woman and two men already seated. She guessed they would be fellow recruits but knew better than to initiate a conversation. At Crewe, they changed to the train for Fort William where they were met by an army truck. The driver checked their papers as they boarded. Two hours later, in the cold of the late January night, they climbed out of the truck in front of a large country house.

'Welcome to Arisaig,' said the driver.

The house, they learned, was the former shooting lodge of a local laird, quaintly named Morag's Nook. She was to share a room with the other woman, Vicky Martin. The latter excused her poor French as due to the fact that her French father had died when she was young and she had spent all her life in England, except for a time at finishing school in Switzerland.

Auriole welcomed this; a native French speaker would soon detect her Alsace roots. A young lieutenant greeted them and told them to come down to the bar as soon as they had unpacked. Once they were all gathered in the warm smoke-filled room, the Lieutenant, who introduced himself as Lieutenant Murray, explained that he would be in charge of the course. They were to have supper and after supper, they would meet again in the bar and he would go through the programme with them.

The bar was an open bar and she noted how her companions made free with the whisky, as they were encouraged to do. She made her double last, feigning a slight headache. The conversations of her companions grew more voluble. She thought them fools. They wouldn't last ten minutes in the "field". Vicky became flirtatious with the men and she noted the Lieutenant's watchful eye on her as she giggled and jostled playfully with them.

The physical training began the following day. This was going to be the most difficult part of the programme for her. She was nearly fifty and her joints were not as supple as the others, who were all in their twenties and thirties. But by the end of the two weeks, she could crawl through the undergrowth, climb the hills, swing on ropes across rivers and fashion a raft to cross the loch. She could scale a wall and enter a house without detection having disconnected the electricity. But she was pleased when that part of the course was finished and knew by the attitude of the instructors that they were satisfied with her progress.

She excelled at weapons handling of course. The pistols were no mystery to her; she had used a .45 Colt and .38 many times. She made a good show of ignorance and won their praise as a quick learner. The Sten gun was unfamiliar to her but she appreciated its usefulness as a weapon; it could be stripped down to small components for concealment and transport and quickly reassembled. Its firepower was devastating. She could strip any weapon, assemble it, load it and fire it, from the hip, shoulder or prone in seconds using the double-tap system – firing two shots to be certain of getting a kill. She excelled at target practice and never missed the menacing silhouettes that appeared in random and rapid succession on the practice range – a film-set-style street around the outhouses of the lodge.

The following week was spent on explosives training. There was much that was new to her; the use of plastics had moved on from the nitrols of the Great War. She enjoyed the feel of the oily putty with its distinct almond smell. She was the first to successfully detonate and destroy the rail track made available for them by the West Highland Line to practise on. Close combat was also easy for her; she knew how to kill a man or woman and had done so many times. She loved the feel of the knife in her hand and knew where to apply it to maximum effect and death. The final week was training in wireless operation and map reading, as well as the use of codes to encode and decode when receiving and transmitting. She found this interesting. The technology around radio had improved significantly since her training with *Fräulein Doktor*.

At the end of the four weeks, she was interviewed by Lieutenant Murray and two others who did not give their names. She was told she had done well and had been accepted as an agent of the SOE. She was now ready to proceed to parachute training, which they explained was necessary as she would be dropped from a plane into enemy territory. She packed her suitcase and joined one of the men who had travelled north with her. She did not ask about Vicky or the other man but suspected they had not made the grade. She did not feel anything for them – failure was anathema to her – but her companion volunteered the information that they had both been taken to what was called a "cooler centre", where they would be taught to forget what they had learned over the past four weeks.

After three jumps – two from a plane and one from a balloon – she was sent to the final stage of training. She had been looking forward to this. She was given a new identity and set to tail a "resistance" character around the streets of Southampton. She had to identify possible dead letter drops and rendezvous points for fictional agents. On the afternoon of the third day, she was arrested and taken to an "interrogation centre". She stood up well to the questioning and never dropped her alias. She deflected the questions and kept up plausible denials of the accusations. She passed with flying colours. All that remained were a few weeks of lectures on the ranks of the German military and the operations of the *Abwehr* and SD. As if she didn't know!

She was recommended for immediate deployment with a cover name of Michelle Dupres as an explosives expert and radio operator, or pianist, as the latter was known. *How appropriate*, she thought to herself.

At the end of July 1941, Auriole and her suitcase wireless were dropped onto a field near the port of Cherbourg. After burying her parachute with the spade that had been clipped to her leg, she made her way through a wooded area where she was met by her contact, René Bertrand of the *Cabosse* group. She followed him to a rundown farm building close to the field where three other members of the group greeted her. The plan was to blow up the rail track linking Cherbourg to Caen the following night. This would hinder the German plans to fortify the port and the beaches around it, as the track was used to carry munitions and materials to the site.

On the night determined for the sabotage, she secured the plasticine-like explosive to a fog signal on the track, she wired up the detonator and wound the coiled fuse into the bushes where the group would wait. The train was due to pass at 21:05. At 20:55, an anonymous caller informed the signal room at Le Molay-Littry Station that the train should be held at the station until 21:15. Under the instruction of agent "Michelle" the group were instructed to adjust the position of the explosive. Whilst they were doing so the explosive detonated and all were killed. The track remained intact and the Cherbourg train passed unscathed.

It was assumed that the newly-arrived agent had died in the explosion. But agent Michelle made her way unobserved to Paris later that night. The SOE had a dangerous new recruit.

For the next six months, Auriole was engaged in identifying SOE agents and Resistance groups. She found a way of blocking their transmissions and replacing them with ambiguous ones of her own devising. But her next and most effective opportunity to disrupt the Allies' plans came in the spring of 1942.

She had returned to Berlin at the end of December after celebrating Christmas in Alsace with her children and invited herself to the Canaris family home.

They were both pleased to see her. Wilhelm congratulated her on her infiltration of the SOE and spoke to her of intelligence that the Allies were expected to launch an operation in the summer of

1942. The operation would land an invasion force of infantry and armoured vehicles at some point on the Normandy coast to establish a beachhead from which they would engage with the German armies. General von Rundstedt expected the enemy to have superiority in the air but the battle would be won on the beaches. He required Auriole to find out where the Allies planned to land and supply false intelligence to the Allies regarding the coastal defences in that area. An agent of *Abwehr* was already in the area and would be looking out for her. Their contact would be through a local fish shop with a beach towel on a bench as a signal for either to go to the shop.

In February 1942, Auriole travelled to Normandy. Under the name of Marie-Claire Darnier, she rented a room in a rundown hotel in the seaside town of Sainte-Marguerite-Sur-Mer. She told the hotelier that she was recently widowed and wished to spend time alone walking the coastal paths to remember the happy times she and her husband had spent there before the war.

After six tedious weeks of walking the windswept Normandy coast, she noted an apparent holidaymaker on a beach near Dieppe. This aroused her suspicions, as the time of year and weather were not conducive to a beach holiday. She took to walking the path every other day to avoid suspicion but observed that the same person was on the beach with her camera on those days. She tailed the woman and saw that she also spent a lot of time around the harbour area. The woman was staying in a rented apartment close to the port and returned there every evening at around 9 p.m. after eating in the hotel. She picked the lock of the apartment door and waited for her to return. Once the woman was in the room, she moved silently from her hiding place as the woman removed her shoes. Before the woman was aware of her presence, the stiletto knife was at her throat.

'Who are you working for?' she asked.

'Nobody, I am just here on holiday.'

'In March? with a British camera?' As she said this she slit the underside of the woman's chin lightly with the knife. The woman reached up to staunch the flow of blood.

'No, it is true. I am here on holiday.'

'With friends?'

'No, I am here alone.'

She moved the knife up to the woman's face. 'Unless you tell me what you are doing here, I will remove first your ears and then your nose, and the last your eyes will see of this world before I kill you will be my laughing face.'

'All right, all right, just take the knife away.'

She knew her not to be SOE. Their agents would not have made such overt blunders, exposing themselves to detection.

'I am with Naval Intelligence to look at the beaches here.'

'And the photographs, the holiday snaps?'

'For the invasion in the summer. Please don't cut me. Please, I have a daughter.'

'And I have two.' She calmly slit her throat. The woman slid to the floor choking and moaning. She waited until she was certain she was dead and then removed the film from the camera. She checked her pockets and cupboards in the room. Tucked inside a cigarette packet was a piece of paper with the woman's code name and in the wardrobe a radio transmitter.

She set up the radio on the table and tapped in a message from "Dorothy".

She omitted the fact of the German gun positions on the cliffs and informed the Intelligence Agency that the beach gradient and terrain were suitable for tanks. She informed that Dieppe was not heavily defended and the beaches in the vicinity were suitable for landing infantry and armoured vehicles. She had photographs to support this and would ensure that they would be delivered to London.

She shut down the radio and packed it up. She locked the door behind her and took the key. It could be days before the body was found. The following morning she threw the key into the harbour and placed her beach towel on a bench nearby. Later that day she went to the fish shop and asked for *Morue*. She took her time choosing a fish and then, having made her choice, quickly placed the film roll inside its mouth. She informed the shopkeeper that she had changed her mind and replaced the fish. She watched as another "customer" entered the shop and selected the fish. The *Abwehr* agent was a double agent. He would ensure that the film roll reached Churchill, and the Allies would be fooled into believing that Dieppe was a suitable host for an invasion.

She returned to Berlin to report to Canaris. He was pleased with her work, but as always with her employer, she sensed ambivalence in his attitude towards her success. She had heard rumours that the spies he had sent to Britain in 1940 were there on account of their incompetence and that he had hoped they would fail. But she also knew that it was not so in her situation. This was interesting and something that could be useful to her in the future. But for the moment, she relished her success and looked forward to another victory for Germany. Her pleasure at being back in Berlin increased significantly when she found her former lover, Reinhard Heydrich, was also in Berlin, without his wife and a guest of the Canaris family. Erika arranged a musical soiree and Auriole was asked to be the accompanist. They found time to speak in private.

'Auriole, *liebchen*, or should I address you as the *Führer's* favourite spy?'

'And you, now Protector of Bohemia and Moravia. We have come far, have we not?'

'Indeed. And now that I remember, after you left Berlin in 1930, you lived in Normandy as the wife of a Jew and as *Schlössherrin* of the Château des Tilleuls, or so I am told. But more interestingly, I had reason to be in Normandy last year. It was in March, following an assassination attempt on the life of my cousin who is *Oberfeldkommandur* in Caen. There was a reception and music recital held in my honour at the cathedral in Bayeux. I was pleased to find that our friend Karl von Werstein was to play the cello, and with him was a most beautiful young woman to accompany him on the piano.'

'Indeed. And who was this young woman?'

'A French girl, Gabrielle, or some such, but I rather felt she was more to him than just his pianist.'

'And what did she look like, this girl?'

'Of medium height, with a beautiful figure and face and red hair and green eyes. I would have liked to fuck her but I feared our friend Karl already had that pleasure and would not be prepared to share her.'

It was hard to feign indifference; he knew her too well.

'Do I detect jealousy or something more than that? I remember how you tried all your womanly wiles to get him into your bed but I also know that you failed.'

'What was Karl doing in Normandy?'

'He is a *Feldkommandur* and lives in your château.'

'So, this young woman lives there too, I presume. How surprising. I did not think she had it in her.'

'What is this young woman to you?'

'Say nothing of this to anyone. I will deal with her.'

85

Auriole waited until her daughters were back at school before returning to Normandy. The assassination of her former lover in Prague had upset her more than she thought possible. No emotion, however, could surpass the hatred she now felt for her former governess. The thought of Helen in Karl's arms, arms which she had longed to have around her, naked and in bed. He was the most beautiful man she had ever wanted. She was sure they were lovers; his wife was dead and Helen was available and she hoped it was no more than that. But the Karl she knew was not a man who used women lightly. She feared the worst.

She rented a room in Villers-Bocage. The town was distant enough from Caen for her to be anonymous but close enough to the château for her to spy on Helen. She wore a black wig and spectacle frames. The tram from Villers-Bocage to Caen stopped in the centre of Sainte-Geneviève-sur-Orne. She alighted there each day and took a walk along the road towards the château. She did not dare to get too close to her former home, but watched the vehicles that passed through the gates.

She noted that Helen – and there was no doubt it was Helen – rode a black horse every day into the woods and the fields beyond. It was September and the sun was getting lower in the sky. She knew what to do. She set off at midday from Caen and followed a narrow track from the city to the field where Helen would ride. She took a large mirror with her. She positioned herself in undergrowth facing the sun. After a while she heard the pounding of hooves and as soon as the horse approached her hiding place, she held the mirror up. The reflection of the sun's rays off the mirror caused a blinding flash. The horse reared in terror, bolted, and Helen fell to the ground.

She waited a few minutes and when Helen remained motionless, she went over to her body. She was not yet quite dead but deeply unconscious and bleeding from a wound to her head. She dragged her body into the undergrowth and covered it with branches from the woods, giving her a kick in the stomach as she did so.

PART EIGHT

Helen

86

Liebchen,

My darling wife, I write to you from Stalingrad where we are surrounded by the Soviet armies. I fear I will never hold you in my arms again. We are to fight on by order of the Führer who will not permit our forces to break out and re-join the armies to the west of us. He will not permit us to retreat from the Volga, so we will stand and fight as good soldiers. But my men are weary, cold, hungry and much depleted in numbers and we have no hope of supplies from the Luftwaffe. The dispatch rider will take this letter to Berlin and I can only hope it reaches your precious hands. Please know, my love, that I long to be in your arms again, but should I die, please love my children and know that my house and land are yours – my family is your family.

Your loving husband,
Karl

I read the letter several times, stroking the page as I did so. The thought that the page had been in his hands made me weep. It was the only tangible connection to him that I had. It was now February and I had only just received the letter. The news from the Eastern Front told of the imminent defeat of the *Wehrmacht* and of possible surrender by Field Marshal Paulus. Hitler had awarded General Paulus the title Field Marshal more as a poisoned chalice than as an honour, in full knowledge that no Field Marshal in German history had ever surrendered. The 6th Army was now trapped in the *Kessel,* surrounded by divisions of the Soviet army. The men were starving and freezing to death but General Paulus had been ordered to fight on.

Dead or alive but in captivity – either could be the fate of my husband.

I took comfort in caring for my friends and in music. The family in the underground room were enduring the cold winter. I had been able to keep them supplied with food and water but feared for their health in such confinement. The teenage son was still hidden in the presbytery of Église Saint-Pierre, but he was well and I was able to pass messages from him to his mother and sisters.

Roundups of Jews continued and there were times when I was tormented by my failure to do more to help. The *Oberfeldkommandur* was solicitous of my well-being and made regular visits to the château. Damian now came once a week. News of Ellana and Ruth was always welcome, but with so few now resident at the château, regular supplies of milk were not justified, and both of us were conscious of the need to be wary of causing suspicion. I had been able to visit Stefan's parents and was pleased to find them comfortable and safe with the Notre-Dame nuns.

An air of apathy had settled over France in this third year of occupation: people no longer anticipated an imminent rescue invasion by the Allies and many were resigned to the possibility of permanent occupation by Germany. The resistants were still active and more united than ever in their goals, but hunger and the brutality of the reprisals suffered by civilians in the wake of their activities caused most of the population to consider that just "getting by" and staying alive were more important than open hostility to the occupiers.

In November 1942, the Germans had occupied the so-called Zone Libre. Now the whole of France was openly and entirely under the control of the German Reich.

I played the piano and discovered among Stefan's scores Schubert's *Nacht und Träume*. Stefan had written the words by Matthäus von Collin to the cello score. It described the radiance of dreams and the comfort of night, which resonated with me. All I had of him were my dreams. I played the accompaniment every night and imagined him beside me playing his cello.

I rode Bathory and Doucette every day and listened to Radio Londres at 9 p.m. every evening. There were often jokes against the German occupiers. The latter had their own radio station, Radio Paris, which they had sequestered after the invasion. The BBC entertainers mocked the station using the tune of a popular song *La Cucaracha* with the words "Radio Paris *ment* (lies) Radio Paris *ment*, Radio Paris *est allemande*". I listened to Radio Paris and heard the voice of Jacques Doriot advocating the destruction of Britain. His catch phrase was *"England, like 'Carthage, must be destroyed'"*, in a paraphrase of Cato. I was surprised to hear Maurice Chevalier singing his latest success *Notre Espoir* which was understood to refer to the hope of a German victory in Stalingrad. *Maman* and I had enjoyed his *chansons* in the past; now I would regard him in a different light.

At the end of February 1943, I learned of the defeat of the German army at Stalingrad following the surrender by General Paulus. After months of fierce fighting, only 91,000 out of the 6th Army of 220,000 had survived, and most of those were now in Soviet captivity. I clung to the hope that Karl would be one of those who survived.

In April, a motorcycle dispatch rider arrived at the château with a letter bearing the insignia of German High Command. It was addressed to *Frau* von Werstein. Lotti took receipt of the letter and brought it to me. I feared to open it and left it to Lotti to read and translate. The letter was from Field Marshal Erich von Manstein and it informed me that my husband had been taken captive in Stalingrad but had been released in exchange for the nephew of Josef Stalin, whose own capture my husband had effected.

Hitler had been outraged by this. Having lost Stalingrad to Stalin, he had felt that Stalin's nephew would have provided some conciliation and comfort in defeat. It was said that for the first time in his war, Hitler had suffered a defeat for which there was no compensation. Manstein had overridden his objections, ignored the ranting communication he had received from the *Führer* and bargained for the release of his esteemed general as well as his surviving men. Manstein mentioned nothing of his circumventing of the *Führer's* wishes in the letter, but assured me that General von Werstein was well, preparing for another battle and hoped to return to his beloved wife as soon as possible.

Lotti held me in her arms.

'There is hope and we must try to hold on to that. I fear the war will be lost and who knows what the peace will bring for such as us. But today, we can celebrate the *Kommandant's* survival and that of his men.'

I listened to the wireless and learned of the uprising in the Warsaw ghetto, where the Jews who remained there had learned that deportation from the ghetto was part of the Nazi extermination plan. On the eve of Passover on the 19th of April, SS and police units entered the ghetto intending to deport the Jews from it but found the streets deserted as all had gone into hiding and were armed. Although vastly outnumbered and outgunned, the Jews had held out against the Germans for a month, defying the machine guns, flame throwers and grenades that were thrown into the buildings.

In July, I learned of the fierce fighting close to the city of Kursk where a tank battle was underway. It was reported that this was Hitler's final throw of the dice in his war on the Eastern Front. Despite the huge tanks the Germans had at their disposal they were no match for the smaller but more mobile Soviet tanks. The massive reserves of fighting men that the Soviets could draw on outnumbered the *Wehrmacht*. Hitler was forced to call up men over fifty years of age and members of the Hitler Youth. As the battle for Kursk moved into August, Hitler ordered a retreat to defensive positions and then deployment to Italy, where the Allies were landing in Sicily and the south. The battle for the Eastern Front was lost, as was the battle in North Africa. The net was closing in on Hitler, but as the wireless news cautioned, he would be more dangerous if forced into a corner and should not be underestimated.

Lotti brought news that panzer divisions were being moved to the Western Front, as Hitler now feared an imminent invasion on the channel coast. She had seen the casualty lists and the *Kommandant's* name was not on them. She felt confident that the *Kommandant* would return to Normandy.

He returned in October. I heard the staff car as it drew up in front of the château steps. I waited for the officer to open the door for him and ran into his arms. He was thinner, much thinner, and his face pale and drawn but he was alive and that was all that mattered. After he had bathed and eaten, I took him to the bedroom. For a while we lay silently together. It was over a year since he had left for the battlefield and I felt tentative in his presence. I could not ask him about the battles he had fought in, the death and destruction he had witnessed and certainly not of the defeats the *Wehrmacht* had suffered in that time. Perhaps he would now be less tolerant of my activities, even regard me as the enemy. But he turned to me and stroked my hair, kissing me gently on the lips, and then moving over me, he stroked my breasts, suckling gently on my nipples. I pulled his lean hard body to me and cried with joy as I felt him deep inside me. Later, after we had slept in each other's arms, he took me again. This time he was less gentle, turning me over to take me with greater force and urgency, as though he had demons to exorcise and only with me could he find release from what tormented him. Later he cried and spoke to me about the war.

'*Liebchen*, I am sorry if I hurt you. The thought of being with you again kept me strong but there were times when I thought that I could never be the man you knew again. You cannot imagine how it was at Stalingrad and after there, at Kursk: the smell of charred bodies, the screams of the men trapped inside their burning tanks and the men crushed beneath the tanks as they ran from the flames. The Russian tanks and infantry came in endless swarms; they had infinite numbers of reserves as their country is vast. Whenever we thought we had the better of them, more came at us.

'We burned Stalingrad around the people who lived there. Stalin would not permit them to leave. Their soldiers would fight all the harder, he said, knowing that civilians remained in the city. They are a strong people and used to war and hardship and it was we who were the aggressors. They were defending their country and I admire their resilience and courage. The women too, they fight and die with the men. We captured one and she spat at and fought with the guards. They wanted to have her to amuse themselves with but I kept her with me and, *liebchen*, I am sorry, but I took her to my bed. She was with me for two weeks. Forgive me but in battle it is necessary to have some release and this woman gave me what I needed. It was the same for her, she said. Svetlana was her name. We exchanged her for some of our men after Kursk. She is the daughter of one of their generals.'

I felt such a powerful surge of anger and jealousy that I thought I would faint. A feeling of nausea gripped me, bile rose in my throat and I gagged slightly; this was something I had not considered could happen, ever. He was my husband and had vowed to be faithful to me. This woman had made such an impression on him that he had bedded her, not once but many times presumably, without a thought as to how I, his wife, would feel about him doing so. He was not the man I knew before, the man I had believed him to be. That man loved me above all others and had promised to forsake all others. How lightly had he taken his marriage vows? I left the bed silently, knowing that my heart had been replaced by wormwood, a bitterness that would not be expunged now supplanted the love I had once felt for him.

I dressed and left the room. He had fallen into a deep sleep, no doubt because he felt relieved of the guilt that had burdened him for however long it had been since he had lain with the woman. I felt defiled. He had used me, no more and no less as the spoils of war than the woman Svetlana. And he had used me again today, to expunge his guilt. Visions of my husband with the woman tormented me. I tried to dispel them but could not.

I wanted to be home, with my parents, far from this place of deceit and violence. I went to the stable and saddled up Doucette. I rode through the woods to the stream where he had so tenderly made love to me. And there I wept: for the life I had known before, with my parents at my home in Berwickshire; for my innocence when I arrived in Normandy; for the babies I had carried and lost; and now this lost love of mine. I would never be able to erase the image of my husband with that woman.

I returned to the château. I fed and settled the horses for the evening. I went into the kitchen and told the cook that from that day I wished to be regarded as no more than a domestic help at the château. I would shop, clean, cook and serve. I would attend to the needs of my friends in the underground room but would be prepared to find another refuge for them if necessary. I then went to the nursery, where I made up the bed and moved my few items of clothing into the cupboard there.

He had apparently slept through to the morning. I had been mucking out the stables when he rose and he was already at his desk in the library when I returned from exercising the horses. I went immediately into the kitchen and started to help the cook. He explained that the *Kommandant* had guests for a meal that evening. I said I would also serve the meal to the guests.

I avoided him for the remainder of the day and he left the château at noon. When he returned, it was in the company of the *Oberfeldkommandur* with his mistress, another officer and the young women who had dined with him previously.

I wore my oldest dress, the one I had worn when I first arrived at the château. I served the food with competence and indifference. I did not get riled by the peremptory tone of the women when they complained about trivial issues. My demeanour was pleasant and appropriately servile, but inwardly I seethed with a bitterness that was as alien to me as the regard I once had for the man who was my husband. And I despised myself for this.

I locked myself in my room after the meal and cried all night. Early the following morning, I went to the underground room to attend to the needs of the people there. I felt acutely the loss of Leah and Raisa; their good counsel would have been so welcome at this time. But the woman and girls were pleased to see me and assured me that they were content just to be safe. The mother fretted about her son but I promised to visit him that day. There had been no news of the men who had been with them in the Erharts' apartment, including the woman's husband

During the next day and those that followed, I kept my distance from him. He was busy in the library and made frequent visits to Caen. I had no difficulty in imagining that he would be seeking his pleasure with one or other of the women who had been at the meal that day, since that was the man I now knew him to be.

It was the *Oberfeldkommandur* who came to talk to me. He arrived without ceremony and came into the kitchen. He took my hand and asked me to sit down. He apologised for his poor command of French and startled me by addressing me as Helen.

'My dear Helen, we need you to forgive your husband. He has been with me every day since his return and is broken by your coldness to him. He loves you and for him there could never be another woman to equal you. I have never seen a man so remorseful. What he did has hurt you and perhaps he should not have shared his guilt with you. There can be too much truth. But believe me, he is truly sorry and his only wish is to be with you again.'

'But you cannot possibly understand how I feel. He took this woman to his bed and enjoyed her company. Perhaps this is the man he is: one who takes a woman lightly to his bed and then burdens his wife with his guilt. From my point of view, he is a man who enjoys sleeping with the enemy.'

The *Oberfeldkommandur* laughed.

'Helen, you are not the enemy. And you have proved that. But neither are you a traitor to your country. War makes us all strange bedfellows. You are loved by the General and he is a good man. Please find it in your heart to take him back.'

'And if I do, how will I not believe that he is capable of the same again, with another woman, here or wherever next your *Führer* decides to do battle.'

'Helen, we are Germans and we do the bidding of our *Führer*. This war will soon be over but however it ends, our lives have been altered irrevocably. I do not know if my wife and my children will be alive. The RAF bombs our cities night and day, but no more than we have done to your cities. Göring promised that no RAF planes would ever reach the cities of Germany, but as we have discovered, this was just another of his boasts, as insubstantial as the *Luftwaffe* planes and their pilots that now lie on the seabed of the English Channel.'

'You did not answer my question. Why should I trust him now?'

'Because he loves you more than he loves himself. I fear he will lose his mind if this continues.'

'Are you blackmailing me? That I must take him back or else have him on my conscience forever?'

'It is he who has you on his conscience, for the wrong that he did to you.'

'And if I take him back?'

'We will have a recital, as in the days before.'

'I will think about it.'

'And do not worry, your secret name is safe with me. Remember that I am your proxy husband.'

He smiled reassuringly as he said this.

Of course, he had known. Why else would there have been such secrecy for the marriage?

'I have been to Scotland. There are many with your hair and eyes in your country. As a boy, I stayed with a family in Edinburgh who were relatives of my mother. It was an exchange arrangement. The boy came to my family in Dortmund one summer and I went to his family the next year. They were very kind to me but I could not understand a word of the Scottish tongue so we spoke German. My own mother was not happy when I returned, that my English had not improved. The Scottish boy returned speaking perfect German.'

I smiled and repeated that I would consider his suggestion.

88

We walked together in the woods every day. This was my idea. I still did not feel I could share his bed but thought it good for us to be together. I could not speak at these times, as the distance between us had become so great that I could not find the words. My mind still dwelt on the image of him with the other woman and I could not dispel the anger and humiliation that this image invoked.

Walking helped to distract me from my sadness and I took pleasure in the birdsong, the sight of the squirrels in the trees and the warmth of the autumn sun on my face. It was now late in October and the woods were glorious in their red and gold tints. The leaves fluttered to the ground in the gentle breeze and crunched beneath our feet. It was still warm by day but already the nights were longer and colder and I feared for the family in the underground room. This would be their second winter there. How many more would they have to endure?

He spoke first, '*Liebchen*, how long must I stay apart from you at night? I cannot bear to see you so hurt, so angry with me. You do not look at me but look down as if you cannot bear to look into my eyes. If you did, you would see a man who loves you above all others, and whose only wish is for his wife to return to him with forgiveness in her heart.'

I found the words to reply, 'You speak of forgiveness as if it were an easy matter, something conjured by a magician from the ether and given substance by the craven, who once forgiven will commit the same offence again. I would liken it to those kings of England who were merciless in murdering their subjects but had their priest to forgive them their crimes, or sins I should say, and who then committed the same crimes the following day. Perhaps this is not a good example. Perhaps I should substitute king and murderer for husband and adulterer.'

I felt myself flush with anger as I said this.

I continued, 'I have only known two men: one who brutally raped me and another who betrayed me with another woman. How do I know that you do not dream of her at night? Imagine her next to you? Wish that you had not married me? And also that I know it was not just once that you lay with her but many times. My father would not have done such a thing to my mother. He loved her too much to wound her as you have wounded me. I feel my life cannot be the same again.'

Suddenly, I could not continue to speak to him in this way. Anguish and despair caused tears to flow down my cheeks. I felt faint with emotion, more desolate than I had ever felt in my life. In a moment his arms were around me and I was sobbing into his chest. He lifted me gently onto a fallen tree and we sat for while holding each other. He kissed me gently, first my eyes until my tears stopped, then my lips and then, after laying me onto the bed of leaves, he slowly undressed me. When he entered me I clung to him, looking deeply into his eyes, seeing only love and his need for me. He was forgiven and I would never deny my love for him again.

After a while, he spoke, '*Liebchen*, I see you have been playing Schubert's *Nacht und Träume*. There is a beautiful arrangement for piano and cello. We shall play it together tonight.'

'That would make me very happy. The *Oberfeldkommandur* suggested that we have another recital. I should like that.'

'The *Oberfeldkommandur* has an excellent tenor voice. Perhaps he should sing while you accompany him on the piano. The words of the song are most beautiful.'

'He called me by my name, Helen.'

'Of course, and he has a great fondness and admiration for you. And before you ask, he does not know of your activities. He would not wish to know.'

I leaned into him as we walked and ached with love.

89

We played all evening together. He explained the words of the song, which was about a man yearning for the dreams he had had and wished to return to them. He likened this yearning to his own, to return to me, to be taken back by me.

'"That, when I waked, I cried to dream again",' I quoted.

'That is your Mr Shakespeare, is it not?'

'Yes, Caliban's speech in *The Tempest*. It is a beautiful speech, especially from a character so malevolent, but it always haunted me to dream of something so wonderful that you cry on waking to be back in that dream.'

'*Herr* Goebbels is a great admirer of Shakespeare. He calls him a genius and the works of Shakespeare and Mr George Bernard Shaw are now the only permitted British writers to be read in Germany. The Hitler Youth has Shakespeare weeks during which the plays are read and enacted. *The Merchant of Venice* is a particular favourite.'

This surprised me until I remembered the character of Shylock.

Later that night, I told him of George's letter warning me that Auriole had been seen in Normandy in September. Both of us were now certain that someone had deliberately caused Bathory's panic and this had been done in an attempt to harm me.

'But why should she wish to harm me?'

'She will suspect that you know who she really is. Perhaps at this time, this is not so dangerous for her but perhaps in another time, it will be.'

'You mean, if Germany is not victorious? But I still do not understand, unless of course, she murdered Odette.'

'Which I am sure she is capable of having done. Auriole Ritter is a spy. She worked with Heydrich and now she works for Himmler as well as for the *Abwehr*. But there is also another reason why she would hate you, which I dare not tell you lest your face goes as red as the autumn leaves and you beat me with your hairbrush.'

'And what is that reason?'

'She wanted me in her bed... But she was not successful.'

'You are safe from the hairbrush.'

I rolled on top him and he held my hips as he thrust deeply into me. I cried when I came and afterwards lay on his chest listening to his heartbeat, and then I slept peacefully for the first time since his return.

90

In December, my husband was ordered to join *Generalfeldmarschall* Erwin Rommel on a tour of inspection of Hitler's Atlantic Wall, the defensive line of fortifications which stretched from the coast of Norway to the sea border with Spain. He would be away for some time he said. I kissed him farewell but was saddened by the occurrence that morning of my monthly bleed. I hoped beyond all else to have a child by him, but, as I reasoned, this was only the first month since our reunion and there would be other times.

Rommel himself came to the château to meet with my husband. I felt in awe of his presence; even the Allies admired him, calling him the Desert Fox. I understood him to be a man like my husband: honourable and loyal to Germany, regardless of who was in power in their beloved country. I showed him around the château and we spoke of music and horses. As they departed, he thanked me for my hospitality, bowing to me as he said so and expressing the wish that we would join his family in Germany for a holiday when the war was over. I found myself wishing for the same.

But life under the Occupation was more difficult than ever. There was no longer any pretence that France was self-governing. The Vichy government was totally discredited as no more than a puppet collaborationist regime and France was now a colony of the Reich, to be stripped of its wealth and natural resources, all of which were shipped to Germany. French men were enslaved in Germany as part of the compulsory labour scheme. Women who were arrested as resistants were either shot along with the men or deported to

Ravensbruck. Many were sent to work in brothels for the *Wehrmacht*. There were arrests and roundups by the *gendarmes* every day as they obeyed the orders from the Centre for Jewish Affairs in Paris that they fulfil their quota of 100,000 Jews to be deported to the East.

The following day, I received a letter from my husband. He wrote of how much he loved and missed me but also that the inspection of the Atlantic Wall would take some time. Rommel had not been satisfied with defences and it would be some months before the fortifications were to his satisfaction.

As I read this, I thought about how the information could benefit the Allies. Was my husband being deliberately indiscreet or did he trust me to keep this information to myself?

PART NINE

Auriole

91

So, she is alive! Why is she not dead? Auriole was spending a week in Normandy before leaving for her next assignment. On a whim, she decided to take the train from Paris to Caen to look at the château. Once the war was over, she intended to take possession of it again, and she relished the thought of taking a recent memory of it to Britain. She saw Helen at the window of the nursery and later riding into the woods on the big horse. It was too late to repeat her previous attempt to kill her but she had another idea. It was time Helen was exposed for what she was: an enemy of the Reich.

An anonymous phone call to the *Gestapo* in Caen alerted them to the presence of a British woman spy at the Château des Tilleuls.

She was dropped by parachute the following day close to the shore in a remote area of the west coast of Scotland. An inflatable dingy was dropped after her and she treaded the freezing water until it inflated. There was a change of clothing in the dingy and a sealed waterproof bag containing English money as well as some Scottish pound notes, her passport and papers. There was also a camera and a gun. Her task was to discover where the expected Allied invasion force would set off from and where it was likely to land.

She was in familiar territory now, not far from the SOE training school. She punctured the dingy with her stiletto knife and pushed it back into the sea, where the tide took it. She buried the parachute and her wet clothing in the sand and made her way across fields in the dark to the nearest bus stop. The bus took her to Fort William. It was 7 a.m. and other passengers regarded her with weary indifference. At Fort William, she took the train to London. She changed compartments a few times during the journey to avoid her face becoming familiar. She was certain she was not being tailed. At Euston, she took a bus to Victoria Station and then boarded a train to Dover where she rented a room at a boarding house close to the port.

Her alias was again that of an unemployed governess but this time by the name of Laure Barbier. To the landlady she repeated the story of a drowned fisherman father and a French mother. She bought a bicycle and spent time on the cliff top watching the boats in the harbour. She noted the numbers of military personnel around the port and armoured vehicles parked in an empty lot. Aerial reconnaissance had reported a build-up of military vehicles in East Anglia and the South East England. From what she had seen around the port, it would seem that the Pas-de-Calais would be the most likely host to an invasion.

As an SOE agent in France she had infiltrated several Resistance groups and uncovered the British "Operation Bodyguard". This had been a deception campaign aimed at convincing German intelligence that the invasion might come in Greece, on the Adriatic coast of Yugoslavia, in the south of France or even in Low Countries, Norway and Denmark.

She cycled over the downland behind the port and pulled over on a narrow country lane to allow a convoy of trucks to pass. Once they were a distance ahead of her, she followed on her bicycle. She did not have to go far. The road led to a vast field, where military vehicles of all types stood with soldiers guarding the entrance to the field and the vehicles. She hid the bicycle in the bushes and watched. She took a couple of photographs. She stayed there all afternoon watching the activity around the vehicles. Men came and went, some taking photographs of their fellow soldiers standing in front of the tanks. She could hear their voices; all sounded American. This did not surprise her. She knew that American and Canadian troops had been in Britain for some time now. Darkness fell and to her great surprise, the troops left the field. Not even the guards remained. She waited a bit longer until she was certain that the field was empty of military personnel and went in. She estimated that there were around two hundred tanks as well as Jeeps and light-armoured vehicles. She approached one of the tanks and to her amazement, discovered that it was no more than an inflatable imitation of a tank. She checked the others, the Jeeps and armoured cars. All were fake. She waited in the field until first light when she took more photographs of each type of vehicle. A field adjacent held a herd of cows. She opened the gate and shooed them in among the vehicles. It was not long before several of them were punctured and deflated by the horns and hooves of the panicked beasts. Her photographs would provide amusement to those in the German High Command. Well-satisfied with her day's work, she returned to the boarding house.

She realised that this roll of film must be placed directly into the hands of *Generalfeldmarschalls* Rommel and Von Rundstedt. The former was Commander of the Western Forces as well as responsible for the defences of the Atlantic Wall. She could not trust this information to radio; there was always the risk of interception. The film roll must be placed into the hands of the generals.

Before returning to France, she had still to discover where the invasion force would depart from. For a while, Hitler had thought that the invasion would occur in Normandy, but Rommel and most of the commanders in France believed there would be two invasions; the main one being at the Pas-de-Calais. She knew that Rommel had ordered fortifications of the Atlantic Wall there as well as in the estuary of the Somme. Hitler's clairvoyants, on whom he increasingly sought advice, had persuaded him that the Pas-de-Calais would be where the invasion force would land. *His drug-addled brain was receptive to such nonsense*, she thought contemptuously.

If Normandy was to be the landing place for the invasion, she thought she should go further west, to Portsmouth; it was very unlikely the Allies would attempt another landing at Dieppe from Newhaven. She excused her early departure from the boarding house as due to an employment that she had found with a family in London. Wishing to avoid London and the possibility of being recognised, she took coastal trains to Portsmouth. As the train passed close to the sea at Pevensey Bay she reflected on the invasion of 1066, when a Norman King successfully invaded England. This time, the invasion was to be in the other direction, but the invaders would not be successful, certainly, if she had a hand in it. She thought how pleased the *Führer* would be with her and the honours he would bestow.

She booked a room in a boarding house using the same alias, bought another bicycle and toured the country lanes around Portsmouth. It was now the middle of April and the weather was very pleasant. The area around the port was heavily guarded, far more so than at Dover. She spent a few days cycling around the lanes and at the end of the week, found the evidence she needed. She had noticed a number of large lorries on the road to Portsmouth. They were all driven by soldiers. On the road back to Portsmouth one afternoon, she was passed by one of these. She stood aside to let it pass and then saw it become stuck between two hedgerows. She put her bicycle into a ditch and watched from the hedgerow. The drivers reversed and thrust forward in an attempt to release the vehicle but to no effect. After a while, one of the soldiers got out of the driver's cab and took a hammer to the side of the lorry, no doubt to release it. There was a sound of splintering wood and the side of the vehicle fell off, revealing a tank.

So now she knew the reason for this unusual traffic. They were secretly transporting tanks to the port and the Normandy coast most accessible from Portsmouth and Southampton would be the location of the invasion. There was no need for photographic evidence. Hitler and his generals would believe her. She had proved her worth at Dieppe and with Operation Bodyguard. All she needed to do now was to return to France as soon as possible.

92

Auriole cycled to Chichester and watched the boats as they were taken out to sea by their affluent owners and watched as they berthed at night. One boat caught her attention; it was put to sea every day by a man who she guessed to be in his fifties. He was always alone and drank late into the evening, before staggering away from the mooring to a local hotel. She followed him to the hotel and caught his eye in the bar. He offered to buy her a drink and later she persuaded him to take her to his boat. Here, she used her stiletto knife to pierce his heart and threw his body into the sea. His death would be presumed a case of accidental drowning due to inebriation. She used the keys to start the engine and set sail for France. It was the 30th of May 1944.

She landed at Honfleur and scuttled the boat. Her *Abwehr* contact informed her that Rommel and Von Rundstedt would be in Normandy at the beginning of June, in Caen, from where they would continue their tour of the Atlantic Wall.

She resolved to make her way there immediately.

PART TEN

Helen

93

I was in the stables grooming the horses when I heard the car draw up. I hurried through the kitchen door where the cook was preparing the evening meal. Lotti came rushing in.

'Gabrielle, it is the *Gestapo*, they are looking for you.'

Her face was pale with anxiety.

My mind ran through the scenarios that could have brought them to the château: perhaps the underground room had been betrayed or one of the families from Paris had been discovered at the convent. I went out into the hall where I was horrified to see two men, both dressed in the black leather coats worn by the *Gestapo*. My heart felt it would burst in my chest. I felt a sweat break out all over my body and was worried that I might faint.

'*Mademoiselle* Doucet, or should I address you as *Frau* von Werstein? But, however you wish to be named, we are here to ask you a few questions.'

I struggled to keep my voice steady and stop my hands from trembling.

'Ask as you wish. I have nothing to hide. My husband is away at the present time and I do not believe he will regard your presence here with favour.'

'Ah, yes, your husband. I wonder how he will feel to discover that his beloved wife is an agent of the enemy.'

This brought me some relief. They did not suspect him. He was safe and they were not looking for the others. A feeling of euphoria engulfed me as I realised that I did not mind what they did to me as long as the man I loved and the people in my care were safe.

'You have nothing on me but malicious gossip. I refuse to go with you. Show me what evidence you have.'

'We have had a call and we follow these calls up. If you refuse to answer our questions here, we shall have to arrest you and take you in for questioning.'

'You cannot do that without evidence. It is not legal to arrest a woman who has done no wrong.'

Both men laughed at this and replied, 'Surely you are aware that in the Frank Reich, we have the power to do exactly that. If we feel that there is a threat to national security then we have the power to arrest suspects. You have wasted enough of our time today.'

With that, they wrenched my arms around my back. The shock and pain of this caused me to cry out. Emilia ran into the hall.

'You will release *Frau* von Werstein at once. She has done no wrong. Her husband will ensure you are punished for this outrage.'

'Then fortunate are we that the husband is not here. Perhaps when this young woman tells us the truth, he will not be so happy to have her as his wife.'

With that, they pushed me ahead of them, down the steps of the château and into the car.

They took me to the new police premises in the centre of Caen. At the desk, they took my fingerprints and wrote the name Gabrielle Doucet with a question mark in the ledger. I was pushed against a wall to have my photograph taken. A woman in uniform arrived and took me into a side room. Here, I was ordered to undress. When I asked why, I was told I would be searched for weapons and valuables. I laughed.

'This is absurd. How can I possibly have a gun or valuables if I am undressed?'

'You will be searched internally.'

I felt weak with terror when I heard this and the abject humiliation of prying hands inside my body.

'I feel I am going to be sick.'

'If you are sick, *Madame*, you will be asked to clean it up. Now, take off your clothes and lie on the table.'

When it was finally over, the woman gave me a towel and left me to wipe myself and after a while, returned with my clothing. She then took me down flights of stairs to a corridor lined with cells. All appeared to be occupied. I could hear a woman screaming and a man's voice shouting at her. The screams got louder; she was clearly in great pain. In another cell, I could a low moaning sound, as though someone had no longer the strength to scream or even cry. The woman opened a door and pushed me inside the cell.

There were no windows in the cell and on one wall was an iron hoop with a manacle attached. The floor was bare and I shivered in the dank foetid air. A bucket stood in the corner. I looked inside and saw that it contained urine and blood. I blocked my mind from speculating on the circumstances of the previous occupant of the cell.

They came for me later that night. I was dragged up the stairs and along corridors to a room where the *Gestapo* officers were waiting for me. They sat at a desk on one side of the room and on the other side of the room was a bathtub. They tied me to the chair and asked my name. I gave it as *Frau* von Werstein. This elicited a hard slap on each side of my face. One of them moved to pull my hair over the back of the chair. They asked my name again. I repeated my married name. This time, my head was jerked violently backwards and one of them punched me hard on the jaw. The force of his fist caused my teeth to crash together and my sight to go momentarily. When I opened my eyes, streaks of blood impaired my vision.

They asked my name again and again, and each time I replied, 'I am *Frau* von Werstein and you will pay for this.'

My head was dragged back again and another fist hit my jaw on the other side of my face.

This time, it was my ears that seemed to be affected; blood pounded in my ear drum so much so that I thought it would burst.

I still refused to give the name they wanted, and in truth I did not know what name they wanted from me, unless Auriole had told them. But if that were so, why the need to question me, apart from the obvious pleasure they took from inflicting pain? I marvelled at my ability to think clearly through the pain in my jaw. No, Auriole had not told them my name but had given them enough information for them to accuse me of being a British spy. And then, through my pain, I realised that I had not questioned the identity of the anonymous informer. But now I understood. It could only have been Auriole who had discovered that I was alive and had decided to try again to destroy me.

They asked my name again and I repeated the same, but the pain in my jaw made it difficult to enunciate. They laughed at me. They stood me up and tore the clothes off me. They took me to the bathtub which was filled with cold, dirty, blood-streaked water and pushed my head under and held it there. I tried to hold my breath as Papa had told me to do when he taught me how to swim.

94

I am in the sea pool at Berwick. I remember it and can now see it clearly. The pool fills up at high tide and makes a safe place for those not confident in the open sea or too young to be allowed to swim there. Papa and *Maman* are there, encouraging me.

'Swim, little fish,' they call to me, 'Swim as fast you can.'

And I call back, 'Right over the dam,' as I go under again, my limbs flailing in all directions in order to stay afloat.

And they laugh. I see them now, watching me holding my breath, but this time for so long that I fall asleep. They said that is how it is in drowning. My friend, Robbie, went out on the fishing boats with his father. He had once fallen overboard in rough seas close to Berwick. He told me that it was so, that it was as though you went to sleep in the water. Then I am out of the water and the voices are demanding my name. I can only find one name, Karl. I call his name, and then there is only darkness.

I woke up in the cell. I was wet and cold and my head ached. I remembered and felt my teeth, they were still there, but perhaps they would be lost the next time. Soon after I woke up they came for me again. I was taken to the same room and they started with the bath. This time the *gendarme* was present. After this, they said, my fingers would be broken. That I would never play the piano again was all that resonated with me. They put me naked into the icy filthy water and held me down while they shouted for my name. And I did not answer.

But then I again remembered Robbie, who told me how his father had lifted him from the water, onto the boat and then carried him home, where his mother had cared for him. But I felt as though I was dying over and over again and I could not say my name, but I could whisper his.

When I opened my eyes, I was in our bed and I was no longer naked but wearing a warm night dress. The pain in my face and head was excruciating and I could not focus my eyes.

There were voices, one voice in particular, and I asked, 'Am I dreaming?'

The other voices were then silent and one voice replied, 'No, *liebchen*, but you are returned to us.'

He sat next to me on the bed and gently held me in his arms.

'It was Rommel who had you released. Lotti and Emilia sent the guards to Calais with a letter. They wrote of what had happened to you and we came immediately. The *Gestapo* have been returned to Berlin and as for the *gendarme*, we will decide later. *Liebchen*, you promised me that you would not be that girl. How could this happen to you?'

And he cried and it was me who comforted him.

I learned from Lotti that Rommel had arrived at the police headquarters with his guards. I had been found unconscious and near death, with my lungs full of water and my airway blocked due to the swelling and bruising of my face. Rommel had instructed the doctors to take me to the château, where my husband would care for me with their help. Rommel had now left for Calais but before leaving, had given orders that I was to be given the best care possible, as a hero of the Frank Reich.

After two weeks, I could eat and talk. My face was still unrecognisable to me; the swelling around my lower jaw and the bruising to my face would take weeks to resolve. The cook explained that my red hair made the bruising more severe but that I would make a full recovery. I had been lucky not to lose my teeth and here he had hesitated; the disfigurement could have been far worse. He had learned from his wife that these interrogations often led to permanent scarring and injuries, if the victims survived.

I felt defiled, even more so than after Mueller; the memory of the *gendarme's* pleasure in my nakedness and suffering as I was beaten by the *Gestapo* thugs, and, above all, the certainty that Auriole had made this happen.

By the middle of May, I was well enough to play the piano. A recital was organised at the château to celebrate my recovery and, as the *Oberfeldkommandur* reminded me, normal relations with my husband. The bitterness and anger seemed so long ago now. I could only consider his solicitude for me and his sorrow at what I had endured at the hands, not only of the *gendarme* but also of his fellow Germans.

We decided to play the Chopin *Polonaise* and then the Chopin *Cello Sonata* to open the programme, and to follow this with the *Arpeggione Sonata*. The works of Chopin had been proscribed under the Nazis but both felt confident that the beauty of the music would transcend racial prejudice. The final piece would be the *Nacht und Träume* with a finale of the *Oberfeldkommandur* singing to her accompaniment.

My husband was happy to see me well, outwardly at least; he alone knew of my night terrors when I awoke screaming and struggling to escape from some unseen force. I had instructed him that he should wake me up when this happened, otherwise I feared falling into a terrible abyss from which there could be no escape. While he could not understand what I meant by this, he did as I asked and helped me to wake up, comforting me, and keeping a night light burning until I felt I could fall asleep peacefully.

The salon was full. The *Oberfeldkommandur* had brought many of his staff officers and their companions, all dressed in their military attire. We greeted everyone as they took their seats and settled down to hear the majestic opening phrases of the *Polonaise*.

It was at times like these that I wondered how war had been brought to their country, to the world, if not for Hitler. I understood at that moment that however this war ended, there would be other wars; there would always be a Hitler and those willing to follow him.

95

Foulden, Berwickshire 25th May 1944

Dear Helen,

I am writing this letter in the presence of your mother and father, who send their love and deepest concern for your safety. We know that the Odette you knew is an imposter and your mother's great sadness is the certainty that her friend is now dead and that Auriole assumed her identity for reasons which may now have become apparent to you. Auriole Ritter has been seen in Scotland and England recently and has used a variety of aliases to disguise her presence. Though desperately worried for your safety, your parents have agreed that I may ask this of you. I cannot explain why I make this request as I am bound by the Official Secrets Act but it is sufficient to tell you that we believe Ritter has in her possession a film roll of vital importance to British intelligence. Should this film roll be passed to the German Military and Intelligence, the tide of war would turn in favour of Hitler. This will portend the end of all that we in Britain believe to be good and honourable. He will do as he has done in other countries where he was victorious and millions more innocent lives will be lost. This letter will be handed to you in person by a reliable courier.

Helen, we ask you to find Ritter and take possession of the film. We believe she will soon return to France and the château. Do whatever must be done to obtain the film.

George Vartis

I read the letter and then burned it on the kitchen range. I sat down until my hands stopped shaking and I could think clearly. I felt sure that Auriole would return to the château, if only to verify that her latest attempt to kill me had been successful.

I did my best to compose myself. My husband was in Caen but was expected to return that evening. Rommel and Von Rundstedt would arrive the following day to discuss the defences on the channel coast. I was looking forward to meeting Rommel again. My husband held him in high esteem. He too had refused to join the Nazi party and was no admirer of Hitler and his methods. He was an honourable soldier and loyal German.

The following day, Lotti and Emilia accompanied my husband to Caen where the Generals were expected to meet with the *Oberfeldkommandur*. The cook went with them to be with his wife but would return late in the afternoon to prepare the evening meal.

I played the piano for a while and later saddled up Doucette and rode into the woods alone. The guards were enjoying the company of girls from the town and I had no wish to disturb them. As I returned to the château I felt that I was being watched. I slackened the reins and sat back in the saddle. Doucette stood very still. There was a faint rustling in the undergrowth but this, I reasoned, could be a small animal scurrying to its lair. I rode on to the stables and rubbed the mare down. The day was warm and I needed to fetch fresh water for the horses. As I drew water from the well, I saw her. Auriole was walking along the path from the woods; I had not been wrong in feeling I was observed.

I remembered the gun and cursed myself for leaving it in the drawer. I must not show fear but would face whatever was to come.

I also knew that I had not bled since April; I must live, for the sake of our child.

96

Retribution

She was smiling as she approached me.

'You have done well, my dear, and I have to admire your resilience, but as we say, third time lucky, ñ'*est ce pas*? Or perhaps you did not realise that those mishaps were my work.'

My mind raced through the possibilities: should I run and hope to get to my room and the gun or should I stay and face Auriole and hope to outmanoeuvre her?

But first I needed to ask the question, 'Auriole, and I know who you are, I just need to know for the sake of *Maman*, what happened to Odette?'

Auriole appeared astonished, as though she had not thought me capable of such insight.

With a complacent smile, she said, 'In that case, I shall enlighten you, but the pity is that your dear *Maman* is not here to learn the truth of what happened to her friend. I killed her in the apartment. She was such an innocent. She welcomed me into her home and even offered me the diamond bracelet that I so admired to save her life. But I got it anyway, as you know. She ran into the bathroom and locked the door but I broke it down and shot her. Her body lies rotting at the bottom of the Seine.'

That was all I needed to know. With a strength that I did not recognise as my own, I hurled the bucket of water over Auriole. The edge of the bucket caught the side of Auriole's face, causing her to stagger, and the water cascaded over her. I seized the moment and ran to the château. Once inside, I made for the staircase but Auriole had recovered and gave chase. As I reached the top of the staircase I could see that Auriole held a sharp blade in her right hand. I had no weapon but I could use my position at the top of the staircase to my advantage. As Auriole came closer I kicked out at her as hard as I could. Auriole stumbled and the knife fell from her grasp. I moved quickly to retrieve the knife but Auriole recovered herself and made to grab at it. Then we were rolling down the staircase in a desperate struggle for survival. Auriole had the knife first and held it to my eyes, but as the knife was poised to pierce me, I managed to twist Auriole's hand and the knife was then pointed towards her. It was only a few seconds but it seemed like an eternity. I moved the knife to Auriole's chest and plunged it into her heart. Auriole grunted in pain and then her eyes glazed over. She was dead.

I pulled the body down the staircase before there could be too much blood and dragged it to the back of the stables. There I removed the clothing. I needed to find the film roll before disposing of the body. I went through the clothing and found what I was looking for. Tucked inside a glove in the pocket of the jacket was the film roll; the last place anybody would think to look, but a spy would know to put it there. I then heaved the body into the cesspit.

I knew exactly what I would do with the film roll.

97

Père François was listening to the confession of a woman when the silence of the church was broken by the sound of harsh voices demanding the whereabouts of the priest, *Père* François.

Without any hesitation in her confession, the woman stood up and announced in a loud but trembling voice, 'He is here, as I told you he would be.' And then she whispered, 'Forgive me, Father, I have no choice, they have my child.'

Père François had time to say, 'You are forgiven,' before two men in black leather coats pulled him from the confessional. He was dragged from the church and pushed into a waiting car, in which he was dismayed to find the young boy who had been hidden in the presbytery. The boy's face showed signs of a recent beating and he was shaking with terror.

The boy looked up at *Père* François and through the blood and broken teeth, managed to say, 'They made me tell of my mother and sisters, and they know where they are.'

'Do you mean where they are hiding?'

'Yes.'

They were driven to the police office and locked in a cell, where around them they could hear the screams of men and women being tortured, interposed with the menacing voices of their interrogators. *Père* François could only think of Helen, of her courage in protecting those in her care. And now it was over. He wondered how long it would be before she too was dragged into a cell and it would be her screams he would hear. He knew of her previous arrest and torture and how bravely she had withstood the agony and humiliation of it. The *Chef des Gendarmes* had been dismissed but his subordinates were still in place, and no doubt he would still have sway over them.

After a short time, the cell door was opened and the boy was dragged out. Then they came for *Père* François. He was told that he was to be deported and that from the police office he would be taken to Drancy and then to Sachsenhausen.

He was told that the boy had been shot, along with all those who had been found hiding Jews.

So, this was the end. He said a prayer for the souls of those who had died, the forgiveness of those who had betrayed them and for Helen's safety.

98

Betrayal

There was no time to consider the death of my enemy or relief at my own survival. I cleaned the staircase and hall of Auriole's blood and having hidden the film roll, removed my blood-stained clothing and put it into the kitchen range to burn. I bathed, dressed and checked around the stables to ensure no evidence remained of the recent desperate struggle. The guards were at their posts, relaxing with the girls in the warm sunshine, and far enough away to have been oblivious to the event.

I heard a car approaching. It was too early for the Generals and their entourage to be returning. I saw the car stop at the gates and two men get out and speak to the guards. I recognised at once that they were *Gestapo*. Panic momentarily paralysed me but my mind raced ahead. We had been betrayed. I ran to my former bedroom and took the gun from the drawer.

I went out through the back door and into the woods to the trapdoor. The entrance showed no signs of recent disturbance. I could only hope that it had not been disclosed. I opened the trapdoor and went down the steps and to the underground room, all the time fearing what I would find there. All five were there and alive. Relief flooded me and I swayed slightly in the doorway.

'There is no time. You must all leave the room now. The *Gestapo* are here. They will know about the entrance in the woods but not the tunnels.'

I took them through the door and along the tunnel to where it bifurcated. I told them to go as far they could along the left fork and to wait there for me. There must be absolute silence no matter how afraid they were or what they heard.

I returned to the room and waited at the bottom of the staircase. I could hear muffled sounds from the grate above the staircase and then they were there. I remembered my history lessons; the men would struggle with the uneven tread of the staircase and I, as the defender, would have the advantage. I waited until they were in my sights, and before they could reach for a weapon fired two bullets into each of them. They fell, their bodies tumbling like grotesque acrobats to the ground.

I went immediately to the women. They had heard the sound of gunfire and feared the worst. They clung to me in relief but I shook them off explaining that there was no time to lose, that others might follow. I took them along the tunnel to the entrance in the rose garden and hugging the walls of the garden, led them through the back door into the kitchen. The cook had returned. He had seen the car and guessed that the *Gestapo* were at the château. He was greatly relieved that I and the women were safe. I explained that first I needed to take the women to a safe refuge, and led them up the back stairs to the nursery. I showed them the hidden cupboard and told them to lock themselves in if they heard anyone approach the room. I locked the door of the nursery behind me and returned to the kitchen.

I asked the cook what he knew of the arrests. He told me that one of the group had been arrested. The man had revealed under torture the involvement of *Père* François in the hiding of Jews at the church and the château. A sympathetic *gendarme* had assured him that no others had been identified and the prisoner had died under torture. He told of *Père* François's arrest and deportation and death of the boy. I related the events in the ruins of the tower and explained that it must be destroyed, along with the bodies of the *Gestapo*. It was now early in the evening and my husband would be returning with Rommel and Von Rundstedt. I would be expected to welcome them and dine with them.

I took my bicycle and cycled to the farm. Damian was there. He knew of the arrests and had feared for my safety. I explained what had happened in the underground room and that the tower had to be destroyed without delay, to remove the evidence of its use as a refuge and the bodies of the *Gestapo*.

I waited while he went into a barn and after a short time, he emerged with his bicycle and carrying a small package. Together we cycled to the woods. He explained that he would go into the tunnel from there and detonate the explosives he had in the package. I should wait in the rose garden for him to emerge. If he did not, I must assume that he had died in the explosion. I wished him luck and promised to do whatever was needed to help Amélie should the worst happen.

I waited trembling by the wall of the rose garden. The minutes ticked by like hours until the ground shook beneath me and the roar of an explosion could be heard underground. Half an hour must have passed before a dust-covered Damian appeared from the ruin. His hair was singed but he was otherwise unharmed. I hugged him and told him I must return to the château at once to attend to my guests.

'Rommel and Von Rundstedt will be here but they are not to be harmed. They are as much my guests as the others.'

And I told him briefly of the letter from George and the instructions he had given me.

'I have hidden the film roll where it will not be found. I do not know its content but I am sure it is of great importance. The body of the spy will also not be found as it is in the cesspit behind the stables.'

I hurried back to the château. The cook had prepared food for the women in the nursery. I took it to them and told them what had become of their former home. It was too soon to tell the mother of the death of her son and the girls of the death of their brother. They were comfortable and had enjoyed the use of a bathroom for the first time in years.

I bathed, dressed and prepared to welcome my guests. They arrived soon after 8 p.m. My husband asked me about the car that remained at the foot of the steps of the château.

'I had a visit from the *Gestapo*. I told them to take a walk in the woods and they did not return. Perhaps they are interested in the rare species of owl that has made its home there.'

'I will ask no more of this. But should more of their kind arrive, they will be told that the Generals and their company are not to be disturbed. It would seem that your day has not been without event.'

'You know your wife well enough to assume that to be true.'

After the meal, I excused myself and went to the tower to listen to the wireless. The Germans had prohibited listening to Radio Londres when they realised that it encouraged and emboldened resistance to the occupation. But despite the Germans' attempted jamming of the airwaves with background noise and static, there had been hundreds of messages broadcast since the beginning of June.

A message came through, '"If you see the stable-door setting open wide..."'

I smiled; they knew I had succeeded. Perhaps Damian had been able to make contact.

Then immediately the radio voice said the words, 'Listen for autumn while you "watch the wall".'

99

The Generals Rommel and Von Rundstedt, and my husband left early the following morning to inspect the defences on the coast of the Cotentin Peninsula.

I needed to find refuge for the group in the nursery. I had not told my husband of their presence and knew that my husband's position would be compromised should any of the Generals' entourage have suspicions. I decided to ride to Sainte-Honorine-De-Ducy to ask Damian for advice. I saddled up Bathory, rode out of the château gates and into the village. As I rode, I noted the V for victory signs daubed on walls and the roofs of houses. The signs had been recently painted, which led me to suspect that people were emboldened and that they must feel an Allied invasion to be imminent. I increased the horse's pace and once out of the town, urged Bathory into a gallop.

Damian immediately offered to take the woman and the girls. He harnessed the pony to his milk cart and followed me back to the château. Once there, we told the woman and the girls that it was no longer safe for them to remain at the château and that place would be found for them at the convent in Bayeux. I wished them luck and bade them farewell. I would miss them but their survival was more important than all else.

My bleed was nearly two months late. I had felt nauseous again that morning and my husband had remarked that the nipples of my breasts were enlarged as we made love the previous night. I had said nothing but enjoyed his tender suckling on them. The thought that our child would soon do the same had made me cry.

'You are weeping, *meine liebchen*. I too feel sad at these times. I enjoy you so much that I am afraid to lose you and the joy you bring me.'

'It is the same for me.'

And I had drawn him to me and encouraged him to enter me again. But he was gentle, as though sensing a fragile life deep inside me that should not be disturbed.

They returned that evening. Rommel announced that he would leave early the following morning to travel to Berlin to be with his wife on the occasion of her birthday. Rundstedt announced that he would leave at the same time, to join his son, Leutnant Hans Gerd, on another inspection of the defences, but that he hoped to return to Caen after a few days. I left them talking in the library and understood that they anticipated an imminent invasion by the Allies, but whether this would be at the Pas-de-Calais or Normandy was still a matter of dissension. Rundstedt did not trust spies and dismissed the intelligence that suggested either location but, nevertheless, favoured the Pas-de-Calais as most likely.

I went to the tower and took the wireless from its hiding place in the alcove. At 9 p.m., I tuned to Radio Londres and heard the first stanza of Paul Verlaine's poem *Chanson d'Automne*, "*Les sanglots longs des violons de l'automne*". This must be the message that invasion was imminent.

The following morning, I served Rommel and Von Rundstedt breakfast. As they left, I had a strong intuition that I would never meet either of them again. They both kissed my hand and clicked their heels as they bade me farewell.

After their cars had left the drive, my husband took my hand and led me to our bedroom.

'*Meine liebchen*, I will soon have to leave you. The Allies are close to landing on the shores of France and you have played your part in this war. My friend, Wilhelm Canaris, informed me that Ritter was on her way here with evidence that would enable their defeat. I understood that he would not judge me for how I used this information. Now I must leave and fight as a loyal soldier of Germany, as I have always done, though it was never for Hitler and his barbarians that I fought. However the war ends, Germany will rise again from the ruins that are of Hitler's making.'

This confused me but then I remembered his words:

"Auriole Ritter is a very dangerous woman."

'So, you knew who she was and what she was and still you would leave me, for her to kill me.'

'No, *liebchen*, that is not so. It was when you showed me the photograph, it was then I saw that the woman you thought to be the friend of your mother was Ritter. I had no reason to believe that you were in danger. All else was unknown, as was the fact that when I arrived and was greeted by a young French girl, I would come to love her and be loved by her. You must believe me. I did all in my power to protect you but no one could have known the malice that Ritter held for you. Please forgive me, *liebchen*. I cannot leave you knowing that will despise me again.'

'I could never despise you. I love you with all my heart. I still do not understand much of this. What of Rommel and Von Rundstedt? Do they know of this?'

'No, they do not. But both despise Hitler, as do all honourable soldiers, including my good friend, Wilhelm Canaris. For Canaris, it was Poland that changed him, the brutality he witnessed there in 1939. He was and is a loyal German but could take no pleasure in a Hitler victory. It was Stalingrad that changed everything for me. Hitler refused the terms of surrender offered to General Paulus, terms which would have saved the lives of thousands of brave men, my men, the men who you saw around the château. We were offered an honourable surrender. The Soviets admired our courage and tenacity, as we did theirs. But from the safety of Berchtesgaden, he refused to permit surrender. He preferred to condemn men to death rather than admit to his own failures as a leader and as a man.'

'But from what you have told me, you wished to betray your country. The Allies will arrive very soon. I do not know where or when exactly, but all resistants have been alerted to this.'

'In what way should I betray my country? I have fought bravely and honourably for my country in the East as well as in the West and I ensured that the beautiful and courageous woman whom I love was able to continue in her work protecting Jews and others.

'I learned from Canaris that Ritter had been tasked with determining where the invasion force would land and he believed she would deliver the evidence on a roll of film to the generals in person, here at the château. We did not speak of this but I planned to kill her with my own hands, to avenge the harm she did you. But it seems she has disappeared and her *Abwehr* contact believes her to be dead.'

So, I told him, 'I killed her and the film roll has been hidden. I do not know what is on the film roll but I was instructed to obtain it. Her body is in the cesspit behind the stables.'

'*Liebchen*, how often have I to wonder at you?'

'What will become of us when this is over? Both of us will be despised as traitors and become citizens of nowhere.'

'The future is not ours to decide. As we say, who knows what war will bring?'

Later, I remembered that the *Oberfeldkommandur* had used the same words and the young soldier. But for now, I allowed him to undress me and watched as he undressed. I took pleasure in his body as he fondled and caressed me, as I did him. As we moved together, my passion rose to equal his and we cried when it was over. He kissed me gently and we slept.

100

The guards came to the bedroom door at dawn to awaken him. The Allies had landed on the beaches closest to Caen as well as the Cotentin Peninsula.

He kissed me tenderly and whispered, 'It is my time to leave. You must take care. I know you to be strong. Look after our horses and remember that I will always love you.'

I watched as his car left the avenue of lime trees and wept. I saddled Bathory, put Doucette on a lead rein and set out for Sainte-Honorine. They would be safe with Damian. When I returned, I awakened Lotti, Emilia and the cook and told them what was happening. They thought it better to go to Caen and tried to persuade me to do the same. But I refused. I would stay at the château and hope to keep it safe from destruction. They kissed me farewell and all hoped to meet again in better times.

I stayed close to the wireless. I learned of the American landings at the beach they named Omaha and of the huge losses the Americans sustained there. I learned of the advance of the Allies from the beachheads and the resistance they encountered by the retreating Germans. I learned of the massacre and destruction of the village of Oradour-sur-Glane. On the 10th of June, the SS Panzer division, *Das Reich*, many of whom were French *Alsaciens,* had locked the women and children of the village in the church and set fire to it. The men of the village had been herded into a barn where they were machine-gunned and then burned. In all, 643 innocent people were murdered, while the soldiers responsible drank wine and ate the food they had stolen from the houses of the villagers. The village had been destroyed and was now a ruin, the bodies of its former inhabitants burned beyond recognition.

I learned of vicious reprisals elsewhere. It was as though the Germans were determined to inflict as much death and destruction as possible in the face of inevitable defeat.

I learned of the summary justice meted out by French people on those accused of collaboration with the hated enemy. I learned that the detested former *Chef des Gendarmes* of Caen had been hanged from what remained of the castle walls, his body showing signs of torture. My regret was that I had not had the opportunity to point my finger at him in court.

During the weeks that followed, I did not leave the château. The wireless informed me of the Allies' progress from the beachheads deeper into Normandy. The aim was to capture Caen from the Germans and battles were being fought around the city. From my window, I watched the tanks of both armies passing the gates. I had no appetite for food but knew that the baby inside me needed nourishment. As time passed I had only a few rotted potatoes to eat and from these I made a weak broth which I could live on for days. As July entered the second week I knew it could not be long. I waited for the inevitable.

101

They sat me down on a chair alongside two other women accused of the same. Two men and a woman came out of the crowd, each carrying a pair of crude, rusted scissors and a sheet of paper. They took their places behind the chairs in this nightmare parody of a hairdresser's salon. In turn, they read out the names of the accused. When they came to my name, there was a loud roar of contempt and derision. It was a man who stood behind me. He pulled my head back and ripped the bodice of my dress, exposing my breasts, which provoked more jeers and crude whistles from the crowd. My crime of prostituting myself to the German command in the town and profiting from the relationship was read out. A woman stepped out of the crowd and slapped me hard across my face. I recognised the woman as one of the stall holders in the market. This woman, I knew, had denounced a neighbour who had been hiding a Jewish family in her attic. The family had been arrested and sent to Drancy. There had been no news of them since. The neighbour and her husband had been shot by the Germans in the town square. The "crimes" of the other women were read out. As the *tondeurs* prepared to begin their work, the crowd became increasingly agitated and I feared that it would become even more violent. Blood trickled from my nose and despite the heat, I began to shiver. I was more afraid than at any time during the last four years. I feared for the child within me.

The noise was now louder, coming from behind the crowd and accompanied by the sound of engines. The crowd suddenly parted as military Jeeps bearing the Canadian flag appeared. Soldiers emerged from the vehicles and came to the front of the crowd where we awaited our fate. They ordered our immediate release and blankets were brought from one of the Jeeps to cover us. Gasps of dismay and jeers followed as I and the two women were taken away.

We were driven through the ruined city, past piles of rubble and makeshift shelters. People were roaming the streets carrying whatever remained of their household goods. A few stopped to cheer the Canadian vehicles. I and my companions hid under the blankets. The Canadian soldiers spoke French and engaged us in conversation. They had the papers with our names and the list of crimes of which we were accused. My two companions responded by denying all culpability in these so-called crimes. I knew better. I had witnessed them arm-in-arm with various German soldiers. Both were reputed to be accepting gifts from them in return for their favours. But I also knew there would be others, those who like myself had loved and been loved. When an occupying army is billeted with you, cared for by you and in whose employ you are, who should judge the choices you make?

When the officer turned to me I astonished him by responding in English, 'My name is Helen Douglas. I took the name Gabrielle Doucet at the beginning of the occupation to protect the people in my care. Please help me to return home. My parents will be anxious for me.'

The officer was astounded. This was clearly beyond his remit, which was to impose discipline and order in the newly-liberated city.

Leaving the other women at a refugee station where they would be given food and protection, he took me to a makeshift operations centre and into the care of his commanding officer, Lieutenant Guy Simmonds. I could hear the sound of heavy artillery fire close by. The battle for control of the suburbs south of the city was still raging.

I told my story as briefly as possible, playing down my role in the war. It was too soon; I could hardly distinguish between fact and fiction, for so long had my life been a lie. The officer picked up his field telephone and asked to be connected with the nearest British

Command Centre. To my astonishment, the voice of Field Marshal Montgomery came over the wire. He asked to speak to me. My voice was shaking as told him briefly who I was, where my parents lived and requested that he make contact with a British Airman named George Vartis who would vouch for me.

I was found a bed in the quarters of the nurses of the Royal Canadian Medical Corps. Food was brought to me and for the first time in weeks I slept without fear.

The following day I bathed and clean clothing was brought for me. I was told that Lieutenant Simmonds wished to speak to me and expected me at the command centre as soon as I was able to be there.

The Lieutenant sat me down and took my hand.

'You are one brave young woman. I sure don't know the whole of it, but in a while you will have a visitor and then we will do what we can to get you home. A telegram has been sent to your parents. They know you are alive and well.'

No sooner had he finished speaking, a man wearing the uniform of a British Air Force officer entered the tent. It was George. He took me in his arms and kissed me on both cheeks in the French way.

Then I told him, 'The film roll, it is at the château. I can take you there when it is safe and give it to you. Rommel and the others, they never got it.'

'And Ritter, what about her?'

'She is dead. She had the film roll with her when she came to the château at the beginning of June. Rommel and Von Rundstedt were there with the *Kommandant*. She knew this was her chance to give it to them.'

'How did she die?'

'I killed her with the same knife she tried to kill me. I threw her body into the cesspit.'

'And the *Kommandant*?'

'He left with his men to fight the Allies. I do not know if he is alive. And I am expecting his child.'

And then I wept.

102

Two days later George and I were driven to the Château des Tilleuls. Remarkably, the château and its grounds were undamaged despite the evidence of fierce fighting in the fields of the bocage around it. I took George into the library, climbed the steps, removed the book from its shelf and passed it down to him.

'You will find the film roll inside the spine of the book. It is a very old book so please take care of it. It is the history of the château.'

He gently probed inside the spine and there it was. He shook the book gently and along with the dust of centuries, the film roll fell out.

He helped me down the ladder and said, 'You not only saved lives, Helen, but you may well have saved the war for us. But this must be kept a secret for a while at least.'

I flew to London later that day. I was debriefed at the War Office and received a phone call from Winston Churchill thanking me for my war time efforts, in particular for eliminating the double agent who would have disclosed Operation Overlord to the very generals who were best placed to undermine its success. I travelled on the overnight train to Berwick. The sun was rising as the train steamed along the track close to the sea, the castle of Lindisfarne just visible through the mist, and then over the Royal Border Bridge with the waters of the Tweed below and into Berwick-upon-Tweed Station. My parents were waiting on the platform for me. They had aged in my absence; I was certain more due to rationing and anxiety than to the passage of time. The village had put banners out to welcome me and posies of flowers lined the road to my home.

In September I started my medical training at Edinburgh University. It was agreed that I would be granted leave from the university from the end of December until six weeks after the birth of my baby which was estimated to be around the middle of January.

News from France told of Damian and Amélie's miraculous survival and that of Ruth and Ellana. The Germans had come to the farm on the 6th of June and accused my aunt and uncle of harbouring "Jews and criminals". Ruth and Ellana were safe in the car repair yard of Agathe's husband at Saint-Paul-du-Vernay. They had been spirited away the previous night after a neighbour warned Damian of his imminent arrest and a planned search of the farm.

The Germans had lined Amélie and Damian against the wall of the farmyard to be shot when a German armoured vehicle drew up and ordered the soldiers to join it with immediate effect as the Allies had landed and they were needed on the battlefield. They had fled immediately, leaving Damian and Amélie in tears of relief and joy.

Of Leah, Raisa and their husbands there was no news. The war raged on into 1945 and broadcasts from liberated Europe described the horrors of the camps where millions of Jews, dissidents and Roma had been taken and murdered. Newsreels showed the full extent of the Nazi killing machine: the gas chambers, the crematoria and the survivors' accounts of torture and medical experiments were terrible to listen to and watch. So many of my friends and those I had tried to help would have perished in unspeakable pain and torment.

Accounts of fierce battles in the Ardennes, named the Battle of The Bulge, reported huge losses on both sides; the panzer divisions taking the brunt of the Allied counterattack. I learned of the massacre of American soldiers, prisoners of the Germans, near a town called Malmedy.

On the 22nd of January 1945, I gave birth to a baby boy at my home in Foulden. The local midwife delivered the baby while an anxious Papa paced outside the room ready to intervene if medical assistance was required.

Maman stayed with me throughout and was the one to inform her exhausted daughter, 'You have a beautiful healthy baby boy.'

Cradling my new-born son in my arms I could already see how much he resembled his father. His eyes were already more grey than blue and his blond hair was surely the colour of his father's as a child. I named him Charles James Francis but he would be known as Karl. He was baptised at the Catholic Church of Our Lady and Saint Cuthbert in Berwick-upon-Tweed on the 2nd of February 1945.

I was able to resume my studies at Edinburgh University in March. I took the train to Edinburgh each morning, having sated baby Karl with my breast milk, and expressed sufficient into bottles for *Maman* to feed him during my absence. My breasts were aching with milk as I returned each evening. If I was ever questioned regarding Karl's father, I replied that he had died in the war. I did not have to say on which side he had been fighting.

I was called to London to a meeting with intelligence officers, who informed me that I had to maintain absolute silence about my life in France during the war years. When I asked why, I was told that others could be put at risk if their identities became known. I signed the document that they put in front of me but not before requesting authorisation to return to Caen to find my friends. A letter to this effect was provided for me.

In September 1945 I returned to Caen. I had heard that survivors of the camps were slowly returning home and also that the Red Cross were putting up lists at train stations of the dead and missing. I arrived at the ruins of Caen Station, where the tracks had been repaired but the building was a blackened shell. Harassed Red Cross and medical workers were helping emaciated and traumatised people from the trains. I went to the boards and read the names carefully. I found Stefan's name immediately. He was listed as deceased at Sachsenhausen Concentration Camp in 1939. I found the name of *Père* François listed as missing. I could not imagine that a man of his age would survive the camps; my dear friend was surely dead. A train pulled in and more ragged, emaciated people emerged onto the platform. To my utter amazement and joy I saw that one of them was Raisa. Her skin was the colour of parchment and her legs wizened and stick-like but it was Raisa. I pushed my way through the crowd on the platform and took Raisa's hand.

'Raisa, it is me, Helen. I came back to find you. Your daughters are safe and well.' Raisa collapsed to the ground, putting her face in her hands and wept.

I helped Raisa to the Red Cross office where her name was added to the list of the returned. Raisa informed the Red Cross officials that she was certain her mother, Leah, had been murdered soon after their arrival at Auschwitz on the *Convoi 9* of July 1942 and that her father and husband had been selected for extermination soon after. Raisa was taken to the hospital to be treated for malnutrition and for the sores that covered her legs and arms. I promised to bring Ruth and Ellana to her that evening.

I asked a Red Cross worker to drive me to the château. He was reluctant to do so until I showed him the letter from the War Office authorising me to go there.

The château gates were locked and the grounds were overgrown with weeds. The driver broke the locks and I asked him to wait while I looked around.

I wandered round the empty rooms which smelled of stale tobacco and unwashed bodies. The château had been used as a base by the Allies during the assault on Caen. I was suddenly overcome by a feeling of loss, uncertainty and extreme exhaustion. It was as though my time in Scotland had only served to put a shell around me and now that shell had broken; I could truly understand the enormity of what I had gone through and what I had lost. The shadows of those days would never leave me.

I looked in the library. The cellos were still there, lined up against the wall. I opened the case of the Guadagnini cello, it was unscathed.

I took it out of its case and held it to me. I had no news of the fate of my husband, whether he was alive or dead. I wept again.

I wondered about the fate of Céleste and Séraphine. They may have been in Berlin when the city fell to the Red Army. The destruction of the city and the rape and carnage that ensued made it unlikely that they could have survived. But they were innocent victims of their mother's crimes. For Stefan's sake, I must do my best to find them.

I returned to the waiting vehicle and asked to be taken back to the Red Cross office. There I requested that a special search be made to find Gisela Erhart, who had been arrested in Berlin in 1939, and her nieces, Céleste and Séraphine Abramsky-Erhart. I then requested another vehicle to take me to my uncle's farm.

I was overjoyed to find them safe and well. Harvest was in full swing and Ruth and Ellana were out in the fields with the family bringing in the first post war harvest. Many of the crops had been destroyed in the fighting as the Allies fought their way inland from the beaches, and much of the dairy herd had perished in artillery fire. But there was new hope. Damian took me to one of the barns where two heifers were giving birth to their first calves. I told him of the return of Raisa and the sad news of the deaths of the rest of the family. Damian promised to drive Ruth and Ellana to the hospital that evening. I then asked if I could stay at the farm while I awaited news of Stefan's sister and his children.

I visited my grandparents in the small cottage close to the farmhouse. Michel and Catherine had learned of my arrival and were impatient to welcome their beloved granddaughter.

A week later I received the news that Gisela had been located in a displaced persons' camp in Austria. She had been very ill due to the conditions she had endured in Ravensbruck but was now well enough to travel to London to be reunited with her children. I was given an address in London where Gisela could be contacted.

There was no news of the girls but I was invited to visit a Red Cross Centre in Paris where children assumed to be orphans were being cared for. Many had been brought out of Germany by French soldiers, presumably because the children spoke French. I travelled by train to Paris. The destruction of the towns and countryside made me weep. How different this journey was from that long ago October day when I had first arrived in France. 1938 was another world away.

At the Red Cross centre, I gave the girls' names and explained that they would now be thirteen and eleven years old and that it was very possible they spoke English as I had been their tutor before they had possibly been taken to Germany. The lady at the desk looked puzzled.

'So how was it that they came to be in Germany?'

I gave a brief account of the circumstances and explained that I was bound by secrecy to keep the main facts from others.

'We have two girls here who could fit the profile you have given but the name is not Erhart, or Abramsky-Erhart, but Ritter. They were found in Alsace hiding in the ruins of a house which belonged to their grandparents.

'Of course, she would have given them her name. Please take me to them.'

The girls were sitting at a table in a large hall where many other children were engaged in the same activity: drawing pictures of family and former homes. It was explained to me that this served both as therapy for the trauma the children had suffered and to identify them and hopefully reunite them with surviving family. I went to the table and touched each girl lightly on the shoulder. They looked up and saw it was their beloved *gouvernante.*

After signing documents testifying to their identity and my authority to take them, we left the centre and returned to Caen.

I took them to the farm in Sainte-Honorine-de-Ducy. Ruth and Ellana delighted in showing the girls around the farm, even engaging them in milking the cows. Both children seemed to be relaxed and happy but I understood how this veneer could so easily crack and how destructive this could be in the young.

I spoke to Damian that evening.

'I have to return to my child and studies in Edinburgh, but before I go, there are things that must be settled. The girls need to be with their family in London. That is what Stefan would wish. I know that the Red Cross will make the arrangements. But before they go, I feel I should tell them the truth about their parents.'

'Do they know their father is dead?'

'Yes, I told them last night. I think they already knew this or suspected at least. They seemed to accept his death. There are so many children who have learned of the same and worse. But they know their grandparents are alive and now back in Paris and that they will be able to see them very soon.'

'And of their mother?'

'I have told them nothing. How can I tell them what she was and that I killed her?'

Damian smiled and put his arm around me.

'There can be too much truth. They need never know.'

I accompanied the girls to London, where they were met at Victoria Station by Stefan's brother and an assortment of cousins, including Gisela's children. They hugged me close as I left to catch a train north. All would be well for them and Stefan's memory would be honoured.

In December of that year my parents and I and baby Karl were invited to join the family in France for *Reveillon*. We arrived late in the afternoon and were met at Bayeux Station by Michel and Damian. Michel insisted on driving the Renault car that Damian had recently purchased. We careered through the narrow country roads to the village, with *Maman* urging caution as her father took sharp bends at speed.

Damian whispered, 'He's finally accepted that cars are the future.'

I suppressed my giggles.

Guests for the *Reveillon* meal began to arrive at 9 p.m. Raisa and her daughters had been busy in the kitchen helping Amélie prepare the traditional food. They had decided to stay in the village and help out on the farm. There was plenty to do. With so many young men lost to the war, the women had to step up as best they could.

At 11 p.m. Damian left the party. I guessed that some secrecy was involved in his departure. He returned just before midnight with a frail bent figure. I knew the voice before I recognised the man and his words removed all doubt:

'"Them that ask no questions isn't told a lie".'

'"So watch the wall my darling while the gentlemen go by",' I replied and crossed the room to hold him in my arms.

My dear friend, *Père* François, had returned.

103

The chimes of Big Ben ushered in the New Year of 1946. The party had celebrated the *Nouvelle Année* an hour before but all considered that they deserved a double celebration, this first New Year of peace time.

I was nursing baby Karl when *Père* François came to speak to me.

'Have you any news of your husband?' he asked gently.

'No, Father. I last saw him as he left the château to face the Allies. I know of Rommel's death and that Von Rundstedt is now a prisoner, but of Karl I know nothing. I feared that he was part of the plot to kill Hitler – they called it the Valkyrie plot – but his name was not on the list of those who were executed. He was never a Nazi and he loathed Hitler but he was a Prussian, and Prussians do not mutiny. He explained this to me. But now I know that some Prussians did mutiny. They were brave but gave their lives and those of their families in vain. The Nazis killed the wives and children of those who conspired.'

'And your family, do they know who the father of your son is?'

'Yes, they do now. It was not difficult for them. Damian and Amélie knew him to be a good man and my parents are happy that I am alive and that they have a healthy grandson.'

'I have news of your friends, Lotti and Emilia. They are well and in Paris. They surrendered to the Resistance when Paris was liberated and for a while, it seemed that it would not go well for them, but the cook and his Resistance wife had them released. They will stay in Paris until they can return to their homes in Germany.'

'I should be pleased to see them again. They were good friends to me, all of them. Without them, I may not have lived and they protected me when I needed them. And what of you, Father? Your time in the camp?'

'I feel this should wait until another time. The world will discover soon enough what horrors mankind can inflict on fellow men.'

'I know some of this. Karl told me of Russia. He found German soldiers hanging little children. He shot the officer in charge and saved the children. He was distraught that one could not be saved. He reported the crime to Von Rundstedt. He told me of the plans to exterminate the Jews and others, and of the camps. He was appalled by this and you also know that he helped to save the Jews and airmen who stayed with me by ignoring what I was doing.'

'Yes, of course. We all knew that without his preference for *fermer les yeux*, your work could not have continued. Helen, this is important, do you know the name of this village you spoke of?'

'No, only he would know, or his men. Why do you ask?'

'Because your husband is awaiting trial in Nuremberg.'

104

He went on to explain that on the 20th of November 1945, the first international war crimes tribunal in history opened at the Palace of Justice in Nuremberg. It aimed to reveal the extent of German atrocities during the Nazi era and the war that followed. By assembling irrefutable evidence of war crimes, it would hold prominent Nazis to account rather than states. Many of those responsible were now dead, having committed suicide or they had escaped to South America, but the tribunal was intent on indicting the remaining prominent members of Hitler's inner circle as well as high-ranking military officers.

'Your husband was captured on the 25th of January 1945 at Bastogne in the Ardennes by the US Army under General Patton. It was the last major offensive by the Germans. His panzer division fought bravely and suffered many losses but his unit had run out of men and equipment and their situation was hopeless. Karl was wounded and taken to a military hospital at Saint-Hubert in Belgium, where surgeons operated on bullet wounds to his chest. He was hospitalised for six months but made a full recovery. He was then taken to Lüneburg prison where he joined Field Marshal Erik von Manstein who is also imprisoned there.'

'Why was I not told of this before?'

'This information has only recently come to my attention.'

'But I am his wife. Surely he would have given my name as his next of kin?'

'I believe he tried but there was no record of the marriage in Caen. The *Mairie* was destroyed in the Allied bombing but the documents had been removed to safety and have not yet been found. But you and your husband did not attend the *Mairie* as I remember.'

'That is because the *Oberfeldkommandur* and the wife of the cook acted as proxy for our marriage. They used my alias, Gabrielle Doucet. Only you, Father, know that our marriage was legitimate, in the eyes of God at least.'

'That may not satisfy the authorities, as in France a marriage has to be legitimised at the *Mairie.*'

'My husband knew of this but we agreed that it could be resolved later. It was done to protect me and my British identity. Also, Karl was not a Nazi. He loathed Hitler. He and his brothers never joined the Nazi party. I am certain that this can be proved as well as his saving of the children in that village.'

'Can you think of anyone who may know of that village?'

'No, there would only be the soldiers under his command at the time. They all left with him on the 6th of June 1944. The others – Lotti, Emilia and the cook – left soon after, when the fighting was getting close to Caen.'

'Perhaps we should ask Lotti and Emilia. They may have spoken with the soldiers. They are young women. I am sure there would have been communication between them and the soldiers'.

'Do you know when the trial is?'

'It is during this month, the 5th of January.'

'I will go to him. I will take our son with me and I will plead his case. Meanwhile, Father, could you please make contact with Lotti and Emilia; whatever they remember may be important. And I also need you to prove that we are married.'

Père François agreed to this but cautioned me that it would not be easy. The members of the tribunal were anxious to convict those in the higher echelons of the military as evidence that justice was at least seen to be done. He explained that he feared to speak of this to me as he did not wish to extinguish the hope I had of reuniting with my husband. He also explained that his case was to be tried by the Soviet prosecutors as well as the French and British. German generals did not return from prison in Russia.

105

The following day I bade farewell to my parents and family. Damian drove me and baby Karl to Bayeux Station to catch the Paris train. I had been loaned a baby carriage, which would serve as a bed and a means of transport for baby Karl. *Père* François gave me a signed letter attesting to the fact of my marriage to Karl Johannes Franz von Werstein on the 20th of February 1942 at the church of Église Saint-Pierre in Caen. I also brought testimonies from Raisa, Ellana and Ruth which would support my claim that my husband had assisted in their survival and that of others during the years of occupation.

The train pulled into Gare Saint-Lazare two hours later and to my surprise and great pleasure, I found Lotti and Emilia on the platform to greet me. They were delighted to hold baby Karl and all commented on how much he resembled his father. Both girls were well but had no plans to return to Germany at the present time. Their parents had died in the fall of Berlin and they were still trying to trace other family members through the Red Cross. I explained that I must first go to the British Embassy to obtain the necessary transit papers to enter Germany. They volunteered to accompany me to the embassy and would look after baby Karl while I applied for the papers.

At the embassy reception, I gave my name to the secretary and requested an interview with the ambassador's deputy. I waited for over an hour and then a door opened and a rotund man with a gingery moustache entered the reception area. He crossed the room to me and introducing himself as Ambassador Duff Cooper, took my hand and shook it effusively.

'So, you are Helen Douglas. My dear, I am more delighted and honoured to meet you than I can say. I have just spoken to Mr Churchill and he has told me of your courage and exploits during the war. My secretary recognised your name but, of course, I had to confirm this with the War Office. Now, please, tell me what we can do for you.'

I explained my intention to travel to Nuremberg to give evidence for the defence at the trial of an officer in the *Wehrmacht*. I told him of the letters I had attesting to his innocence and that I hoped to find others who could also support his case.

'And who is this officer?'

'His name is Karl Johannes Franz von Werstein. He had the rank of General in the *Wehrmacht*. He is my husband and the father of my son.'

The ambassador's face took on a look of utter disbelief.

'Do others know of this marriage?'

'My family in Scotland and in France, and my close friends know of our marriage.. It was necessary that we married as I had to be protected from... others, and my safety meant that those I was caring for could survive. He was aware of what I and the resistants were doing but he pretended not to know. He is a loyal German but he was never a Nazi. There is more: he was on the Eastern Front with his division and they came to a village where he found German soldiers hanging the children. He managed to save all but one. He shot the officer who was in charge of this brutality and contacted General von Rundstedt to report it. I am trying to find evidence of this, someone who was there perhaps.

My husband will need all the help I can get for him. Also, I need proof of my marriage. I have a letter from the priest who married us in church but we could not go to the *Mairie* to legalise the marriage as my identity had to be secret. Instead, the *Oberfeldkommandur* and a member of the Resistance, a woman who had married the château's cook, who is German and was part of the *Feldkommandur's* entourage, were proxies for our marriage at the *Mairie*. The building was bombed in the battle for Caen but the records were saved. I was married there by proxy under my alias, Gabrielle Doucet.'

The ambassador's face looked even more astonished, if that were possible. He took out his handkerchief and mopped his brow. The idea of a collaboration or cover up, whatever word could be used to define this apparent digression from what was known to be the norm during the occupation, literally defied credibility. That the *Oberfeldkommandur* was party to this charade was equally beyond belief.

'Are you telling me the truth, young lady?'

I felt my face flush in anger.

'Do you dare to doubt me? Do you think I would travel here with my son just to entertain you with lies? Have you any idea how it was here during the occupation? While you and your socialite lady wife enjoyed parties in England, people here were starving, they were tortured and I was tortured. Our Jewish friends were taken from their homes and sent to camps to be murdered. So you endured the blitz, but you did not have the enemy at your gates, in your homes. How do you know what choices you would have made? I know that many of your class wished to appease Hitler. War was inconvenient for you. The servants went to fight instead of waiting on you hand and foot. You would have been pleased to marry your daughters to high-ranking Nazi officers once Hitler had agreed to the terms of a ceasefire. Churchill alone stood against that and well you know it. Thank you but I will leave now. Remember that I am also French. I will seek my permission from France.'

At that, I turned from him and strode out the door. He followed immediately.

'Wait, Miss Douglas, Mrs... Von Werstein. Wait. Perhaps I was hasty. Churchill spoke highly of you. It is just that your story is completely outside of my comprehension. I apologise. Please come with me and I will do what I can.'

I took a deep breath and allowed myself to be ushered into his office. He read the testimonies of Raisa and her daughters and looked at the attestation of marriage that *Père* François had given me. I told him that he could check other facts with the RAF officer, George Vartis. Anything else was still subject to the Official Secrets Act. He nodded in understanding when I said that.

He asked me to return to the embassy the following day, by which time he would have the necessary papers for travel and, if possible, make enquiries on my behalf regarding my husband.

I thanked him and left.

Lotti and Emilia were waiting for me outside the embassy. I suggested that we visit the apartment where Stefan's parents lived. The couple were overjoyed to have me with them again and more so to meet my baby son. The fact that his father was German added to their pleasure. They regarded it as a new beginning for Europe, a blending of the old and the new order. Their unquestioning acceptance of my marriage and the circumstances around it was in marked contrast to the suspicion and scepticism of the ambassador. Their sorrow over the death of their son, Stefan, was mitigated by the survival of their daughter and their grandchildren.

Céleste and Séraphine, as well as Gisela and her children, had spent the school holidays with them and they themselves had been able to travel to London for *Hanoucca* and Christmas.

They chatted in German with Lotti and Emilia.

'And we look forward to meeting your husband and to speaking German with baby Karl when he is older.'

I asked if I and my child could stay that night in the apartment as I had to return to the embassy the following day. They made up a bed for both of us in the salon. Looking around the room I shivered as I remembered that this room had witnessed the murder of my mother's dearest friend: the Odette I would never meet, whose last act before dying had been to secret the Star of David bracelet in the wall for me to find. The decision had been made to give the bracelet to Céleste. She was, after all, the daughter of Stefan and had been brought up in the Jewish faith, and would continue to be so.

The Château des Tilleuls had been offered to me to use as I wished. Raisa and her daughters lived there at present but they hoped to find a smaller place to make their home. They found the vast empty rooms intimidating and Ruth was certain it was haunted. I had not felt any otherworldly presence there and felt that the château needed to be occupied by a family again, with children's voices echoing through the rooms and the sound of the piano and cello heard from the library. Arpeggione, the word caused my heart to contract and memories of those days suddenly overwhelmed me. I cried myself to sleep.

106

The following day I returned to the embassy. The ambassador greeted me and ushered me into his office. He handed me a large envelope explaining that inside were transit visas to Germany and letters of introduction for the court. He had reserved a room for me at the Hotel Victoria in Nuremberg which was close to the Palace of Justice. I was welcome to stay there throughout the trial. He added that it was not possible to obtain legal papers to support my marriage, but perhaps, all being well, this could be done at a later date.

'You mean if my husband is released?'

'Yes, I am afraid that is all we can hope for.'

He then apologised.

'I apologise most sincerely for my rudeness yesterday. How could any of us imagine what you and all those who lived under the Nazi occupation had to endure, and the choices you had to make! I should like to know your story one day, perhaps when the restrictions are lifted.'

I promised to do so and left to collect baby Karl. I arrived in Nuremberg late that night. I was met on the platform by a British Army officer who introduced himself as Major Tristan Mackenzie. He took me and baby Karl to a waiting car and drove us to the hotel. Through the car window I could see the ruins of the bombed city, its magnificent buildings now reduced to piles of rubble around which street vendors had improvised makeshift street cafés and bars. A salvaged front door made a counter supported by upended armchairs and the smell of hot sausages and malty beer filled the evening air.

Before he left me, the Major assured me that I would be collected from the hotel the following morning at 11 a.m. His wife, Edith, would care for baby Karl, if I was in agreement. I thanked him.

I found it difficult to sleep. My son was restless having slept for most of the train journey. But it was the anxiety of what faced me in court the following day that prevented me from sleeping, that and the excitement and longing to see my husband again.

The Major and his wife arrived just before 11 a.m. I found it difficult to hand my son over to a stranger but Edith made it easy for me. She had children of her own, she explained, and there was also a young nanny at their home who was eager to have a baby to care for. He would be in safe hands.

As we walked the short distance to the court, the Major explained that my husband was being tried for war crimes along with three other defendants. The crimes he was accused of included participation in an illegal war. This was defined as a crime against peace. He was accused of planning and waging a war of aggression, of war crimes, which included the killing of hostages and civilians and crimes against humanity, which included massacres of civilians in the camps and occupied countries. These were the main indictments.

'And what would his punishment be, if he is found guilty?'

'He will be hanged, as others before him have been.'

I felt a wave of nausea and feared that I might faint. The Major noticed this and held my arm.

'Perhaps you should not attend the trial. It may be too upsetting for you.'

'He is my husband. I know him to be a good man. There are others who can testify to this. How has he pleaded?'

'This was most surprising. The other three pleaded not guilty to all four charges. Your husband pleaded guilty to the first two. This has not happened before. They have all invoked "*ein Befehl ist ein Befehl*" and "*tu quoque*" as their defence. But your husband has done neither.'

'Does he have a lawyer?'

'Of course, he has. Dr Hans Laternser. He is excellent. Your husband is in good hands.'

'And who are the prosecutors?'

'There are four, one for each of the Allies. I won't trouble you with their names. In any case, you will be given an agenda for the trial. He will not be questioned by the American prosecutor, I believe.'

'What of the papers I brought with me? When can I submit them to the defence?'

'Dr Laternser already has them. The British Ambassador in Paris sent mimeographs to the defence by special courier.'

'When can I speak to my husband?'

'We will go to him now, before the trial. He is not expecting you. All the prisoners have been held in solitary confinement since their arrest.'

I was taken to a waiting area inside the court building. Secretaries sat at a long desk typing furiously. One or two of them looked up with an air of indifference and dismissal when I came in. *No doubt they think I am another apologist for the Nazis*, I thought to myself. But my heart was beating furiously and waves of nausea beset me again. It seemed so long ago that I had said goodbye to him. He had not even known that I was with child.

A door opened and the Major beckoned to me. I followed him along a corridor lined with guards from the Military Police and then down a steep flight of stairs to a long corridor of rooms, each with guards posted at the door. He stopped at one, signalled for the guards to open the door and invited me to follow him in.

107

Restitution

My husband was standing by the window with his back to the door.

'Karl, my love, I am here,' and I rushed into his arms.

'*Liebchen*, how is it that you are here?' He held me tight, caressing my hair and kissing me.

'*Père* François told me. He came back from Sachsenhausen. We celebrated New Year in France with him. I must tell you that we have a son. It was too early to tell you of the pregnancy when you left. I was not certain and did not dare to hope. He was born in Scotland on the 22nd of January 1945. His name is also Karl. My love, I will not leave here until you are with me. I have brought letters testifying to your innocence. Lotti is trying to find your soldiers to testify about the children you saved. She is in Paris with the Red Cross every day looking for records of your division. Some may still be in captivity but others may have already returned to Germany. Lotti and Emilia will do their best.'

'We have a son? *Liebchen*, I cannot begin to say how happy this makes me. Is he here, in Germany?'

Yes, Major Mackenzie's wife is caring for him while I am in court. He is so very like his father, you will see that.'

'And Lotti and Emilia, you have been with them?'

'Yes my love. They met me in Paris. They are well and send their love. One day we will all be together again. Just know that I am in the court and close to you.'

I clung to him. The feel of his body next to mine and everything that made him the man he was, I wanted to keep close to me.

'We will play music together one day, whether that is in this life or the next, who can tell.' He said this as he kissed me, with the familiar, slightly mocking, ironic air that had so confused me in the early days of our relationship but that I now found utterly, infinitely endearing.

I was allowed a brief moment to kiss him once more and then the Major indicated that my time was up and I should leave. My throat felt tight and I needed to cry but I was determined not to show any emotion. If I were to speak to the court, my voice must be clear, it must be heard.

I took my seat in the visitor's gallery in Courtroom 600, a vast wood-panelled chamber with ornate carvings in grey around its doors. The Major explained that I would not be called to give evidence until much later in the proceedings. He pointed out the witness stand in front of the huge film screen and explained that windows had been built into various parts of the walls for taking photographs and to allow for radio reports. He cautioned that I should not be intimidated by this. He handed me a set of headphones and explained that an IBM system had been installed that allowed for simultaneous interpretation into four languages: English, French, German and Russian, and assured me that he would stay with me throughout the day.

I looked down at the courtroom as it filled up slowly. Lawyers took their seats in a large stand on the left-hand side from where I sat and reporters filed into the seats below the gallery. After an hour, a door opened and the four defendants filed in. Karl was the last to appear. Then a door opened on the left side of the court and the four prosecutors appeared and took their seats in a row in front of the defendants. All in attendance wore headsets with microphones.

Karl was the first to be called. The French prosecution counsel began with the two charges to which he had pleaded guilty. He replied briefly that he agreed that the war was illegal, that it was a war of aggression against peace and that, yes, he had participated in this war, as an officer and loyal soldier of Germany.

'I am a Prussian soldier and we fight for our country no matter who is commanding us. We do not mutiny but neither do we engage in acts of barbarity and sadism. I admit to participating in the war; if that makes me guilty of a crime then I am guilty.'

The prosecuting counsel looked surprised.

'You had the rank of General, did you not? Surely that would mean that you had a high degree of autonomy in your role. Perhaps you could have refused to participate in the bloodiest and most brutal war that Europe has ever endured.'

'So, I should have refused to fight and surrendered my men to captivity? Would any General do that? But let me say now, I am pleased that Hitler's war was lost. The world should not have suffered such a man to be born, let alone be the leader of Germany. And evil begets evil, as we have seen and now know so much about.'

'Were you a member of the Nazi party?'

'No, I was not. They threatened to remove my rank and commission, but after a while, they forgot about me.'

The prosecutor then moved on to the indictments to which he had pleaded not guilty: the killing of hostages and civilians and the failure to protect civilians in his sphere of operation.

'While I was *Feldkommandur* in Sainte-Geneviève-sur-Orne, no hostages were killed but many of your Resistance were guests at my château, along with others. I was not permitted to meet them. In May 1941, I was summoned to my home in Germany as my first wife was dying. After her interment, I was sent to command my division on the Eastern Front. I was injured, spent time in a field hospital and was then sent back to France to recover. This was the end of December of that year. During my absence, *Oberstleutnant* Otto Mueller took over my command. His ways were not mine.'

'You say you were not permitted to meet them, the resistants, at your château but you knew they were there. How could that be?'

'You need to ask my wife that question.'

The French prosecutor shook his head in disbelief and sat down. The Russian prosecutor took over.

'You were the General in command of the 19th Panzer Division, were you not?'

'I was, that is from June to November 1941.'

'And your division entered the village of Ljubarov in the Kharkov Oblast on the 22nd of August 1941. The village was burnt to the ground by your men, and children as young as two years were strung up to die while their parents watched. You are charged with this crime against innocent civilians.'

'Your information is incorrect. It is true that my soldiers entered this village on that day, but when we arrived, an *Einsatzgruppen* unit was there. They had the children on rope and piano wire and the parents were being held at gunpoint. I ordered the immediate release of the children, but one could not be revived. I shot the officer in charge of the operation and reported the incident to *Generalfeldmarschall* von Rundstedt. My soldiers were not sadists. There will still be records of this communication perhaps.'

'There are no records as I understand.'

The Russian prosecutor spoke for over an hour, detailing atrocities committed during the war on the Eastern Front but my husband denied all involvement in the events.

The court adjourned until the following day. I felt a sense of utter exhaustion and despair. If there were no witnesses to the events that my husband was charged with, it could go very badly for him. The Major drove me to his home and I was invited to stay for supper. As he drove me and baby Karl back to the hotel, he surprised me with the news that I would be able to see my husband again the following day and to bring the baby with me.

He sat with baby Karl on his knee and jigged him up and down. Karl giggled with delight and put his plump arms around his father's neck.'

'So, this is our son, *liebchen*. I am so happy for this moment. I agree, he is much like me. His legs are already long; he will be as tall as I am.'

'And as handsome,' I added, kissing him, and then went on to say, 'Lotti is trying to find a witness from the village, but even if a soldier is found, the prosecutor could accuse him of collusion and collaboration. We need someone from the village to testify. The prosecutor said that the village was destroyed, is that correct?'

'Some houses were burning, yes, but otherwise, the village was intact. Other villages were destroyed by the same group. We were too late to save them.'

'I will speak with the Major.'

A military police officer knocked on the door to inform me that it was time to leave. I kissed him goodbye, holding onto him for as long as I could. The Major and his wife were waiting for me. I handed Karl over to Edith to take to their home.

It was the turn of the British prosecutor, Sir Hartley Shawcross, to question him.

'Were you in command of the *Wehrmacht* 19th Panzer division that crossed the Ardennes in May 1940 and surrounded the BEF at Dunkirk?'

'Yes, but we were ordered to withdraw as *Herr* Göring thought he could annihilate your army with his air force. For us, it was a welcome break from the hostilities, for your men fought bravely; we were well-matched. And as you are aware, a fortuitous cloud cover protected your armies from the *Luftwaffe* and enabled a mostly successful evacuation.'

'And after that?'

'We fought through Northern France and eventually to Paris. At that time Hitler was in control of Europe. You feared he would turn his attention to Britain. It was a very troubling time for you. But here we are, *Vae Victus,* and you the victors have the opportunity to call us to account. We meekly await our just deserts.'

'You are arrogant and vexatious, sir.'

'My wife, who is Scottish, would maintain that vexatious is a term British men such as yourself use to describe women who have the courage to speak their minds.'

'Your wife is Scottish? This is not possible. My notes tell me that your wife was a Prussian lady, sadly now deceased. There is no record of your marriage to a Scottish woman.'

'I do not think this court is the place to discuss my marital status but I can assure you that my wife, who is in fact of a French mother and Scots father, is here in Nuremberg with my son who was conceived in France and born in Scotland.'

'And what was your wife doing in France during this time.'

'She lived at the château and was saving Jewish families as well as your British airmen, resistants and others.'

'Were you aware of these activities?'

'"Them that ask no questions isn't told a lie." I was not confronted by her activities.'

'You know Kipling?'

'Of course, I visited his house, Batemans, many times. My first wife and children were tutored in his poetry.'

'So, what were you doing in Normandy during that time?'

'I was a *Feldkommandur* in the town of Sainte-Geneviève-sur-Orne. My wife may one day tell her story, but for the moment, she is bound to secrecy by your government. Some details related to your invasion on the 6th of June, I believe, but of course, I knew nothing of those activities of hers. But we met there and fell in love. We played music together, I on the cello and she on the piano.'

'This is fascinating. Will she be taking the witness stand?'

'Why should she not.'

'No further questions.'

That evening, I asked the Major whether it would be possible to make contact with the village where my husband was accused of war crimes.

'Surely, there would be a mayor or a village council who could vouch for my husband.'

'That would be impossible. Stalin would not allow such a thing. You really need a member of the *Einsatzgruppen* unit responsible to confess and exonerate your husband. I will make enquiries, but do not be hopeful.'

The second day was even more harrowing than the first. The Russian prosecutor stood up again. My husband was confronted with film and photographic evidence of massacres of Jews and other civilians across Ukraine. I knew I would be haunted forever by the pictures of Jewish women and children, as well as men, standing naked by the pits they had been forced to dig in forests, and then watched as they were shot, their bodies falling into tangled heaps. I watched the film of a young boy standing next to a pit where his entire family had been shot, a gun is put to his head and he falls slowly and gracefully, like a leaf from a tree in autumn, into the pit beside them. Families and communities lost forever.

He denied participation in any of these events, but it was clear that the prosecutor did not believe him.

That night, I could not sleep; my mind played out the images of what I had seen that day in a continuous reel. The women undressing, their clothes taken away to be sent to Germany, naked, they run towards the pits, the soldiers pushing them and jeering at them, and then their final moments before they fall into the pit. I wondered how it felt to know it was your last moment of life and to watch your children die in front of your eyes, and then it is your turn.

The same prosecutor stood up on the third day with more photographs and film evidence, this time of a place called Babi Yar, a ravine outside of the city of Kyiv.

On the 29th of September 1941, nearly 34,000 Jews were marched from the city to the ravine. They had been told they were being relocated and to bring clothing, valuables and food. Men, women and children were herded in a long column by soldiers as well as Ukrainian guards. I watched the grainy film in horror, of the line of unsuspecting Jews as they were led out of the city and along the narrow road; a river of death, they flowed into the ravine.

The prosecutor explained that the crowd was so huge that most of the victims could not have known their fate until it was too late; by the time they heard the gunfire, there was no chance to escape. The film showed soldiers standing on the bodies of the dead and shooting those still alive who had been made to lie on top of the bodies of family and friends. When all in the line were assumed to be dead, the soldiers covered the bodies with earth.

At the end of the film, the prosecutor informed the court that the massacre was at that time the largest of its kind in the war, only to be surpassed by the massacre of 50,000 Jews in Odesa the following October.

I listened as my husband, visibly distressed by the footage he had seen, denied any part in the massacre and insisted that he would never have condoned such an atrocity. He was then allowed to speak in his own defence.

'As an honourable soldier, I had the misfortune to fight for my country when it was governed by barbarians and sadists. I do not use the "you too" as my defence but I am sure you all accept that to fight for their country is a soldier's duty. I am guilty of fighting an illegal war, a war against peace, but I and others were fighting for the

Germany of our ancestors, our homeland, where our families wished to live our lives peacefully. The victors have decided the terms of peace and I am pleased that it is not Hitler's peace.'

It was then time for the defence lawyer, Dr Hans Laternser, to stand. His first witness, a young woman who had been a theatre actress in Kyiv told her story. She had managed to escape from the Babi Yar pit during the night, but as she had lain there, she could hear the moans of children who had managed to survive the shooting but now found themselves surrounded by the dead and covered in blood. A child could be heard crying "mama, mama". The woman had clawed her way through the soil, run naked into the woods and to the home of her Russian mother-in-law. On her way, she had found a young child who had also managed to escape from the pit and had taken him with her.

The lawyer then asked the young woman if the defendant had been present at the massacre.

'No, sir, he was not. The commander in charge on that day, I remember well. I knew him by name and I will never forget him by sight: *SS-Obergruppenführer* Friedrich Jeckeln. He and the Military Governor of Kyiv, Kurt Eberhard, were in command that day. I never saw the defendant at this place.'

The next witness was led to the stand in handcuffs by a military policeman. He gave his name as former *SS-Standartenführer* Josef Kreuzer. He had already stood trial for war crimes and was awaiting sentencing. He had agreed to testify for the defendant, as in his own words, "I have nothing to lose but this is my chance to die with some dignity"

He explained to the court that as a commander of an *Einsatzgruppen* D unit, he had been responsible for following the *Wehrmacht* as they fought eastwards, deep into Soviet territory. Their role was to hunt down and kill all those whom Himmler and Heydrich had defined as undesirable, the *Untermensch*. These were not only Jews but also Slavs. He and his unit entered the village of

Ljubarov in the Kharkov Oblast on the 22nd of August 1941 and began to burn the village and kill the people there.

'The children were to die first. My men enjoyed this, making the parents watch as their children suffered. After a short time, General von Werstein arrived with his panzer unit. He ordered the release of the children and their parents and had the fires put out. When I argued with him, he shot me, not enough to kill me but enough to incapacitate me. I later heard the men say, "*Mit Von Werstein legt man sich nicht an*".'

I heard this translated as "you don't mess with Von Werstein".

Kreuzer went on to say that Von Werstein had a reputation for discipline and would never permit civilian deaths in cold blood. They called him the "Jew lover" behind his back and some even questioned his Prussian ancestry because of this. But it was acknowledged that he was a Prussian nobleman and feared and respected by those under his command.

Kreuzer was led away from the stand.

The lawyer then read out the letters of Raisa and her daughters, attesting to the fact that Von Werstein had known of the secret room and their presence there, along with others, namely Resistance workers, airmen and soldiers evading capture. The *Kommandant* had indicated to Helen Douglas, now *Frau* Von Werstein, that he wished to ignore the activities in the old tower.

The letter from *Père* François verifying the marriage of Helen Douglas to Karl von Werstein was read out and, most surprisingly, a letter from the British Ambassador in Paris attesting to Helen's contribution to the D-Day invasion and that Churchill himself was prepared to support her testimony.

Gasps of astonishment from the court followed this last presentation.

I was then called to the witness box. I gave my married name but explained that in 1938, as Helen Douglas, I had been employed in the Château des Tilleuls as governess to the children of the family Abramsky-Erhart. I told of the circumstances of the family's departure and how I had been left in charge of the château. I briefly described the people I had helped to survive the occupation by the Germans. I admitted that the resistants had persuaded me to become the mistress of the *Kommandant*, so I would be well-placed to assist their activities and help those who needed to be hidden.

'I was supposed to hate him but I came to love him.'

I also described the time under Mueller's command.

'He was brutal and I suffered in his hands. And not only Mueller, the *gendarmes* had me arrested and tortured. It was not just the Germans who perpetrated these crimes; they were well-supported by the police and fascist militia groups, and ordinary citizens too. My husband was never a Nazi but he is and was an honourable soldier. He told me what happened to his cello teacher in Berlin. The man was a Jew and my husband tried to save his life but was too late. Nevertheless, he used his influence to get papers for the cellist's family to escape to Switzerland.'

The lawyer then posed the question regarding my husband's knowledge of my activities.

'Of course, he knew. He even used the code the Resistance gave me. To this day, I do not know how he discovered this code.'

'And what was this code you speak of?'

'It was from the poem by Rudyard Kipling *A Smuggler's Song*. We used lines from the poem to communicate and to inform of the safe arrival of agents and airmen in Britain. It would be broadcast on Radio Londres. My husband used to tease me with the line "them that ask no questions" and I would know what he meant. He also used the phrase "watch the wall" which is another line in the poem. By this, I knew he meant that what his eye did not see, he could ignore, which he did. But he explained to me that he would never betray his country, that he was a loyal soldier of Germany.'

The lawyer thanked me for my testimony and I returned to the visitor gallery. I found it hard to control my nerves and sat shivering and shaking during the judge's summing up. The jury then retired to deliberate.

The Major took me to a nearby café but I could neither eat nor drink. We walked along the banks of the frozen Pegnitz River where the black-headed gulls in their winter plumage swooped and cried over the ruined bridges.

Then a woman appeared, calling to us as she ran, 'Major Mackenzie, the jury is returning to the court, it is time for you to take your seats.'

I felt my heart contract with fear. They had not taken long over their deliberations and had reached their decision quickly: guilty or not guilty.

The foreman of the jury rose and was asked if the verdict had been unanimous, to which he replied that it was.

He was then asked if the defendant had been found guilty or not guilty of war crimes and crimes against humanity.

He replied, 'Not guilty to both charges.'

'What does this mean?' I asked tentatively of the Major.

'I think he will go free. He pleaded guilty to the two lesser charges but the judge knows that to have refused to participate would have meant death for him and his family, and very likely many of those in his command. A soldier is obliged to fight for his country. Had the Germans been the victors, God forbid, we would all have been strung up by now but without a trial. Wait here. I will ask if you are able to visit him.'

He returned shortly after and took my arm.

'He is waiting for you.'

The following day, the court was reconvened for sentencing. The judge acknowledged that Karl von Werstein was a soldier and had no alternative but to fight and that he was a man of honour and courage who had evidently done his best to save civilian lives. He had been found not guilty of the most grave charges, that of war crimes and crimes against humanity. He did not think that a custodial sentence was appropriate with regard to his plea of guilty to participation in an illegal war. He wished him well in civilian life.

A round of applause and a few cheers were heard from the visitor gallery and from among the press benches.

I ran down to the exit of the courtroom and was joined by my husband. I put my arms around him and clung to him, never wanting to let him go. He raised me up to meet his eyes.

'Now, *meine liebchen*, let us join our son and return home.' He lifted me into his arms and carried me to the waiting car.

EPILOGUE

6th June 2004
Arromanches, Normandy

Helen and her granddaughter leave their seats when the parade and ceremony are over and make their way to a small restaurant on a side street near the square. They order food and sit with their drinks in a sheltered area of the terrace. The rain has stopped but a cold blustery wind blows from the sea. All the tables inside the restaurant are booked by members of the press and their guests. Most are young and their loud voices and raucous laughter can be heard over the clink of wine bottles and glasses.

'It is unfair, Granny; you did so much in the war. I know you don't like to speak of it but *Grosspapa* told me you were brave and saved lives. And now those young people sit in the warm and you are in the cold.'

Helen is about to reply that she is content where she is when a figure in the uniform of Wing Commander approaches.

'Helen, I would know you anywhere and at any time. How are you?'

'I am well, George. This is my granddaughter, Claire. And you? It has been many years.'

'I am well enough, getting old takes courage, perhaps even more than fighting a war, or perhaps a different type of courage.' He smiles as he says that.

'Are you here alone?' she asks.

'Yes, my wife died many years ago. I assume Karl is now dead.'

'Yes.'

'You must miss him.'

'Of course I do but I have our family.'

'I often wondered about your life after we last met. Perhaps you could tell me about it one day.'

She smiles.

ACKNOWLEDGEMENTS

I thank my editor Vicky Richards and all at Cranthorpe Millner. I also thank my husband Jeremy for his infinite tolerance of my many meltdowns on account of my poor IT skills. Many times the document was consigned to the ether when I pressed the wrong button and equally many times did he succeed in retrieving it.

ABOUT THE AUTHOR

Jan Stirling Locke was both a trained registered nurse and teacher of English throughout her long working life in the UK and in a variety of countries around the world. As a young woman she travelled alone through Europe into former Iron Curtain countries, in the pursuit of love and adventure.

As a child of the '50s whose father, uncles and aunts had fought and/or played a role in the Allied victory, Jan grew up imbued with the concept that the Germans were the 'baddies' and 'all of them Nazis'. As an adult, during frequent visits to her cottage in Normandy, Jan attended the commemorative ceremonies of the D-day landings with her family, hosted veterans, and became an honorary member of the now sadly disbanded Grimsby Normandy Veterans Association. A walk along one of the lanes beside the cottage sparked her consideration for the German soldiers who had also died during World War Two, whose bereaved families would not be permitted to mourn their loss. They too were fighting for their country, albeit one ruled by Hitler. This prompted her to read about life in Germany in the 1930s, and to begin working on *Deception*.